THE JOSHUA COVENANT

A NOVEL

THE JOSHUA COVENANT

DIANE / DAVID MUNSON

MicahHouse
m e d i a

Grand Rapids, Michigan

ISBN-13: 978-0-9835590-0-9

ISBN-10: 0-9835590-0-7

Scripture quotations, unless otherwise indicated, are taken from the HOLY BIBLE, NEW INTERNATIONAL VERSION®. NIV®. Copyright ©1973, 1978, 1984 by International Bible Society. Used by permission of Zondervan. All rights reserved.

This is a work of fiction. Names, characters, places, and incidents either are the product of the authors' imaginations or are used fictitiously. The authors and publishers intend that all persons, organizations, events and locales portrayed in the work be considered as fictitious.

Printed in the United States of America

17 16 15 14 13 12   7 6 5 4 3 2 1

DEDICATION

To the countless boys and girls, who as children applied themselves in school and who joined in productive and broadening activities offered by their communities. To those who as adults applied to the military, to the law enforcement and intelligence agencies, passed the stringent application process and background investigation, endured the grueling and continuing training and who now serve twenty four/seven to keep our communities and nation safe, and often can't tell us about their deeds, for which we owe them so much. You have our thanks.

ACKNOWLEDGMENTS

It is one thing to write a novel. It's quite another to see that novel take the form of a book to hold and enjoy. We thank Micah House Media and those supporting them for assembling The Joshua Covenant into the book we delight in promoting and you will enjoy reading. Thank you, Pamela Guerrieri, for your editorial adjustments to what we created, and to Ginny McFadden for creatively making our story fit between the covers. Once again, Randy Groft has exceeded our expectations with a beautiful cover design. We are grateful to M.D. Van De Mae, M.D., for her expert opinions regarding medical issues.

ABOUT THE AUTHORS

ExFeds, Diane and David Munson write High Velocity Suspense novels that reviewers compare to John Grisham. The Munsons call their novels "factional fiction" because they write books based on their exciting and dangerous careers.

Diane Munson has been an attorney for twenty-eight years. She was a Federal Prosecutor in Washington, D.C., and also served the Reagan Administration, appointed by Attorney General Edwin Meese, as Deputy Administrator of the Office of Juvenile Justice and Delinquency Prevention. She worked with the Justice Department, the U.S. Congress, and the White House on policy and legal issues. More recently she has been in a general law practice.

David Munson served as a Special Agent with the Naval Investigative Service (now NCIS), and U.S. Drug Enforcement Administration over a twenty-seven year career, where as an undercover agent he infiltrated international drug smuggling organizations. In that role he traveled with drug dealers, met their suppliers in foreign countries, helped fly their drugs to the U.S., then feigned surprise when shipments were seized by law enforcement. Later his true identity was revealed when he testified against the group members in court. While assigned to DEA headquarters in Washington, D.C., David served two years as a Congressional Fellow with the Senate Permanent Subcommittee on Investigations.

As they travel to research and cloister to write, they thank the Lord for the blessings of faith and family. David and Diane Munson are collaborating on their next novel.

www.DianeAndDavidMunson.com

GLOSSARY

Agency	Insider's name for the CIA
Boker Tov	Good morning (Hebrew)
Bucar	Car provided to FBI agents
CIA	Central Intelligence Agency, America's spies
FBI	Federal Bureau of Investigation
Foggy Bottom	Insider's word for the State Department
ICE	Immigration Customs Enforcement
IDF	Israeli Defense Force, Israel's military units
IFF	Information Friend or Foe
Institute	Insider's name for Mossad
Knesset	Israel's parliament
Kremlin	Seat of the government in Russia
MSG	Marine Security Guard, protects U.S. embassies
Mossad	Israel's spy agency, similar to America's CIA
NCS	CIA's National Clandestine Services
PLO	Palestinian Liberation Organization
POTUS	President of the United States
SCIF	Sensitive Compartmented Information Facility, Special room for secret conversations
SEC/NAV	Secretary of the Navy
USAF	United States Air Force
Whitehall	Insider's name for the British government

1

Julia Rider bounced onto the cable car with a smile, her dream of journeying to this old-new land finally coming true. She marveled at the aqua sea rolling against Israel's northern coast. Suddenly the steepest cable car in the world lurched and she rocketed down the sharp cliffs. Panic erupted, crawling up her throat. How could she remain calm in front of her children? Though Gregg and Glenna giggled at the fast approaching water, Julia tried to steel herself. Strong winds jolting the cable car roiled her stomach. She squeezed her eyes shut.

"At the bottom, I'm searching for gold coins," Gregg shouted over roaring winds.

Julia gripped the middle railing, wishing she hadn't listened to Clara Cohen. The Ambassador's wife had coaxed her and the kids to join the last-second tour with other embassy wives to the towering Rosh ha-Nikra and the grottos. Her husband, Bo, toiled at the U.S. Embassy in Tel Aviv, completing an urgent project for his new boss, Ambassador Hal Cohen.

Someone shook Julia's arm and she popped open an eye.

"Mom, look! You're missing the best part." Gregg pointed at rugged cliffs zooming by.

Julia blinked. In her eleven-year-old son's shining gray eyes she glimpsed a much younger version of Bo. Would he follow his father's footsteps into the CIA? A shudder ripped through her. Bo lived to take risks and she didn't want Gregg living in constant jeopardy. At least Bo's new assignment in the State Department kept him close to home. Well, on most days.

"Cool! Watch those jets diving," Gregg chirped, his nose plastered against the window.

Julia's daring glance upwards was rewarded by the sight of a jet swooping dangerously low. She reached for Glenna, and her thirteen-year-old daughter hurtled toward her just as two more fighter jets roared overhead. A moment later a huge explosion and fireball erupted in the sky.

"Wow!" Gregg jumped. "The second jet blew the first one out of the air!"

"Mom!" Glenna screamed.

Heart pounding, Julia clutched her daughter as debris crashed around their wobbling cable car. Sharp pieces of metal and she knew not what else fell into the blue Mediterranean waters below. Fear climbed her throat and she felt powerless to save her kids before they were killed.

She'd always heard the Israeli military was superb. Could this be some excessive training exercise? The car docked at the bottom and screaming tourists pushed out of the exit. A hand gripped Julia's shoulder and a raspy voice croaked, "Follow me back to the bus."

"We will!" Julia cried, looking into Clara Cohen's black eyes. Julia whisked her kids from the clumsy car, planting her feet on the path back to the bus. A loud siren wailed, mimicking the panic in her heart and mind.

A voice barked orders over an intercom, intensifying the chaos. She couldn't understand one word of the Hebrew. Then miraculously Moshe, their Israeli tour guide, began directing them in English.

"Run! Get to the shelter. This is no drill."

Clara caught Julia's hand and together with Glenna and Gregg, the four of them sprinted past a group of gun-toting Israeli soldiers herding tourists through a metal door. They shot down concrete steps into a dimly lit shelter, where Julia tried to catch her breath. Lungs heaving, she asked, "What's going on?"

"Nothing to worry about I am sure." Clara shrugged.

Moshe confided in a hushed whisper, "An Israeli fighter shot down an Iranian plane."

"But we are nowhere near Iran."

Julia grabbed Gregg's shirttail, but her son flitted away. Moshe had more to tell.

"Iranians are the puppet masters of Lebanon, only a few kilometers from here."

Julia huddled Glenna to her side, certain her ultra-sensitive daughter was as frightened as she in the dank shelter. A noisy mix of Hebrew, English, and other languages swirled around them. She desperately wanted Bo. Yanking out her cell, she was lifting her phone to call him when Clara jabbed an arm toward her.

"Your cell will not work this deep below ground."

Julia had to try. She punched in Bo's number, pressing her cell to her ear. It didn't ring. She slid the phone back in its holder, her heart sinking. Was this shelter even secure? How long would they have to remain below ground—hours, days? Before she could express her worries to Clara, the Ambassador's wife cajoled Julia and Glenna to a quieter corner.

"At four years old, I survived a tornado ripping apart our house. Living in Israel on and off for twelve years, I am prepared for abrupt change."

"I can handle storms," Julia groaned, "but explosions in front of my children are terrifying."

"You must be bold in the face of your enemy or you will expire."

What a strange comment. A sudden movement prompted Julia to glimpse Gregg punching the walls as if searching for a secret chamber. Glenna sniffled at Julia's side. Moshe strode around acting important with his badge and bullhorn.

"Israel will meet any test Iran throws at our defenses. Because we shot down their plane, they will leave us alone for weeks. Once the all clear sounds, we board the bus. I do not suppose anyone wants to see more of the area, do you?"

"I want to see more jets," Gregg said, whistling loudly just like Bo might have done.

Glenna looked up asking, "Can we go home?"

In the meager light Julia saw tears hovering on her lashes. "You heard Moshe say we could leave once they announce the all clear."

"I mean *home*, to Virginia."

What could Julia say? Words of truth she'd read a few hours ago swelled in her heart and she hugged her trembling daughter in a tight embrace.

"Sweetie, God sees us in this shelter. He'll protect us from all harm."

"You think so, Mom?"

"With my whole heart," she said stroking her hair. "Remember when the Israelites crossed into the Promised Land? God told Joshua that He would never leave or forsake him."

"Yeah, thousands of years ago. You told me."

Julia patted Glenna's head. "God sent Jesus to be our shepherd."

"I know," Glenna sniffed, wiping her eyes with her hands. "In Nazareth yesterday, Dr. Van Horn said a shepherd protects sheep from wolves."

"There are no wild animals down here," Gregg blurted.

"Mom means from danger," Glenna corrected. "We shouldn't be so scared."

Gregg laughed out loud. "You're the 'fraidy cat, not *me*."

"Gregg, leave your sister alone," Julia said, her voice echoing around the shelter.

"Dad will think the exploding jet was awesome. You'll see."

Gregg dashed over to Moshe and pulled on his sleeve; however, Julia couldn't hear what he asked. Her mind alerted to the future. How could they survive in the Middle East where violence sprouted like poison mushrooms? Embroiled in the terrible possibilities, Julia was haunted by her words of moments ago. She must rely on her new faith in God and not just say so.

Besides, she didn't want Glenna growing into a fearful young woman. On the other hand, her son parading around the dark shadows made her pause. She didn't relish Gregg becoming a soldier or secret agent as Bo had done, emulating his own father, Douglas MacArthur Rider.

"You are wise to rely on your faith," Clara said, giving Julia a moment's respite from thoughts of danger. "My mother took me and my sister to Temple and we kept every Sabbath."

"Do you attend Temple with the Ambassador?"

"Hal is too busy with his job. Perhaps I should make an effort to attend myself."

Clara turned away. Julia pondered how her own faith in God had deepened in the two weeks since arriving in Israel. Still, hiding in a bomb shelter with her children made her heart pound. She wiped clammy hands on her slacks. With Bo's new assignment in such a dangerous place, would they face more explosions? Someone started shouting in Hebrew and Julia flinched.

"Are more jets flying overhead?" she asked Moshe.

"No. Our IDF is protecting us. Follow me upstairs and head right to the bus."

Julia took Glenna by the hand, then grabbed Gregg's shirtsleeve, herding them upstairs. She quickly scanned the blue sky for fighters. Seeing none, she phoned Bo, bursting to tell her husband about the Iranian attack. His voice mail didn't even click on.

Clara held her cell phone high in the air, a scowl marbling her forehead. "The signals are jammed. I cannot reach Hal either."

Julia hurried to the bus. Gregg kept his eyes aimed at the sky and Julia had to push him on board, where she sank into a cushioned seat behind Clara. Gregg barreled to the window next to Clara, insisting he had to see any new action.

As soon as the driver turned the large bus, Clara swiveled her head to Julia. "We are going straight to Tel Aviv. In the embassy I have something to take your mind off trouble."

"Okay," Julia said with little zeal for another of Clara's schemes. Look how their excursion to the northern border of Israel had turned out. Julia dearly hoped no more surprises would erupt on their way home. She shut her eyes, trying to calibrate Bo's reaction when he learned the Israeli military had shot down an Iranian fighter a fraction above their heads. Did he even know of the explosion?

The bus tore down the highway and Julia opened her eyes, shaken by Glenna's thin, pale face. In the morning they were supposed to go with Dr. Van Horn to visit the famous King Solomon's mines, but Bo's work plans meant he couldn't join them. Should she cancel the plan?

When Bo first shared they'd be coming to Israel, Julia had laughed with delight. Easy to do in the safety of Virginia; she'd so longed to see the cradle of Christian civilization firsthand. Dr. Van Horn's books and teachings had stoked her appetite to explore the lands of the Bible.

The bus jerked around a corner. Julia jolted and her mind veered from her safe suburban home to unknown trouble looming ahead. She smoothed the gleaming hair of her sleeping daughter with an unwavering conviction: Coming to Israel had been a terrible mistake after all.

2

On the bright October morning, Bo Rider parked in the visitor section of a ritzy condominium with a burning question. Would his work here in Tel Aviv ever amount to anything? So far, he passed his days in one boring meeting after another pretending to advise Hal Cohen, the U.S. Ambassador to Israel on national security matters.

Bo felt more like a glorified babysitter. This morning he'd fled his cubbyhole at the compound trusting the CIA Station Chief, Mike Spencer, would serve him rare meat, something to sink his teeth into. He pulled the keys from the ignition with a chuckle. The Chief invoked a cloak-and-dagger routine, refusing to be seen with Bo at the embassy.

He locked the car, grateful Julia and their two kids were touring Israel. Tonight he'd get to hear all about their day's adventure. Guess he should thank Clara and Dr. Van Horn for showing his family the sights while Bo plunged ahead with his mundane duties at the embassy.

Normally, a more junior agent would have been sent to the embassy posing as a State Department diplomat, but Bo's boss, Wilt Kangas, had insisted Bo fulfill the opening. As CIA's Director of National Clandestine Services (NCS), Kangas' unwavering faith in Bo made him want to succeed. This new gig came with a new peril: For the first time he worked for the Agency not as Skip Pierce, but as Bo Rider, his real persona.

After clearing through security, Bo hopped on the elevator and hurried off on the third floor per the Chief's instructions. Bo knocked, noticing a camera mounted near the ceiling by Mike Spencer's door, recording his visit. The Chief opened the door, all six-foot-five of him, but Bo made it no farther than the foyer.

"No time for chitchat, Rider. What do you have?"

"Mossad called me the other day. Saul Goldberg, who I met at an embassy reception, hinted he wanted to meet soon."

"Nothing arranged yet?" Spencer folded his arms.

"He was vague. I don't know what's on his mind or if he'll call. Do you have much contact with Mossad?"

"Not as much as Kangas would like me to have," the Chief said. "I find them aloof."

Bo shifted his weight. "Duly noted."

"Be careful, Rider. Mossad may act like they believe you're with the State Department. Play that role. You decide when it's time to admit you are Agency."

With the Chief towering over his head by almost five inches, Bo didn't balk at his suggestion, simply replying, "Using my real name doesn't sit well, but I'm honing my diplomatic skills, sir."

"Kangas promised you'd have my back. Never forget Tel Aviv is a hotbed of secrets."

"I'm feeling my way around, slowly. As Hal's alleged advisor on national security, I'm on his calendar every day, but he never meets with me."

"He won't confer with me either. Any ideas what he's up to?"

"None. He doesn't keep me in his loop."

"Then burrow in, Rider," Spencer growled.

"Is that your order, sir?"

Asking that of the CIA Chief sounded more like Bo's Army Ranger days, but he needed to know where he stood.

Surprisingly, Spencer grinned. "No. It comes straight from Director Kangas. He knows I'm on my way out of here in two months. I'm pulling the pin."

Kangas hadn't told Bo about the Chief's retiring from the Agency.

"I'll keep you posted on Ambassador Cohen, sir."

"Make that a top priority, Rider."

"What am I looking for, specifically?"

"Follow me."

The lanky Chief stalked into a room where he dropped into a wing-back chair near the door, motioning for Bo to sit opposite him and provided Bo with a bird's-eye view into why Hal needed watching.

"The Berkeley grad recently testified before Congress that the U.S. should cut off all assistance to Israel. Can you believe our ambassador to Israel would dare voice such a thing?"

"Why keep him around then?"

The Chief narrowed his beady eyes. "He's carrying someone's water—Secretary of State, SecDef, or even the President. Kangas and I are frantic to learn who is pushing Israel, our only democratic ally in the Middle East, out into the cold."

Bo did some fast thinking. Spying on Hal might be Kangas' ploy in sending Bo to the embassy. While most station chiefs were approaching retirement, perhaps Mike Spencer had real guts. Bo felt a surge of uneasiness. Here he was in Israel using his real identity and beholden to three masters—the Chief, Ambassador Cohen, all the while reporting everything to Director Kangas back at Langley. Something seemed out of whack.

The Chief's gaze didn't waver. "Never let Cohen know you know me. Never, I repeat, never contact me at the embassy."

Bo nodded. He got it. He'd never even acknowledge the CIA Station Chief unless he came to his residence for a briefing.

"Shellie Karnack, the Special Agent in charge of Diplomatic Security, is reliable."

"I've not met her yet," Bo admitted.

"You will. She's been attending an international security meeting in Brussels."

Bo reflected on what Frank Deming, Kangas' assistant, had said about Shellie. "Her grandfather was a moving force in Israel becoming a nation back in 1948 and she grew up in Miami, which is everything I know of Special Agent Karnack."

The Chief stood on his long legs. "She had applied to the Agency, but we turned her down. A big mistake."

Bo followed him to the front door, asking, "So she's bitter toward the CIA?"

"Not in the least. She feels a kinship to us, which is nice for a change."

"What does Shellie know about me?"

"Rider, she hasn't been told you are Agency, but she'll make it her job to unmask you."

"Then what?" Bo didn't like the idea of Shellie poking around in his life.

"Don't worry. Once she does that, she'll let you know. Consider her an ally."

"Yes, sir."

"See you here in another week, same time. Keep a trained eye on Cohen."

Bo stepped into the hall, the bolt clicking behind him. He hustled down to the car curious if the Chief was paranoid about Hal. If so, why had Kangas never hinted the Chief had an axe to grind? Maybe Bo's fortunes were about to change. Political intrigue at the embassy would make for interesting days ahead.

AN HOUR LATER back at his uncluttered desk, Bo ramped up his computer searching for important messages. He had none. Another idea surfaced. He locked the morning's notes in his office safe and headed out, passing the receptionist on the way to feed his caffeine habit.

"Zaveda, I'll be back in ten minutes. If anyone needs me, send a text on my cell."

"Where are you going?" the Israeli woman asked, tossing her swirls of black hair.

"For coffee. Want some?"

"I do not share your American obsession with that drink. Do not be gone long. Ms. Karnack has returned and wants to meet you at eleven."

Zaveda seemed abrupt and unlike her usual self where she'd laugh about nightclubbing like froth bubbling over. The elevator took him to the ground floor, where he paid for a tall cup of java at the Daily Grind and wandered to the inner courtyard. He sat on a bench sipping hot brew, a lone sentinel keeping the embassy safe.

What a joke. Bo had no business masquerading as an embassy official. He belonged at Langley, digging out America's enemies around the world. The thought of being exposed under his real name brought out a crawling sensation on his arms.

Then again, maybe it was the unusually cool temperatures. Too bad he'd left his jacket in the car. Winter was on the march, but the cloudless sky above him looked as boring as his life had become. A throaty voice at his ear startled him.

"You planning a rendezvous out here?"

Bo looked up into a woman's smiling dark brown eyes.

"Hardly. I'm taking a break from my hectic schedule as National Security adviser to Ambassador Cohen."

"Mr. Rider, I have looked forward to getting to know you. I am Special Agent Karnack, but you can call me Shellie."

"And I am Bo, at your service."

With that, she held out a hand, pumping Bo's as if he was her dearest friend.

"Zaveda told me you were back and scheduled a meet at eleven."

"Hmm, I hadn't told her that," Shellie replied, shrugging her shoulders.

"She's a real mind reader and a bit intrusive into my comings and goings."

"Zaveda thinks she is doing her job. Hey, don't sit out here by yourself. Anytime you want to kibitz over coffee, give me a ring."

Shellie snapped on a pair of stylish sunglasses, leaving Bo to ignore her invitation and sip his hot drink slow and easy.

"I've returned from Brussels. Want an update on the latest security techniques?"

"Set the time and I'll be there."

"How about three this afternoon?"

"Works for me," Bo said, draining his coffee.

Shellie removed her sunglasses to stare. "You weren't looking for me?"

"No. Why would I be?"

"I don't know. Zaveda said someone was looking for me."

"Well she knows me and knows that I wasn't."

"I think you are right. Something is up with her," Shellie said with a frown. "If you sense anything unusual about her actions, will you let me know?"

Bo gave a fake salute. Shellie stepped closer, her high heels tapping on the tile.

"A word of advice. You won't be here long before someone tries to stab you in the back. You need me." With that Shellie grinned coyly and went inside the glass door. Bo refused to be flustered by Shellie's cryptic words. He looked at his cell, thinking he'd heard a text alert. Nope. Unlike Shellie, no one was looking for him. Every ticking second brought him closer to nothing, except for Shellie's new charge: Keep an eye on the receptionist.

He knew little about Shellie Karnack, the Diplomatic Security Director, other than her grandfather's key role in the creation of modern Israel. The Chief had insisted she was a friend to the CIA, yet she seemed too keen, like some wannabe spy.

He'd just stood when his phone chirped. Bo opened it and read: *U have call on hold. Come now. Z*

So Zaveda texted. Useful info, but the caller was probably a local reporter wanting background on the upcoming Middle East peace conference. Bo guzzled the foam lingering at the bottom of the cup. When he walked off the elevator he found Zaveda pacing by her desk.

"You received my text?"

"Yeah, that's why I'm back."

"Mr. Rider, first the male caller refused to tell me who he is. When I went back to say you would be right with him, he was impolite. This line should not remain tied up."

"Which paper is he with?"

Zaveda's brown eyes widened. "From the way he demanded you, he is no reporter."

"Transfer his call to my office."

He hurried to unlock his office hoping for a real challenge. The light on his phone was flashing and he grabbed it, announcing, "Bo Rider here."

A slight pause. "This is Saul Goldberg. Was that your secretary who answered?"

"I have no secretary," Bo said, breathing hard. "My phone diverts to the embassy's receptionist."

"She ordered me to give my name. I refused her demands."

"Wise of you to tell her nothing."

"I have something to share of the utmost urgency. When can you arrive at my office?"

"You name it and I'm there." Bo grabbed his PDA, gearing up for a change he hoped would use skills he'd gotten to use recently in Iran.

"How about in five minutes?"

That fast?

"I'm on my way," Bo promised.

He relocked his office and ran to the elevator without telling Zaveda where he was going. Let her wonder. He secured an embassy car, curiosity growing about why Mossad wanted him ASAP, and headed out the rear entrance leading through the courtyard and to the parking lot. He'd just passed the security office when he heard his name.

"Hey, Bo Rider."

Against his better judgment he stopped. There stood Shellie in her brown pantsuit wiggling her index finger, requesting his presence. Bo battled within himself: Race to Mossad or placate Shellie, who the Chief promised would be an important ally. Bo's work ethic winning out, he strode into her high-tech office. She closed the door after him.

"Zaveda is upset by someone phoning for you."

"Did he cuss her out?" Bo asked, boring his eyes into Shellie's intense dark ones.

"She wants to know who called."

"Why?"

"He hurt Zaveda's feelings."

"Shellie, I know you run security here, but my caller's identity is immaterial. He doesn't have to give Zaveda his name."

"You're right of course, but here's another tip." Shellie pulled herself up to her full five-feet-five inches as if she needed to look important.

"For you, Shellie, I'm all ears."

"I thought you'd be eager to fit in after your time at Langley. Zaveda is Israeli. I treat her and the entire staff like family I trust."

Bo made sure his facial muscles didn't give away his surprise: Shellie already knew Bo worked for the CIA. He rested a hand on the doorknob.

"I'm a team player. Ask anyone at *State*," he stressed. "But you told me earlier to keep an eye on Zaveda. Here's a tip for you. Both my eyes tell me she's crossed the line."

"We are to keep records of everyone who visits or calls. Zaveda maintains a log."

"When you can guarantee Zaveda is absolutely trustworthy, then maybe I'll let her know my caller's names."

"We run background checks for all Israeli nationals working in the embassy."

"Whoop-de-do." Bo glared at Shellie. "Are you vouching for the men she spent the night with? Who are they, Shellie? Any of them members of Hamas, or don't you know?"

"You are being ridiculous," Shellie lobbed back.

"I have confidence in your ability to protect the embassy, but I'm not trusting Zaveda with any information. As the Ambassador's advisor on national security, I resent her even knowing *my* name."

Shellie flinched and leaned against the edge of her desk. "This is going to be a problem."

"Look," he said, rattling his car keys. "I'm late for an important meeting."

"I'll smooth things over with Zaveda for you."

Bo didn't budge. "Tell her to stop harassing my callers for their names. Then her feelings won't be hurt."

"When you return from your meeting, you and I will have a nice, long talk," Shellie said, opening the door with a beaming smile.

"Glad you understand my point. I'm sure we can work together."

Bo left her to calm Zaveda's feathers. Still, why had the Agency rejected Shellie? Her bloodhound instincts seemed a positive trait, but he wondered if her being rebuffed meant she'd constantly meddle in his job here in Israel.

3

Bo wheeled his unmarked car into a tight parking spot near Moss-ad's HQ, Shellie's barb about his being from Langley ringing in his ears. Score one for Shellie, but he wouldn't let her outwit him. He slammed the car door, a grudge building against the Security Director.

At Langley, no one peered over his shoulder. Kangas trusted Bo to perform his covert jobs with excellence and Frank Deming, assistant to Kangas, was as close as a brother. Shellie might hold the title "Special Agent," but she was starting to pale in comparison with two other agents he respected, ICE Special Agent Eva Montanna and FBI Special Agent Griff Topping.

As he sauntered past concrete obstacles, Bo paused. Israeli security teams had built barriers along the perimeter so bomb-laden vehicles couldn't puncture the heart of Israel's intelligence service. He should do the same with Shellie and not let her penetrate his defenses.

That decision made, Bo stepped with renewed purpose through the wrought iron gate when he noted a flaw. Any idiot approaching Mossad could guess the unmarked building held Israel's secret spy agency. It would be Bo's first time inside and excitement grew as he handed his State Department ID to a guard. The khaki-clad soldier, who boasted a beret and an assault rifle on his shoulder, stared intently at Bo.

"Saul Goldberg is expecting me."

The guard inspected Bo's eyes before typing on a keyboard and briefly consulting a computer monitor. "Ah, you go in," the soldier finally said in fractured English.

Cleared to the main entrance fifty yards away, Bo presented his phony creds to a female officer wearing a similar uniform, minus the assault rifle. She allowed Bo into the reception area where he pocketed his ID and waited. Minutes upon minutes passed and he began doing a slow burn. Saul insisted on Bo getting here in five minutes, yet here he stood killing time.

Finally an escort brought Bo upstairs to what he instantly recognized as a Sensitive Compartmented Information Facility (SCIF).

Saul Goldberg, a clean-shaven man, accepted delivery of Bo, ordering the escort to leave them alone.

"*Boker Tov*, Bo Rider. Our meeting last week must have been preordained," Saul said in flawless English. Obviously he'd been educated in the West.

Bo shook his hand, analyzing the Mossad agent's shiny bald head and two hoop earrings made of gold.

"*Boker Tov*," he replied grinning. "I owe you thanks."

Saul flexed his eyebrows downward. "You are certain of that already?"

"Yeah, for saving me from another boring day."

"Your mind works like mine," Saul laughed. "But one second may change a lifetime."

"You are right, but my time at the embassy seems to be wasting mine."

"I predict you will reach an opposite conclusion before you leave."

Saul hurried to a side office, then sat behind a metal desk. After shutting the door behind him, Bo found a plastic chair, which barely held his six-foot frame. He was eager to discover what Saul had up his sleeve. Perhaps Bo's diplomatic role had more purpose than being a sham assistant to Hal.

"In the SCIF, we can talk shop. I was delayed by a concerning development."

"Egypt's new regime? They've gone from living in peace with Israel to arming Hamas."

Saul flashed his brown eyes. "I bring greetings from our friend Judah Levitt."

"Pass along my warm regards. He won't join us?"

"Judah is not allowed to be seen in this building."

Then why invoke Judah's name, Bo wanted to ask. Rather than be provocative, Bo gazed at Saul, curious if Judah Levitt would contact him through other means. While previously posing as Skip Pierce, corporate recruiter, Bo had met the secretive Mossad agent on a hair-raising Op where Judah had discovered Bo's real identity. Last he knew Judah had infiltrated a radical group in an unknown country.

Saul inserted a key into his desk drawer. Metal scraping sounds pulled Bo from his mental travels and he decided to unlock what was in Saul's mind.

"Are you going to connect me with Judah or not?"

"At the proper time," Saul said, an ominous look sweeping over his face.

Bo fidgeted, uncomfortable on the undersized chair. "My respect for Judah fills an entire file cabinet, so I'll assist however he thinks I can help."

"A given."

The Mossad agent drew out a thin brown envelope. Saul seemed prone to riddles or evasion, Bo wasn't sure which. A spy himself, stealth usually intrigued Bo, but he'd had too much caffeine and was in no mood for games.

"What's so urgent that we meet without Judah?"

"I believe your embassy assignment is the first time you have worked overtly for the Agency."

Bo narrowed his eyes. Where was Saul going with the cross-examination?

"Are your days on the dark side over?" Saul asked, fingering a gold earring.

Bo didn't like a counterpart from a foreign power interrogating him, but most likely Judah had told Mossad of Bo's covert status with the Agency.

"I'm unsure what comes after my embassy assignment. What about you, Saul? Spend any time in covert operations?"

Saul's nod was more of a flick of his shiny head. "Briefly. My superiors arranged for me to fully experience Mossad."

"Your English is superb," Bo said, feeling his way along as if on a professional first date.

"Who knows? Perhaps we met each other earlier in our lives."

Bo's mind revved into high gear. Was he missing some code to open the spigot before Saul would divulge the reason for this meet? Saul pushed back his chair, resting one calf on the other thigh.

"I attended grad school at George Washington in D.C.," he said.

"When?" Bo asked, making his next move in the chess game Saul was playing.

"Twelve years ago I worked for the IDF. Mossad recruited me and sent me to GW."

"So you worked covertly for the Israeli Defense Forces?"

Saul threw his head back and laughed. "On the Institute's payroll, I studied international finance."

Okay, Saul didn't share Judah's covert role at the Institute for Intelligence and Operations, Mossad's official moniker. Bo crossed his arms, nearly fed up with the charade.

"The Agency recruited me while I was an officer with the Army Rangers."

Saul simply wove his fingers together as if wanting to hear more. Bo complied.

"My dad served in the Pentagon. I visited my folks in D.C. when you were there."

"Your father, Captain Douglas MacArthur Rider, was Navy, right?" Saul knew his dad? Bo blinked, not wanting to reveal how that startled him, so he managed a tight grin.

"Yup. He commanded subs. In later years he hated being at the helm of a desk."

"Bo, follow me. It is time for you to talk with Judah."

"Ah, hah," Bo laughed. He must have unlocked the secret passage.

Saul clutched a file under his arm, leading Bo down a far hallway that ended by an elevator, which brought them to a lower level. Here Saul placed his eye against a retina scanner. A heavy steel door opened.

Beyond this door they walked through a series of corridors, some a half block long. Bo guessed they'd passed under the street to the bowels of other buildings. At another elevator, they rode to yet a lower level. This elevator opened and at last, Bo clapped eyes on Judah Levitt, his lips spread in a mighty grin between his robust beard.

"Your beard is longer than when I last saw you." Bo strode to his friend.

Saul handed the file to Judah and said, "This is where I leave you, Bo."

Elevator doors swished open and closed. Judah embraced Bo in a giant bear hug.

"The last time we were together, we spent days without bathing. We smell much better this time."

"We stunk but were lucky to be alive," Bo chuckled. "What's with the maze?"

"It is imperative I am never seen at Mossad."

Bo assumed Judah had entered through a secret corridor or nearby building. "Where are we, in the belly of Mossad?"

Judah put a finger to his lips and led Bo to another door with an optical scanner. Inside the windowless room, they took seats around a long conference table in front of a large monitor.

"This reminds me of the secure communications room beneath the White House," Bo said. "Judah, isn't all this secrecy a bit extreme?"

"Israel is a young nation, not yet a hundred years old. But we are an ancient people. You may know this because the Old Testament of your Bible contains our Jewish Torah and Tanakh, which describes our history. We have been spying for thousands of years and have learned how to survive. Saul was making sure you were you."

"I accept Saul's vetting of me. America, not yet three hundred years old, can learn much from our Jewish friends and allies."

"The truth of your statement will soon be revealed. First some history. Do you mind?"

"I'll try to memorize what you tell me."

"It is life changing, my friend. In Mossad training, we study a leader named Joshua. Your Bible has an entire book about how Jehovah appointed him to command the Israelites after Moses gained their release from Pharaoh's captivity in Egypt."

"Charlton Heston played Moses in the movie. I liked the part where Pharaoh and his warriors were swallowed by the sea."

Judah ran a finger along a jagged scar in one of his eyebrows, which Bo didn't recall seeing before. He wanted to ask what had happened, but the Mossad agent had more to tell.

"Years after Moses died, Joshua sent spies into the city of Jericho to discover their weaknesses before attacking the heavily fortified city. The spies consulted with the woman Rahab to probe the city's defenses. You see, she was a prostitute. Some things never change."

"I never studied your Joshua in any of my training. Why is he important?"

"To us, he is equal in stature with George Washington."

"The movie ended after Moses received the Ten Commandments. That gives me an idea of who Joshua is anyway."

"Put your mind a thousand years ago in Jericho when the Israelites are about to take the Promised Land. Someone told the enemy king about Joshua's spies."

"What we'd call a mole," Bo replied evenly.

"Exactly. Rahab knew God had sent the spies. She hid them from the soldiers and later helped them escape by lowering them down the city's outer wall on a rope from her window. For her aid, the spies promised to save her when the Israelites attacked the city if she would hang a scarlet cord out her window. Joshua's army saw the cord, sparing Rahab and her family. She lived and became the great-great-grandmother of King David."

Bo leaned forward. "What do you want me to take away from this story?"

"This is a scarlet cord moment."

"You want me to save you. From what?"

Judah lowered his head, looking suspiciously like a bull ready to charge. "Our countries are both in terrible danger. I want to protect you, my friend."

"I'm at risk from one of your enemies? Is that what you're telling me?"

"I have a source from the Gaza who I recently met in Cairo. He told me that Bo Rider was on his way to the American Embassy here in Tel Aviv as a diplomat. My asset bragged how you were really CIA."

Bo sat back stunned; Judah saying this shot through his heart. "You knew my cover with the State Department was blown before I ever arrived?"

"I wasted no time calling you in."

Bo did some rapid-fire thinking. No doubt Judah had ordered field agents to monitor Bo's actions and to report back. Bo leapt up, striding about the enclosed room, concern and anger pummeling his chest.

"I arrived two weeks ago as advisor to Ambassador Cohen. Now you're saying I've moved my wife and kids to ground zero. Who is leaking my identity?"

"My asset does not know but is confident it is the work of a spy."

"A mole has burrowed into Mossad?" Bo sat back down across from Judah asking, "How can I help you uncover his identity?"

"Not Mossad. Someone in *your* embassy is smuggling out intelligence."

A spy in the U.S. Embassy? Under Bo's watch? Shocked for a second time in as many minutes, Bo was speechless. Who was to blame? The Chief considered Hal Cohen treacherous. Although Bo found Hal a nice enough guy, he seemed clueless about securing an embassy in the midst of terrorizing neighbors. Bo had a sinking feeling about Hal's true allegiance but wouldn't share his misgivings with Judah. Not yet.

"I wish I could say it's impossible, but the spy trade will never go out of business," Bo said. "What else did your source tell you?"

"That Hamas could have a source inside."

"The Islamist paramilitary faction of Gaza, in my embassy?" Bo swallowed, feeling violated as if he'd been mugged.

Judah opened the file folder, removing a photo of Hal sitting next to a man in the rear seat of a Mercedes Benz. Bo stared at the grainy photo, obviously taken with a zoom lens.

"Who is the man Hal's meeting with?"

"A Turkish arms dealer organizing flotillas seeking to arm the citizens of Gaza."

"You show Hal's photo because you suspect he leaked my identity?"

"I cannot say with certainty. We shot the photo six months ago. Some in Mossad believe Hal could have been urging the Turk not to support the flotilla. You know what happened. IDF responded with force. Several citizens lost their lives."

"Could your source have been testing your reaction about me?"

Judah spread out his hands. "I trust him. He knew you were coming to Tel Aviv before Mossad. I do not know who your embassy spy is; however, you should clean house."

"Keep me advised if you learn anything," Bo said, wiping sweating palms on his slacks.

"I trust you will do the same."

"Other than the leak about me, has other intelligence been compromised?"

A thundercloud erupted in Judah's deep set eyes. "Six months ago Sadie Lamb, the American teaching at a Gaza mission school, was kidnapped. She is still being held hostage."

Bo met Judah's eyes without revealing any knowledge of the teacher.

"Hamas believes Sadie Lamb worked for the Agency."

"Why?" Bo feigned surprise.

"The week prior to her capture she met your Station Chief at a restaurant a half mile from your embassy."

Bo knew Judah spoke the truth from his briefing prior to departing the U.S. Still he asked, "Who alleges she is connected to the Agency?"

"My source who claims your embassy leaks worse than an old boat. As a result, Mossad will no longer engage with your embassy."

Bo raised his eyebrows. "And I thought we were having a friendly chat."

"I will always meet you, my friend, but no one else."

Bo swiped a lock of hair from his forehead. His mind was reeling at the idea of a spy running roughshod through the embassy for six months before Bo even set foot in Tel Aviv. This was too hot to tell the Chief and he certainly wouldn't breathe a word to Hal. He'd fly straight to Kangas, avoiding any encrypted messages or the telephone. Bo turned his mind from the difficulties ahead to what Judah was saying.

"This goes deeper than a mole in your embassy. I was delayed because an hour ago, our Air Force shot down an Iranian fighter trying to penetrate our northern air space."

"Where?"

"At our northern border with Lebanon. This time Iran's IFF, their Information Friend or Foe, squawked out a frequency from your Air Force, trying to convince us they were friendly."

"There's a leak in our Air Force too?"

"Enemies all around us, my friend. Whom do we trust?"

Bo offered a hand. "Each other, and we go from there."

"A wise reply and one I do not take lightly." Judah stood and the agents shook hands. "You will savor our friendship the longer you are on Israeli ground."

"I won't mention your suspicions to anyone at my embassy. Everyone is a suspect."

"You have arrived at a crucial time. Can I assist your planned house cleaning?"

"I'd like to take a copy of Hal's photo."

"Both our lives are at risk while your embassy remains infiltrated."

Their lingering handshake cemented Bo's quest to root out and disable a spy in America's embassy. He'd need Judah's expert help in remaining a step ahead of whoever had leaked Bo's real identity. He shoved a copy of Hal's photo into his pocket and left the bowels of Mossad's Headquarters a different man, no longer feeling like a useless and bogus diplomat. Bo practically ran out the wrought iron gate, a man on a deadly mission.

4

Bo roared back to the embassy, his brain firing as if on ten cylinders. Under Shellie's watch, she'd allowed the embassy to be infiltrated by an enemy spy, which at a minimum questioned her competence. With the Chief vouching for her, Bo intended to go easy, but he needed to eyeball her and ask about security after the tussle in the air with Iranian fighter jets. Of course, he wouldn't admit Judah's startling mole revelation to Shellie.

He entered the Com Center with a whistle so as not to alert staffers of his goal. He slid into the secure phone booth and placed a call to Kangas at Langley. It wasn't quite eight in the morning in Virginia and Bo expected to leave a voice message.

When he heard, "Clandestine Services, this is Frank Deming," Bo waited for the beep before leaving a message. But then he heard again, "Hey, it's Frank. Who's calling?"

"I didn't think you'd be in yet."

"Sorry, but I don't recognize your voice."

"Bo Rider. You forgot me already?"

Frank laughed. "I'm here early because Director Kangas is meeting with agency heads. I drove in to assist with coffee, Danish, all the important stuff. Hold on a sec."

He muffled the phone and Bo strained to hear what was going on in Frank's world. When he returned to the call, Frank sounded flustered when he said, "Gotta go, but what's up?"

Bo glanced at several tech-types loitering near the door of the secure booth. So he carefully chose his words. "I'm reminding you that my flight leaves tomorrow night and I meet the Director the next morning."

"Hate to tell you this, but you're not on his schedule."

"I know that. I'm calling to *remind* you to put me on his schedule."

A moment's pause and then Frank chuckled, "I get it. You can't talk."

"Glad you haven't lost your touch."

"You're in luck. The Director will hear firsthand what you can't say over the phone."

"I'll call back with my flight time and I'll try not to make it so early."

"Thanks, and Bo, stay safe."

Bo clicked off, dread seizing him. Not only did he have to break it to Kangas that an unidentified spy had invaded America's embassy in Israel, but he had to tell Julia he was leaving her and the kids alone in Tel Aviv on such sudden notice.

First, he made his flight arrangements and shot out of the Com Center to corner Shellie, wanting to discuss with her what security measures were needed for Ambassador Cohen and the staff. Shellie was not in her office. Bo hurried up to ask Zaveda if she had seen her.

"No." Zaveda rolled her eyes, stuffing buds in her ears.

Bo spun on his heels. Hoping to locate Hudson Engle, the Marine Security Guard, Bo could only hope his wife hadn't heard about the IDF shooting an Iranian fighter jet. If she had, Julia would never agree to let him out of her sight, let alone fly to Langley.

JULIA GAVE UP TRYING to acquire a signal on her cell phone. The bus finally dropped them at the U.S. Embassy in Tel Aviv and she barreled out with the kids. Clara swept them through security without signing in. All of Julia's energy had disappeared. Her mind kept replaying the horrific explosion in the sky as their cable car had plummeted toward the sea.

As she passed a rigid and motionless Marine guard, Julia's heart rate finally slowed. They'd made it safely back to the embassy, which was U.S. soil. Clara faced the Marine.

"We just witnessed the Israeli Air Force shoot down an Iranian plane at Rosh ha-Nikra, near the Lebanon border. Have you increased security?"

"Security is always tight here, ma'am," the Marine said without a smile.

"We shall see about that, young man. Julia, come with me to Hal's office."

Clara dismissed the Marine with a wave. Julia trailed behind Clara as the confident woman hurried down the hall to the elevator, which would take them to the second floor. Glenna and Gregg grumbled at each other over who knew what.

"You two behave," Julia said. "Dad works here every day. This won't take long."

"You always say that," Gregg said, squeaking his rubber soles on the tiled floor.

"Sshh." Julia pushed a finger against her lips.

In a sparsely decorated room outside Hal's office, Clara challenged Joe Adams, her husband's young assistant. "Where is my husband?"

"I cannot say, ma'am."

"Never mind," Clara said, arching her brows. "Please round up cold juice and snacks for these children. They can wait out here with you, Joe. Mrs. Rider and I will be right out."

"Remember what I told you both," Julia cautioned Gregg and Glenna.

Inside Hal's plush office, Clara snatched up a photo, showing it to Julia. Clara radiated joy in the photo, standing between two serious-looking women wearing white jackets.

"Are they doctors?" Julia asked.

"Specialists who treat breast cancer. I want to help Israeli women fight a terrible disease."

"What do you hope to accomplish?"

"Nothing short of a miracle. Less women dying from breast cancer. These doctors and I raised almost a million dollars in our race for the cure. You missed my foundation's event this summer, but perhaps next year you will run in the half marathon."

Julia burst out laughing. "I'm no athlete like Bo. My hobby is scrapbooking."

"You won't help?" Clara asked, her sunny face growing cloudy. "I had thought—"

"I know calligraphy. Is that of any use?"

"Marvelous." Clara clapped her hands. "You design the place cards for our reception tomorrow evening. You will come?"

Julia wanted Bo to succeed here in Tel Aviv and although she doubted she could help in any meaningful way, she agreed on the spot. Clara told her to arrive by seven.

"That should be no problem," Julia said with a smile. "Bo can stay home with the kids. What you're doing is heroic. I'll come alongside, but now I'd really like to find my husband."

"I knew I could count on you," Clara said beaming. "I'll take you upstairs myself."

Minutes later in the reception area outside Bo's office, Julia said good-bye to Clara and hello to Zaveda, who wore a haggard look, hair drooping in her eyes. Gregg and Glenna laughed jovially as they examined a mini-Jerusalem on a side table.

"This is not a playground and I have a headache," Zaveda grumbled.

"Sorry to hear you are not well," Julia replied, "but we had a frightening experience. Is my husband in his office? I see his door is closed."

"He is not and he never tells me where he is going."

Julia's hopes fell. They were supposed to ride home with Bo, but he wasn't expecting them for hours. Before she could think what to do, the elevator pinged and the doors swished open. Julia jerked her head around. Bo's manly face and eager smile made her heart leap. She wanted to fling herself into his arms as tears sprang to her eyes.

Instead, she called to the kids, "Dad's here."

She hurried over to him, whispering, "Can we go right in your office? Something terrible happened and I've been trying like mad to call you."

"Honey, what's wrong?"

She aimed her eyes at Zaveda. "Not here."

"Hey guys, I want to hear about your day."

"It was awesome, Dad!" Gregg plunged through the door first.

Glenna broke down into tears as Bo closed his door. He hugged her and coaxed his daughter to tell him all about it. Tears flooded Julia's eyes also and she fought for calm.

"We were hurtling down the cable car. An Israeli fighter fired on an Iranian jet. It burst into flames over our heads. Soldiers pushed us into the shelter. It was real scary for the kids."

"Glenna acted afraid, but I didn't!" Gregg said, pumping his fist into the air.

Julia handed Glenna a tissue to blow her nose.

"We're thankful God answered our prayers and protected us, right?"

Gregg launched into a tale. "Dad, metal parts crashed all around us. I wish you could've been there to tell us what kind of planes they were."

"I have just heard about those fighters, but I had no idea you were in harm's way." Bo's forehead creased.

"My cell signal was jammed all the way back." Julia sighed. "Clara's on the hunt for Hal, but no one knows where he is."

Bo hurried to the phone and called someone, leaving a voice message, "Shellie, it's Bo Rider. Please call me right away about an urgent matter."

He made a few other calls, but Julia didn't listen, more important matters crowding her mind like how to keep her family alive. She jumped as Bo touched her moist cheek.

"Honey, I'm taking you home. If I have to, I can return here later."
That sounded like a lifeline and she hoped Bo didn't have to leave
them alone. She and their kids really needed to talk with him about
what happened. Out in the reception area, Bo hurried past Zaveda.

"Where are you going?" she demanded.

"I'm on my cell if you need me or you can text me."

Zaveda stood by her desk. "That's not what I asked."

"Taking my family for an early supper. Don't worry about me."

Julia pressed the down button, anxious to exit the building before
someone returned Bo's messages. They stepped onto the elevator
where Glenna held onto her dad's hand. Bo gave her a hug, which
prompted a smile on her peaked face. Safe in the embassy car with
Bo driving out of the lot, Julia felt certain they'd make their getaway.
Then Bo stomped on the brakes.

"There she is!" he cried.

"Who?" Julia twisted her neck to see.

"Shellie Karnack. She's getting into that car with a man. Recognize him?"

"Nope," Julia said. "But I met so few people at the embassy reception."

"I need to speak to her."

"You'll have to run to catch up to them!"

"Wait here."

Bo jammed the car into park and ran to the garage exit. Julia could
see the black car, long like a limo, speed away before Bo reached
them. He hobbled back to their car and eased in.

"I pulled a leg muscle."

"Daddy, can we go home now? My stomach hurts."

Julia reached back to pat Glenna's arm. "You'll feel better after a
nice warm bath."

When she straightened, she noticed Bo's tense profile and his
white knuckles as he gripped the wheel. He must be hiding something about the battle in the sky. Could she convince him to tell her?

5

Bo stretched his legs beneath a circular glass table, hardly noticing the view from the spacious balcony of their Tel Aviv apartment. Though dark clouds threatened rain, no drops fell, giving Bo a chance to sit with his family outdoors and watch a storm blowing in across the mighty Mediterranean.

After he'd dropped his family at home, Bo had returned to the embassy for a briefing by the military attaché. Then he'd sped to a meeting with Hal about the Iranian's ulterior motives. Hal had wanted Bo to stay and have a meeting with Shellie, but she failed to reappear. So he jetted back home to eat an early dinner, only he wasn't hungry.

His eyes scanned the water, his mind mulling over the shoot-down. Julia tapped his shoulder and he tore his eyes from the gray, foaming water.

"You aren't eating," Julia said, worry lines etching around her eyes.

"The chicken and avocado are good."

"Then why is your salad bowl still full?"

She searched his face as if looking for a clue to his thoughts. Bo winked, turning quickly.

"Wow! Look at that guy jump those huge waves on a jet ski."

Glenna and Gregg whipped their heads to watch a phantom rider and Bo swiped a ripe olive from each of their plates.

"Daddy," Glenna grumbled, "you fooled us again."

"Lesson two for the day. Keep your eyes open for the possible. And thanks for the olives." Bo smacked his lips. "Tasty."

"I'm getting dessert so we can watch a movie."

Bo watched Julia hurry from the table, going inside. How thankful he was that his family hadn't been hurt. Coming on the heels of Judah's scarlet cord affair was almost too much to absorb. A spy within the U.S. Embassy would hinder Bo's relationship with his Israeli counterparts. It was probably no coincidence that he'd learned of a traitor on the same day Iranian fighters engaged the Israeli military.

Gregg kept up a running banter about their escapade at Israel's northern border boasting, "I thought it was cool, but you could hear Glenna's scream for miles."

Glenna dropped her head to her arms and Bo jostled the top of her head.

"Pumpkin, you had a shock with those jets fighting each other, but you're home safe. Last year, I was scared when a plane flew too close to my plane. The pilot flew me safely home."

Bo didn't admit he'd almost been blown out of the sky by a Russian MiG. Most likely he'd never tell his kids about the hazards he faced everyday with the CIA.

"Glenna's such a girl."

"Gregg, stop it, or you'll have no apple pie," Julia warned, returning with dessert.

"Okay, my sister rocks," Gregg said, grabbing his plate. "Can I have a big piece?"

"I don't want any." Glenna folded her arms. "My stomach aches."

Julia knelt by her daughter. "Want some ice cream?"

"I dunno." Glenna shrugged her thin shoulders.

"Enough quarreling." Bo thrust a hand on their shoulders. "I'm proud of you both. Want to hear lesson three?"

Gregg rolled his eyes and Glenna lifted her head. But they chimed in unison, "Okay."

"Good answer. Mom will serve you both pie."

Julia flung him a smile, giving him the first piece. Bo tried a bite before saying, "Your Grandpa Popeye taught me to respect my mom, Grandmama Rider, by never wrinkling up my nose at what she spent hours making."

Glenna's blue eyes watered, but she stabbed the pie with her fork. Gregg attacked his dessert with gusto as if he was hollow inside. Bo toyed with his fork, forcing himself to eat the delicacy, even though he didn't care for dessert. The timing couldn't have been worse for his flying to Washington. Was it safe to leave his family alone in Tel Aviv?

"Please rinse your plates in the sink," Julia said after they'd eaten the pie. "Get ready for bed so we can watch *Black Stallion*."

"Sweet," Gregg called, racing inside.

While Glenna slowly trudged inside, Julia came over and hugged Bo's neck.

"Thanks for saying what you did to them. It was an awful moment, Bo. I was afraid we wouldn't make it back here alive, but God spared us."

Bo stood, enveloping Julia into his arms.

"Believe that if you want. When I face danger, I stuff it into a corner of my mind and move on. Otherwise, I might never leave my bed in the mornings."

Julia touched his chin. "That's what I mean. We don't have to face scary stuff alone."

"I'm glad you're all okay," he said, wiping tears from her cheeks.

"I love you, Bo. And I cherish our times together."

"Me too." Bo lightly kissed her on the lips.

When he added, "I hate to say this, Julia," she went limp in his arms.

"Where to this time?"

"Washington to meet Kangas. My plane leaves at midnight."

"You see how shook up Glenna is." Julia dabbed her eyes. "Can't you postpone leaving until Wednesday night? Clara's reception is tomorrow night and I need you home with the kids."

Guilt stabbed Bo. He should stay home, but surely a spy in America's embassy trumped his personal desires, especially with Iran flaunting its muscle in Lebanon. What stung was that while he looked like a callous heel to Julia, he couldn't tell her why he needed to talk with Kangas eye to eye. But then, would twenty-four hours make a huge difference?

Rain drops began splashing on their heads and Julia pulled away, dashing to collect the dishes. Bo caught her hand.

"You're right. It's unbelievably urgent, but I'll sleep home and catch a flight in the morning. You all need to feel how much I care for you."

As Bo scurried to shelter the rest of the pie from the rain and Julia rounded up dirty plates, he thought he heard her whisper, "Thank you, God."

He had to wonder, would Kangas abandon his wife and children right after they'd witnessed an act of war? Bo thought he wouldn't. He could only assume that Kangas would agree Bo shouldn't either and resist placing a demerit in Bo's file.

BO HAD JUST FINISHED browsing online news when the clock struck eleven. He shut down his laptop and climbed the stairs, certain Julia would be asleep. But, she lay awake with the lights on, armed for battle.

"Are you exposing the kids to a perilous way of life over here?"

"Just a minute." Bo closed the door tightly and padded on bare feet into the bathroom. Brushing his teeth, he searched for the right words to mollify his wife during his absence. In the mirror, he glimpsed a side of himself he did not like. Once again he had to disappoint Julia, but what could he do? Quit the Agency?

Pressing a washcloth against his eyelids and letting the warmth refresh him, he hoped once she said her peace, Julia would accept his decision. After all, he wouldn't be gone more than a few days. He joined her in the bedroom where she let him have it with both barrels.

"You forgot to tell me that we'd be living in a war zone."

"It's not a war."

At least not yet, but he didn't say that aloud.

"I'm unnerved by a plane exploding a breath away from our children."

"You're right. I wasn't there. Wish I could've been, but I wasn't."

Bo didn't reveal that everyone north of the capital city had fled into shelters. Instead, he snapped off the light and slipped into bed, patting the sheet next to him.

"Lie down and we'll talk."

Julia's body seemed to relax and she plumped her pillow beneath her head.

"I'm not afraid for myself or Gregg. Glenna cried and was frightened."

Bo reached for Julia's hand. "When I tucked her in, she laughed about being tougher next time. She enjoyed the grottos and riding on the cable car."

"Of course she'd tell you that. She knows you expect her to be strong, but Bo, she's a growing girl, not some federal agent you work with."

"Don't you want her to be a courageous woman like you?"

Julia lapsed into silence. Bo could almost hear her mind working and see her tight lips in the dark. He tried to stay awake, but his eyes kept slamming shut.

When Julia finally whispered, "Yes, I do," he was startled awake. Bo squeezed her hand, but he had no more words to encourage Julia. He didn't wait for her to bring up anything else. He rolled over and in seconds, sleep provided him a needed respite from his ever-mounting problems.

6

Bo stepped off the elevator, arriving at the CIA's executive suite a few minutes past nine in the morning, jet lag weighting his legs. He stomped his feet to get blood flowing and tried to cast off qualms about leaving Julia and the kids behind.

With Frank Deming on the phone cajoling a clerk, Bo recalled Clara Cohen's promise that she and Hal would look after his family in his absence. Still, how safe were they if Hal Cohen was the mole? Bo had few options with the Chief not able to admit he even knew Bo.

Frank barked into the telephone, "Get that tech up here on the double," before ending the call and darting around his desk to shake Bo's hand.

"Sure isn't the same around here without you."

"Miss your spunk too, Frank. If Kangas wants to send you on embassy duty, claw your way out of the trap."

Those words had barely left Bo's lips when he recalled Frank had spent time at a U.S. Embassy, with deadly results for his wife. Fortunately for Bo, Frank let the unfortunate reference go with a shrug of his shoulders.

"The guy who took over your duties is a lightweight. Anyway, Kangas wants you, so we'll catch up later on what's eating you about working for State."

"Frank, it's simply that I work with State people *every* day." Bo snickered.

With a shake of his head, Bo entered Kangas' tidy office and stood before the massive desk carved from mahogany. The NCS Director was talking on the phone. Shirtsleeves rolled up, he jerked his head toward a leather chair opposite his desk. Bo sat. The door behind him closed with a metallic click, convincing him that Kangas tapped his foot on a button beneath his desk.

"Understood," Kangas hissed into the phone. "I'll be there by ten."

He slammed down the phone, wiping his forehead.

"You flew from Israel to tell me something urgent. I'm all ears, Rider, but be quick about it. The President's called a National Security Council meeting, wants my opinion on the chances for achieving a peace accord given the IDF killed a Lebanese pilot."

"Sir, it was an Iranian fighter pretending to be U.S. Air Force."

"What?" Kangas roared. "Why was I was told otherwise?"

"I heard it firsthand from Mossad. And listen to this. I doubted I could do the Agency any good working from our embassy, but that's been erased. We have a spy within our walls."

Kangas leaped from his chair.

"Here at Langley?"

"Mossad's source claims the leaks are pouring from Tel Aviv. I was shocked at first, but in retrospect we can see Hal runs a loose ship. Plus, Shellie Karnack, his security guru, is too busy micromanaging interpersonal relations and has lost sight of the big picture."

"I expected this to happen, just not so quickly," Kangas said, settling back into his chair.

"You knew?"

Kangas tented his hands, dropping his voice. "A recent fissure damaged our relationship with Mossad. They're not as forthcoming with critical intel and they've not asked for our help."

"Judah Levitt admitted they don't trust working with our embassy staff, me excepted."

"Exactly!" Kangas pounded his palm against the top of his desk. "I suspect your predecessor caused the breakdown, which is why I brought him home and sent you in his place."

"Why me?"

"Simple. You achieved one of our greatest successes with Israel."

Bo appreciated the compliment for past work, but so far he'd accomplished zip in Israel.

"I had no contact with Mossad officers, but I spoke to Saul Goldberg at a reception. He invited me to Mossad and took me to a secret chamber where Judah dropped the leak on me."

"Superb!" Kangas punched his fists together. "They couldn't tell just anyone or Mossad risked alerting the spy. As I planned, once they learned you were the replacement, they checked you out within their ranks, then beat feet over to warn you."

"Except I did the walking."

"Mossad won't be seen anywhere near our embassy," Kangas shot back, spinning around in his chair, glancing at his monitor. "You were briefed about the schoolteacher who was abducted?" he asked, turning back toward Bo.

"Yes, but I hadn't been told Sadie Lamb was one of ours."

"Sadie's schoolteacher cover was blown the moment she met the Chief," Kangas spat in disgust.

Bo sucked in a deep breath. "Judah knew of her meeting. It appears Hamas did as well, which means the leak came from within the embassy."

"Hamas snatched her, betting they held a valuable pawn. The Secretary of State surmised Hamas would think our failure to act confirmed she was a teacher, end of story. Based on what Judah told you, that boneheaded strategy is no longer viable."

"Hamas holds her for a bargaining chip, but for how long?" Bo asked, fighting a yawn.

"State shut down my plan for Sadie's release."

Bo considered Kangas' position. It wasn't unusual for State to buck anything CIA tried to do. That's what made Bo's pretend role at State so disturbing.

"Hal never mentioned Sadie's detention, sir."

"No big surprise. Hal is the President's man in Israel rather than a true diplomat."

Bo recalled what Mossad had discovered about Hal. "After a successful career on Wall Street and contributing to the President's election campaign, Hal goes over to Israel and cozies up to a Turkish arms dealer. Here's a copy of the photo Judah showed me."

Kangas perused the photo. "This fuels my suspicions. Pass everything about Sadie to me. I am furious our agent is held hostage for so long and the President ties my hands."

"Is freeing Sadie my mission?"

"Rider, conditions on the ground in the Middle East change as quickly as lightning strikes. Don't get burned."

That was no answer. Bo fixed a steady stare into Kangas' eyes and was rewarded with a hurried blink. Okay, Kangas wouldn't break with the chain of command, but would he back Bo in Israel? To smoke him out, Bo veered to another problem.

"I've an idea how to trap our embassy mole, but I need to work out a snag."

"Fair enough." Kangas rapped his knuckles on his desk as if deciding how much rope to give Bo. "We need to identify and neutralize this leak. Look at everyone."

"Including Hal?"

"Trust no one over there, not one soul. The way State is hanging Sadie out to dry is a crime," Kangas said, opening a drawer and shutting it with a bang.

"And Mike Spencer, our Station Chief?"

Kangas smiled sheepishly. "He's served us well but is approaching retirement. Don't bother him. Report to me."

Bo needed to disclose something else.

"Cohen is hardly ever around, especially if something happens."

"Explain."

"The day before I arrived at the embassy, white powder showed up. I understand Shellie went berserk, shoving citizens outside, shutting down the entire building. When the Iranian fighters tried penetrating Israel's defenses, Cohen went missing and couldn't be reached."

"Hal's idea of glory is forging Middle East peace, which will never happen."

"He might jeopardize our national interests to achieve peace." Bo rubbed his sore neck.

"Meaning he would sacrifice Sadie Lamb?"

"Hamas holds her, but the mole could also be selling information to other players in the region. Sir, I'll need all the help I can muster to solve this puzzle."

Kangas leaned forward, his eyes ablaze. "Don't involve any FBI agents posing as legal attachés. I'll ask my reliable contact in State's Security Division to float a rumor about an impending audit. They'll tighten up the embassy's security systems as a housekeeping matter, thinking they'll earn good marks on an inspection they're not supposed to know about."

"A clever ploy. Is there an empty office I can work out of here?"

Kangas pointed to the door. "Tell Frank what you're up to, but no one else. Understood?"

"Yes, sir!" Bo said, rounding his fist to keep from saluting, his habit from Army Ranger days hard to break. He rose to his feet, figuring he'd better get a move on his Ops plan.

"Another thing. Everyone in the embassy and their families are at risk. If this spy hacks into a roster, terrorists could invade your homes. Hamas thrives on creating chaos."

Kangas walked Bo to the door, where he clasped Bo's shoulder.

"Have your plan ready for me by two o'clock tomorrow."

"You want me to prepare a *comprehensive* plan, right?" Bo asked, seeking to learn if Kangas wanted Sadie Lamb included.

Kangas' eyes never shifted. "Describe only our mole trap in writing."

"I understand completely." His marching orders entrenched in his mind, Bo left in awe of the impossible task before him.

"Hey, Frank, can you line up some digs for me to work in?"

"Give me thirty minutes."

Bo hustled to the fitness center where he showered and geared up to pull an all-nighter.

BO BLINKED RAPIDLY trying to moisten his dry eyes, staring at a mostly-blank computer screen in a stifling, windowless office. Frank opened the door and with a sympathetic shrug gave Bo the combination to a four-drawer safe and a password for the Agency's network. He also plugged in a landline phone.

"Kangas said you'd brief me on what you're doing," Frank quipped, his brows arching in an air of expectancy.

"I've twenty-four hours to smoke out a mole in the U.S. embassy in Israel."

"Wow!" Frank shut the door.

"My kids think I'm superman. Here's my chance to prove it, but here's the dilemma. Am I after a man or woman, Israeli or Arab, insider or outsider? Who stands to gain?"

"In the Middle East, everyone has a claim including Iran, Egypt, and don't forget Russia," Frank said, pushing out his bottom lip. "With the prospect of peace, their arms trade shrivels to nothing."

Bo's fingers hovered at the keyboard. "I haven't come across any Russians lately."

"Just be sure you don't make a mountain out of a molehill."

"Right." Bo forced a laugh. "I need a sense of humor to keep me sane."

"I'm on stand-by if you need anything."

Frank disappeared out the door, leaving Bo to consider his digs, adorned with a narrow cot and musty green Army blanket. He'd recruited spies in Russia and China, but Bo had never been confronted with unearthing a mole working by his side; worse yet, a terrorist mole. He had to do something, so he typed a few more cryptic words:

Ops Plan – OPERATION MOLE BE GONE

He swept a hand through his wavy hair, reaching for an elusive answer that failed to materialize. Only one fight came to mind. Days before they had left for Tel Aviv, a mole had eaten its way through Bo's expensive Virginia lawn. When he'd brought home a metal trap to spear the beast, Julia had insisted he use something less lethal. If he ever finished this Ops plan, he'd swing home and see if the grub killer he'd spread on the lawn eliminated any moles.

But who was wreaking havoc from within the U.S. Embassy? Hal Cohen's aide leapt to the forefront. Bo had traded stories with Joe Adams over lukewarm coffee. The smart staffer wore a perpetual smile, which Bo found disconcerting. Or could the char force that cleaned the offices after hours be to blame? The cleaners could smuggle in a bomb and detonate it during the busiest working hours.

Bo typed more notes to his Ops plan until a loud rap on the door interrupted Bo's mental hunt. He launched out of his chair, pulling open the door. Frank stood with his hands in his pockets and a grin on his worn face.

"Want to hit the cafeteria for lunch?"

"I'm on a roll. Come in, but shut the door."

Frank perched on the one extra chair as Bo hit "save" on his computer.

"Kangas said I could tell you what I found."

Frank's eyes widened. "You've discovered already who it is?"

"Gotcha. Frank, I've got nada. What if it's an American?"

"Yeah, some loon developed by Hamas as a youth who lied his way into a high-level diplomatic position."

"Or worse, a security position," Bo added, flinching at the thought of Shellie or a Marine guard spying on him.

Both men stared in silence until Frank muttered, "Go ahead. Ask me, Bo."

"Are you sure?" Bo wet his lips.

"Yup. I'm handling grief much better these days."

Bo was one of the few people at Langley who knew Frank's wife had been kidnapped and killed by jihadists.

"Was an intelligence leak to blame for your wife's kidnapping?"

"I don't think Kangas knows for sure what happened in Pakistan. He brought me back to the States for safety reasons."

"Frank, wasn't your assignment in Pakistan what I'm doing in Tel Aviv? I mean, weren't you the only CIA person posing as a State employee?"

"I'm not sure. Probably," Frank said, lowering his eyes, his face turning red.

"To think a mole could access my personnel file. It's unnerving!" Bo bellowed, bounding from his chair and stalking around the room, a confined tiger.

"Settle down, Bo. Walls have ears and no one else is supposed to know."

Bo stopped in his tracks.

"This is serious. I picture this ghoul downloading my home address, names of my kids. All that stuff's in my file."

"True. A spy could be responsible for embassy dependants being kidnapped and held for ransom or their homes bombed," Frank said, wiping his face with both hands.

Bo imagined Frank was reliving the horror of what happened to his wife. Another picture clouded Bo's mind, one which he hardly dared speak aloud.

"Or the mole might discover our sources in the Middle East and kill them, making it look like an accident. Even the State Department's sources are at risk."

Bo's breathing came hard, his heart pounding in his chest like a jackhammer. None of the myriad possibilities had a happy ending.

"We have to find this guy," Bo finally declared with a firm voice.

"Or woman. Remember your last case in Iran."

Bo punched his fist into his hand.

"Give me another twenty minutes and I'll meet you for lunch. Search your mind for *anything* that might have crossed Kangas' desk recently."

"Bo, this time lunch is on me."

Frank swung open the door, closing it softly behind him. Bo dropped in his chair and wheeling it to face the computer, he typed:

IMPERATIVE: Security at our Tel Aviv Embassy is compromised. All its personnel are at great risk.

GOAL: Identify and eliminate enemy agent. Likely handlers of the agent are Lebanon's Hezbollah working at the direction of Iran or Hamas, which rules the Gaza and West Bank. This agent might be a U.S. citizen, but he/she could be Israeli or Palestinian. Said agent most likely has pro-Palestinian leanings.

OBSTACLES: Author is responsible to execute this plan. Director Kangas will be the only other person briefed about this problem and will take responsibility for notifying the Ambassador. Any other briefings might alert the mole to our knowledge of his/her presence.

Bo stopped typing. Had his true identity as a CIA officer instead of a State Department wonk already been passed to Hamas or Hezbollah? Even now, were Julia and the children safe?

On impulse, he reached for his cell phone but remembered he was in a dead zone. The government clock behind his head whirred and Bo suddenly realized he was supposed to meet Frank for lunch. He'd try Julia later.

Bo scrambled to lock up the dingy office and then headed for the cafeteria, the strangeness of walking the halls of Langley dogging each one of his long and determined strides.

7

Bo burst through the cafeteria doors, finding Frank hovering by the salad bar, his hands behind his back.

"Sorry, I couldn't shut my mind off," Bo mumbled, sliding his tray along the metal bars.

"My brain's a whirlwind too. Grab some chow and I'll fill you in."

"I'm going for carbs. Spaghetti and meatballs is on special."

"Doctor's put me on a low salt diet," Frank said hesitantly. "I better eat a salad."

He set a small bowl of greens on his tray with a warning, "In case you've forgotten, Chef's bread is heavy on garlic."

"Thanks." Bo shrugged. "I feel like a raw recruit visiting Langley for the first time."

"Forget about it. Let's sit in the back, by the Picasso print."

It didn't take long for both men to dive into lunch, with Bo relishing the spicy meatballs and telling Frank how well Julia and the kids were adjusting to Israeli culture.

"Except the IDF blasting an Iranian jet out of the sky pushed Julia off her game. Glenna freaked, but Gregg thought it was cool."

"Wall-to-wall news coverage is claiming the pilot flew in his own air space."

"A total fabrication. Julia and the kids saw it live."

"You're not surprised the media makes stuff up, are you?" Frank speared at a grape tomato with his fork. It rolled off his plate and onto the floor.

"Another one bites the dust," Bo quipped.

"That's an old song about the Detroit Lions."

"I promise not to sing if you won't."

"Who do you like in the World Series?"

"Being in Israel, I'm out of the loop. Wanna fill me in?"

The two men talked baseball until Frank pushed his bowl away.

"Bo, let me correct something I said earlier. Director Kangas dumped you in the Middle East, *not* Russia."

"Did he say why I'm there?" Bo asked, his brain ready to memorize Frank's every word.

"He's impressed by your can-do attitude and previous success with Judah Levitt."

"That deal with Iran turned out better than I hoped."

"From my years in Pakistan," Frank cleared his throat. "I can't stress enough you're dealing with a whole different ethic in the region and I'm not just referring to Mossad."

"Disagreements lasting for thousands of years aren't the easiest to crack."

The enormity of Bo's mission settled in his stomach and he shoved aside the meatball.

"So Mossad dropped a mole-bomb on you. Do you trust their agent?"

Did he? Caught off guard by Frank's sudden question, Bo recalled Judah's intense stare when he'd revealed the mole burrowed deep into the U.S. Embassy. Bo tossed down his fork.

"Why should he lie?"

"He could use you to seek vengeance against an unrevealed enemy."

Kangas' earlier words flowed into Bo's mind and he decided to ask Frank.

"When I told Kangas, he said he'd expected this to happen, just not so soon. He claimed he meant the disruption between CIA and Mossad, but is there more I should know?"

"He brought home your predecessor, assigned him to domestic recruiting."

"So he said. Anyway, Kangas thinks Mossad's intel is plausible. I won't quit digging until I ferret out the truth."

Frank downed his soda before saying, "Don't forget that competing groups use violence to elevate their cause in the Middle East."

"Don't you forget, Frank, that I almost died in Kirkuk. A homicide bomber there killed seven people yesterday."

"I heard."

As much as Bo wanted to discount Frank's warning, the mere thought of his near death experience soured Bo's mood. However, he appreciated Frank's concern and told him so.

Frank dropped his voice as a group of analysts chose to sit nearby. "Iran's toehold with Hezbollah is firm. They're calling the shots in Lebanon. I'm not supposed to say, but don't be surprised if Iran completely rules Iraq by year's end."

What else did Frank know? Bo socked him lightly on the arm.

"Out with it, Frank. My life's on the line."

"Hamas controls Gaza."

Bo rapped his fingertips on the table, in no mood for another chess game. When Frank dipped into his cup of fruit, Bo sipped his ice tea, waiting for whatever classified intel Frank had ensconced in his mind to roll off his tongue.

Frank finished his melon and with his lips hardly moving he whispered, "A few miles from Israel's northern border, Iran landed a thousand Revolutionary Guards into Lebanon. A satellite picked up the movement."

"Why didn't Kangas tell me?"

"It came in an hour ago. Kangas is still at the White House, no doubt trying to slice a word in edgewise between the Secretary of State and the SecDef."

Bo's mind thundered over a hundred different angles. The fighters Julia and his kids witnessed were the real thing. He pushed back his chair, skidding it over the vinyl.

"I've gotta call Julia. Make sure she's all right."

Frank lifted a hand. "Get with me later."

Back in his cubby hole, Bo phoned Julia, the ringing tones on the other end jarring his worried mind. Why didn't she pick up? He'd never have flown to Langley if he'd known Iran had moved in those troops. At a voice message prompt, Bo growled, "Julia, call back. We have to talk."

JULIA WRIGGLED NERVOUSLY on the hard-backed chair in the embassy's smaller meeting rooms, wondering if Glenna and Gregg were having fun at the circus performance. Though Julia tuned her ears to Clara's remarks, she glued her eyes to her wristwatch, wanting to be home before the kids returned with Naomi Rabin, the embassy's interpreter.

"And a hearty thanks to Julia Rider," Clara announced. "She's agreed to help us plan next week's reception."

The other ladies turned their heads, lightly clapping. Julia smiled and pulled out her pocket calendar, writing in the date for the reception. She'd agreed to contact the mayor of Jerusalem, inviting him and his wife to attend.

"Thanks for helping," one of the ladies said graciously.

"I'm happy to help," Julia replied, anxious to leave.

Several other well-wishers shook Julia's hand, welcoming her to Israel. At that moment, she no longer felt like a stranger in a new land, but part of a larger community. Joy filled her heart to overflowing, even with Bo away in Virginia. He said he'd be home in a day or two and that helped the jet episode recede in her memory. This would be a fabulous time in their lives.

"Julia, let me show you something interesting," Clara said, keeping her voice low.

"Okay, but I want to be home before Naomi brings my children back."

"This will not take long."

Clara pulled on her plaid wrap, leading Julia to Hal's office, but a tall Marine guard stopped them with his arms held out.

"Sorry, I can't let you in. Ambassador Cohen is out of the office."

"I know that," Clara dismissed his stern objection. "I am his wife. You must be new."

She snatched her embassy identification from her purse, holding it up to the Marine's eyes. He examined it closely and then straightened.

"Sorry, ma'am. No one told me you would be here this evening."

"Mrs. Rider's husband is on the embassy staff too."

He allowed both women to pass. Clara waded right into the Ambassador's office, shoving her ID into a side pocket of her slacks.

"I announced next week's reception on my media page. Let's see if we have any posts."

Clara hurried over to her husband's computer, logging onto her social media page.

"Wow, twenty replies," she said, her voice rising in excitement. "Look at this one, Julia."

Julia leaned over to focus on tiny letters on the screen, reading aloud one of Clara's messages. "Your group brings together women of Israel and transcends our religious differences. Count on my support."

"Dorothy is one of my closest friends."

"How do you know if she'll come to the event?" Julia asked. She wasn't a fan of social media, not understanding how it worked. Both Glenna and Gregg were too busy to be immersed in computer technology and Julia intended to keep their interest on history and outdoor activities.

"I'll check Dorothy's name against my donor list in the morning," Clara replied, opening an unlocked drawer.

She pulled out a piece of ivory paper with the Ambassador's name and seal on top, and writing with a flourish, quickly handed the sheet to Julia.

"Here are the names and numbers of the donors you agreed to call."

Julia took the list with a tentative hand, unsure how to avoid being drawn in by Clara and her good deeds. Julia's main focus was raising her children and caring for Bo. Before she could say she wanted to leave, Clara deftly navigated to another site on Hal's computer.

"Traffic spiked after I announced our reception. More than one thousand hits total."

"I leave technology to Bo. He doesn't want us identifying ourselves on the web."

Clara stopped and looked into Julia's eyes. "Oh? Is that because of his job for the government?"

On second thought, Julia folded the list, uneasy talking about Bo's job even with Clara.

"Sometime you'll have to tell me about your exciting lives," Clara added, whirling back to the keyboard and typing with rapid-fire fingers.

"We are quiet people, enjoying family time."

"Leave social networking to me, Julia. I am a whiz at computers, having studied journalism in college. I am always taking classes and using Hal's computer. The embassy's other computers have filters, but his does not."

With a flick of her wrist, Clara zoomed over to another website.

"Here's something new, the design for the planned cancer hospital. My foundation raised ten million dollars."

Before Julia could make out the giant facility, Clara zoomed off the page.

"I'll drive you there sometime. This site shows us all around the world. Watch."

Julia's eyes and head were spinning. She desperately wanted to be home, but she was at the mercy of Clara who was driving.

"Write your address for me and I'll bring up your apartment."

Julia wrote the address for their Tel Aviv apartment on a scratch pad while Clara watched and typed. Suddenly Julia saw their high rise apartment pop up on the screen.

"That's amazing! If I were sunbathing on the deck, someone could see me."

As Clara typed, the picture changed to a blurry image. "Here's our old house in Chicago. We used to live in the same neighborhood as the former governor when he was a boy. Of course, now we live on Long Island when we're not in Tel Aviv and I love it."

Julia had no idea where the Cohens lived. She could only stare in amazement as a large brick home emerged, becoming so crisp Julia saw stately trees out front.

"Is that a tennis court?"

"Oh, Julia, I would love to play with you sometime."

"Don't get your hopes up. I lob a tennis ball with the kids at the park. I'm not athletic, remember?"

"You can do anything you put your mind to, that's my motto. Want to see your house?"

To humor her, Julia agreed, but sought an end to Clara's computer searches. "I really must be going."

Clara shot her a surprised look, prompting Julia to add gently, "If you don't mind."

"Okay, where do you live in the States?"

Julia told Clara their home address in Great Falls, Virginia, and in seconds, the Rider home appeared on the screen, even the swing set in the backyard.

"Oh, no!" Julia exclaimed. "Someone moved my car into the driveway."

"Let's bring it up closer and see if you are correct." Clara enlarged the image and Julia pointed at her car.

Julia wrung her hands. "We locked our cars in the garage when we moved."

"My dear," Clara burst out laughing, "I am sure your car is still in the garage. We are seeing a satellite picture taken months or perhaps a year ago."

Blood rushed to Julia's face. She really knew nothing about the Internet or satellites. Clara clicked the mouse, taking her screen back to their gorgeous Long Island home.

"I will help you on social networking another time. Ready to hug your kids? They are probably on their way to your apartment this very moment."

"Great." Julia sighed, stuffing her contact list into her handbag.

She would help Clara on the upcoming reception and then draw the line with no more events until after Christmas. Bo's parents might be visiting. A sudden idea flitted through Julia's mind, but she discarded the notion of inviting Clara over. Because they'd moved mid-term, Julia homeschooled Gregg and Glenna, giving their apart-ment a schoolroom glow. Still, it might not hurt to stay on Clara's softer side. Julia sensed that with Clara, she was holding a tiger by the tail.

THE NEXT HOUR DRAGGED for Bo as he bent over his computer, half-listening for Julia's call. He couldn't keep his eyes off the noisy clock, each second passing with a loud clunk. Forty minutes past four in Virginia meant it was almost midnight for Julia in Israel. She still hadn't called.

He could stand it no longer. On his office phone, he punched in her number, hoping this time she'd answer, but no, he left yet another message with his callback number. He had to believe they were okay. Turning his mind to something he could control, he dove into the Ops plan with gusto, every keystroke highlighting his lack of contact with his family.

Adrenaline surging through his veins, he struggled to push aside family matters. It took effort, but finally time sailed toward his dinner hour and the plan coalesced, his earlier conversation with Frank jogging his creative juices. Ideas flowed from his brain to his fingertips and onto his computer screen. He'd just saved the document, intending to review it again the next day, when his phone rang. Bo lunged for it, answering without reading the call screen.

"Julia?"

"Sorry, I had my cell along, but the light just popped on alerting me I had a message."

"You were out then? Alone?"

"I went to Clara's meeting for breast cancer research." She sighed.

"What about the kids?"

"They had more fun than I did."

Her light tone suggested all was well, but he had to be sure.

"What did they do while you held Clara's hand?"

"You've got that right. Hal went to a meeting in Jerusalem. Naomi brought Gregg and Glenna to a circus play at a theater. They watched acrobats climb ribbons from the ceiling and swallow fire. Shetland ponies raced in a ring."

So Cohen went to Jerusalem on sudden notice. Bo found that tidbit intriguing. To Julia he asked, "You're sure everything is all right?"

"Glenna and Gregg are tired. Dr. Van Horn is taking us to Nazareth in the morning."

"Okay. Did Clara mention anything about Hal's meeting?"

He waited, then Julia said breathlessly, "I nearly forgot in the flurry of coming home. Clara called Hal as she dropped me off and she asked about a warning. Should I be concerned?"

"Lock the doors and keep your phone on in case I call you."

"I'll never sleep now. I wish you were here."

Bo swiped at his hair. "I should be home soon. You enjoy Van Horn's new book about the new nation of Israel. Read until your eyes get heavy. I'll be at this number all night long."

"You always know the right thing to keep me steady in the water."

"Frank found a crummy cot for me to sleep on," he joked, trying to keep their banter light. "It's so old, it looks like it saw action in Korea."

"I miss you," she whispered.

"Me too. Call me for anything."

After Bo hung up, he logged onto an international news site, finding no stories about Iran's soldiers swarming along Lebanon's border. Did Frank have the right intel? Bo switched over to his Hotmail account using the fictitious name, and ICE agent Eva Montanna caught his interest with the subject line: *Need your help!*

He hadn't heard from her since before he'd left for Israel so he quickly opened the urgent sounding message. *Bo, can you find someone in Israel? Call in the next two days before I leave for Dallas. Eva*

He dialed an outside line, chancing that she'd be in her office at five minutes to six. Like Bo, she worked plenty of overtime. After two rings Eva answered, "Special Agent Eva Montanna. How can I help?"

"Your wish is my command," Bo chuckled, thinking he'd surprise her. "It's more like how can I help you?"

Silence for a split second before Eva burst out laughing. "Aren't you up past your bedtime? It's the middle of the night where you are, Bo."

She'd thrown him a curve by recognizing his voice so quickly.

"Wrong," he finally managed.

"Not according to my watch. Or are you on a secret mission around the world?"

What could he tell her? Bo reflected on how, unlike most CIA covert agents, Bo had gotten tangled up with other federal agencies a few times, including Immigration Customs Enforcement (ICE). A talented investigator, Eva shared Bo's love of family.

"Ah, I'm in your time zone, arriving yesterday to put out a fire. I just opened your cryptic e-mail. What's up?"

"I'm on my way to meet Scott and my kids for pizza."

"Who are you looking for?"

"Will you be here in the morning?"

"Yes, but unavailable."

"I'd like to explain my request in person. Can you make lunch?"

"Eleven thirty works. I have a two o'clock meeting that can't be changed."

"That works for me. How about Rob's deli, Griff's favorite place to eat?"

"Great. If our buddy Griff isn't busy, bring him along. There's nothing finer than seeing that man inhale Rob's Duffer."

"I'll see if the FBI has him ensconced in some case. I hope he's free, because we always get better service when Griff's with us," she said and Bo imagined her grinning.

After ending the call, he put final touches on his Op plan to snare a deadly mole. At midnight, he shut things down, crashing on the narrow cot. But he woke suddenly, drenched in sweat.

Shaking his head to blot out a vivid dream where Julia had fallen from a cable car in the mountains of Israel, Bo stumbled to turn on the light. Four in the morning. Another hour before he could buy fresh java at the cafeteria.

With few options, he fired up his computer and spent the time tweaking his plan designed to draw the mole from the shadows. As he saved his document, Bo rubbed his lower back, aching from the decrepit cot, an appalling thought seizing his mind. Waiting for results over the next sixty days would be sheer torture.

8

Bo inhaled a lukewarm breakfast of sausage and eggs in the cafeteria and then showered in the fitness center. Somewhat refreshed, he stormed back to his cave-like office seeing no one he knew in the hallways. The Lone Ranger again.

He dove into reviewing his Ops plan, time slipping by. The whirring clock clunked loudly and Bo swiveled his head. Yikes! He was late to meet Eva. Flipping off lights and locking the door, he scrambled to the pool car and wound his way through heavy traffic to Rob's Deli.

Ten minutes late, Bo wheeled into the crunchy gravel drive, dodging a gaping pothole. The last time he'd eaten here he'd been cautious about a tail. At least this morning, he felt safe no one had followed him.

The same weathered golf flag for the nineteenth hole hung above the door and the sight of a hand painted sign, *We Serve Duffers Here*, made Bo's mouth water. He'd come to enjoy this deli as much as Eva and Griff. Not only was the food homemade and delicious, but it was also unlikely they'd be spotted by anyone they'd ever arrested.

Bo burst inside and Eva waved from the far back corner. Rats. Her annoying habit of snagging a seat along the back wall gave her a clear view of everyone in the place. Of course Bo had no one but himself to blame for being late. Griff, towering above Eva a good six inches and smiling beneath his brown mustache, extended a rock-solid hand to Bo.

"Have a seat." Griff smiled, pointing at a chair, its back to the diners.

"Thanks," Bo grumbled. "I have enemies too, you know."

He pivoted his head, looking around for a better seat, but gave up with a shrug. "It would look strange for the three of us to sit lined up in a row."

Griff snuggled into his chair with a laugh. "You snooze, you lose."

"Whenever I meet with you two, I arrive a half hour early, just to be seated with my back to the wall," Eva joked, resuming her prime spot.

"I didn't plan to see either of you so soon after my new State Department gig."

Wally, the lanky waiter formerly from Sudan, appeared at the table, bringing Bo an Arnie Palmer and Griff a tall cola. Eva gestured at Bo's drink.

"If that's iced tea and lemonade, I'll have one of those."

"Yes, ma'am."

Wally turned to Griff asking, "Your usual sandwich, the Duffer?" And to Bo, "You want the Birdie, right?"

Both men nodded.

"I'd like a Reuben," Eva said, scanning the menu, "but don't see one listed."

"Oh, you mean our Mulligan," Wally said, flashing a generous smile. "It is filled with corned beef, Swiss cheese, and sauerkraut."

Eva's mouth hung open. "That's a Reuben."

"Rob adds his special dressing, which makes it a Mulligan. Just like his hamburger has the same dressing and grilled onions, making it a Duffer."

"Sold." Eva lifted her hands. "A Mulligan with fries and coleslaw."

"I love your hearty appetite," Griff said, handing Wally the menu.

"That's what happens when I'm getting three kids off to school by seven. No time to eat."

Her eyes followed Wally as he hurried into the kitchen. "Griff, your mentoring of Wally sure has paid off. You'd never know his tragic story as a lost boy from Sudan."

"You helped him receive a scholarship to your alma mater," Bo said before sipping his icy drink. "What's he up to these days?"

Griff put down his glass. "Wally has plans for medical school. Why are you here and not in Israel?"

Bo glanced over his shoulder, sliding closer to the table.

"First of all, aside from Julia," he lowered his voice, "you two are the only agents who know where I work. If we hadn't bumped into each other officially, you still wouldn't know it."

Griff rapped the table with his knuckles. "Here I thought you were in Israel toiling to whip our State Department into shape."

"I'm in Tel Aviv on diplomatic status, as liaison to Mossad and other Israeli agencies. I happened to be at Langley when Eva sent an e-mail asking a favor."

Bo stopped abruptly when Wally returned with Eva's drink. After placing the chilled glass by her hand, he hustled away. Eva sampled her Arnie Palmer, patting Bo's arm.

"It's no coincidence you're being home when I need to talk with you."

"Have one of your visions, Eva?" Griff asked, raising an eyebrow. "What's that about?" Bo stared at Eva, thinking of the nightmare he had about Julia.

"She won't say much, but Eva receives special insights into future events through dreams and stuff. I've only recently come to understand spiritual matters myself."

Was Griff for real? Bo shrugged off religious talk.

"I don't understand half the church stuff Julia is into. She's more content, which makes my traveling life easier."

Bo drained his drink just as Wally appeared, sliding a platter of hot food in front of him, placing all of their orders perfectly. Then he was gone. Eva bowed her head as though saying a silent blessing. So did Griff. Bo stared at his food as if he didn't get the memo. Curiosity stirred in his mind. What was the interest in spiritual things that had a grip on these two and his wife?

When Eva and Griff raised their heads, a strange silence fell upon Bo. He bit into his Birdie sandwich, enjoying the flaky crab.

"Grandpa Marty received a call from a man claiming to be Israeli and trying to establish a relationship," Eva blurted, holding one-half of her sandwich.

"Did he demand money?" Griff snapped.

"No, but I wondered if you could track him down for me, Bo."

Bo set down his sandwich. "Is Marty at risk from scams? Does he have diminished capacity?"

"Hardly." Eva frowned. "He's moved back to the family farm in Michigan, living alone in Zeeland. He volunteers making scooters for amputees in third world countries."

"If you tell me more, I'm happy to consult with my sources in Israel."

Eva removed a paper from her purse and Bo snatched it up. "Eli Rosenbaum sounds Jewish," he said.

"I don't want Grandpa Marty getting hurt. After being orphaned, he left the farm to visit his aunt in the Netherlands, being forced to remain there during the war. He and Aunt Deane hid Jews in the attic of her home to keep Nazis from finding them."

Bo was taking notes. "Is his legal name Marty or Martin?"

"Martin, the name he used in the Netherlands. Supposedly Marty hid the caller's father. They gave an e-mail address to contact them and when he said he didn't use e-mail, they asked if one of his children could contact them. I'm uncomfortable doing so until I know they're legit."

"Does Marty recognize Eli's name?"

"They helped so many people back then." Eva shrugged.

Griff wiped his mouth on a napkin after finishing the last bite of his sandwich. "Eva, be careful. We never release info about our families because you never know when someone we've arrested might find our relatives. Eva and I once neutralized terrorists in the Middle East."

"I'll ask an Israeli counterpart to learn if the man truly immigrated to Israel after surviving the Nazis. I'll e-mail you from my Hotmail account."

Wally arrived to clear plates and offer dessert, finding no takers. Bo picked up his tab, telling Wally, "Good luck in med school. It's a long haul."

"Yes, sir," Wally agreed, "but I am determined to return and help my people in South Sudan. They need so much."

"Wally has a chance to work at a mission hospital in the new South Sudan between semesters." Griff winked at Wally with pride.

Eva reached out for Bo's bill. "I'm paying yours as a down payment for the work you're doing for Marty."

"That's not necessary," Bo said.

"This once," Eva insisted, her hand outstretched.

But Bo shook his head. "Agency rules."

"Hey, how long will your assignment last?" Griff asked. "Eva and I miss bumping into you as we chase criminals and spies."

"Two years, but the way things are going, I might return sooner."

Eva's eyes rounded. "Oh? I sense a story here."

"Classified." Bo shrugged with a grin. "And Griff, congrats on your marriage. I've gotta run."

9

With a promise to stay in touch, Bo roared off in the Agency pool car. Twenty minutes later, he pulled into the driveway of his Virginia home, ready to do a quick run-through and hurry back to Langley. Cold wind whipped around the front trees and through Bo's hair. With no plants on the porch and no one inside, his house looked forlorn.

Before he left for Israel he'd spread grub killer on his lawn and apparently the potion worked. Bo saw no signs of mole tunnels in the front yard. He inserted a key into the side door and once inside, punched in the code turning off the alarm. The kitchen looked neat, everything in its place, but the house felt cool as the heat had been turned down. He closed his top shirt button.

Then Bo hustled upstairs and in Gregg's room, the red dragon kite Bo had bought him for his birthday hung neglected on the wall. He poked his head into Glenna's purple room, spotting the journal she'd asked for. He scooped it off her bed and hurried to the master bedroom where nothing seemed amiss. Then he stopped to listen. Was that the window rattling?

With a quick pull, up went the blinds. Funny, he thought he'd secured the windows before they'd left for the airport weeks ago, but this one was unlocked. Bo flipped the lock and closed the blinds before hiking downstairs two steps at a time.

Next, he wandered to the basement, relieved no mice had been caught in the traps. He examined the furnace air filter, which looked pristine. Back upstairs in the empty kitchen where Julia had enjoyed making homemade lasagna and pies, no pleasant smells wafted to his nose. Homesickness overpowered him. That was absurd. He was home. But not with his family.

To shake off the gloom settling like sticky glue into his mind, Bo wiggled the front door handle and the locks. Tel Aviv and the mess at the embassy held enough trouble for him without fighting shadows. On a whim, he flipped his wrist, his watch telling it was nine o'clock in Israel. Julia might feel like talking.

He punched in her cell number, which rang. She didn't answer. Bo left a hurried message: "I'm at the house. Need anything?"

Ending the call, he wondered if this was the day they'd gone to

Solomon's Mines with Dr. Van Horn. Or was that yesterday? He'd lost track of time.

After resetting the alarm he dashed to the car, not wanting to risk being late to meet with Kangas. His tires were almost out of the drive when he glimpsed his neighbor, Carver Washington, swinging his arms and veering straight toward him. Bo jammed the car into drive.

Carver ran behind him shouting, "Stop! Stop! We have'ta talk."

What was Bo thinking? Carver had promised to keep an eye on the house. Bo stepped on the brakes and lowered the window.

"I went through the place, Carver. All is well."

"I walked through on Monday, but that's not what I need to talk to you about."

Bo saw trouble in Carver's coal black eyes. "You're not moving away, are you?"

"Not in this market. The State Department transferred you temporarily to Israel, right?"

Bo nodded, with no appetite to answer questions from the nosy accountant, such as why was Bo back in Virginia.

"Should've worn my jacket." Carver rubbed his hands together. "It is cold!"

"Sure is and I should be going. Can't miss my flight."

"Wait," Carver implored, his hands dropping to the open window edge. "Why did they send a guy asking about you?"

Bo's mind flipped. What was State up to?

"Ah, probably routine with me going overseas. What did they ask?"

"The more I think about it, I may have misspoken."

"Oh?" Bo rammed the car in park taking his foot off the brake, but keeping the motor running.

"He really didn't approach me."

"I don't understand how someone asked about me without approaching you."

"Okay," Carver said with a shrug. "Here's what happened."

"Out with it!" Bo roared.

His neighbor flinched and Bo relented. Carver was nice to check on his house. Bo should be more patient.

"Sorry, Carver. I'm due at Dulles pretty soon to catch my flight. What about the guy asking about me?"

Carver's hands clapped his arms to keep warm. "I saw a car idling in your drive and because it was mostly dark outside, I walked up and tapped on the window. The driver lowered the window like you just did."

"You mean a government employee was working that late?"

"He flashed an official looking ID and said he was doing a background investigation." Carver lifted his chin. "He asked did you live there and with how many people."

"Oh." Bo's hand gripped the gear lever. "He's probably a census taker."

"Nope. When he started asking where your father lived, I grew wary and asked to see his ID again. That's when he said he had no more questions and left me watching him peel outta your driveway."

Something was wrong. Bo didn't want to reveal concerns to Carver, especially since his neighbor had no idea who Bo worked for.

"You know, State updates our background investigation every five years."

"Wait," Carver hissed, narrowing his eyes. "Then why didn't he ask about your loyalty to our government or if suspicious foreigners visited your house?"

Carver was right.

"Did you get a license plate?"

"Nope," Carver said, hanging his head. "In the dark I can't be sure, but I think he drove a red sedan."

"Thanks for everything, Carver. Feel free to call in the future if you're troubled by anything."

"Bo, I will. How do you like Israel? I'm surprised to see you back so soon."

"Julia will have my hide if I miss this flight."

With a wave, Bo shoved the selector into drive, raising the window as he rolled away and heading for Langley with a nagging question. Who had been nosing around asking about Bo and his father? It made no sense.

The subdivision receded in his rearview mirror as he pushed his mind forward to Operation Mole Be Gone. Writing his plan was one thing, but actually identifying and arresting the real mole was something else all together. Bo hit the gas and pulled away from a stop sign with a troubling question. Was the mole a loner or somehow linked to a spy network seeking to disrupt the upcoming Middle East talks?

AT FIVE MINUTES TO TWO, Bo raced into Headquarters. During the trip in, he'd thought of a way to verify what Carver had told him. He stopped by Frank's desk.

"Can you find out if the Agency is updating my background investigation?"

Frank raised his eyebrows, which told Bo nothing.

"Come on, Frank. My neighbor was up in arms how he stumbled on a guy parked in my driveway," Bo said, motioning with his hands. "He showed some government ID, claiming he was conducting a State Department security investigation."

"They're supposed to redo our clearances every five years." Frank turned toward Kangas' door. "You better go in and I'll work some kind of magic. Good luck with your plan."

"I need a miracle." Bo flashed a grin.

He found Kangas immersed in a computer program. Without waiting for instructions, Bo handed over Operation Mole be Gone, having placed his Ops plan in a red folder marked Secret.

"Don't have time to read it, Rider. Give me the highlights."

Kangas didn't even look up, but Bo launched into the details anyway.

"We strategically insert several phony memos throughout the embassy's computer network. Each will snag the interest of Hamas or Hezbollah, or whoever. The fake memos will have increasingly lower security classifications."

"Bravo." Kangas flipped open the red folder, scanning its contents. "After I've read it carefully, Frank will implement things here and at State."

Kangas posed additional concerns for Bo, stopping mid-sentence as Frank rushed in.

"Sorry to interrupt, but I thought you should know what I just learned."

Kangas leaned back in his leather chair. "It's official then? Iran is ruling Iraq?"

Frank shook his head. "Someone was asking questions about Bo at his Virginia home. We thought it might be for his security clearance."

"Is he up for review?" Kangas barked.

"Not for two more years. None of our people or contractors went to his house."

"I smell an even bigger rat." Kangas bounded from his chair and strode around the corner of his desk, glaring into Bo's eyes. "Is a PI onto you for some personal mischief?"

"Sir, no, sir!" Bo fired back like in his Army days.

How could Kangas even think he'd cheat on his wife?

Kangas blinked. "Of course not, but I had to be sure. Give me the details."

Bo explained what Carver had said. "Unfortunately, due to darkness, my neighbor didn't see the license."

"Security Programs assured me Agent Rider's security clearance is in top shape." Frank nodded at Bo.

"Rider, you have bigger problems at our embassy. Frank will follow up on the identity of the questioner."

Kangas returned to typing on his computer and Bo left the office with Frank, a sharp sword sticking in Bo's mind. Should he be concerned about the man Carver saw? Kangas had sure blown him off.

"Don't worry," Frank said, resting a hand on Bo's shoulder. "Maybe he was the tax assessor trying to ante up your property tax bill."

"Why didn't he just say so?"

"Would you admit you were a tax assessor? Their job is more dangerous than ours."

Frank dropped his hand and Bo tried to figure just who had been at his house.

"I've been away a few weeks and it feels like months. How can I solve this from across the pond?"

"Here's a thought." Frank's chin jutted upward and Bo waited.

He had to get to Dulles, but he didn't want Frank thinking he didn't care to stay and listen.

"If you're not sure about this Carver fellow, let me stay at your house."

"I trust my neighbor, but Frank, does Kangas trust me?" Bo asked, unsure of the answer.

"With his life. Otherwise, he'd never send you to Israel in the middle of a firestorm."

"Then he shouldn't have made that wisecrack about a PI investigating me."

"Forget it," Frank said with a warm smile. "He spoke on impulse. Listen, the lease is up on my Arlington apartment. Do you think Julia would approve of my staying there?"

"Sure, but I'm not telling her about the guy asking about me."

Frank nodded evenly. "Tell her that I'm staying in your home until I find a new place."

"It's a good idea," Bo admitted, "but I have to make you a new key."

"Leave yours with me and I'll send it after I have one made. My stuff's already in storage. I could use a new start."

After all Frank had been through with his wife being kidnapped and probable death, Bo had a sudden urge to accept his proposal. His friend needed a break. Having Frank at the house would give Bo peace of mind.

"I'm happy you'll be staying there, but don't feel pressured if you find something better." Bo reached out a hand.

When Frank clasped it, Bo sensed he and Frank were as close as brothers. He passed along his security code for the house, which gave him an idea.

"We should adopt code names in future communications. What do you think of 'Wolf' for Hal Cohen and 'Dolphin' for Shellie?"

"Those work. I'll pass them to Kangas."

"I have a favor to ask, Frank."

"Name it."

"Watch for moles in my lawn." Bo ran a hand through his hair. "Call a landscaper and don't let the tiny beasts tear up my yard."

"You'll be too busy catching the embassy mole," Frank replied in all seriousness.

"I'm running down to meet Maureen Hall before I catch the shuttle."

"Stay in touch, Bo. I'm a phone call away."

Bo said good-bye and hustled downstairs to meet the intelligence analyst. Handing Maureen a slim file, he told her how to dribble his memos into State's system on certain dates.

"Any questions, contact Frank in the Director's office," he warned.

She stared from behind black and gold glasses, snapping her gum and blowing a big bubble, which popped.

"Please, Maureen."

"My father calls me Mo," she said chewing her gum.

"Which rhymes with Bo and we'd make a good team if you'd follow my instructions without your usual lip."

"Didn't your new assignment take you far away?"

Bo pocketed his hands, frustration building. "This is top priority."

"Like everything else around here?" She jerked her head at a locked cabinet behind her desk. "Thirty files are awaiting my special touch."

"We must watch for whoever opens these file memos. It's not my real address in Israel, but when someone shows interest that will help me identify who is tracking me and my work for the Agency."

Her eyes grew round behind her glasses. "You sound deadly
serious. I was having fun."

"This number belongs to a prepaid cell phone I bought as a trap."
Bo pointed to the file. "But if anyone uses or refers to this phone,
we'll know they snuck into the files."

"Wow." Maureen licked her lips.

"Right, and if you move my project to the top, I'll send you a dozen
packs of gum. Watermelon is your favorite, right?"

"Thanks for remembering, Bo. I'll get started on yours before the
clock strikes midnight and I turn into a pumpkin."

"Maureen, you're the best. You really are working so late?"

She gurgled out a sigh, her fingers flying over her keyboard with
great speed. Bo bustled off to Langley's parking lot where minutes
later he slid into the seat of the agency's shuttle.

"Dulles airport, ASAP," he told the driver. "I can't miss my flight."

The driver sped off and Bo felt hopeful that he'd make the Tel Aviv
flight. If he missed the plane, he'd have to wait until morning. No way
he'd spend another sleepless night on the rickety cot. He punched in
Frank's number, leaving him a message.

"Hey, Frank. Let me know when you're settled in my place. And
could you pick up a dozen large packs of gum and take them to
Maureen, preferably watermelon? I owe you, buddy."

10

Bo ate a skimpy salad and guzzled a few bottles of water during the entire flight back to Tel Aviv, but his mind stayed glued to his Ops plan. Only Kangas and Frank knew the details, with Maureen Hall knowing enough to assist Bo's mission. Could he pull off his scheme without Hal and Shellie being tipped off? He'd been ordered by Kangas to keep things mum and this would be one time Bo followed orders to the letter, except one other person needed to know.

He'd tell Judah he was working on a way to identify the mole, since the Mossad agent had been the one to alert him. After clearing security at Ben Gurion Airport and hustling to his embassy car, Bo made a scheduled stop at Mossad HQ. This time, Saul met him immediately and brought him to the lower level where Judah was waiting. Without a word, Saul left Bo to be briefed by Judah.

"I just flew in. What's new?" Bo asked, settling into a chair.

"Iran has installed their Revolutionary Guard along our northern border after the plane incident. They are eager to escalate tensions."

"I heard they put in roughly a thousand troops."

"Closer to two thousand, my friend."

Bo's hand plunged through his hair. He needed to know what else Judah knew. "And our embassy's response?"

"Pathetic. Diplomatic talks are under way."

"With Iran growing in strength with every second." Bo heaved a sigh.

"Russia is still hawking their weapon systems in the region."

Bo flexed his calf muscles aching from being cramped up for hours on an airplane.

"Judah, have there been more leaks?"

"I have received no new intelligence from my source."

"That's something, I guess. I have a favor to ask."

Bo briefly explained how the son of a man named Eli Rosenbaum had contacted Martin Vander Goes, a federal agent's grandfather who hid Jewish families from the Nazis.

"I know Eli Rosenbaum's son very well," Judah said, surprising Bo. "Give me the telephone number and address that you have. I will ascertain if he is the same man."

"I appreciate your help. Also, my Ops plan sprinkles poison peanuts for the mole."

Judah narrowed his black eyes to slits. "Let us hope your mole is hungry."

Bo stood, pocketing his hands. "If he is on a starvation diet, I will implement plan B."

The two agents agreed to stay in touch, and Bo returned to the main floor of Mossad Headquarters where he signed out. He'd just started the car, when a text from Julia popped on his phone.

Meet us at King David Hotel. Tour bus arrives at six.

Bo found a parking spot near the hotel with a mere fifteen minutes to spare. He sprang from the car and strode into the lobby where he bought a newspaper and bottle of juice. Back in the car, he gulped the warm apple juice and read the paper, which was crammed with the Iranian President's warnings and Israel's tough verbal response. Did the escalation in rhetoric mean war was inevitable?

What a time to be a backstage player to the intrigue. Bo cleared his mind of politics and checked his rearview mirror, watching two buses disgorge Western-looking tourists. He didn't spot Julia, so his thoughts wandered to his globe-trotting where he'd recruited his own spies for the U.S. But who had recruited someone to spy against America? And who was the "someone"?

A loud whoosh of air brakes jolted Bo to attention. An even larger bus rolled to a stop behind his car. The driver swung open the door, but was that Julia stuffed into the seat behind the driver? Bo glimpsed her sunny smile as she peered around the driver's head.

No one left their seats as a man with thick wavy hair stood by the driver with a microphone. Bo imagined him addressing the tour group. What a great day of seeing the sights. Meet the bus at eight in the morning. Blah, blah, blah.

Julia gazed up at the tall man as if he held her future in his hands. Bo saw his kids pointing toward Bo's back window so he waved a hand out the window. Gregg pulled on his mother's arm, but she appeared mesmerized by the tour guy's every word.

Weariness taking root in his legs, Bo's eyes locked onto the stream of pedestrians filing past his car and the enormity of what lay ahead hit him. Questions multiplied like bees swarming the hive. How could he possibly finger a spy among the many people employed at the embassy? The State Department hired locals to answer phones, process visa requests and other clerical tasks. What if the spy never used computers?

His whole plan could implode before it ever left the ground. For all he knew the traitor could be an Arab, an Israeli, or even a State Department employee. It wouldn't be the first time an American sold out his country for cold hard cash.

The passenger door flew open and Bo nearly jumped out of his wrinkled shirt when Gregg called, "Dad! Mom wants you to meet Dr. Van Horn."

Must he chat with her book-hero this very second? Bo slid his long legs from behind the wheel, pocketing his keys and sauntering behind Gregg toward the front of the bus. Julia beamed beside a distinguished man. If he was Van Horn, he sure was animated talking to an elderly couple. Bo caught a few snippets.

"Sign up for future tours, but there is no guarantee I will be here."

"Are you retiring from ministry?" The elderly woman's powdered cheeks fell in disappointment.

"Oh no!" A lock of the tall man's wavy hair fell into his forehead as he gestured broadly with his large hands. "I refer to events in the Middle East. You will see what I mean in the morning when we visit the Jezreel Valley. The Book of Revelation predicts that is where world powers will clash in the final Battle of Armageddon. Napoleon fought there and said there was no place on earth better suited for war. Of course, I won't be here."

"Do you mean the rapture of the church?" Julia asked, staring up at the man.

"I do. My latest book explains how Bible prophecy is playing out here in Israel on a grand and rapid scale. I pray you and your family won't be here either during the Tribulation."

The couple wandered off and he turned to grab a valise from the open baggage compartment. Julia ducked her head toward him.

"Dr. Van Horn, I would like to introduce my husband Bo."

"Too bad you missed much of the tour, but it is a pleasure." Van Horn extended a strong hand, his blue eyes penetrating into Bo's.

Bo shook hands, stunned by the man's presence, more powerful than he appeared on his book cover.

"I've studied Napoleon and his battle at Megiddo," he managed.

"That is the same place as the Jezreel Valley. Studying historical military battles is a hobby of mine." Van Horn's intense gaze never wavered. "I hope you realize God's blessing to you. Julia's gift of hospitality encourages me and others on the tour."

"You work for the State Department?" Van Horn asked brusquely.

With Van Horn knowing about his once closely-held cover, Bo forged a pretend smile but thought it wiser to stay silent.

Van Horn paused, assessing Bo with his piercing eyes. "You have a grave responsibility, young man. The U.S. alliance with Israel is critical."

So Van Horn had other interests in Israel. "What else do you do here besides take Americans on tours?" Bo asked, probing Van Horn's connections.

"We're the only power standing between Israel's annihilation by their neighbors." Van Horn turned to Julia. "Are you available for our trip to the Jezreel Valley?"

"The kids and I won't miss it," she said, admiration shining in her eyes.

"Honey, don't forget the embassy shindig starts at eight tonight."

Julia lobbed Bo a look he couldn't decipher. Van Horn patted Bo's shoulder in a way Bo didn't appreciate, figuring the doctor was an intellectual type who considered others inferior.

"Stay vigilant, Bo. Keep looking up, because we're going up."

"You don't have to believe everything he says," a gruff voice intoned. "Every generation before us thought the so-called 'rapture' would occur any moment."

Van Horn twisted suddenly and Bo turned, eager to learn who challenged the good doctor, whose face wore a puzzled look, his bushy eyebrows raised.

"Ted!" Van Horn cried, looking down at a shorter man. "I thought you were in Dubai."

"I'm flying back to Tennessee," the man said. "Thought I'd stop and see you."

"Bo, Julia, this is my son, Ted."

Handshakes all around and Bo eyed the newcomer. Where Dr. Van Horn was tall and distinguished, his son barely reached his earlobe. Ted sported a muscular build, like an athlete's. Bo snickered. He liked Ted's surprise appearance. Van Horn wasn't infallible after all.

As they headed to the car, Bo heard Van Horn say to his son, "Did you lose your cell phone? You could have called me."

"Move it," Bo called to his kids. "I'm taking your mom to a swanky party later."

As Bo opened the car door, Julia shot him a pained look. She settled into her seat and buckled in.

"I forgot about the dinner. My party dress is being cleaned after Clara's reception."

"Don't worry, love. You look terrific in whatever you wear."

She batted her eyes with a tender smile. "Bo, I am so glad you arrived safely. I wish we didn't have to go out."

Bo hit the gas. He viewed the party as a lineup for potential suspects. Traffic congealed and he concentrated, dodging a taxi veering into his lane and then deftly turning onto their street.

"How nice to meet Ted Van Horn," Julia remarked. "He's part of his father's ministry."

"The guy I saw didn't look too happy following in his old man's footsteps."

"You're wrong. Dr. Van Horn knows a great deal about the Bible and Israel's key role in the world's future. Look how you followed your dad into his military career."

"Do you think Gregg will follow Mac and me into serving our country?"

"Sshh. I don't want you giving our son any ideas."

"Do you approve of my career or do you wish I'd become a minister?"

"What?" Julia snapped her head to face him. "You've flown too long at thirty thousand feet. I leapt for joy about coming to Israel. We should discuss it later, when we're alone."

Bo rubbed his eyes with one hand, gripping the wheel with the other.

"Our kids have their noses into their handheld games and have no idea we're alive."

Julia turned around and sighed. "Their recent obsession with electronic gizmos is why I take them on tours. Getting them off the couch and observing history up close is good for them."

"You're doing a fabulous job, too."

Bo eased into the garage under their apartment building, passing a black sedan that looked like the Ambassador's car. But Julia distracted him by touching his arm.

"I'm saving your compliment in my precious memory book."

Bo quickly looked to see if the car had left the gate, but the sedan had disappeared.

"Something bothering you?" Julia asked.

"I'd rather stay home too. After the long flight, I'm beat."

"Take a hot shower and I'll heat pizza for the kids before the sitter comes."

"You don't think they're old enough to watch themselves?"

"Not in a foreign country with jets exploding I don't. Clara's friend has an eighteen-year-old granddaughter who's been accepted at Duke. She speaks perfect English and wants to be a pediatrician."

"Okay," Bo said with a yawn. "Hey kiddos, ready to ride the wave runners?"

Both Gregg and Glenna jerked their heads up and wailed, "Dad, we're in the garage!"

"Glad you're awake. Grab your gear. We're heading upstairs."

"What's for supper, Mom? I'm starving," Gregg said bursting from the car.

Bo locked up without listening to Julia's menu. He'd thought of a few ideas on the return flight that he wanted to swing into action at the embassy party, but for the life of him, he couldn't recall what they were.

11

Bo straightened his tie in the mirror for the third time. He'd razzed Julia for not being ready and here he was fussing with his outfit. Something else flitted across his conscience, but before he grasped what bothered him, Julia waltzed in from the bathroom. Bo stared at his wife.

She'd drawn her normally free-flowing hair up onto her head, clipping the back to keep her brown tresses in place. Bo's heart thudded as she adjusted a gold drop earring. She smiled at him shyly.

"Do I look okay to mingle with your muckety-mucks?"

Bo swallowed. In her black dress and yellow shawl draped across her shoulders she was a knockout. He tenderly touched her bangs, wanting to fold her into his arms and not let go.

"Honey, you look stunning."

"It must be this silk shawl you brought me from on your Asian trip last year."

"Are you hinting I should buy you something in Israel?"

"They're known for excellent prices on diamonds," she giggled, grabbing Bo's hand.

She had a compliment of her own for him. "Wear your navy-blue suit more often. It brings out the blue tint in your beautiful gray eyes."

Bo gazed into Julia's appealing eyes. Love for his wife thundered over him, blocking out all thoughts of duty. That is, until she reminded him.

"The sooner we head to the party and do whatever it is we do at these things, you and I can come home and enjoy my lemon cake on the balcony. Unless it's too cold to sit outside."

Bo dipped his head in a mock bow. "My lady, your chariot awaits."

BO CAST A FLEETING LOOK around the lavishly decorated State Room at the U.S. Embassy. His eyes swept over the long buffet table laden with sliced turkey and beef, bowls of salads, decorated cakes, and chocolate desserts. Julia hovered by his side, tossing him a grin at the sound of his stomach growling.

"Hal had a great idea to celebrate the upcoming holidays with the embassy staff." Bo piled turkey and stuffing on his plate.

"It was Clara's idea," Julia said, nibbling on a celery stick. "If only the kids could have come. I hope the new sitter works out as well as Naomi did."

"Let's take our plates out of the main traffic flow. I'm famished and want to eat before someone grabs me."

Bo brought Julia to an empty table, where she lowered her head to pray like she had since she'd started reading Van Horn's religious stuff. Bo sought to satisfy his hunger, so he plunged a fork into creamy potatoes relishing the buttery taste on his tongue. Hal, Clara, or whoever hit a homerun in his stat book; he'd not eaten anything this delicious in a long time.

Julia sipped hot apple cider, glancing sideways. "Who is that woman talking to Hal?"

Bo twisted his head to see, but kept his fork near his lips. "The one in the black pantsuit?"

"She has his ear on something important."

"That's Shellie Karnack, head of Diplomatic Security Corps. She let me know that she knows I'm a Company man."

Julia seemed to analyze Shellie. "Is that okay? You both work on the same team, right?"

"I guess so," Bo replied, sampling a bite of turkey.

"Does she carry a gun?"

"Let's not talk about that in here."

"Bo, have your forgotten my lemon cake? I see pumpkin pie on your dessert plate."

Bo grinned. "Um, pumpkin is my favorite."

"Then enjoy it," Julia said smiling. "The kids can have your cake and eat it too."

"You're the funny one. I'm surprised Clara hasn't snagged you for one of her causes."

As if his words conjured her appearance, Clara rushed at Julia, her tanned arms dangling with heavy bracelets.

"Julia, come meet Shalom. I didn't think he'd be here. His latest painting of Moses parting the Red Sea will be auctioned off for my foundation."

"Do you mind if I leave you to finish your pie alone?" Julia asked, her eyes twinkling.

"Go ahead. I have some folks to see, so have fun."

He gobbled his pie, free to people watch. Shellie still had Hal corralled in a corner, bending his ear. Perhaps the Ambassador's upcoming trip to London gave them cause to ignore the festivities. Or was it something more sinister? Bo returned to the buffet table intending to test his theory. After selecting a second slice of pumpkin pie, he ambled past Hal as if looking for somewhere to sit, catching a juicy morsel.

"The Secret Service will make those decisions while the President is here," Hal corrected Shellie.

Her eyes blazed. "But I'm in charge of security at the embassy."

"Shellie, I have pressing concerns." Hal wiped his forehead. "Iranian troops are swarming all around Israel's northern border."

The man looked ready to flee.

"Why leave in the morning? With the President's visit a week off, I need you here."

Hal didn't sound convinced. "I must resuscitate my peace efforts, which are fast disappearing. I'll be away just a few days."

Bo had seen the Ambassador's schedule. It mentioned no travel. Hal suddenly seized Bo's elbow.

"Shellie, you've met Bo. His wife helps Clara with her fundraising and I am grateful."

Shellie gripped Bo's free hand with a crunch, asking, "Will Hal have you interfering with me during the President's visit?"

Bo stepped back out of reach of her iron fist and considered her question. What had Hal told her about Bo's role at the embassy?

"Bo is my go-to-guy for national security," Hal boasted. "He even did a stint with the Army Rangers before joining the State Department."

Shellie smiled pleasantly. "Bo has so many talents. He will be a swell asset to us both."

Bo shifted his pie plate to his right hand, while Shellie waged a final battle with Hal to protect her turf. "Mr. Ambassador, please inform the Secret Service I have the lead for POTUS' security."

"Nobody doubts that, Shellie," Bo said. "How long have you been assigned to Tel Aviv?"

Hal used that moment to make a quick getaway.

Shellie tossed her head. "Longer than Hal's been Ambassador here."

"Any tips for me and my family?"

"Here's one. Convince Hal that he should trust me to do my job."

Bo measured his words carefully. "Surely he knows your role is to protect him."

"Secret Service shouldn't assume the lead when the President visits. It's my duty station."

"Shellie, you wouldn't like it if the FBI attaché at the embassy tried to run over your responsibilities. The Secret Service is tasked to protect POTUS within and outside the U.S. If you appeal to their sense of duty, you'll have no problems working together."

A waiter passed with a tray of coffee, and Bo plucked off a cup to go with his pie. As he drank some, he noticed Hal in a heated conversation with Joe Adams. Bo tilted his head in their direction.

"Does Hal bring his aide in on sensitive matters?"

"Not that I've noticed," Shellie replied, smoothing her long hair. "Why?"

Bo simply changed gears. "What's it like living in Israel for so many years?"

"No day is ever the same. You know who to trust and who you don't."

Shellie seemed bent on protecting her career, but could Bo trust her to defend his back?

"Anyone I should watch out for?" he asked, hoping to learn some clue, no matter how small, about the mole.

She lifted her chin as if weighing her answer. Bo detected a cynical glimmer in her eyes and was on the verge of asking another probative question when Hudson Engle, the Marine Corp Company Commander, marched up looking official in his dress blues.

"Excuse me, Mr. Rider, but someone left a threatening note at the guard station out front. It needs Ms. Karnack's attention."

"Who has the note?" Shellie demanded.

"The duty guard received an envelope with a note tucked inside," Engle replied. "It's secured in my office. Follow me so the guests don't catch wind of the situation." He stopped and added, "Oh, it's in Hebrew, which I do not read."

Pure U.S. Marine in his blue jacket, white cap, and white belt— Bo faced a sobering question. Did Engle hold a grudge against his country and seek revenge by becoming a spy? Bo made a mental note to spend time with the commander.

Shellie turned toward Bo, her eyes filled with concern. "Can you find Naomi Rabin and bring her to the security office? She is our Hebrew expert."

Bo put down his pie and coffee on a nearby table. Then he hustled to find Naomi for reasons of his own. Getting a bird's-eye view of

Shellie and Commander Engle interacting with staff might be one way to unearth the mole's identity. He found Naomi engaged in a deep conversation with a swarthy man that Bo did not recognize.

"Naomi, please come with me."

"Babar, wait for my return." She collected her purse from the table.

The man dipped his head at her and Bo led her toward Engle's office. Outside the door, he laid a trap for Naomi.

"I think Babar performs with the circus where you brought Gregg and Glenna. Something to do with elephants, right?"

"I think, Mr. Rider, that you are making a joke. Babar works at the Jordanian Embassy. He is helping me improve my Arabic."

Bo did not consider her close association with Babar humorous. He added Naomi to his mushrooming list of would-be traitors. Vowing to keep a close eye on her, he swung open the door to Engle's office where the commander was showing the note to Shellie. The threat turned out to have been pieced together from letters, possibly ripped from Hebrew magazines.

"What does it say?" Shellie asked, thrusting the note for Naomi to read.

"It spells out 'Death to America. All Jews must die.'"

Surprised the torn letters weren't from Arabic magazines, Bo realized the threatening note was unsigned. Whoever concocted the vile words knew Hebrew. That might eliminate a few suspects, including Commander Engle.

"What should I do with the note, Ms. Karnack?" Engle asked, straightening his back.

"Secure it in a glassine bag. We'll analyze for fingerprints, but I doubt we'll find any."

Bo watched Engle zip the bag shut, then posed a question, "Did you match any prints from the white powder incident a few weeks back?"

"Don't overstep your bounds, Rider." Shellie lifted her chin.

"No, ma'am, his point is legitimate. You did not brief me on those results."

Engle rose a mile in Bo's estimation. That didn't mean he'd cross him off the list yet. Years ago, a Marine guard had gone way over to the dark side in Moscow.

12

The next few weeks passed at a snail's pace for Bo. Not only did he learn nothing about the threatening note, he'd also spent precious little time with Hal since the Ambassador's return from his supposed trip to London. It might be his vivid imagination, but it seemed Hal went to extra lengths to avoid talking with Bo alone.

By Tuesday morning, suspicions were mounting against the Ambassador, especially with warnings from the Chief Spencer and Kangas. Still Bo had no proof. He gripped a tall cup of the Daily Grind's special brew, heading for his office. Shellie swirled by looking glum.

"Have a nice night?" he greeted Zaveda, measuring her response. "Want me to fetch you coffee?"

She snatched off her headset. "I prefer tea. What is on your calendar this week?"

"If I knew what the Ambassador had scheduled, it would be easier to plan."

"Shellie just told me that he is flying to Istanbul to meet with the Turkish Foreign Minister. If you need to talk to him, I could arrange that for you."

Zaveda actually smiled and Bo did a double take. Had he passed the gauntlet with her?

"I appreciate that, Zaveda. Set it for ten, and in the meantime, I'll make some calls."

She instantly punched in an extension, talking to Joe Adams, Hal's assistant, and in seconds Bo had a conference scheduled with Hal. Maybe Bo could find out what Hal was up to in Turkey. Meeting the arms dealer?

Zaveda looked up, her dark eyes gleaming. "Joe is unhappy, but what can I do? Should I tell Shellie to be there at ten?"

Bo's mind spiked to high alert. Why should Shellie be included? But perhaps Zaveda was on to something; he could observe Shellie and Hal together.

"Yes, and thanks for the good idea."

Bo walked into his office, where he fired up his computer, musing over what had happened in the last few days. Clara had invited Julia to constant meetings, which Julia honored, asking Naomi Rabin to watch Gregg and Glenna on some evenings when Bo was unavailable. The Israeli interpreter seemed dedicated to her role at the embassy, making no more mention of Babar.

Yesterday, Bo received a phone call from Judah. His friend's father, Eli Rosenbaum, had survived WWII because of an American. Bo had passed the details to Eva in an e-mail. He was now about to call Maureen Hall, the computer specialist at Langley, when his phone rang.

"You have a call from Eva Montanna," Zaveda said.

Odd. Why hadn't Eva called him on his cell?

"Put her through."

Eva said hello in his ear.

"Don't you have my cell number?" he asked.

"Yes, but it went right to your voice mail."

"I never heard it ring. What's up?"

"I only have a minute," she replied. "How are things in Tel Aviv?"

"Up to my neck in alligators. You?"

"Thanks for the update. I called Eli's family. Grandpa Marty is visiting them in Israel."

"I'm happy to help. Does Grandpa Marty need a place to stay?"

"It's all arranged through Yad Vashem, the Jewish Holocaust Museum in Jerusalem. Bo, I'm flying with him."

"That's fast work. Julia will want to host you at our place one evening or whatever works. I can't wait for you and Grandpa Marty to meet my kids."

"We would love it. Are things as heated over there as the media pretends?" she asked.

"Israelis live in dangerous times, but you get used to it. I know of a place in Old Jerusalem where we could meet. Esther's Bakery has the best lentil soup I've ever had."

"Sounds like a place I'd like to try. Bo, I'm praying for you over there."

They agreed to stay in touch before Eva ended the call. Bo heard a tap at his door. Zaveda turned the knob, looking in, her eyes red. "Hal has already left and will not meet with you."

Bo sized up the receptionist and in a flash saw that someone had been bullying her.

"Close the door."

She did and sniffed.

"Who told you the Ambassador was gone?"

"Joe, just a minute ago."

"Had you already told Shellie to meet us at ten?" Bo narrowed his eyes.

Zaveda merely nodded. What game was being played here? A ringing phone out in the reception area interrupted his exam of Zaveda.

"I should answer that," she said wistfully.

"By all means and don't worry about the Ambassador. Find out from Joe when he returns and reschedule my time with him."

Zaveda disappeared, closing the door behind her. Bo decided to call Maureen at Langley for an update on the "Operation Mole Be Gone" memos she'd inserted into State's computer. He locked up and zoomed past Zaveda who was still on the phone, speaking in low tones. He thought he heard her say, "Joe, you need to break it off."

Down in the Com Center, the secure booth was being used by an embassy staffer. On a secure phone at a nearby desk, Bo dialed Maureen, alert to a technician scanning computer screens and looming near Bo's shoulder.

Bo opted for a ruse, not wanting to reveal his efforts to find the mole. Hopefully Maureen would be smart enough to play along.

Maureen answered with an abrupt, "Yes?"

"It's Bo Rider. Had a chance to stop by my house and water my plants?"

"I've chewed all the gum you sent. By the way, are you on a secure line?"

Of course she worked in a secure area, but Bo didn't have that luxury.

"For the most part I like it here," he quipped. "How are things with you?"

"I thought of you," she said, apparently getting his drift. "I asked our information technology people. I've been adding your memos as scheduled in State's system, but nobody has discovered them."

Bo could hardly believe that *none* of the top secret, the secret, or even confidential memos had been read. That left non-classified memos, which would be accessed mostly by clerical types. Had any clerks seen the original directive about his assignment to Israel? He should ask Maureen the classification of his transfer orders sent by State to the embassy, but he had to be mindful of snooping ears.

"I can't check from here, but a contractor is supposed to repair my fence and latch. Next time you stop by, can you let me know if the gate is secure?"

"I can't decipher your code."

"Give it a whirl," he muttered.

A pause, and then she said, "How's this? The memo notifying the embassy of your transfer to Israel is classified as 'Secret.' If anyone found out you're with the Agency, could it be a case of careless gossip from someone who rightfully knew? Loose lips sink ships."

Anything was possible, but Bo was convinced the leak was not from carelessness.

"Maureen, you've answered my question. Let me know if there's ever evidence the contractor's been in my house."

"Got you covered. Will you ask Frank Deming to stop by and see me again?"

"You want more watermelon-flavored gum." Bo laughed.

"Yes, but he's nice. Frank is the only person who asks about my kitty cat."

Bo looked over his shoulder. The tech had moved away.

"Maureen, I'll tell him you appreciate his kindness."

"No! Please don't give me away."

"Okay, I'll ask him to keep you supplied with gum."

"Heading to an early lunch, Bo. I'll alert you to any news."

With a click, she was gone. Bo approached the coffee station in the Com Center and raising an empty cup, he asked the lone tech, "May I?"

He shrugged and Bo filled the cup, leaving no room for cream or sugar. He left the Com, nearly bumping into Hal. Hot coffee trickled onto his fingers. Bo steadied his cup.

"Bo, I need to speak with you."

Bo was flabbergasted. Hadn't Zaveda told him Hal had already gone to Turkey?

"We can talk in my not-so-spacious office."

The two of them passed Zaveda, who shot up in protest when she saw the Ambassador. Bo waved her off, shutting his door. Bo set his cup on the desk and pointed for Hal to sit.

Hal fumbled with his tie. "The West Bank trade delegation is waiting in my office."

"So you're not going to Istanbul to meet Turkey's Foreign Minister?"

"Where did you get that crazy notion?"

Bo folded his hands in mock surrender. "What can I help you with, sir?"

"Do you have anything to report you have not told me?"

Bo mentally replayed the events of the last few weeks. Though he'd not divulged one whit of the mole, had Hal found out somehow?

"About what in particular?" Bo asked, deflecting the heat from Hal's glare.

"The security problem around here."

"That's Shellie's turf. Ask her."

"Commander Engle showed *you* the threatening note."

Bo leaned on his desk, folding his arms. "Shellie hasn't briefed me on fingerprint results."

"I need your expert set of eyes as the region destabilizes." Hal pursed his beefy lips and waited.

"Are there new developments that I should know about?"

Bo picked up his cup, drinking half of it.

"Iran recently installed a proxy government in Lebanon, using Hezbollah to fan the flames of hatred against Israel."

"Many are pressuring Israel to return to the sixty-seven borders. That will be the end of Israel," Bo replied, probing Hal's loyalties.

With his hand resting on the doorknob, Hal grunted. "You hold a simplistic view."

"But you admit the note threatened death to Israel and the Jewish people."

"Keep me advised of all progress," was Hal's terse response.

Bo wasn't satisfied. "Because America has always been Israel's staunch ally, the embassy and staff are experiencing the brunt of Israel's enemies."

Hal opened the door, leaving Bo to watch his disappearing back. What a strange conversation given what Zaveda had told him. Hal might have loosened his lips in the wrong quarters. He could have told Naomi or others in the embassy the CIA was sending Bo to "be a set of expert eyes" as Hal had just told Bo.

Perhaps Naomi worked for an intelligence service, maybe even Mossad. Bo's sensors on overload, he didn't know who he could trust. At the very least, he'd tell Julia not to let Naomi be a sitter in their home ever again.

THAT AFTERNOON, BO DUG THROUGH his incoming mail. One half-opened envelope held a photocopy of an invitation to a reception at the British Embassy. Bo tossed the crumpled invite in the garbage can. During his years as a covert operative, he shunned all events that might hint to his government service. Suddenly Bo changed his mind.

He yanked the invite out of the can. The party, offering plenty of drinks and hors d'oeuvres, started in thirty minutes. Because it looked like someone didn't want him to attend, Bo decided to be there for one very good reason. The arrival of Britain's new Ambassador to Israel might be a prime way for intelligence officers to gather a true sense of what was happening among Israel's power players. Bo let Julia know with a phone call.

"Honey, there's a meet and greet at the British Embassy I should attend."

"You don't need my permission."

"I won't be messing up your night?"

"Glenna is writing an essay on the Continental Congress and Gregg is waxing eloquent about discoveries of air travel. I'll be grading their papers."

"Oh, I can't say more on the phone, but Naomi is not available to sit with the kids."

"Is she all right?"

"She's super busy here at work. I'll be home by ten."

Bo replaced the receiver and then rummaged in his desk drawer, pulling out a clean tie, which he knotted quickly. He raced to his pool car, biting down on a breath mint, and drove to the British embassy. Pocketing his keys and approaching the front entrance, he saw Shane Rollins taking a last puff before snuffing out his cigarette. Bo recoiled.

The FBI Special Agent was the Legal Attaché at the U.S. Embassy who had one major flaw, his big mouth. In Bo's one previous encounter, Rollins had whispered, "Your secret's safe with me," meaning the Legat knew Bo was Agency to the core.

Bo thought of asking Rollins if the FBI had fingerprint results from the threatening note, but thought better of sneaking behind Shellie's back. Let her prove she had the stuff to be a team player. Better to talk to Rollins socially in hopes he might reveal tidbits about embassy staffers. Bo would watch and listen.

"So you decided to suffer for the Bureau," Bo said dryly.

Rollins looked around furtively. "What's your excuse?"

"One of the lousy perks I put up with. Ready to indulge in free drinks and food?"

Both agents showed their photocopied invites and diplomatic IDs to the British security officer and were allowed to enter the embassy. Rollins faced Bo with a tight grimace.

"Most people here know I'm FBI, but I'll introduce you as the Ambassador's national security advisor. Many foreign intelligence officers are scattered among the diplomats. If anyone drills for more info, impress them with your stories of the Army Rangers."

Did Rollins think Bo was such a simpleton? Instead of arguing, he nodded and left Rollins behind to go mingle among U.S. Embassy staffers. He found Joe Adams downing several glasses of whiskey over ice, keeping mostly to himself. A lush could easily pass along secrets. And Joe had instant access to the Ambassador's computer.

Bo drank soda water, eyeing Joe's solitary ways. Liquor rarely passed Bo's lips. He needed his wits about him at all times. His mind snapped to attention. Shellie entered the room, immediately latching onto a server. Bo headed in the opposite direction, where he found Rollins in a fiery exchange with some Bureau agents Bo knew.

"The Brit's former ambassador dug in his heels," Rollins complained. "He wanted a separate Palestine or nothing."

A man Bo didn't know said in a clipped British accent, "If America dillydallies reining in Iran, it will be too late."

The wiry man stopped speaking when Rollins clapped Bo on the shoulder.

"Another proud Yank. Bo Rider is the guru advising Hal Cohen on national security." Rollins gestured to the others. "Bo, you've met our guys, but this other gent is British MI5."

Familiar with Britain's version of the FBI, Bo grasped the man's hand, trying to figure what his role might be here in Tel Aviv.

"Nice meeting you, chap. I am Brewster Miles, visiting from White-hall. My close FBI friend mentioned your name."

Bo knew only one FBI agent who'd use Bo's name. "Was his grand-father a well-known British Admiral?"

Miles tossed a brief nod. "Yes. Griffin Topping and I shared several cases abroad."

The others returned to their conversation, giving Miles a chance to maneuver Bo away from the crowd where he lowered his voice.

"You are a Company man. While I am usually interested in Brit-ain's domestic matters, I am on loan to MI6, our intelligence service."

First Rollins and now a Brit. Bo might as well hand out business cards advertising his role with the Agency.

He crossed his arms. "How did my name surface?"

"You and Griff saved the day involving the UN. I had a mutual interest in the outcome."

His China caper. Before Bo could reply, Shellie stalked past with a man, her face an inch away from his. They settled at a high corner table where they placed their drinks. The man reached over and ran his hand up and down Shellie's back, resting it on her hip. Bo checked to see if Miles noticed, but the tea drinker was snagging a hot cup from a passing waiter.

Bo noted Shellie's closeness to the man but said to Brewster, "My New York case with Griff had an amazing ending, much like a spy novel with twists."

"I saw you gazing at the woman in the corner," Miles said. "Know her?"

"She's our embassy's Diplomatic Security Director. She's so wedded to her job I'm surprised to see her off duty."

Bo was about to ask why Miles noticed Shellie when the British agent handed him a business card, which he slid into his pocket.

He returned the favor, telling Brewster, "When I see Griff, I'll mention we met."

Miles finished his tea, setting the cup on a table. "A word of advice, Rider. Your boss is mixing with a known arms dealer."

"Again?"

"I am aware Hal Cohen met with a Turk on the day Israeli fighter jets scrambled to shoot down the Iranian fighter."

Bo knew that exact date. Even Clara couldn't locate Hal when she'd returned with Julia.

"My family was riding a cable car and the explosion erupted above them."

"The arms dealer your boss met with is on my radar screen for reasons I choose not to divulge here. You have my card and I welcome your call."

Miles tipped his head, slipping through the bustling crowd of revelers. Bo looked for Rollins, but didn't find the FBI agent. Shellie also had disappeared. Bo headed to the car, his mind buzzing with the clues he'd picked up. Gripping the wheel and driving home, he realized a dreadful fact. He was far from ensnaring any elusive mole in a steel trap.

13

The following morning, after a restless night of waking and dozing in spurts, Bo grabbed a bagel and hot coffee, heading to the embassy where he hunkered down to unmask the mole. His memos hadn't provoked any hits. Meanwhile, Sadie Lamb stayed in captivity, which was unacceptable. He needed to devise a new plan and he'd use old-fashioned shoe leather.

After a brief call to Brewster Miles, Bo sped over to the British Embassy to confer with him. The two spies lunched in a quiet corner, Bo picking Brewster's brain and learning that the arms dealer Hal had met with was connected to Egypt's new regime. Bo filed that in his near-photographic memory and hurried back to the embassy where he cornered Joe Adams.

"Let's have coffee."

"Why me?" Joe put down the phone receiver. "I'm some threat to national security?"

Bo pasted on a grin. "With the President's upcoming trip, you and I should coordinate."

They agreed to confer in fifteen minutes at the Daily Grind downstairs. Bo darted down to the Com Center, placing a secure call to Frank Deming, relieved to find Kangas' assistant had already begun his day at Langley. The secure booth was occupied by a Legat, but this time the Com tech wore a headset, giving Bo freedom to talk on another secure line.

"I need to speak to the Director. I've learned something urgent."

"He's attending a ceremony at Quantico, but I can reach him for you," Frank offered.

"MI6 passed something I won't send via diplomatic pouch. The Wolf met a second time with the arms dealer."

Bo detailed Hal's clandestine meeting, adding, "Nothing new on the other front."

"I learned last night the President canceled his trip to Israel."

"Really? I'm about to meet with a staffer about that very trip. No one mentioned POTUS isn't coming."

"It is not common knowledge," Frank whispered, "but the President is convening a session in France with heads of State. The Secret Service pulled the plug on his going to Israel."

Maybe that was why Shellie had looked shell-shocked yesterday. Had the threatening note tipped the scales after the white powder incident? Bo cast a look at the technician, noting he'd pulled off his headset. He'd end the call.

"You do the briefing for me and I'll stay in touch."

He signed out of the Com and found Joe near the Grind, looking like a wounded dog, fleshy bags protruding under his eyes. Bo paid for two coffees and came right to the point, testing what Joe knew.

"Are you and the Ambassador ready for the President? Need my assistance?"

"Special Agent Karnack just told me. The President isn't coming."

"Really?" Bo feigned surprise. "Do you know why?"

"Some security issue. Ask her."

"I will. Did you enjoy the embassy shindig last night?"

Joe blinked his eyes and guzzled his coffee.

"A bit hung over? When I saw you last night you were really into the sauce."

"Mr. Rider," Joe wiped his mouth on a napkin, "I don't usually drink that heavy."

"Something wrong, Joe? You can tell me."

Sweat formed on Joe's upper lip. Bo leaned in for the kill while Hal's aide felt weak.

"You're plagued with regrets about something."

"How did you know, sir?" the young aide gulped.

"It's written all over your face. Why not fling it off and be free."

Joe wilted like a dead flower in his chair. "My girlfriend dumped me last weekend. She's home in D.C. and e-mailed me that she was through."

"That's rough. Why so filled with regret?"

"She wanted me to turn down this job and remain at Foggy Bottom."

From the profound relief in Joe's eyes, Bo believed the young man.

"You wanted adventure and a higher paying job, right? That's nothing to be ashamed of."

Joe shrugged. "I guess."

"My dad always urged me to shoot for my dreams and never give up. Is that what you're doing or are you letting a failed relationship steer your future course?"

"I see what you mean." Joe straightened his shoulders. "I need to re-organize the Ambassador's calendar."

"I'll tag along and see if I can find Special Agent Karnack."

"You won't tell her what I said? She delights in ribbing me, like I'm some schoolboy."

Bo bit back an acrid retort about Shellie needing to mind her own business. Rather, he pumped Joe's hand. "Nah, it's between us guys."

Back upstairs, Bo interrupted Shellie locking her desk drawer with a key. When she heard Bo, she whirled around.

"You don't believe in knocking?"

"The door is open."

"That does not mean you can swagger your way in. What do you need?"

"I understand the President changed his mind about Israel. Care to enlighten me?"

"He's joining the economic summit in Paris instead."

"I think the Secret Service got spooked by the infamous white powder incident and the threatening note," Bo replied, leaning against the doorjamb.

Shellie's face blanched. "I briefed them, but the change occurred because the Prime Minister of Israel is traveling to France. POTUS will meet him there."

"Did the FBI send their fingerprint results to you?" Bo studied her dark eyes.

"As a matter-of-fact, I have received a report. Read it yourself."

She handed over a sheet of paper before powering up her computer.

"No identifiable prints. What do you make of it?"

"We are dealing with a pro and not some nutcase."

"Obviously, but do you have any suspects in your crosshairs?"

"The usual pro-Palestinian militants. You know Israel haters are legion."

"So you're sitting on this and doing nothing because it's too over-whelming?"

Shellie lit out of her chair, thumping her palms against her desk and growling at Bo as if she were a German shepherd about to eat him for lunch.

"Rider, don't tell me how to do my job. You've been here, what, less than two months, and are suddenly a know-it-all about Israel? I turned both the white powder and the envelope to the FBI for finger-print analysis. They came up with nothing. We move on."

"What about requesting more Marine guards?"

"Security is tight enough."

Weary of the banter, Bo backed out her door with his usual grin. "Glad you're on top of things, Shellie."

He wasn't about to tell her of his plans to stay as close to Hal like stink on a skunk. Brewster had dropped that sizzling intel about the Ambassador cozying up to an arms dealer the day Iran showed its military might. Fortunately, the IDF had eliminated the threat first. That is exactly what Bo needed to do with the mole.

He returned to his office. Zaveda was not at her desk, but she'd left Bo a note:

Eva called. She and Marty land at Ben Gurion tonight, nine thirty. Call her hotel number and confirm time for lunch at Esther's Bakery. Z

Bo called Eva's cell number, leaving her a message that he would collect her at her hotel at noon. Then he locked his office, noticing Zaveda had returned.

"Bo, did you receive my note?" She thrust her hands on her hips.

"Yes. After I have lunch with Eva, she and I are meeting Julia and my kids. Not to worry."

Zaveda's shoulders sagged. "I could tell you were an honorable man like my father. Joe is so hurt by his girlfriend dumping him over the Internet. I wonder if he will be ready to date anytime soon."

Her eyes turned dreamy and Bo knew better than to play matchmaker. He turned, heading for the elevator, telling Zaveda, "Send me a text if anything unusual erupts."

BO DODGED PUDDLES along Jerusalem's Hadassah Street, thankful rain had quit falling. He ducked into Esther's Bakery with Federal Agent Eva Montanna trailing behind him. Unease shadowed his steps. Wiping raindrops off his face, Bo couldn't shake the sense he and Eva were being watched. He assessed the diners sipping drinks and eating pastries. Everyone appeared normal.

Eva spoke to a hostess while Bo gazed over a curtain hiding the lower half of a large window. Two teenage girls skipped down the wet sidewalk, listening to music through buds in their ears. They posed no threat. His eyes traveled to cars parked across the busy street.

"Bo."

His body jumped.

Eva lightly touched his arm. "Our table's ready."

He reluctantly followed the hostess to a noisy corner of Esther's, which he'd found one day while waiting for Julia and the kids to return from one of Van Horn's tours. In fact, at this moment his family was touring Jerusalem's ancient tunnels with the famous doctor.

Eva snagged the seat facing the door, forcing him to take the chair beside her.

"Do you always have to face the door?"

"Get used to it, Bo. It's my survival instinct."

Had he been wise to meet Eva in a public place? He supposed nervousness was natural, flowing from his days posing as Skip Pierce, corporate recruiter traveling the world for the CIA. But with each passing day he began to regret working in Israel using his real name.

"Being in the Middle East brings back memories of my sister dying on September 11th." Eva wrung her hands.

Bo had his own vivid memories of that horrible day when terrorists killed thousands crashing planes around the nation. "Some might forget. You and I never will."

"One day my sister and I will be reunited," Eva said softly.

Her eyes traveled upward. Bo opened a menu not knowing what to say. Julia often tried, after spending time with Van Horn, to talk about eternal destiny with Bo. He sympathized with Eva losing her twin sister in the Pentagon, but he refused to dwell on the past. As an Army Ranger, he'd chased the Taliban and these days, he hunted down terrorists and America's enemies for the CIA. But so far he'd come up short running the mole to ground.

"Bo, are you all right?"

"I need food." He motioned for a waiter.

None came. An awkward silence at their table mingled with pungent smells of lemon and garlic. Bo studied Eva's pale face and heavy eyelids drooping over her vivid blue eyes. She was usually a hard charger, busting the chops of criminals with no thoughts for her safety. The flight across the Atlantic must have taken its toll on her.

"Enjoying your time with Grandpa Marty?"

"Thanks to you. Eli's memory is so clear of fleeing the Nazis with Grandpa's help. I'm amazed by how much Grandpa did to save God's chosen people," she said, rubbing her eyes.

"Then what's eating you?"

"Grandpa acted so tired this morning when I left the hotel room."

"Your hands are shaking because you left him alone?"

Eva snapped open her menu. "Quit it. You're making me as nervous as my cat is around strangers. I drank too much coffee."

"Me too." Bo laughed.

"Thanks for taking time out for more coffee," she said with the first hint of a smile. "Grandpa is not alone; he's lunching with Eli at the retirement village."

"We're both edgy, but you seem off your game."

"Guess I miss my three kiddos."

Could it be as simple as being separated from her family? Bo leaned forward.

"We've worked together enough that I sense you're wired. Julia accuses me of being aloof, so I won't pry." Bo looked around. "Where's our waiter anyway?"

Eva's eyes swept across the room then stopped in an intense stare behind Bo.

"Head's up." Eva shifted her eyes. "There's something we don't see often in Virginia."

Bo turned. A woman dressed entirely in black, only her black eyes exposed, sat erect at a table close to the front door. With her unblinking eyes, she seemed uncomfortable in the Jewish bakery. Bo's eyes returned to Eva's worried face.

"You see women totally covered here. She's probably a Palestinian from the West Bank. Israel permits them to enter as day laborers."

"Anyway, what should I order? I need a change."

"I tried hummus during one of Julia's tours with some religious guy." Bo stretched out his legs.

"You're not interested in the sights?"

"Embassy duty keeps me too busy with minutiae. Julia is always coaxing me to delve into Israel's ancient places. She's convinced my assignment here is no coincidence."

Eva tapped the plastic menu with her fingertips. "My turn. I sense you're not enthused with your new job."

Bo spiked a hand through his wavy hair, his mind seizing upon his failure. He'd like Eva's opinion as a seasoned federal agent. Of course he couldn't go against Kangas and tell her about the embassy leaker, but posing a general question wouldn't blow his covert Op.

"When you have a suspect and surveillance turns up nothing, what's your next move?" Bo folded his arms on the painted table, eager for Eva's take.

She stared, her lips turning up at the edges. "Depends on the target."

"A slippery type, identity unknown."

"It's a skill I have developed with years in the business. It would be impossible for me to recruit as you do."

She was right. He was no investigator and Eva was no spy. However, chasing the mole would be his chance to improve his investigative techniques. Without warning, Eva's periwinkle eyes locked onto the front of the bakery.

Bo swiveled around. The hostess gestured to an extremely tall man, his unusual height and girth drawing stares from other patrons. With his large head covered by a brown fisherman's cap, scruffy clothes, and round face hidden by a full beard, he looked like a cartoon figure.

"He stands out in a crowd."

Eva breathed deeply. "Have you seen him before?"

"Nope. In my line of work, I'd hate to be so tall. It's impossible to blend in. My stomach is growling. Let's try another restaurant."

"The Palestinian woman shares your sentiment," Eva said, jerking her head toward the table where the covered woman had been seated. "She went up to the bakery counter to complain. She must be buying food for an entire household. Look at that large bag full of stuff."

The bearded man sat at a table less than two feet from Bo. Just as Bo sniffed, detecting smells of diesel fumes, a dark thundercloud passed over Eva's features.

She leaned close to Bo's ear. "I remember where I saw him. He was standing on the corner when I paid my taxi fare. I imagine he looks to me like Goliath might have looked to David, the shepherd boy, thousands of years ago."

Bo studied the large man's profile, wondering if he'd been following them. Eva seemed tense about seeing him near her cab. Instead of voicing his concerns, he said instead, "So you think he looks like some ancient giant."

"Last night, I was reading my Bible. David killed Goliath with a slingshot. I turned out the lights and dreamed of a giant man chasing me and Grandpa through Jerusalem. I tried to call for help, but my cell phone caught fire. We ran into a cave outside the city, which flooded with rising water. Grandpa couldn't breathe. Bo, I thought he was going to die."

Bo shrugged off her worries. "When my kids have nightmares, I tell them to move on with life. Dreams aren't real."

"My dreams mostly come true." Eva clasped her hands in front of her.

"If this modern Goliath is following you, why risk being seen in the same restaurant?"

He hoped to get her thinking more like the federal agent he respected. Besides, he'd eaten no breakfast, having briefed the U.S. Ambassador about a new flotilla heading for Gaza. But he kept from Eva how Hamas was poised to confront Israel's IDF any second.

"From my law enforcement experience, the guilty do the obvious for two reasons. One, they're dumb criminals or two, they are intentionally in your face."

"I'm finding the manager of this joint. I'm starving."

Bo hurtled from his seat and out of the corner of his eye, he saw the burly fisherman leave, maybe to find a restaurant that actually served food. After a few words to the hostess, Bo returned to the table telling Eva, "Your creepy follower just left so nothing to worry about."

The waiter appeared with an apology, sweat streaming down his wrinkled face.

"We each want chicken soup, pita bread with hummus, and orange juice. I get the tab," Bo said, handing the menus to the waiter who hurried to the kitchen.

"I want to buy your lunch as thanks for helping Grandpa Marty find Eli."

"It's on me. I have a favor to ask."

As if she hadn't heard, Eva asked, "Does Israel ever have earthquakes?"

"Excuse me?"

"Are there earthquakes here?"

"Are you looking for trouble?" Bo demanded, drumming his fingers on the table.

"A terrible roar started under the Old City. It crumbled before my eyes. I—"

The waiter brought steaming bowls of soup laden with matzo and thick pieces of chicken. He set down a platter of bread, hummus, and chopped salad with onions. Bo barely noticed Eva close her eyes. Without thinking about her praying, he blew on his soup and dipped in his spoon.

His soup was half gone when he finally said, "I don't remember hearing anything about the Old City being destroyed."

"You wouldn't. I dreamt it."

Bo was about to jazz Eva when the Palestinian woman passed by their table striding to the door carrying two large circles of flat bread. Eva leapt to her feet.

"Ma'am, you forgot your package!"

Bo turned. Over his shoulder he saw the woman dressed from head to toe in a black robe clinging to her ankles open the door. Eva snatched up the woven reed bag and started after her. Suddenly, she plunked it down with a thud and peered inside.

"It's a bomb!" Eva screamed.

14

A bomb! Bo launched to his feet, tipping over his chair. Adrenaline pushed him toward the door, his mind reeling. How did Eva know it was a bomb? Was it meant for him?

She tugged the parcel with both hands, running toward the door. Out in the street, Eva tossed the bag high into the air, hurtling it down Hadassah Street, shouting, "It's a bomb! Run!"

Eva sprinted to her left, running after the veiled woman. Bo charged after them, breathing hard. Hordes of people, their arms flailing and mouths open, were fleeing in the same direction, but they jumped aside as Eva cried out, "Stop that woman!"

Suddenly, Eva grabbed the covered woman in a choke hold and both went tumbling into the street. Bo dove and held down the woman's feet, but she kicked at him fiercely, striking his chin, brawling like a man.

Pain rocked through his jaw. The woman leapt to her feet. Eva dislodged her head covering and she had a full-length beard!

· The female imposter spun Eva around and curled his fist to strike her. Bo grabbed his black robe from behind, yanking him around. Eva pounced at his chest, her hands balled into tight fists. The man leaned into Bo's grasp, propelled his feet outward, and kicked Eva in the stomach. Bo tipped him over backwards and both men fell to the ground.

An enormous blast ripped through the air.

Covering his ears with his hands, he spotted Eva sprawled flat on her stomach in the road. Before he could tell if she was hurt or even alive, the bomber stood and started to run. Bo seized his arm, but the man turned, pounding Bo in the face. Bo fought back swinging, struggling to get the upper hand.

Without warning Eva leapt on the man from behind, distracting the bomber long enough for Bo to cock his right arm. With tremendous might, he landed a blow against the man's head, crushing Bo's fist.

Throbbing pain shot through his fingers and wrist, but he shook it out. In those few seconds, the bomber tossed Eva to the ground like a feather and raced down the street. Bo hurried to help her up.

"You all right?"

Her eyes flew open. "Yes! But he's getting away!"

Bo sped after him, dodging folks crying and holding their heads. The fleeing man tripped on his long black skirt. Bo jumped on top of him, hunter and prey splashing down in a puddle. He punched the guy's abdomen, a sure place to weaken him. Eva joined in the fray, pinning the bomber's arms. Bo ignored rocking pains in his side and fingers, wasting no time ripping off his belt and securing the man's legs.

Eva sat on the bomber's chest. Bo straightened, quickly surveying the scene. Less than a hundred feet behind them a car burned, hot flames sending stink and black smoke into the air. The front of the café was in shambles. An armed Israeli carrying an Uzi scurried toward Bo and Eva, casting a dark look at Bo.

"He's dressed like a woman, but this man left a bomb in the bakery," Eva huffed, sitting on the bomber.

"I will handle from here."

The officer pulled Eva away and busied himself handcuffing the bomber's hands. The suspect began shouting words in Arabic and Bo instantly grabbed Eva's arm, tugging her behind a gathering crowd. He didn't stop until they reached an alley.

"My ears are pulsating. I can hardly hear," he complained.

Eva leaned over, shaking her head. "It feels like a lead balloon is in my ear."

"Come on," Bo shouted. "I parked on the street beyond Hadassah."

"I can run."

He looked over his shoulder. "But did you leave a purse in the bakery or anything to identify you?"

"Oh!"

Eva quickly reached for a fanny pack attached around her waist. She patted it, a look of relief passing over her brow. "Everything I have is still here."

Sirens blaring one street over got them hustling out of the alley toward Bo's car. They hurried inside, slamming the doors against the din. Bo let out a deep sigh and wiped his face before turning to Eva with a sheepish grin.

"Whenever we're together there is drama."

She rolled her eyes and dusted off her clothes.

"A casual lunch so far from Washington almost wiped us out. Good thing I prayed over my meal for our protection."

Bo pushed his fingertips into his ears, massaging them, hoping the ringing would stop. He let his mouth hang open and felt *pop*, *pop*. His heart racing, Bo yanked his keys from his jacket pocket.

"Unbelievable!" he hollered. "We're plunged into some terrorist case in Old Jerusalem."

Eva licked her bloody lip, full of questions. "Was that bomb was meant for us? Did Goliath speak to the man, ah you know, the one pretending to be a woman?"

"I don't think so." But he mentally replayed the past thirty minutes and shrugged, that simple move shooting pains through his neck. "Eva, if one of us were followed, that wouldn't have given anyone time to prepare a bomb. I guess the ongoing dispute between Palestinians and Jews caught us in the crossfire."

"We can only hope so." Eva steadied her shaking arms.

She leaned her head against the car seat, briefly closing her eyes. Bo wondered if she needed a moment of quiet. He looked out the rearview window, not seeing anyone on their tail.

He started the car, but before driving away he asked, "Eva, when you looked at the covered woman, did you see murder in her eyes? I can't believe I missed it."

Eva faced him, rubbing the back of her neck. "I didn't recognize the hate as murder, but I saw something amiss. That must be why I focused on everything she, I mean he, did."

"From now on you can grab the seat watching the door. You saved my life."

"I can't take credit," she objected.

"In my book you should and I thank you." Bo held out his hand adding, "My wife and kids thank you, even though they will never know what you did."

Eva dropped her hand. "Yes, I detected the bomb in his bag and ran after him. But Bo, God was prompting my spirit to be on the alert. What should we do now?"

"Avoid the mob. I'm taking you to your hotel."

"Good idea," Eva said. "I'd better clean up before collecting Grandpa Marty."

Bo pulled from his parking spot and he drove in silence, listening to a cacophony of sirens, sounding like they'd landed inside of Bo's throbbing head.

"I mentioned a favor. Gregg, my eleven-year-old, is interested in cops and crime. Sometime could you send him an ICE shoulder patch? I can't tell him what my job really is, but he might think I have influence with important federal agents."

Eva chuckled softly. "I brought along miniature lapel pins. I give the replicas of ICE badges to law enforcement officers who are helpful to me. Think he'd like one?"

"That would be great. Bring one tonight. You and Grandpa Marty are our guests for dinner. Julia found a nice place here in Jerusalem and she's anxious to meet you."

"Running from danger always brings on my appetite."

As Bo turned onto her street, his heart finally stopped hammering.

"Say, didn't you forget to give your police pal one of your ICE pins?"

"He missed out. But I promise to bring one for Gregg."

"My son likes to search for treasures. Maybe one day he'll be wearing a badge."

Eva wiped her face and pulled her hair behind her neck. "My son Andy wants to be a pilot. Maybe he'll fly fighter jets like Scott once did."

"I hope you and I can provide them with a safer place to live," Bo said, driving under the portico. "After today, I'm not sure we'll succeed."

JULIA RIDER DUCKED, passing under an archway carved from ancient stone, her hand resting on Glenna's shoulder. Yellow lights lit the tunnel, casting eerie shadows on rough granite walls.

Their group stopped, with Moshe the tour guide cautioning, "Be careful near the gaping shaft. Romans toppled the large stones you see below as they destroyed the second Temple."

Gregg sped forward, slipping away from Julia.

"Take a look, but move along," Moshe warned him. "We have three hundred more feet to enjoy in the tunnel."

"Those rocks are huge." Gregg leaned over the barricade to the large opening.

"Get back!" Julia gripped his arm, pulling her son from the hole.

Even looking down at the monstrous boulders made her dizzy. Their group began shuffling along.

"Stay within my sight," she told her eleven-year-old son. "Don't be getting lost in here."

Gregg kicked a pebble on the narrow rocky path. "I want to find treasure."

"Silly," Glenna snickered. "Any gold's been found by millions of tourists before us."

"Did not. Dad said I might find a gold coin."

Julia rolled her eyes at the endless banter between her two growing children. It wouldn't be long before Gregg joined his sister in the difficult teen years. Soon, Glenna would want to drive.

"Mom, Gregg's gone!" Glenna cried, pointing down the curving tunnel.

Julia squinted ahead trying to see in the dim light. Was that him around the bend? A sharp movement startled her.

"Boo!" Gregg jumped from behind a supporting timber.

Glenna's scream echoed down the tunnel and Gregg bounced with delight on his tiptoes. Julia sighed. This day was going nothing like she'd planned.

"Hey you two, you're doing something none of your friends can do. We're below the Western Wall, which is part of the ancient Temple where Christ taught."

Julia swallowed nervousness, seeing no one. The tour group had vanished.

"Gregg, your horsing around caused us to become separated and lost."

Someone tugged on her sleeve and she flinched in the close corridor. Julia wanted out of the narrow tunnel.

"Lady, I show you holy antiquities."

Julia peered down at a boy about Glenna's age with tightly curling black hair. She didn't recall seeing him when their tour began. What had started as Gregg's lark was quickly turning into a trying situation. Her nerves fluttering, Julia wished Bo had come along.

"I am Bennie," he said by her side, performing a bow. "I take side trips for Moshe, your tour guide. You speak of treasure. Lady, I show you amazing things."

"Mom, can we?" both Gregg and his sister chimed.

"Not today, thank you," Julia said firmly, hoping the boy would scamper away.

She consulted the folded map in the flickering light, seeing a way out.

"We walk ahead twenty feet and turn right."

"No, you get lost. Follow me." Bennie shot by Julia like a whirlwind.

Glenna whispered in her ear, "He knows, Mom. I saw him talking with Moshe before we ducked in here. Let's go. I want to find Daddy."

"I agree. He should be finished with his appointment by now," Julia told her.

"Lady, I hear sirens."

Julia paused to listen. "I don't hear anything."

"Yes, it could be an attack. Follow this way. Hurry."

Gregg first and then Glenna shot past her, trailing on Bennie's heels. Julia had no choice, so she went as fast as her trembling legs would take her along the underground labyrinth. In minutes, she scurried behind her daughter out of the tunnel, rejoining their group. Relief washed over Julia. How dreadful to be below ground and not know the way forward.

She wiped her perspiring forehead and breathed deeply of the fresh air. While listening to Moshe instruct the group about the next day's arrangements, she scanned the street for Bo. Two police cars with flashing lights roared by in tandem, and a policeman on foot ordered Moshe to dismiss the group. Julia wondered if Bennie really had heard sirens in the tunnel.

The teen engaged the policeman in Hebrew and then turned to Julia.

"A bomb exploded one street over."

A bomb! Julia gasped, drawing Glenna to her side.

"Where?" she asked Bennie.

"On Hadassah. A man is already arrested." Bennie waved a hand as if violence was routine in his young life.

Then he needled Gregg in the side. "Show you something."

Bennie hopped across David Street, running up to a vendor who sold wooden toys. Gregg and Glenna followed being entertained by the bent-over man who showed them how to nestle a ball on a string into a wooden cup. Nervous, Julia joined them, watching Bennie dig beneath the man's table and remove crude spikes and long spear-like thorns.

"He allows me to keep these here," Bennie said. "I sell them to Christian tourists. The thorns are like those that were crushed into Jesus' head like a crown. People think the spikes are like the ones that nailed Jesus to the cross."

Gregg tapped a thorn on the end. "Ouch! That hurt."

He shook his finger and a small drop of blood bubbled to the surface, which he wiped on his pants.

"Gregg, let me give you a tissue," Julia told her son. She pulled one from her pocket, wrapping it around Gregg's bleeding finger.

Bennie gingerly took back the thorn, saying in a low whisper, "I am paid five shekels for each of these. If you sell them to your tourists, I will give you a dollar for each one you sell."

Gregg and Glenna looked at her with such eager eyes Julia found it hard to say no. "You may so long as Dr. Van Horn doesn't object. I will speak to him about it."

"Thanks, Mom!" Glenna chirped.

Julia gazed down the street. "I'm going over to the Tourist Office where your dad is meeting us. Stay right here."

She walked a half-block to the Jaffa Gate, keeping her eyes trained on the kids. Gregg bounced the ball into the cup, his face alive with fun. But Julia couldn't tear her mind from the bombing. When she didn't see Bo or his SUV, she recalled he was meeting Eva Montanna at Esther's Bakery. That was on Hadassah!

Fear pulsed through her. What should she do? She dialed his cell, but his voice mail answered. She looked at Moshe, but the guide was helping a couple from Michigan find a taxi. Then she heard a distant beep. Down the street she saw Bo's hand signaling out the window. She waved to her kids. "Dad's waiting down the street."

Julia dashed down the block, sliding into the front seat as Gregg and Glenna dove into the back competing to tell Bo about the drama of being lost in tunnels.

"We heard about a bombing," Julia croaked in a whisper.

"Something happened back there," Bo replied, pulling out in a break in traffic. "Seems the police have things in control."

"Dad, you'd like Bennie," Gregg bellowed in Julia's ears. "He showed us the way out."

"No need to shout, son." Bo covered an ear. "But why were you lost?"

Julia simply shook her head, a dull ache pounding behind her ears.

"I don't like my family gallivanting around the country with Van Horn."

"But Dad, there's treasure still to be found!" Gregg moaned loudly.

Bo put a hand to his other ear, driving with one hand.

"Is something wrong with your ears, Bo?" Julia asked.

He sure was acting edgy.

Before Bo answered, Glenna giggled. "Mom was scared, but not me. I had fun."

"We'll talk about it later," Julia said, her heart torn.

Though she wanted the kids to experience Israel firsthand, something they couldn't do from studying books, she had been afraid. First exploding jets and now a bomb. Of course they'd been safe beneath the tunnel.

Julia gazed out the window at passing residents of Jerusalem: Women wearing shawls and carrying baskets and two men talking on the sidewalk, their long black coats and fur-rimmed hats revealing they were orthodox Jews, all living as if nothing unusual had happened.

Where was her faith? Dr. Van Horn had shared verses from the book of John where Jesus told his disciples toward the end days, the love of many would grow cold. That seemed to be happening around the world, especially in the Middle East. Julia rubbed her temples, wondering how to let Jesus sustain her more than food or drink or even policemen in times of trouble.

She eyed Bo's chin. Was that a red welt?

"Bo, are you all right?" she asked, fearing he'd been close to the bombing.

"Little ears, Julia."

He refused to say more and tears stung her eyes. Danger lurked all around her family.

Bo nodded toward the children, bickering in the backseat. "They're wound up. How about going to Sacher Park until we meet Eva and her grandfather for dinner in an hour?"

Julia simply wiped her eyes. She didn't know what to do. Go home and hide in the apartment? Bo tried again to engage her.

"The park has beautiful rose gardens. The kids can blow off steam. Maybe I can whisper in your ear about the exciting lunch I never finished."

"Maybe we should race home and lock the door," she replied, her heart thudding.

"The park is in New Jerusalem, miles from the hubbub. Besides, Eva is bringing Gregg a surprise."

Julia settled into the seat, desperate to erase worry clouding her mind. This was her chance to meet Eva, Bo's colleague, something Julia rarely had a chance to do. She willed her heart to be calm and brave. With a deep breath, she leaned over, patting Bo's hand on the steering wheel.

"We'll have a great time, so long as we stay together."

15

The next morning Bo fidgeted in Hal's reception area, weighing the bombing's fallout. He'd divulged to Julia little of the danger he had survived. At last evening's elegant dinner, neither he nor Eva hinted to the horrific explosion. Instead Marty regaled them with stories of his time in the Netherlands during WWII. Bo's mind came back to the present when Hal's receptionist ushered him to Hal's massive double door.

"Mr. Rider, please be brief," she said scowling. "He leaves soon."

Bo stepped into Hal's spacious office, the meeting spot for high-ranking foreign dignitaries an opulent palace compared to Bo's dingy office. Hal was threading his arms into his suit jacket behind his desk, looking haggard and older than his mid-fifties.

Bo had to wonder. Were his many secrets wearing on him?

"What is so urgent?" Hal blurted, buttoning the suit coat.

Bo sat across from Hal's desk, a bit uncomfortable with his so-called "boss" standing.

"I've reached out to my contacts, but no data has been released about the terrorist who bombed Old Jerusalem yesterday."

Hal paid little attention, gathering up loose files. "Leave the arrest to the Israelis."

"I thought you should know. An ICE agent and I were present."

"Are you saying that you and an ICE agent were involved operationally in Old Jerusalem? I never approved that. What is an ICE agent doing here?"

"Agent Montanna is a tourist with her grandfather. She and I met for lunch. We spotted a male Palestinian covered in veils, who chose that time and that bakery to set off a deadly bomb."

"Yes, killing a vendor's mule. One man has been arrested. End of story."

Bo crossed his arms. "As a Foreign Service officer I have immunity from questioning. Still, the IDF might contact me for evidence."

"Why should they come to you?" Hal pulled off his jacket, his brow furrowed.

"When Agent Montanna discovered the bomb, she hurled it down the middle of the street, warning people," Bo answered, desperate for caffeine. "The two of us chased the bomber before subduing him."

Hal dropped in his chair. "I will have to explain your involvement to the authorities?"

"That's why I came to see you first thing. Once we nabbed him, we turned the bomber over to the Israeli police. The officer didn't even take our names."

"All right." Hal stood, once again squeezing his arms back into his suit coat. "Otherwise, you would be headed stateside. Brief Shellie and advise me of all changes."

Bo left Hal for the Com Center where he entered the secure booth, sending an encrypted message to Frank Deming. After explaining his involvement in capturing the bomber, Bo asked why Kangas still hadn't contacted him, ending with: *Glad you're in the house. Julia and I won't be charging you rent. Please watch my yard for moles. Bo*

LATER THAT AFTERNOON Bo explored the Old City of Jaffa, modern Tel Aviv a few clicks to the north, its borders snuggling up against the ancient city built of stone. He was getting a close-up view of the once thriving seaport, but a question seared his mind. Was his search for the elusive mole linked to the bomb? He should be finding out instead of loitering by the shops.

Still, Julia had wanted him along as she showed Eva and Grandpa Marty the sights. So he trudged behind the entire bunch, gazing over his shoulder at the narrow stone steps he'd just walked down. Had he heard footsteps? No one was there. He lingered by a bookshop until Julia came out smiling.

"I found an old book in Hebrew," she said, holding up her prize.

Bo's eyes searched the streets. "You read Hebrew?"

"No, but I want to learn."

"Good for you, Julia." Eva sauntered by, holding Grandpa Marty's hand. "Thanks for inviting us to Tel Aviv. And Jaffa is a wonderful change from Old Jerusalem."

Yeah, the quiet seaport had no bombers trying to kill them, Bo almost blurted.

Rather, he said, "I'm glad you're comfortable in the guest room. The apartment building keeps a suite of rooms for visitors."

"Bring the rest of your family next time. Our kids will have loads of fun with yours." Julia clasped her books under an arm. "I want to hear more about your church."

At that, the two women walked off arm in arm, chatting as if they'd been friends for life. Not surprised they hit it off, Bo took Marty's arm.

With his thinning white hair and unsteady gait, he seemed fragile. Bo tried to picture him as a daring youth dodging German soldiers. "How do you intend to stay in touch with Eli?"

"We gather at Yad Vashem tomorrow. Can you meet us for lunch?" Glenna interrupted, "See that pretty glass bottle? It's the color of the sea."

Bo peeled out some shekels, paying the vendor so his daughter could admire the costly bargain on her windowsill. Gregg skipped along the stones, his eyes glued to the crevices. Outside the restaurant, Bo pondered an earlier call from Judah.

"We must talk," Judah had said, his voice edged with concern.

"We're off to shop and eat dinner at the Angler's Pier in Jaffa," Bo had told him.

"No matter, I'll be waiting."

A cormorant flew above Bo's head, pulling his mind back to the wharf. Stiff breezes blew and he watched boaters struggle against the building waves.

"Bo," Julia called. "Our table's ready."

He wasn't hungry, but once surrounded by aromas of spices and hot olive oil, his growling stomach signaled their table had come just in time. He and Julia ordered St. Peter's fish with everyone else opting for perch. A server brought them all glasses of fresh orange juice.

Eva raised her eyebrows. "Julia is starting as a tour facilitator in Old Jerusalem for Dr. Van Horn."

How could his wife even consider doing so after the bombing? Where she'd suddenly gotten such courage Bo couldn't fathom, but this wasn't the place to probe the inner workings of Julia's mind. He opted for a safer approach.

"Julia is homeschooling, which gives us a chance to see Israel together."

Julia beamed a smile. "I'm glad you contacted us, Eva. If we had known sooner, we could have shown you some real exciting places."

Eva's periwinkle-blue eyes sparkled as she traded a look at Bo. Surely, she must have been thinking the same thing he was: They'd seen enough excitement in Old Jerusalem.

The server brought their dinners and as if on a silent command, everyone except Bo bowed their heads in prayer. He watched as even Grandpa Marty folded his knobby hands and closed his eyes for a few seconds.

Feeling left out of something, Bo didn't know what. Eva was a devout Christian, but being interested in religion was newer for Julia and the kids. Since their arrival in Israel, Julia spent lots of time hanging out with Van Horn and his religious tourists. But Bo shouldn't grumble. This newfound faith brought her more fulfillment than serving on Clara's committees. He began eating, enjoying the tender fish, crisp salad with olives, and creamy goat cheese. At least Julia didn't insist he share her beliefs.

Marty sipped his juice, his blue eyes crinkling with happiness. "What a thrill to see Eli again after so many decades."

"Did you really hide him in your attic?" Glenna asked, her face serious.

"Yes. My Aunt Deane taught me courage in dangerous times, something like what the Jews face today." Marty sat up straighter, his eyes shining with enthusiasm.

Gregg's eyes grew huge. "Did Nazi soldiers search your house like in the movies?"

"All the time. It was difficult for everyone in the Netherlands. Some of our Christian friends gave us some of their rations so we could feed Eli and his family."

"Did you meet any fighter pilots?" Gregg asked.

Marty took a bite of fish and Eva sliced in a comment, her eyebrows again raised in a question mark.

"Bo, it must be nice living where no one knows you and you don't bump into friends each time you're in a restaurant."

Her eyes held his before shifting abruptly across the restaurant.

"Oh, we have met many new friends. Sometimes we see them around town," Glenna said, shoving pita bread into her mouth.

Bo's eyes followed Eva's gaze. There sat a large man, who looked something like the man Eva had tagged as Goliath in Old Jerusalem. This clean shaven guy wore no fisherman's cap as he laughed over a candlelight dinner with a woman. Was he their Goliath from the bakery or was Eva being paranoid?

Believing it was mere coincidence, Bo returned to the last of his salad. Old Jerusalem was nearly an hour away. Yet, he couldn't shake the sense they being watched. He excused himself, thinking he'd discover what Judah wanted. In the men's room, after making sure he was alone, he punched in the number. Judah didn't disappoint, answering right away.

"There is a new development with Iran."

"On the northern border?"

"No, but it has security implications."

"We could meet in the morning," Bo replied at the same moment a man walked in.

The sight of the enormous man that Eva had pointed out with her eyes made Bo's heart surge. But as the tall diner grew closer, Bo realized this large man had blue and not black eyes. Also his skin appeared so smooth it seemed unlikely he'd just shaved off his full beard.

Bo pressed his cell close to his ear. Judah suggested he arrive at Mossad HQ around nine. Bo agreed and returned to the table, convinced the burly diner wasn't Goliath following him from Old Jerusalem to Old Jaffa. Draining his orange juice, Bo felt ill at ease about Judah's cryptic phone call and his mysterious "security implications."

16

At Yad Vashem, Israel's Holocaust Museum, Bo zipped his jacket to his neck, reflecting on Judah's casual shrug when they'd talked earlier about the bakery bomber, the Mossad agent being more concerned about Iran. Why? Because Israel's number one enemy had just formed a secret pact with former Soviet Union countries. The purpose of their alliance: Wipe Israel off the map and weaken Israel's ally, America.

Cold wind sliced through Bo's thin jacket as he and Eva walked behind two aging men on the walkway. Julia and the kids were at a museum with Van Horn to see the Dead Sea Scrolls.

Bo pocketed his hands, telling Eva, "Marty and Eli seem oblivious to the biting wind."

"It sure whips through the trees." She pulled on her gloves and scurried up ahead.

Bo gazed at the sky, glad for the sun poking out from thick cumulous clouds, providing some warmth. He heard Eva ask the men if they were up to more walking, but being out of earshot he couldn't hear their answer.

Eva fell in step with Bo. "They want to see the Dutch memorial around the bend."

"The children's exhibit chilled me to the core." Bo rubbed his arms. "I never realized over a million children died in the Holocaust."

"Enemies against Israel and America never stop coming."

"I aim to uncover who nearly wiped us out," Bo grunted, puffing his cheeks in anger.

"God protected us," Eva replied softly. She tapped her ears with her gloved hands. "But my ears are still ringing."

"Mine too."

"On a positive note, you did something wonderful in connecting Eli with Grandpa Marty. Look at them. They've eaten lunch together every day."

"Then I've accomplished something meaningful here."

"Give it time, Bo. You've been at the embassy, what, going on two months?"

"Seems like years."

They reached the Nieuwlande Monument where Bo stopped with the others to read how Israel had honored all one hundred and seventeen citizens of the tiny village who risked their lives to save Jewish families from the Nazis. Stories of people facing personal jeopardy to help others stay alive gave Bo pause.

In the quiet place and in the presence of a hero, he remembered Sadie Lamb, a CIA agent like himself, who'd been captured because of a careless mistake. Vowing to press on until he freed her, Bo faced Marty.

"Did you live in Nieuwlande?"

"No, I lived farther south in Zeeland. I met Arnold Douwes, the pastor's son mentioned on the plaque. He threw himself into providing Jews with food and forged ID papers and vouched for me with the underground."

"Because of Martin, I am alive," Eli said, his voice trembling.

Marty laid a brown-speckled hand against Eva's arm and Bo glimpsed tears in the rugged agent's eyes.

She put a slim hand over Grandpa Marty's. "Ready to go inside?"

"Not just yet."

"Marty, how many people did you help escape?" Bo asked.

Eva answered for him. "That's precisely what he's trying to recollect for his memoirs."

Marty gaped heavenward, the sun's rays lighting his rosy cheeks.

"I rode my bicycle for the Dutch underground passing messages stuffed in my socks. When Aunt Deane learned of the dangers I faced, I thought she would take away my bicycle. I was wrong. She dedicated her life to the work, leading the pipeline in our village."

"She was a strong woman," Eli whispered in Bo's ear. "She hid my parents and me in her attic for weeks. We never wanted for food."

Eli blew his nose on a handkerchief and without warning his legs seemed to fold beneath him. Bo rushed over, gripping Eli's arms to keep him from falling.

"You okay, Eli?"

"A little weak. My blood sugar runs low."

"We passed a cafeteria on our way here. It's time for lunch," Bo announced.

He placed a strong arm around Eli's right side with Eva guiding his left arm down the path to the cafeteria. Soon they positioned Eli and Marty around a square table.

"Cocoa for everyone?" Eva asked, snatching her wallet from her purse.

Both men nodded and Bo joined her in the food line, where she selected blintzes and fruit for Marty and Eli. "That should rev up their systems."

"Looks healthy, but I need something more substantial." Bo chose a hot roast beef sandwich with Eva copying his lead.

"I like horseradish," she said with a smile. "Spices up my boring life."

Bo managed a grin. "Thanks for the invite, Eva. I'm seeing Marty and Eli living out history. If your grandpa finishes his memoirs, I'd like to read them."

"Not if, but *when*. I want my kids to know what a hero Grandpa is. He rarely talks of it."

Bo paid for his meal, feeling an urge to tell Glenna and Gregg about his more difficult assignments. Well, maybe he would when he reached his late eighties, like Marty. Bo carried two trays to the table and had just given Marty his food when his cell phone whirred.

"Hi, Julia," he said. "We're having lunch with Eli and Marty. Yad Vashem really has me thinking."

"Bo!" Julia howled in his ear. "Dr. Van Horn cancelled our tour. An earthquake destroyed part of Haifa."

"An earthquake? I didn't feel anything." Bo didn't want to react in panic.

Eva stared at him from across the table and he held up a finger.

"Are you and the kids okay?"

"Yes, but Gregg insists we head to Haifa to see for ourselves what happened."

"Where are you?"

"At the museum."

"You're not far from me. See if the bus will drop you out front of Yad Vashim."

Julia talked to someone in the background and then said, "Dr. Van Horn will have the driver bring us straight to you. We'll be there in a few minutes."

"I'll meet you in the circle drive. And honey, try not to worry."

"When we're together, I should be calmer. I don't care to deal with another crisis alone."

She ended the call and Bo locked eyes with Eva. "An earthquake hit Haifa. Just like your dream."

"Eva, you said nothing of your dream." Concern flickered in Marty's watery eyes.

"I try not to worry you. Was anyone hurt?" she asked Bo.

"My family is fine. They're on their way here."

"When did you have this dream, Eva?" Marty pressed.

"The night before we flew to Israel."

Marty rattled down his cup. "That same night I dreamed an earthquake hit Israel."

"Grandpa! You didn't tell me!"

"I do not like worrying you. Jesus carried me in his arms like a lamb."

Eli seemed confused. "What are you speaking of? Has an earthquake struck Israel?"

"Near Haifa north of Tel Aviv. We should be in no danger in Jerusalem," Bo assured.

Eli clasped his crooked hands. "Jehovah speaks to His people during times of trouble. He is the great God who saved me from the Nazis and the slimy pit."

"Although you and I do not agree that Jesus, the Messiah, already came to save us, I pray God will shower you with His blessings," Marty said tenderly.

"Finish your cocoa," Bo said, bolting from his chair. "I'll be right back."

Bo sprinted to meet Julia, with Eva and Marty's peculiar dreams dogging him. He swerved to avoid a man, sideswiping his tray and sending apples crashing to the floor.

"Sorry."

Bo scrambled to pick up the rolling fruit.

"No problem," the fellow said, adjusting his glasses. "May God bless your day."

Bo shot through the glass doors with those words, similar to the ones Marty had just spoken over Eli, echoing in his ears.

TWO DAYS PASSED in a flurry for Bo. Fortunately, no one in Tel Aviv had been hurt in the earthquake. A few buildings toppled in Haifa, but there were no casualties. Some elderly folks who could not flee fast enough suffered minor abrasions. Julia declared it a miracle and Bo wondered if she was right.

A ringing phone startled him and his brain changed gears. He snatched up the receiver, hearing a voice in his ear declare, "Rider, I need you in the Ambassador's office."

"I can be there shortly," he told Special Agent Shellie Karnack.

"Not in five minutes. Now!"

Shellie clicked off. Rather than jump up, Bo's left hand levitated above the keyboard and he finished the encrypted e-mail with a grin. Perhaps the message to the Agency's admin office about his fuel purchases during his recent trip to D.C. wasn't urgent, but on principle Bo refused to cave in to Shellie's demand.

He took his time shutting down the computer and locking up. Inside Hal's office, he found Hal and Shellie whispering with their heads together around an open laptop computer on the conference table. Bo drew closer; they seemed to be running a computer program with audio. A muted TV set broadcast headline news off in the corner.

"About time you made it in here," Hal snapped. "We have an incident brewing that you'd better shed light upon."

Shellie rapped her hands on the table as if playing bongo drums. "Hal said you and an ICE agent were having lunch when a male suspect left a bomb at the bakery."

"Correct. Then we chased down the terrorist after Special Agent Eva Montanna threw the bomb into the street."

Hal shot darts at Bo with his eyes. "No one cleared Special Agent Montanna for her trip to Israel."

"I told you before Eva traveled on a tourist visa with her grandfather," Bo said, trying to keep exasperation from his voice. "An Israeli citizen whom Martin Vander Goes saved from the Nazis invited them."

"Oh really?" Hal's voice rang with sarcasm.

Exactly what was Hal trying to pin on Bo? He stood his ground.

"After the bomb went off, I briefed you that following morning."

"Somehow you forgot to tell me." Shellie smirked.

Bo fired back. "I left you several messages, but you never called me."

"Forget the miscommunication," Hal said, shoving on his half-glasses. "The issue is whether the federal agent is still in the country."

"Eva and Grandfather Marty flew out yesterday. Is there a problem?"

"See for yourself."

Hal played a video from the Internet. Bo watched the street scene in Old Jerusalem, a typical day along the wet stone road, vendors hawking their wares and shoppers haggling for the cheapest price for leather bags and spices. Without warning, Bo saw a blond woman racing out of Esther's Bakery carrying a bag, yelling at the top of her lungs, "Bomb! A bomb!" She threw something dark into the street. Bo watched in horror as he saw the man running behind Eva.

"That's me!" he roared.

On the video, men and women, young and old scattered in every direction as the package landed in the street. He heard a woman's scream and then an explosion. The camera fell to the ground. Bo vividly recalled the horrendous blast; however, the video made the bang sound muffled more like a firecracker.

Hal stopped the video, pointing over his shoulder at the silent TV.

"You and your tourist friend have gone viral. Your faces have hit the Arab news, which are gleefully reporting the female bomber is American. Israeli authorities know better."

"They'd better," Bo growled. "Eva and I tackled the terrorist. Israeli police arrested him."

At these words, Bo's mind grasped the terrible truth. His face and Eva's face plastered on global television meant trouble. Shellie punctured his swirling thoughts.

"The bomber is Palestinian. He dressed in female garb, traveling into Israel from Gaza using a daily work pass. Hamas is pressuring the Palestinian Authority to know more about Eva, her name, address, employer, everything. Hamas is convinced Israel arrested the day worker to cover up the truth that she, an American, is the bomber."

"Ridiculous!" Bo cried, leaping from his chair.

Shellie slapped her palm against the table. "The embassy is fielding inquiries and denying she works here. Good thing your image is grainier. Nobody's asking for you."

Bo dropped in a chair at the computer and replayed the video, his pulse rate nearly returning to normal. That is until he saw a number rising under the small picture.

"This video has been watched more than seventy thousand times."

"Just think, this is the first day it's aired." Hal turned off his computer. "Wait for wall-to-wall broadcasts on twenty-four-hour news channels. Reporters will swarm like bears to honey, demanding that I investigate the American."

Dread filled Bo and he furiously calculated his options. He'd notify Kangas immediately, but he didn't admit that to Shellie or Hal.

"I have to call Eva." Bo stood to leave.

"Not through official channels," Shellie warned. "Let someone outside the embassy loop contact her."

"I hadn't considered that. What are you going to do, Hal?"

The Ambassador leaned on the edge of the table, looking green around the gills.

"The region is a tinderbox. Iran incites Hezbollah in Lebanon; Hezbollah riles the Palestinians. The bomber is Palestinian, but they're blaming America for derailing peace."

Shellie folded her arms. "We hope no one connects you to the man in the video."

Her concern was touching, but she probably didn't want any stink ruining her career. Bo grabbed the doorknob, deciding he needed Frank's opinion, trusting him more than Shellie or Hal, possibly moles themselves.

He'd also call Maureen Hall back at Langley and find out if there were any hits on the memos she'd inserted for him. It seemed impossible, but with the flick of a camera button, Bo had become the hunted and not the hunter.

"We're notifying *your* headquarters." Shellie stared, tapping her fingers on the computer.

Hal piled on. "Be circumspect. The Secretary may send you home."

Hal planned to contact the Secretary of State? With Hal and Shellie squeezing him, Bo had to wonder why. Judah had told Bo two days ago the bomber was a Palestinian day worker but didn't know who the terrorist had been targeting. Shellie seemed to read Bo's mind.

"We don't know the day worker's motive and he isn't talking. Perhaps he planned to kill you or the federal agent. What cases is she working on?"

Bo suddenly recalled his folks were coming in a few days. He'd have to tell them of the violence. Would they still want to travel to Israel?

"I have family visiting for Christmas." Bo glanced back at the mute TV as if expecting his face to appear any second.

Hal looked at his watch. "It might be wise for you to take a few days off. Shellie will brief me on any further results of your short film career."

With that, Hal stalked from his office and Shellie shut her laptop with a sharp click.

"It's a shame you landed on Hal's wrong side. I will do my best but it may be impossible for me to continue smoothing the way."

Bo pressed his lips together, debating whether to thank or deride her. Refusing to be drawn into her intrigues, he strode to the elevator, with Shellie trailing behind. She selected the down button, cracking a smile.

"I sent an encoded message to Foggy Bottom."

So she'd already notified State about the video. Bo hopped into the elevator ignoring her out-of-tune humming. They reached the first floor. Bo hurried to the Com Center, anxious to reach Kangas before Shellie's message to State zoomed over to Langley. He sucked in a ragged breath and dialed from an encrypted phone, hoping Kangas would be in.

Because Eva was a true friend and colleague, Bo wanted nothing more than to protect her, yet her trip to Israel couldn't have gone more wrong.

17

Glenna Rider loved being with her mom at the tourist kiosk. This was her fourth week helping. Since they'd come to Israel, each day was a wild adventure. Scared at first, she was trying to be more brave and have fun doing new things. Best of all, she and Gregg rode on the bus with Mom from Tel Aviv spending days making money with Bennie.

Glenna thrust a hand into her pocket, suppressing a giggle. Already she'd earned thirty shekels selling thorns and spikes. She couldn't wait to buy a sixth blue bottle. Her beautiful collection was like having the green-blue sea and the light-blue sky in the bedroom with her.

"Bennie and I are gonna look for treasure in a special place," Gregg whispered.

"Can I come?" Her hand flew out of her pocket.

Bennie hustled over. "I will take Gregg under the ground. He says you do not like to go."

"Yes I do! I'll give the thorns to Mom."

"Okay." Gregg kicked at the ground. "But hurry."

"Bring your tools," Bennie ordered.

Glenna shoved her container of long spikes and thorns under her mom's stool, putting two items in her pocket. She spotted a white-haired lady pushing an old man in a wheelchair and skipped over to them asking, "Can I help you?"

The man's hands trembled in his lap and the lady said slowly, "Is there a tour where the wheelchair can go? We have two hours before our bus brings us to Nazareth."

"Follow me. My mom helps arrange tours."

Glenna brought the couple to the kiosk where her mother sat perched on the high stool reading a book with Dr. Van Horn's picture on the back.

"Mom," Glenna chirped, "these nice people need a tour that allows wheelchairs."

"I know just the one."

Her mom snapped her book shut and the white-haired lady handed Glenna a dollar.

"Thank you, young lady. We are from Iowa and you folks sound American."

"We live in Virginia when we're not here." Glenna stuffed the dollar in her pocket, telling her mom about Bennie taking them on a search.

She held her breath, hoping if Mom stayed busy helping the tourists, she'd say yes.

"Be back in one hour because the bus is leaving to take us back home."

"Sweet!" Glenna bounded off, hopping over the curb in her pink canvas sneakers, excited to join Gregg and Bennie on a new escapade. Being in the Old City was way better than a stuffy classroom back in Virginia. She ran after Gregg and Bennie who scurried behind a rock.

In seconds, Bennie took them down worn steps to the public tunnels. When she'd gone under the old Jewish Temple with Mom and the tour group Gregg had scared her, but she wouldn't let him do that again. With Dad's help, she was learning to explore new places.

Her eyes became used to the dim light, but she felt for her flashlight in her pocket just in case. The tunnel smelled of damp earth. She plugged her nose for a second.

"Did you bring the tools?" Bennie hissed, sounding like a snake.

Glenna shuddered. She hated creeping reptiles. Something tickled her leg and she muffled a scream. Gregg laughed, holding up a string.

"Gotcha!"

"Stop it. We're here to find treasure, not pull tricks. Here's my screwdriver and flashlight."

"Last time we were here, I saw a hunk of metal in a crack. Let's find that spot." Gregg aimed his skinny flashlight against the wall.

Bennie shook his head, pointing up ahead. "Arrowheads are farther down the tunnel."

"Let's go." Gregg pushed Bennie forward.

They left the public tunnel with its yellowish lights and Bennie slid into a lower tunnel. Glenna clicked on her flashlight, barely breathing in the gloom. Were snakes crawling around? She snapped her head to look for the creatures. Glad she didn't see any, she started breathing again.

As Bennie scooted over big boulders, Gregg followed and Glenna stayed close on his heels. Bennie squeezed between the wall and a large rock.

"The tunnels used to be canals. Long ago, my people filled them with water to keep enemies from climbing the wall." He stopped, flashing his knife. "This is where we searched before. Start digging."

Glenna shone her light on a crack while Gregg felt between the rocks with both hands. He bent down and picking up a rock, he hammered the screwdriver into the crack.

"I found one!" Gregg bounced on his toes.

"Sshh," Glenna warned, shining her light in another split in the rock.

"Hey! Shine your light back here," Gregg hollered. "Use your mouth like Bennie does."

Glenna watched Bennie for a second. His flashlight stuck out of his mouth as he worked with both hands. Wouldn't that injure her teeth? She'd just gotten her braces off.

Instead she edged away from the boys, finding a crevice running to the ceiling. Soon, she felt something hard and Glenna stabbed it with her screwdriver. Tapping sounds bounced off the rocks. Excited, she slowly brought her teeth down against the plastic flashlight. It didn't hurt and her hands started flying to pry out that arrowhead. Bennie had bragged they could make lots of money on them.

No one spoke; their mouths were too busy holding the flashlights.

"I found one too!" Bennie yelled, stumbling over the rocks.

He held out a hand, shining his flashlight on a rusty metal arrowhead.

"This relic has been waiting for us to find it for thousands of years. Back when our enemies attacked the ancient Temple they shot arrows. I dig out the ones stuck between rocks."

Gregg resumed his tapping and Glenna returned to her treasure trove. Yet the more she tapped, the more discouraged she grew. Finally she plunked down her flashlight.

"I found a stupid root. It must have grown in the crack."

"Here's mine!" Gregg announced, showing his arrowhead.

Bennie compared his to Gregg's. "Mine looks older."

"But Gregg's is the biggest." Glenna shook her flashlight. It was getting really dim.

Bennie pushed past Gregg and Glenna. "We should go. Our lights may run down before we leave the tunnel."

"I'm walking between you boys," Glenna said, her voice trembling. "My light's out."

Fear crawled along her arms, making large goose bumps. She began counting as Dad taught her to do, but being in the tunnel without much light was really scary. They tripped over rocks and she struggled to keep pace with Bennie.

"I know a man who will buy these for one hundred American dollars," he boasted.

At last she saw lights coming from the public tunnel, but she had to climb behind Bennie up slippery rocks to reach it. Bennie was almost near the top when he crashed into her. She tumbled, falling against Gregg. The three of them sprawled along the tunnel floor.

"I dropped my arrowhead!" Bennie howled.

"Are you hurt?" Glenna asked her brother, brushing dirt from her legs and hands.

"I'm okay," Gregg said, "and I saved my arrowhead."

Bennie scooted over, demanding, "Let me see."

Gregg shone his light on the arrowhead in the palm of his hand. "It's the one I found."

"You took mine, the one I dropped. Where did you hide your other one?"

"I only have one!" Gregg insisted.

"Shine your light along the floor," Glenna said, trying to keep peace in the tunnel. "We'll find yours, Bennie."

"I will look, but Gregg has mine."

With Gregg's flashlight she looked all around. Glenna's heart fell. She could find no arrowhead. She touched Bennie's arm.

"Yours must have fallen into a tiny opening between the steps. We'll return later with fresh batteries and search behind the rocks."

Bennie climbed up into the lighted public tunnel, pulling Glenna up. "If we do, it will be your brother's arrowhead we look for."

After he pulled Gregg up, Bennie stuck out his hand and blurted, "I want my arrowhead."

Gregg almost knocked Bennie over to reach the exit, but Bennie pinned Gregg against the wall, trying to rip the arrowhead from his clutched hand.

"Stop it!" Glenna cried, afraid her brother would be hurt.

Gregg elbowed his way clear and ran. Glenna lunged along the tunnel until reaching the bright sunlight, her heart beating as fast as it had on the cable car.

"Those two robbed me," Bennie yelped behind them.

Gregg almost collided with their mom who was helping tourists climb into the bus. He wiggled up the steps, blasting onto the bus.

"Mom," Glenna raced over breathing hard. "Gregg found an arrowhead. Bennie lost his and pushed Gregg to get his."

Bennie ran to Julia's side. "I will tell my father and then you will all be sorry."

"Glenna, be seated on the bus right now. We are leaving."

Glenna listened to her mom, dashing up the steps and stumbling over her brother's legs to reach the window. She plastered her ear against the glass.

"I can't hear what Mom is saying to Bennie, but from the look on her face, I'd say you're about to be grounded for life."

"Am not. It's my arrowhead."

"I tried to stick up for you, but Bennie is freaking out."

Seconds later, her mom hurried onto the bus, telling the driver, "Please hurry us home. Trouble is brewing."

JULIA DARTED INTO THE SEAT behind her children. "I never should have let you run off with Bennie, though you've gotten along well in the past. What happened out there?"

Gregg pushed out his bottom lip. "Bennie took us to find arrowheads. He lost his and tried to steal mine."

Dr. Van Horn picked up a microphone and Julia settled in her seat to listen as he explained about a discovery in Old Jerusalem. "In the morning, we will touch and feel ancient stones at the Ophel Archaeological Garden. The staircase from the second Temple is stunning."

The driver started rolling away from the curb when he jammed on the brakes. Julia's eyes shot forward. She saw through the large front window a throng of men, some wearing traditional black Jewish hats, their grey locks blowing in the breeze, coming straight at the bus. A few men brandished sticks above their heads, shouting loudly as if angry.

Dr. Van Horn lowered the microphone. "Is this another confrontation in Old Jerusalem? Try driving past them," he told the driver. The driver did not budge.

Julia gasped, "There's Bennie charging up front, pointing right at us."

"You know that young lad?" Dr. Van Horn asked.

"He is friends with Gregg and Glenna, or used to be."

Bennie fixed his eyes on Gregg, plunging forward and spreading his arms in exaggerated motions. He planted his body by the door. Just then, a man ran up, swinging a large stick. With force he struck the front of the bus.

"What in the world?" Dr. Van Horn charged down the steps.

Julia followed, tugging on his sleeve. "I have an idea what's causing the trouble."

Before she could explain, an elder in a long black coat and beard raised his voice, jabbing a long finger at Julia. "She is the mother of the boy who desecrated the Temple wall."

Dr. Van Horn glared at her, scorn written over his face. Shame burned Julia's cheeks, prickling her scalp.

"Gregg injured the Temple wall? How dare he!" Dr. Van Horn scolded.

"It's nothing like that!" Julia cried, trying to be heard above the ranting crowd. "That boy took my children into the tunnels. Gregg found an ancient arrowhead Bennie claims is his."

The man with the stick tried penetrating their circle. Julia, her mother bear instincts revving into high gear, held out her arms. She'd protect her children at all cost.

The religious leader pushed the man back into the crowd and spoke in agonizingly slow and heavily accented English pointing at Gregg and Glenna.

"They damage tunnel wall with tool. They steal ancient relic."

Dr. Van Horn stepped forward, speaking gently. "Sir, we have traveled halfway around the world to see the Temple wall for which we have great respect. The forefathers of our faith, including Jesus Christ, worshiped here. We would do nothing to deface the Temple."

"Ask children if they have relic," the elder said.

Dr. Van Horn faced Julia. "Please bring your children to the steps."

Julia's motherly instincts trusted Dr. Van Horn to straighten this out. She climbed the first step while he continued talking in reassuring tones to the elder and the crowd. She wiggled her index finger and without a word, Gregg and Glenna rose. They came out, but stood behind Julia on the street.

Dr. Van Horn leaned over to Gregg. "Why is that boy claiming you took an arrowhead from the tunnel?"

Gregg pulled out his pockets, which looked like tattered elephant ears sticking out on each side. Nothing fell to the ground.

"Did you take an arrowhead from the Temple wall using a tool?" Dr. Van Horn probed.

"Bennie taught us how to dig out arrowheads," Gregg said, squaring his shoulders. "He lost his and wants the one I found."

The elder gripped Bennie's shirt collar. "This boy desecrated wall?"

"Yes!" Gregg nodded fiercely. "He sells arrowheads for money."

Julia turned to Glenna. "Please tell me what happened."

"Bennie dropped his arrowhead beneath the rocks when he fell on me."

"It is unlawful to remove sacred relics." The elder shook Bennie's collar. "You as Jew know this."

Bennie's skinny arms began to tremble as the elder raised his fist to Bennie's nose.

Julia lifted Gregg's chin, gazing in his eyes. "You could be arrested if you take the arrowhead away. You must return whatever you found to this elder."

Gregg shot into the bus. Through the open door, Julia could see him clawing between seat cushions. Seconds later, after dodging over the feet of several passengers, he hopped off the bus with his hands gripped tightly together. He uncurled his fists, revealing an ancient arrowhead. Dr. Van Horn lifted it gingerly, examining the artifact. Murmuring men watched from behind as he gave Gregg's find to the elder.

"This belongs with King Solomon's ancestors. We are sorry it was taken."

"Shalom. Go in peace." The elder bowed and turning to Bennie intoned harshly, "Bring me to the place where you lost the other arrowhead."

One man with a stick trailed behind Bennie and the elder, but the rest of the mob faded away. Dr. Van Horn wiped his forehead. Julia took Gregg's hand, leading her children to their seats. She dropped in hers next to the window. The bus lumbered away and Dr. Van Horn seized the microphone.

"You just witnessed a lesson I never could have planned. Thanks to these curious children I held in my hand a twenty-five-hundred-year-old arrowhead, probably fired by Nebuchadnezzar's Babylonian army. Removing antiquities from the City of David or from Israel is illegal, so we returned the arrowhead to an elder of the Synagogue."

He turned off the microphone, stopping to talk with Julia.

"What a close call." He sighed. "In the future, leave the children in Tel Aviv. They will no longer be welcome in the Old City." He pulled something from his side pocket, which he handed to Gregg. "This has helped me to know that God's love is the most important treasure I will ever find."

Julia watched Gregg shove what he'd received in his pants pocket. Dr. Van Horn stepped down the aisle encouraging the other passengers.

"I don't approve of you taking an arrowhead," Julia said, leaning across the aisle. "But being honest is what Dad and I always expect from you."

"Wait until Daddy hears." Glenna rolled her eyes at her brother. "You won't be playing video games for weeks."

He glared at his sister, folding his arms across his lap like a shield. "How could I know Bennie would become my enemy, calling me a thief?"

"What did Dr. Van Horn give you?" Julia asked.

Gregg pulled out a shiny gold coin, a smile of wonder on his face.

"Looks like you have your gold treasure after all." Julia leaned back exhausted, sadness weighing her heart. She planned to talk to her kids about forgiving enemies, but not on the bus. How would Bo respond when he found out Gregg and Glenna caused such a ruckus? She closed her eyes. Rather than worry over his reaction, she brought all her concerns to the throne of grace.

18

Late the following evening, Bo dealt with his photo being blasted on the news by sneaking out the embassy's rear door. He slid behind the wheel of his car, adjusting the mirror. Yikes, was that really him staring back? He'd donned a pair of dark sunglasses and wide brimmed hat and with his unshaven face he looked like some decrepit tourist from a foreign country.

The mêlée out front made disguise essential. The noise was deafening. Bo placed an index finger horizontally above his upper lip. That clinched it. He'd grow a moustache; maybe even a beard. A guard opened the gate and Bo passed through, bending over the wheel as he inched down the street toward the embassy's front facade. The angry crowd shouting and waving Palestinian flags seemed to have doubled in size from an hour ago.

He turned on a side street, phoning Julia. "Keep the kids in the house. Don't ask why."

"What's going on?" she asked, taking in a breath.

Bo could picture Julia's worry lines etching the middle of her forehead.

"Can't say on the phone. I'll be home soon. Julia, lock the doors."

He hit the gas full throttle, speeding away from the mushrooming America-haters. Minutes later, he wheeled into the garage and scurried to their apartment. Dressed in one of Bo's sweatshirts and jeans, Julia challenged him.

"What's so secretive? Why are you wearing that costume?"

This wasn't how Bo planned to begin this conversation. He edged past her to sit down.

"An incident erupted at the embassy. I'm being sent back to the States."

"A week before Christmas? How long will you be gone this time?"

Julia had hijacked his presentation. Bo tossed off the wide-brimmed hat.

"Not just me. We *all* must leave. Permanently."

Her hands flew to her hips and she spread her feet apart, like Custer taking his last stand.

"No way! We're finally settled, making friends, and the Agency jerks us back?"

Glenna had walked into the room without Bo realizing she was there. Her eyes grew round and she ran to her bedroom. Bo let her go, intent on convincing Julia this had to happen.

"It's no arbitrary decision. The Palestinians think I set off the bomb in Old Jerusalem. They're swarming the embassy, calling for death to the Americans."

Julia sagged next to him on the sofa as if life drained from her. "The synagogue leaders called for Gregg's scalp yesterday. This is scaring me."

Gregg and Glenna hurried in, circling around their mom, their faces ashen. Adrenaline pulsed through Bo's veins and he enfolded his family in his arms.

"Daddy, it was terrible," Glenna sniffled. "A man rushed at us with a big stick. I thought he was gonna beat Gregg."

Bo smoothed her hair. "You're leaving with Mom on a flight tomorrow night."

"See Gregg, it *is* your fault," Glenna accused him.

Bo released his arms. "None of that, you two. We handle this together as a family. Something happened at the embassy and that is why we must go."

Julia grasped Bo's hand. "Dr. Van Horn saved us from those enraged people doing us serious harm." Then her hand flew to her mouth. "What about your mom and dad's visit?"

"They're in the air as we speak, arriving in the morning at ten. You'll be able to hug and kiss them good-bye."

"Daddy, I love it here!" Glenna wailed, running to her room.

Gregg kicked the table leg. "Sorry, Dad," he said and stalked off.

Tears clung to Julia's eyes. Bo pulled her up and she leaned against his shoulder.

"What are you going to do?" she asked.

"Kangas wants me here another week to finish an important assignment. Then I'm heading back to Langley."

"What happened at the embassy? Why are we being sent home?" Julia whispered.

Bo looked up at the direction of the kids' rooms.

"You know Eva and I met for lunch in Old Jerusalem," he said, keeping his voice low. "A terrorist dressed as a woman placed a bomb in the café. Eva spotted it. She ran outside, throwing it into the street, saving countless lives. A tourist was shooting video and captured her throwing the bomb. In the video I'm standing right behind Eva in the street."

Julia's eyes widened, tears flowing down her cheeks. "You could have been killed."

"Eva and I tackled the terrorist who is in custody. The video is spreading around the world on TV and social media sites. Hal told me agitators discovered that I work at the embassy. We're being sent home for safety reasons."

"Will we be safe until our flight? Should we stay at a hotel?"

"Shellie is helping. She's assigned plain-clothed security outside for us until we're gone. I'm growing a beard and mustache. I want you to take the kids and visit your folks."

"We won't be together on Christmas?"

"It looks that way, honey."

At that, Julia broke down crying. Bo hugged her, wiping away her tears.

"I told Dad about the bombing and he won't be deterred. Said their tickets were prepaid. I'm sure when they learn you and the kids are flying home, they'll only stay a day or two."

Julia straightened. "Can you think of a way to convince the kids this is a good thing?"

"Yeah, Gregg should be happy to get out of Dodge and not be arrested."

When Julia simply stared, Bo knew he'd blown it again.

"Promise them I'll come to Florida and we'll have fun on a dolphin cruise."

"They should like that." Julia sighed. "After we tuck in the kids I'll call my mom."

"I already notified Frank. He's cool about it. Said he'll find a new place soon."

They talked about the dangers, sharing their concerns. When Julia finally dried her eyes, Bo snatched her hand. Together they found Gregg and Glenna asleep in their rooms.

"I'm pretty tired myself," Bo whispered in the hall. "I'll go close up."

After securing the doors, Bo phoned Shellie's cell, but she failed to answer. He'd just left a message when the apartment phone rang. He grabbed it and said hello to Clara Cohen.

"Hal told me Julia is leaving tomorrow. I'd like to tell her good-bye."

"She's upstairs, but I'll bring her the portable."

He hiked the steps two at a time, reaching their loft bedroom swiftly. He handed Julia the phone mouthing, "Clara."

He didn't stay to listen. Probably Clara would bemoan losing Julia's help. Back downstairs he switched on the news, instantly recognizing the shouting throng at the embassy. He snapped off the TV and walked out to the balcony, the disappearing sun painting the sea an incredible bright blue. Bo couldn't help but think how Glenna would have to leave behind her bottle collection. Maybe he'd package the glass and ship them home for her.

Bo tore his eyes from the shimmering water, desperate to protect his family from grief. But he, Bo Rider, ace spy and failed diplomat, had used up his entire bag of tricks.

JULIA HUNG UP ON Clara gripping the phone. When Bo had said Clara was calling, Julia hoped her friend would be consoling. After all, she'd moved many times following her husband's career. Yet Clara only wanted to talk about her foundation and how she couldn't survive without Julia to rely on.

Julia slumped on the bed pillow, not wanting to face the looming deadline: packing for home in one day. Then she thought better of her sour mood. She scrambled to her knees, something she should have done before.

"Lord," she whispered, "strengthen me to weather these storms. I trust you and need your help."

If only Bo understood her reliance on God. Yet so far he showed little interest in spiritual matters. She admired his independence and while he had read Dr. Van Horn's book about the life of Jesus, Bo seemed content in his self-sufficiency. Julia rose with a deep desire: for him to share her joy in realizing Jesus died to save her.

She brought the phone downstairs, catching a glimpse of Bo leaning on the balcony rail. Eager to discover his thoughts, she pushed open the slider door.

"It's a grand sunset for our send-off," she said, touching his arm. "I've been upstairs polishing my ruby slippers. I'm ready to go home."

Bo didn't move. "I thought we would see Israel together. We never did."

Gold and lavender rays colored her world, one she needed to say good-bye to. Julia swallowed her heartache, slipping her hand into Bo's. In a flash she knew she could rely on the same God who created the beautiful display for her final night in Israel to guide her and her family. She stood at Bo's side, searching for courage to take the next step without him.

Hadn't she kept their kids on course when he'd traveled overseas? Yes, but this time Bo had been home nearly every night. Both Gregg and Glenna were thriving in their dad's constant presence. She had to be satisfied with his promise to join them soon.

Julia squeezed his hand, giving a final nod to the fireball in the sky.

"You are quiet," Bo said. "Regretting the day you married me?"

She dropped her hand as if scorched. "How can you even think such a thing?"

"You seem upset at leaving so abruptly. It's a lot to take in, even for me."

"Bo, you have my love and respect until our last day on earth."

She fought the urge to tell him their love could last for eternity, but this wasn't the time. Instead she rubbed his back, enjoying his warmth beneath her fingertips.

"Take a good look, Bo. My Jesus once walked along the seashore. That's what I was thinking moments ago."

He pulled her into his arms, holding her tightly against his chest. Neither Julia nor Bo had room for any more words that night.

JULIA PERCHED ON THE EDGE of Glenna's bed the next morning, brushing her daughter's hair for a final time in Israel.

"What about my bottles the color of the sea? They won't fit in my suitcase."

"Daddy will pack them up safe and sound. Then he'll come see us in Florida."

Glenna sank against the bed. "I want to see the Galilee. Gregg wants to catch fish."

"He can fish with Granddad Crockett," Julia replied, holding the brush. "You need to start packing."

"All because Gregg found that stupid arrowhead."

Glenna's blue eyes drooped with sadness.

Glenna's dejection pulled at Julia's heart and tears rose to her eyes. She dabbed them away. "No, I'm afraid it's because the embassy is not safe."

"What are you afraid of, Mom?"

"I don't mean I'm scared of anything. Oh, it's hard to tell you."

Glenna propped herself up on her elbows. "Tell me. I'm no baby like Gregg says I am."

"I know, honey." Julia patted her daughter's hand. "Some people do not like America and want to harm us."

"Like Bennie was mad at Gregg?"

"Something like that, only different."

"You never tell me anything."

"I have told you enough. Gather your summer things for Florida."

"Will we ever go home to Virginia?"

"Daddy and I thought it would be fun to visit your Granddad Crockett and Grandmama in Treasure Island. Besides, Frank is at our house until he finds a new one. We'll finish this school term homeschooling."

Her daughter thumped back to her bed, and pulling the covers over her head, she murmured, "I don't want to go."

"Daddy is taking us on a dolphin cruise when he comes."

"Dolphins!" Glenna popped out from the blankets, jumping around her room. "I can't wait to swim with them."

Julia laughed out loud, feeling for the first time her kids would flourish no matter where they lived. She threw open the closet, pulling out a suitcase.

"I'll help you pack after I wake your brother."

"Mom." Glenna stopped hauling clothes out of a drawer. "It might not hurt if you let him think we're leaving because of that arrowhead."

"What about telling the absolute truth?" Julia thrust her hands on her hips.

"My brother is too big for his britches. He should be taught a lesson."

"Brothers tease their sisters. I ought to know. I grew up the younger sister to three older brothers and I survived. Don't forget your toothbrush."

Julia left Glenna rolling up socks into little balls, finding Gregg burrowed in his blankets, facing the wall. No doubt he was worn out from the thrills of finding the arrowhead and the sorrow of losing his former friend.

"Gregg, are you awake?"

He rolled over. "I heard you and Glenna talking."

"We need to pack. We leave after Popeye and Grand fly in."

"Yeah, because of me."

Julia saw him swipe at his eyes and she flew to his side.

"Sweetie pie, that arrowhead business has nothing to do with our change in plans."

"I heard Glenna say so."

Julia rubbed his hands in hers. "What have I told you about listening at closed doors?"

"That it's rude. I was heading for the bathroom and her words popped into my ears."

"Listen, Daddy's work is sending us back home."

"Where is Dad? Let me ask him."

"When he returns from picking up Grand and Popeye, I'll have him talk to you man to man. You and Bennie should have resolved your differences by talking things out. "

"Bennie is not my friend," Gregg said, smacking his pillow.

"That is a hard lesson, one we'll talk about when we're on Treasure Island."

"Like in Florida? Can Granddad Crockett take me fishing?"

"Yes, and you can comb the beach for shells."

"Watch me find something cool!" Gregg blasted out of bed and ran to his dresser. "I need my compass and pocketknife."

"Those go in here." Julia pulled his suitcase from the closet.

"Dad says pirates camped on Treasure Island. Will I find gold coins left by the Spanish?"

Julia ruffled his hair. "I'm sure it will be a lot safer if you do."

Although she put on a happy face for her children, Julia blinked back tears climbing the loft stairs, her heart battling loneliness. She hurried to the dresser, stopping by a photo Eva had taken in Jaffa.

Julia smiled alongside her family, happiness radiating from four pairs of eyes. Now they were stealing away from Israel and it hurt. She opened her Bible, hungry for answers. Her finger touched a verse in Jeremiah and her eyes gobbled the God-given promise: God had a plan for her, one giving her hope and a future.

She pulled out her black sweater willing her faith to buoy her spirits. She had to fly with the children all the way to Florida. As she stuffed her carry-on with every conceivable essential, she tried counting her blessings in between dashing away tears. Julia perched on the bed, longing for Bo to hold her one last time. How hard it was going to be apart from him, with danger swirling around him on every side.

19

Bo drove back home from the airport for a second time that day. Thankfully his folks had arrived safely and were resting at the apartment. Julia and the kids, after saying tearful good-byes, were on their way to Florida. As he parked in his assigned space in the garage, Bo's hand touched his neck right where Glenna had clung to him before clearing security.

The worst of it was Bo didn't agree they should leave without him. But Hal had insisted his dependents had to go. With Kangas' backing, Bo would remain at the embassy until after Christmas, making a last-ditch effort to uncover the spy.

He nudged the car into park, a question burning in his mind. Was Hal trying to kick Bo out before he could finger Hal? The others at the embassy had quit talking to Bo. Only Shellie remained civil. Bo grabbed the keys and headed into the waiting elevator.

Upstairs his mom was preparing a light supper, trying to use up fresh food Julia had recently purchased. She'd also promised to help Bo arrange a mover to pack and ship their stuff. He opened the door to mouthwatering smells of cooking apples. Bo found Vivian, his mom, in the kitchen filling mugs with hot chocolate. She gave him a quick hug.

"I'm sorry your family is already gone, but I'm glad you're going skiing with your dad tomorrow at Mount Hermon."

Bo swiped a piece of cheese from a plate. "Yeah, then it's Christmas. I reserved a swanky place for brunch. Most restaurants are open."

"I suppose that makes perfect sense in Israel. Your dad has on one of your war movies in the living room."

Bo hurried in, greeting Mac. "Dad, you're watching *A Bridge Too Far*. I love that movie."

When Mac Rider stood, he didn't quite match Bo's height. "Too bad we lost that battle led by the Brits. Montgomery was fuller of himself than ideas of how to win. Did you stay to watch their flight leave?"

"I followed your rule: Be prepared for contingencies. I'm heading to the embassy to make a secured call."

"Take your time, son. Your mother and I are at your disposal. It's wonderful spending time with you. Just watch your six."

Bo cranked Dad a half-salute in honor of his time in the U.S. Navy before retiring as a captain. Fifteen minutes later, Bo closed the door to the Com Center booth and punched in the numbers to Frank, who answered as efficiently as ever.

"It's Bo. My family is on their flight."

"The Director and I are concerned for your safety and theirs."

Bo drummed his fingers on the phone. "I'm not convinced they had to leave."

"Don't be a blockhead. I wish I'd been more concerned for my wife's safety, but it's too late. We start believing we're invincible. I learned the hard way we're not."

"Frank, you should've warned me."

"What?"

"I'm used to being Skip Pierce, international career recruiter. Here as a State Department schmuck, Dolphin and Wolf, along with everyone else, have guessed I'm with the Company. I feel totally naked and vulnerable."

"The Director sent you to Tel Aviv for a reason. He's is mighty unhappy with Wolf insisting you leave before your assignment is complete."

"Wolf wants me gone to protect his hide. Who would predict I'd be eating soup in a café targeted by a terrorist? I know if I kept at it, I could expose the mole."

Frank sighed into the phone. "Bo, are you sure the bomber wasn't targeting you or the ICE agent you were with?"

Bo pulled on his earlobe. Of course he'd considered that.

To Frank he replied, "The Israeli police have their ways of finding the truth. They and Mossad think the bomber is helping Hamas destabilize Israel."

"When are you due back? I need to find you an office and me a place to live."

Bo explained how he'd be joining Julia in Florida for a few weeks. "I have months of unused vacation. Does that give you enough time?"

"Plenty. I'm making an offer on a Falls Church townhouse."

"Frank, do me a favor. Change my Israeli address to the old safe house address we decided on. Nobody is staying there. Let's see who queries where I'm living."

"Remind me, is that address mentioned in your Mole Be Gone Ops plan?"

"Yup. I'll park an embassy car at the safe house, making it appear I live there, but I'll be staying in my place until after Christmas."

"You'll be alone over the holidays?"

"My folks just flew in. Two trips to the airport in a couple hours, but Dad and I are heading to the slopes in the morning. How about you?"

"You may find this a hoot, but Maureen Hall invited me to her sister's for Christmas." Frank chuckled nervously.

"Good. Have fun, but remember to see if anybody takes our bait and searches the database to find me."

He heard *clickity clack* then Frank said, "Your address is changed. Stay safe."

Bo returned to his office where he logged off his computer, scrutinizing the gray walls and bleak furniture. Perhaps he needed a change after all. Shellie turned out to be an ally as the chief had predicted. Hal turned out to be a bigger lone wolf than Bo. What was the Ambassador hiding with his arms dealing friend? Had Clara's interest in Julia been a ruse?

BO ATE HIS MOTHER'S DELICIOUS MEAL of omelets and apple pancakes with his folks, catching up on Dad's retirement, which he wasn't too happy with.

"Vivian, how about more cocoa?"

Mom glowed as she poured Dad a steaming cup. "Bo, should I pack this carafe?"

"Oh, I nearly forgot," Bo said sheepishly. "Julia left notes about that. I'll run upstairs."

"After dessert. I baked a chocolate tart and we need to finish the ice cream," she said, laying a hand on his arm. "And you should relax."

"Sitting with my feet up isn't my strong suit."

"Mine either," Mac cracked.

"Ask Dad," Vivian said, her brown eyes smiling, "why he always found reasons not to visit the Holy Land with me."

"All I wanted was for you both to share Christmas with me and my family." Bo drained his cocoa, gloom stealing into his mind.

His dad stared at him over the cup. "What did I predict when you pulled this crummy assignment?"

Why couldn't Bo remember? His mind had suddenly become a black hole.

"Sorry, Dad, but what you said is gone."

"I'm glad you're taking time off for skiing." Vivian cut thick slices of the tart.

"Never mind, Vivian," Mac said with a thrust of his hand. "Bo, I told you the Middle East is a quagmire. Your being sent home proves I'm right."

Bo gazed into Dad's brown eyes. "Sounds like you've had personal experience here."

"We're ready for ice cream." Mac jumped up, suddenly interested in opening the freezer.

Bo would ask him in private. For now he enjoyed the rich dessert and telling his folks about the unique places Julia had taken the kids for school projects. Bo brought his dishes to the sink and then motioned his dad to the living room.

"Do you mind following me a couple blocks from here?"

"Sure. What's up?"

"I'm driving an embassy car to a safe house, letting my co-workers think I've already moved out of here."

"Is that necessary?" Mac raised an eyebrow, giving Bo his trademark stare.

"Seems a safer plan. Some State Department employees aren't the most reliable."

Mac laughed. "Tell me about it. When do we leave?"

"Right now."

Bo grabbed a small case with extra clothes he'd packed, telling his mom they'd be back in thirty minutes or so. Down in the garage, Bo stowed the case in the backseat and hopped up front, with his dad slipping into a car Bo had rented at the airport. They drove to the safe house, where Dad waited out front.

Inside, Bo flipped on the lights and opened his case pulling out a Jerusalem newspaper, which he scattered across the couch. He placed a rolled up tissue in a trash can along with an empty cup. In the bathroom a quick wash of his hands and a toothbrush and paste on the sink provided evidence he lived here. Socks and briefs he tossed in a drawer. He hung a few shirts and a pair of pants in the closet.

He left Julia a message to call him as soon as she and the kids landed. Then he phoned his father-in-law, Crockett Taylor.

"Calling to make sure you'll pick up the family when they land."

"Julia didn't answer her cell when I called. She also failed to tell us why you're avoiding your family on Christmas."

"I need to clean up a few things here first."

"You have it your way. Always have, always will, but we'll care for your kids like they're our own."

"Believe me, I'd be there if at all possible."

The last thing Bo wanted was to rehash with Julia's father the stale argument over how much he traveled for his corporate recruiting job. Her parents had lived fifty years in the same house until they moved last year to Florida.

"Glenna and Gregg can't wait to go fishing with you, Crockett. Call if you need me."

"Hmmph. Not likely. Sheryl's calling me to set up the checkers table. Gotta go."

A loud click and Julia's dad was gone, leaving Bo with an empty feeling. He'd thought her father had finally accepted him as a son-in-law. Some things would never change.

But Dad was outside. Bo felt enormous thanks to Douglas MacArthur Rider who friends and family called Mac. His dad was the man he admired, looked up to, and tried to emulate. With Julia and the kids flying halfway round the world without him, trust of his parents gave Bo a lifeline to grab hold of. He flicked on a light, setting a box of cereal on the counter. He opened the fridge surprised to find it stocked with butter, soda, and a few apples. He locked the safe house and once outside, eased into the passenger seat.

"What are you up to here in Israel?" Mac shifted the car in drive.

"Nothing has gone right. You know about the Palestinian putting a bomb at the café and the federal agent tossing the bomb, saving people. Well, that fiasco has imploded my career."

"Remind me, left or right at this corner?"

"Left. I'm in the middle of an Op, which I had to cut short. It doesn't sit well, Dad."

Mac turned. "Sounds like you're up to your eyeballs in enemies around here."

Bo stroked his chin stubble. "Spend much time in the Middle East for the Navy?"

"Nothing to write home about. How long since we skied together, son?"

"Too long." Bo sighed.

They reached the parking garage, with father and son riding up in the elevator. Mac slapped Bo on the back.

"It will be like old times, slicing downhill. Is this Mount Hermon for real?"

The doors swished open and as they stepped out in the hall, Bo thought he saw someone dash into the stairwell.

"Did you see him?"

"See who, son?"

"Probably my imagination. Shellie Karnack, our Security Director, assures me the slopes are adequate. We're not talking the Rockies, but we'll have fun while Mom packs."

"Exactly." Mac grinned as Bo opened the apartment door. "Too bad she hates to ski."

"You know full well, Mac Rider, why I don't like to ski. When we were first married, I was happy going down the bunny hill until you convinced me to risk the ski lift at the top."

"You should've seen her, skiing on her buttocks all the way to the bottom."

Mac howled with laughter and Vivian patted his cheek.

"He loves telling that story. It was pretty scary for a Midwestern girl who never put her feet into ski boots before."

"Looks like it's you and me on the slopes again, Dad."

"I wouldn't miss racing you downhill for the world."

Bo leaned against the stair rail. "You're all settled into our master bedroom, Mom?"

They were and Bo said goodnight. He plodded down the hall to Gregg's old room. In the hall bath, the guy in the mirror had two days growth of beard. Bo washed his face, running his hands over the prickly hairs. If only he could drink a glass of some miracle liquid and make his beard grow faster. He reached for his toothbrush, but it was gone! His mind whirled. Had someone snuck into the apartment while Mom was here? Had he seen someone dart into the stairwell?

Okay, there must be a simple explanation. There was. Julia had probably grabbed his toothbrush by mistake. Then he remembered. He'd taken it to the safe house. He ran his tongue over his teeth. Grungy teeth fit in with his scruffy beard. Then he remembered. He kept a tiny reserve brush in his travel kit. And that was upstairs in the master bath.

Waves of strangeness overpowered him. His family was flying over the ocean and here he was worried about plaque on his teeth. If only he could be in the plane with them, to make sure they arrived safely in Florida. Bo ran some water on his finger, using the tip to brush his teeth. In his line of work, he had to adapt at all times.

20

Bo loosened the ski boots pinching his toes. The small rental shop at the foot of Mount Hermon didn't carry his size so he'd opted for a smaller boot with a thinner sock. With fresh snow overnight, Israelis were flocking to the resort, wanting to christen the slopes before year's end.

"Ready, Dad?"

"Let's squeeze in a run before the snow melts." Mac jetted up the trail to the chair lift using giant strides like a cross-country skier.

The lift attendant checked their passes and in seconds, Bo eased onto the swinging seat next to his dad, hoping this outing would bridge the twelve-month gap since they'd last seen each other. He also didn't want anyone recognizing him as the "mad bomber" from Old Jerusalem.

At least racing downhill would be exciting and not filled with danger, unlike the threats that drove his family to Florida. The lift took them up the snow-covered mountain, the sun's rays warming Bo's cheeks.

"These slopes are tiny compared to the White Mountains."

"Time with you is what I'm after, not trophies."

"You prefer steep runs." Bo grinned. "We haven't skied together in years."

His dad sought Bo's eyes.

"Not my choice. When I suggested skiing or whatever, the Agency had other ideas."

"I teetered on the edge of burnout, which is why my boss sent me here, Dad." Bo thrust out a sigh. "This embassy duty is boring and cutthroat at the same time. Did you ever detest going to work in your naval career?"

"Not when I defended our country, but national security consulting wears thin."

"Sorry about Julia and the kids leaving. I'm sure Mom wanted to be with them too."

Mac's voice deepened. "We're disappointed to miss time with our grandkids. But we make the best of things. Seems like this lift is slow going."

Bo dangled his skis above the snow-brushed mountain, wondering if Julia was safely in Florida. He'd left her a second message earlier, but she hadn't called. Maybe with the time difference, she and the kids were still asleep.

"You've never confided much in me, Bo. I wonder if my long deployments kept us from bonding like most fathers and sons."

"But Dad—"

"Wait, I'm not talking about our relationship. I'm concerned for you and Julia. Did something else happen to make her vamoose?"

"You saw me take the car to the safe house."

"Wasn't that for my benefit?"

"No way. When we get home, I'll show you the news about the bombing. My face is all over the Internet. That's why I'm growing a beard."

"What else is going on besides the bombing? You don't run from a fight."

The lift jerked to the top of the hill where Bo and Mac dismounted.

"On the ride back up, I'll fill you in. Julia and I are in love with each other."

Mac crouched slightly and took off. Bo followed, shocked how nimble his dad was on skis. Dad's comments on the lift stung. Bo had failed to keep in touch with his parents these last few years. Now Dad was trying in his clumsy way to counsel him.

Bo pulled next to Dad, waiting for the lift to take them up again. His cheeks felt numb, his neck chilled. When he gazed upward, dark clouds swirling over the sun caught him off guard.

"These runs aren't long. We should beat any inclement weather," Bo said.

"That's one job where you can be wrong a hundred percent of the time and not get fired," Mac quipped. "Sure wasn't that way for me as a Navy captain."

The chair approaching from behind quickly boosted their skis from the ground. Before Bo could tell him things were changing at the Agency with younger agents, a gust of wind rocked the chair, throwing Bo into his dad's side.

"Watch out!" he cried.

"I'm okay. Remember when you were six and we got stuck on that Paris roller coaster?"

"Two long hours way up in the air. I'll never forget it!" Bo yelled, his words ripped away by winds.

Mac grappled with his poles. Worried more for Dad than himself, Bo reached for the side railing, trying to steady their chair. Sharp ice pellets stung his eyes. Then without warning, the lift screeched to a stop. But they hadn't reached the top.

"Oh great," Bo fumed.

History repeating itself, only this was no mild day in France. Their skis swung above the earth. No way they could drop and ski down. Too near the top, they bobbed like torn kites on fierce winter currents. Bo put a hand over his eyes and gazed at Dad, who also wore no woolen cap. At least sunglasses protected his eyes.

"Guess we should've brought protective gear. You all right?"

"We're talking about you and Julia, not me. Why did she leave? I won't tell Mom."

"Dad," Bo's heavy breath blew away in the wind, "they fled because of the bombing."

Mac spun in his seat, bouncing the lift in the wind. "Violence is common in these parts. The embassy is evacuating dependants over that?"

"Sit still and I'll tell you. Let's not fall out of this lift."

"Promise." Mac crossed his arms.

"Not all dependants. Just my family. And I don't like being a CIA Agent living openly as a bogus State Department employee."

"Wow! I had no idea you were here without cover."

"My boss in clandestine services is pleased with my past work. He sent me here for national security reasons that I can't share. But this development could dump a load of garbage into my personnel file."

"Son, I'm proud of you. First when you made Army Ranger and these days you protect our country against terrorist assaults. But danger seems too real for you and my grandkids."

Without warning the chair lurched forward. Bo couldn't recall Dad speaking such glowing sentiments about him before, yet he'd been a rock, always there cheering Bo on.

"Off we go and I'll race 'ya to the bottom." Mac flashed an enormous grin.

Snowflakes landed on Bo's face, blinding his vision. He wiped his eyes and slid from the chair, coasting with his dad in harmony up to the apex of the next slope. Mac sidled alongside and Bo turned, looking down at his athletic dad with respect and awe.

"I learned duty and honor from you."

"Come on."

Mac smiled, the returning sun shining on his cheeks, and father challenged son to the bottom, the time spent skiing and riding lifts easing tension from between Bo's shoulder blades. Dad acted young, like he enjoyed the outing too. They chomped roast beef sandwiches slathered with horseradish before a blazing fire, then skied more runs. At the bottom of their fourth run, Bo had reached his limit.

"How about getting out of these skis and heading home?"

"I'm ready for another if you are," Mac said, thrusting his ski pole in a snow bank.

"Don't you think we should quit? Mom's planning dinner for us."

"You are right there, son. I haven't had so much fun in years."

Bo laughed at Mac's wide smile punctuated by his reddening cheeks.

"Maybe next time you can take me fishing out in the Atlantic."

His dad clapped Bo on the shoulder. "I want to see you and your family back together first. Then you all come for a visit in Hampton."

"Back to my place, we'll phone Julia, and you can talk to the kids."

They turned in their gear and waited for the valet to bring Bo's rental car.

"Doesn't it seem odd to be free of the ski boots?" Bo bounced on his tiptoes. "I always feel more agile when back in my loafers."

"My toes are numb," Mac replied, cold vapor escaping from his mouth.

The attendant rolled up in the rental car and Bo asked his dad if he wanted to drive.

Mac nodded, tipping the attendant before sliding behind the wheel. From the corner of his eye, Bo noticed a giant of a man bending his head to get into a parked car. Would he be forever assaulted by memories of Goliath?

Bo turned and got comfortable in the passenger seat. Mac patted both breast pockets, then opened the door and hopped out. He searched his pants pockets as if looking for something, then leaned in, telling Bo, "I left my sunglasses back in the shop, on the counter."

Bo took out his cell phone to see if he had messages when he noticed Dad about to enter the lodge, sunglasses propped atop his head. He chased after his dad, catching him near the entrance.

"Hey," Bo huffed. "They're on your head."

Mac's hands flew to his sunglasses. "Whew, that's a relief. I wore these on the bridge of my last command."

As he shoved the glasses on his nose, their rental car disintegrated in a huge explosion. Bo felt his body launching into the air until he hit something hard. He couldn't hear or move. Everything melted to black.

21

The stethoscope probing Bo's chest felt cold, making him shiver. A male nurse was inflating a pressure cuff on Bo's right arm. Dull pains throbbed in his shoulder. *Hiss hiss.*

Bo struggled to open his eyes.

"You are awake," the nurse said with an accent. "Do you remember what happened?"

The man's face blurred and then cleared.

"Ah, where am I?" Bo managed to ask, his tongue feeling thick.

He heard more hissing and the pressure against his arm dissipated.

"You are in a hospital in the town of Karmiel."

It meant nothing to Bo. "Am I still in Israel?"

"Yes. You were brought here after a bomb blast at Mount Hermon's ski resort."

The nurse typed something on a handheld computer. "Do you recall asking me the same questions earlier?"

Bo closed his eyes hoping to form some mental picture. None came and when he opened his eyes, the nurse stood staring.

"Seems I don't remember much."

"You were badly injured, but the man with you is worse."

Bo fluttered his eyes closed again. "Where am I?"

The nurse put down his computer. "In a hospital. You were brought here from Mount Hermon ski resort. You are in Israel."

The nurse lifted a bandage on Bo's head. Did he have a wound? Instinctively, Bo's hand flew to his head and fumbled with the bandage.

"What's wrong with me?"

"The doctor will explain your injuries. You suffered a concussion, broken clavicle, and abrasions. Your chart indicates you were thrown hard against a building."

"When?"

"You have been here since yesterday. You must be someone important."

"I am?"

"I think so. An American soldier guards this room."

Bo's mind tried to cut through the fog. "I'm alone?"

"You were one of four people brought here. Two have been discharged."

"Were they a woman and two children?"

Bo remembered his wife Julia. They had two kids, but what were their names?

The nurse put a finger on Bo's wrist, saying, "Two were Israeli employees from the resort. One man shares your same last name."

"Could you ask the guard to come in here?"

The nurse released Bo's wrist, grabbed his computer, and turned to leave. "I will send in the Marine."

Quickly, a young man dressed in casual clothes stood next to Bo's bed.

"Mr. Rider, good to see you finally awake."

"You are a Marine?"

"Yes, sir."

"What is your name?"

"Corporal Jason Knight. The embassy assigned me to guard your room during your recovery."

Bo studied the young man's military bearing and haircut.

"I'm assigned to the embassy in Israel?" Bo asked.

"Yes, sir. You and your father were targeted by someone who placed a bomb in your car at the Mount Hermon ski resort."

Bo blinked. "You're sure I was with my father? Where are my wife and kids?"

"Safe in the States. Apparently they'd just flown back."

Bo nodded his aching head, which was not a smart move. Sharp pains shot down his spine. He gripped the side railing, feeling sweat break out under his arms. That was okay. The pain and sweat meant one good thing: He was alive, even if his mind didn't know it.

His family leaving was a gaping hole in his memory. Oh yeah, he had a son, Gregg, who loved to fly kites. And Glenna, looked like Julia, didn't she? Which child was oldest? He couldn't recall.

"We are spread thinly, sir. Our Marines are on high alert because of riots at the embassy. Do you remember your previous bombing in Old Jerusalem?"

"No." Bo didn't move his head even a fraction.

"Your mother is at your father's bedside."

"Has she been to see me?"

"Yes, sir. I'll notify her and Special Agent Karnack you are conscious. They both have been asking."

"I want to call my wife. She'll be worried sick."

"Rest first. Then I'll help you make that call."

Bo resisted sleep. He had to find out what was going on. In seconds, his heavy lids dropped and things turned black again.

JULIA SHOOED THE KIDS into her parents' home in Florida, nestled along Treasure Island's Inter-coastal waterway. Gregg jabbed his fishing pole like a sword, dragging his feet along the indoor-outdoor carpeting in the porch.

"Can't I try for more fish? Granddad Crockett said we're having a fish fry and I only caught one."

Julia closed the door. "We're going to a dinner buffet. Please wash your hands."

"Do I have'ta?"

Gregg gripped the pole, his hair sweeping into his eyes. Her heart tumbled for her vulnerable young son. It had been hard on the kids leaving their dad behind. Julia bit down a harsh retort. Instead, she walked over to Gregg, gently taking the pole and setting it in the corner.

"Later, if it's not too late Granddad will help you catch your biggest fish yet. Then when Dad calls in the morning, you can tell him all about it."

"Cool! I'm getting my Redskins cap, the one Dad gave me."

Gregg scampered away and Julia's mother hurried in, handing her the telephone.

"It's from Israel, but it isn't Bo calling."

Julia's heart started pounding. She held the receiver to her ear. "Hello?"

"Mrs. Rider?"

Not recognizing the voice as Clara's, Julia hesitated.

"Mrs. Rider, if it is you, I have news about your husband."

"Tell me what's happened!" Julia cried.

"This is Special Agent Shellie Karnack. Another bomb went off, but Bo is conscious. His father isn't and your mother-in-law is by his side."

Julia's knees buckled and she groped for a chair.

"Agent Karnack, please put my husband on the telephone."

"I can't. He's conscious, but sleeping. When he awakes, we'll let you speak to him."

"*Let* me speak to him? Of course you will or I will call Ambassador Cohen."

"No need to get huffy. I'm doing you a favor."

"The only favor you can do for me is to put my husband on the phone."

"Mrs. Rider, please calm down. Bo is in the Karmiel hospital. He and his father survived a bomb blast. I'll provide details, if you'll listen."

Adrenaline pushed through Julia's veins like wildfire. She imagined steam erupting from her ears, but she silently counted. *One, two, three.*

Finally she said, "Please tell me everything."

With a finger to her lips Julia motioned for her mother to take a seat as Shellie rattled off the facts and Julia battled to absorb the gruesome details. Because the kids were laughing in the kitchen with their granddad, Julia had to press the phone against her ear, catching Shellie say, "broken clavicle."

"How hurt is Bo? Do you need me in Israel?"

"No!" Karnack shouted. "That isn't necessary."

"Thank you for letting me know, Agent," was all Julia could say, tears welling in her eyes. "Please have Bo call right away."

Julia hung up, a flood of tears pushing to be released.

"Bo's in the hospital. Someone tried to kill him!"

She sagged into her mother's arms, crying. Her mother smoothed her hair, speaking words of comfort. "Sshh. Mom is here. He is okay, right?"

Julia heard footsteps and she pulled away from her mother. But the footsteps receded.

Her mother retrieved a box of tissues from the table. "Is there anyone else you can call? Whoever you were talking to gave you more grief than answers."

"Yes! I can phone the Ambassador's wife. She's a friend of mine."

Julia wiped her face, crushing the tissue in her hand. However, the call went right to Clara's voice mail. Julia hung up, facing her mom.

"I know it's Christmas Eve, but can we order pizza delivered? I need to gather my wits before I tell the kids anything."

Julia bustled to her guest bedroom, collapsing on the bed, hardly able to think or feel anything but her grieving heart. She wanted to fly to Bo's side, but her children needed her here.

She sobbed in pain and confusion, "Oh Jesus! Save Bo! He's not ready to meet you!"

Someone rustled her hair. Julia shot up from the bed, dreading the kids seeing her in such a crumpled state. No one else was in the room. Her skin prickled. What had just happened? Julia perched on the edge of bed, amazed. She realized something had dramatically changed.

She felt total peace. Not the throwaway kind, but peace as solid and real as her two children. Julia scooted to the bathroom where she splashed water on her face. Looking in the mirror, she saw only her old self, her eyes red and puffy standing there.

Yet deep in her heart a truth bloomed as beautiful and fragrant as an apple tree in spring. She knew without a doubt, she wasn't walking alone. Jesus was helping her, guiding her, comforting her every step of the way.

22

BO'S SLEEP WAS BATTERED by a hodgepodge of trauma. He dropped into Kuwait by parachute. He flew in a B-1 bomber strafed by Russian MiGs. Then an IED exploded near him in Iraq. Someone was tapping on his arm and he awoke drenched in sweat to a familiar voice.

"Bo, it's Mom. Can you hear me?"

He opened his eyes, recognizing his mother's face. Her warm brown eyes set far apart were ringed with dark circles. She seemed to be on a chair next to his bed, patting his arm. He lifted his left hand, which collided with a steel bed rail.

"Where am I?" he asked, swallowing.

"Good afternoon to you," she said, a smile showing her white teeth. "You must have been dreaming because you were moaning and panting. I thought I should wake you."

"Am I in a hospital?"

"You are injured, though not severely."

With Mom sitting by his bed, Bo felt like a child again. But his tortured dreams were anything but childlike. Were they really dreams? It seemed those awful things had happened to him. He licked his dry lips.

"Mom, are you okay?"

She placed a foam cup with a straw to his lips. "Drink some water, then we'll talk."

Bo sipped, sensing liquid dribbling down his chin. He'd turned from a child to an infant in seconds. She took the cup away.

"Yes, I'm fine. Even your dad is improving."

Bo's mind searched for some solid thought but came up empty. "Where is Dad?"

"Upstairs in the ICU. Do you know what happened?"

Bo blinked, his brain stuck in low gear. Where had he been before this hospital bed?

"I think I was shot in Iraq. But Dad wouldn't have been with me." He shook his head. "It makes no sense."

"Bo, your wife and two children are in Florida."

"Yes! I remember someone telling me that. Was it you?"

"I was here a few hours ago and we talked. Son, your dad is a survivor, but the doctors amputated his left leg below the knee. He lost lots of blood and had a concussion too."

"Oh Mom."

Tears pricked Bo's eyes. He tried sitting up, but the hose streaming oxygen into his nose stopped him. He felt pains in his back. With a tender hand, Mom lowered him to his elevated bed and pillow.

"Please keep still. I was having fun packing up all your photo albums and Glenna's blue bottles when a nice lady called from the embassy. Her name's Shellie. She said there'd been a bombing at the ski resort and an ambulance brought you and Dad to this hospital. The embassy immediately sent Marine guards protecting you both. Shellie drove me here. She's been a rock."

Bo didn't know Shellie, but his earlier talk with a Marine was coming back, if a bit hazy.

"Why Marine guards, Mom?"

His mother hesitated. "I'm not sure, Bo. They are being tight-lipped about that."

The curtain was drawn back with a flurry. There stood an American-looking woman and his mother said, "This is the wonderful lady who helped me."

"Thanks for saying so, Vivian."

Bo stared at the woman with almost-black eyes and a swarm of dark hair, unable to conjure up where he knew her from.

"What's your name then?" he managed.

Her eyes narrowed a fraction. "Special Agent Shellie Karnack, Diplomatic Security Director. You and I work together at the embassy."

His mother spoke for him. "He's just awake. I started telling him of the explosion."

Shellie surged forward, past the hanging curtain. "Vivian, maybe you could attend to your husband upstairs. I need time with Bo."

His mother leaned over and as she lightly kissed his forehead, Bo smelled lilacs. Hadn't he smelled flowers like that as a kid when Mom baked bread in the kitchen?

"I'll be back soon, buddy." She gently straightened the sheet.

"I wish you'd stay, Mom."

"Vivian, please. What I have to tell Bo is classified."

With that, the woman named Shellie followed his mother to the door and closed it, the smell of lilacs receding. In its place, he detected foul odors of medicine. Shellie came right to Bo's bedside, leaning over in his face.

"Do you know why your rental car was bombed?"

A rental car? Bo shook his head a fraction to the side. "I'm told Dad and I were skiing, but I don't even recall snow."

"We're sorting through the myriad of enemies you or your dad made through the years," Shellie said, stealing his mom's chair. "We think it's related to the previous bakery bombing."

Another bombing? Bo closed his eyes, his mind flashing a picture of people running. A woman threw a package down a street. Her hair was blond. Suddenly, he knew her name: Eva. He fought to recall the rest.

"It's coming back slowly. You mean the one in Jerusalem?"

"Yes." Shellie nodded. "We received intel that your dad was the target, due to his run-in with Palestinians years ago."

"My dad a target? I don't think he was with me in Jerusalem."

"No. I mean the ski resort bombing."

Bo thought about his dad, Douglas MacArthur Rider. Hadn't Dad retired from an honorable naval career?

"You shouldn't have sent Mom away. She can tell you better than I, but you must mean someone besides my dad."

"Your memory is dim." Shellie jumped up, gripping the steel bar. "But don't be gaming me. I'm talking about nineteen seventy-eight. Your dad's sub rammed a Palestinian fishing boat in the Mediterranean Sea off the coast of Israel."

Bo stared at her. "Sorry, ma'am. You're confused."

"Listen, Bo. There's been chatter among Hamas for years that someone would avenge the loss of the fishermen. Problem is they weren't really fishermen."

If only Bo had a better memory of Shellie, he'd know how to react. What she was blabbing was strange to him. "I've never heard any of this and I think I would have."

"Let's not kid each other. I know you are with the Agency. You want me to believe you passed their extensive background checks and no one ever talked to you about your dad taking out a boat loaded with smuggled weapons and disguised as a fishing boat?"

Bo racked his brain. "Ma'am, I have no idea what you're talking about."

"You don't seem to even remember me. Bo, this is sad."

She sat in the chair by his bed, looking like a lost puppy.

"Shellie, I want to help," Bo said, shifting on the bed. Pain savaged his shoulder and he let out a moan.

"Should I call the doctor?" she asked.

Bo felt weaker by the minute. "Maybe, if we're done."

"One more question. Do you mean Mac never told you about his little sub accident?"

"My dad was Navy, traveled a lot. Mom reveres him and I guess I do too."

"The Navy always claimed the collision was an accident, but we at State assumed it was the Agency's scheme to assist Mossad or Israeli Defense Forces."

"Shellie, perhaps my dad was protecting me. I doubt I've told my kids what I have done, some of which is returning to my memory as we speak. In fact, you do look familiar."

"You'll be yourself in no time." Shellie smiled. "I don't care if Mac kept it from you. It's a fact. Hamas or other Palestinian rebels bombed either of you for revenge."

A sudden rapping on the door and it swung open. A pretty woman stepped in, her shoes making no sound. She wore a white physician's coat and a stethoscope glistened around her neck. She approached Bo's bed, carrying a handheld device.

Shellie faced the doctor. "Excuse me, but we're having an important meeting here. Could you come back later?"

The tall doctor glanced down at Shellie, scowling.

"Excuse me, but unless you are Dr. Hebron, the consulting neurologist I requested, *you* will return later."

Bo felt his head swoon as the doctor told him, "It is your decision. However, I must discuss your treatment. If you want your friend to stay, then she may."

He struggled upward on his elbows. The doctor pushed a button to raise his bed.

"I am in pain," he muttered. "This woman is from the American Embassy and will help me transition from the hospital when you release me."

The doctor gave a curt nod to Shellie. "I am Dr. Rehkopf. Let me complete my examination and then you may return."

Shellie stepped behind the curtain and the doctor set her device on the tray. She felt Bo's pulse and asked him to sit up. It pained him, but he breathed deeply as she listened to his lungs with her stethoscope.

"Your lungs are clear, which is a wonderful sign. I have treated you since you arrived."

"I don't remember seeing you," Bo said, easing against the pillow.

"You had a concussion. Also you have contusions," she pointed to his hairline, "and a broken collar bone. The blast may have tossed you against the ground or a building."

"My memory is shot." Bo fingered the bandage on his forehead.

"Give it time. We are pleased with your recovery so far. You will have another CT scan and a consultation with Dr. Hebron. You might be released as early as tomorrow."

Relief surged through Bo. "So my back is okay? It hurts."

"You have muscle trauma and I will order relaxers for you. Your friend may return."

The doctor slid open the curtain and Shellie walked up, an anxious look in her dark brown eyes. What else wasn't she telling him?

"Have you also been treating my dad?" Bo asked the doctor.

"He wasn't as fortunate," she replied, typing something on her device. "He lost his foot and an excessive amount of blood. His shrapnel wounds are deep."

Bo's heart thudded against his chest. "Can I see him?"

"Not yet."

"Did I donate blood for him?"

"With you unconscious at first, we did not think that was wise. We have ample supplies of blood available." She consulted her computerized device, pushing some buttons. "You could not have donated blood anyway because you do not match your father's blood type. Do you know what type your mother has?"

"Type A, I think."

"Are you sure?" The doctor's head volleyed from Bo's eyes to her device.

"She's upstairs," Bo said. "Is it important?"

Dr. Rehkopf paused. "Your father is type A; however, you have type B blood. So you could not give him blood. That is often the case with adopted children."

"I'm not adopted."

Bo shifted his gaze from Dr. Rehkopf to Shellie, whose face looked pinched. The doctor typed something on her device.

"Then your mother is not type A. If she is A and your father is A, you cannot have type B."

"Look," Bo struggled to wrap his mind around the doctor's statements. Had he been bombed only to end up in the Twilight Zone? "I was born to my folks in the Philippines when my dad was stationed there. My birth certificate says so."

"It is of no matter," the doctor intoned, heading toward the door. "Let us not be sidetracked by your parentage. I will see you in the morning, after the consult. Maybe we can release you then."

Bo slumped on the pillow, stunned. The door closed behind the doctor and Shellie crept to his bedside.

"I'm surprised none of this adoption stuff surfaced in your background investigation."

Bo sized her up, regretting she'd been present during the doctor's visit.

"I'm not adopted. I must be wrong about my mom's blood type."

Shellie patted his hand. "Don't worry. Your brain is overexcited. I'm heading to the embassy. Hope you're released tomorrow. Your Marine guard will drive you home."

She left him alone. Bo lay staring at the closed door, his mind and body rattled by what the doctor had implied. The last few days of his life were blank. Maybe he'd been adopted and couldn't remember. He shut his eyes, recounting his life from his earliest memories. The door squeaked open.

Thinking it was the nurse with pain meds, he said, "I need something for pain. My back is killing me."

"Bo, it's Mom."

His eyes flew open and she simply leaned against the door, gazing at him.

"Shellie stopped me in the hall," she stammered. "Why is she asking about my blood?"

"Mom, am I adopted?" Bo asked, lifting up his hand.

She rushed to him. "That's absurd. Why?"

Bo moistened his dry lips and she gave him the cup of water to drink, aiming the straw to his lips. The water tasted warm, yet the liquid soothed his scratchy throat.

"The doctor said I couldn't give Dad blood because you're both type A and I'm a B."

"So?" She shrugged.

"Never mind," Bo said, biting his lip.

"Son," she said, soothing damp hair off his forehead, "I spent twelve hours in labor with you in the Philippines. Dad was stationed there. I loved you from the first moment they laid you in my arms. *You* are not adopted."

"That special agent dropped another bomb on me. Was Dad involved in a boat accident in the Middle East?"

Vivian briefly shut her eyes. "Shellie told you that too?"

"Yeah. I wondered if you'd mentioned it to her on the drive here."

"I did not." Vivian adjusted his sheet, glancing toward the closed door before lowering her voice. "You were a year old. Your dad's sub crashed into a Lebanese fishing boat. An international clamor arose for Dad to be turned over to Lebanon for trial."

"How come I never heard about it?"

Vivian took glasses from her purse, thrusting them on her nose as if shielding herself from something. "It was difficult." She sighed. "We wouldn't burden our little boy."

Bo sank back against the pillow, worn out and filled with questions. With Dad in serious shape, he didn't want to bring Mom any more anguish.

"You're tired. Can I bring you anything before I head back to your dad?"

Bo gazed at his mom, thinking she looked more tired in her glasses. Who was holding her up in a strange land with no friends?

"Are you okay?" he asked gently.

She blinked back tears and pressed her lips tightly before telling him, "We'll survive this together. I spied an American burger chain on the corner. Want one, piled with onions?"

He pressed a finger to his forehead. "You used to kiss my owies and make them feel better. Give me a kiss right here and then I'm taking a nap. Tell Dad I'll come see him soon."

23

Bo's trip back from the hospital passed in a blur of shadowy memories. He watched from the front seat as snowy mountain peaks blended into wide plains, becoming stone villages. Nothing looked familiar. Why not? On the ride to Mount Hermon Dad had driven and Bo had watched the same countryside. His mind ached as he tried recalling details of his life.

He'd wanted to stay near the hospital and support his mom, but Special Agent Karnack insisted the Ambassador needed to talk with Bo ASAP.

"Ever ski Mount Herman?" Bo turned to Corporal Knight, who was driving.

"We Marines don't stray from the embassy, sir. I haven't been this far north in Israel before protecting you."

Bo checked the side mirror for cars following them. A blue sedan stayed back a hundred feet, but Bo trained an eye on it. Was he on the lookout from instinct? Garbled words flitted through his mind. An African-American man said a red car sat in Bo's driveway. He pictured his house. The man was Carver Washington, his neighbor. What had he said about the driver?

He asked about your father and who lived here with you.

Knight jabbed the brakes. "We're nearing the suburbs of Tel Aviv. Traffic is congealing."

"I'm surprised you were assigned to guard duty so far from the embassy."

"It must be because of your status, sir."

"What are you talking about?" Bo adjusted the sling under his left arm.

The Marine corporal turned gravely quiet as his fingers tapped the wheel.

"If you don't mind rumor, they say your cover is blown, which made you a target."

"What do you mean 'cover'?"

"Don't know, sir. I'm repeating the rumor."

Bo slipped into his own thoughts. Why should they assign Marine guards outside of the embassy? Could a new generation of Hamas terrorists be after Dad for an accident that happened more than thirty years ago?

Miles passed and the Tel Aviv port came into view. Miraculously the rolling waves brought a revived memory of sitting on the balcony watching the sea with Julia and his kids. But he'd been told they were in Florida with Julia's parents. Something about a mob demanding Bo's head at the embassy. Okay, he remembered. He'd appeared in a video of Eva throwing the bomb. The Arab street found out he and she were Americans. Then a traitor leaked it that Bo Rider worked at the U.S. Embassy in Tel Aviv.

Bo could envision his orders: Locate and neutralize the spy within the U.S. Embassy. And what Kangas had told him flashed into Bo's mind word for word: *Trust no one, not the Ambassador, not the Security Director.*

Corporal Knight screeched to a stop behind the embassy and Bo let out a groan.

"Sorry, sir."

An Israeli contract guard checked their identification before opening the gate. Once the car was parked, Bo slid from the front seat being careful not to jostle his left arm resting in a sling. He saw his reflection in the car window, startled by his ashen face and spotty beard. He fumbled in his front pocket for his magnetic ID card to open the embassy's rear door.

The corporal stepped in front of him. "Excuse me, but your access card is deactivated."

"Why?" Bo simply stared at his card.

"Follow me directly to Special Agent Karnack's office, sir."

Bo thought of dozens of questions for Shellie, but he chafed at taking orders from a corporal. He ran his free hand over his stubble, forming a quasi-plan. In moments, they walked into Hal's office, bursting his huddle with Shellie around a long conference table. Hal looked up from papers in Shellie's hands, nervously adjusting his bowtie.

"Corporal, you may leave," Shellie nodded pleasantly, "but remain in the embassy."

Hal dropped his hands, pointing at a chair. "So you're out of the hospital."

"How is your father?" Shellie asked, pulling out a chair for Bo.

"He's conscious. Hal, I'd like to be there with him, but Shellie said you needed me."

Shellie sat beside Bo. "You look better today than yesterday."

He shifted to face her.

"Why did you deactivate my entry card? I'm working at the embassy for another week."

"For your safety," Hal snapped.

"I don't understand, sir."

"Since you arrived, you've been the center of nonstop violence," Shellie spoke softly. "I know your agency and the FBI think you're the best at developing intelligence sources."

Bo's antennae pulsed on high alert. No way he'd be drawn into Shellie's tennis match. Let her lob another ball before he responded.

She kept her voice low. "I discovered a leak in the embassy and items have been changed in our computer system. It's all happened since you arrived."

The door flew open and in filed several embassy staffers, a tall man, a short and younger guy, and a woman with darting eyes. Bo didn't recognize them, so he quickly read their name tags hanging around their necks.

Mike Spencer. Oh yeah, he was the CIA Station Chief ready to retire. Bo's eyes flipped to the younger male, Joe Adams, but only an obscure tidbit surfaced. Joe was Hal's aide. The woman with fluttering eyes saw Bo staring at her tag and turned it over, but not before he glimpsed her name, Naomi Rabin. Had she babysat the kids? Bo thought hard. Yes, she was the embassy's Hebrew interpreter, but was there something about her learning Arabic?

Hal motioned the others around the table, clearing his throat. "I asked you all here because our secrets have been compromised."

Bo wasn't about to tip his hand. He didn't even glance at Hal who said, "Don't you find it strange it's happened since Bo Rider took up his assignment?"

Five pairs of eyes flew to his, but Bo waited, poking the stitching on his sling.

Shellie drummed her fingers on the table. "In baseball it's three strikes and you're out."

"I prefer chess. Make your next move, Shellie."

"You are good, Rider." Hal chuckled. "I'm sorry to lose you. But you see, yesterday I met with the Israeli Defense Minister about Israel's contingency plans for Jordan. Today my meeting is in all the Israeli papers."

"I was in the hospital, or did you conveniently forget that fact?"

Shellie shook her head. "Not so fast, Bo. You had visitors."

"Yeah, you."

"And others." Shellie held up a finger, her short nail painted pink. "Also, you're in Old Jerusalem when a bomb is left at your restaurant. Then, you're skiing at Mount Hermon when a bomb is secreted in your rental car."

"Have you found out who put it there?" the Chief fired. "Or are you too busy pointing a finger at Bo?"

Hal tossed the Chief a hard stare. "Stay out if it, Mike."

"At first we thought the latest bomb was meant for you," Shellie added, "but now we know Captain Douglas MacArthur Rider has a checkered past here in Israel."

"I was surprised to hear that." Hal stared at Bo over his puny half-glasses.

Bo lifted his chin, testing Hal's reaction. "Sir, don't the bombings suggest I am being targeted by our nation's enemies?"

"All diversions," Hal replied, grappling with his tie. "You're alive, aren't you?"

Bo opened his mouth to probe Shellie's thinking but stopped. He still had too many unanswered questions. Hal looked at the others.

"If anyone has evidence to help me pinpoint the leaker, now is the time to step forward."

An awkward silence enveloped the room. The Chief nodded at Bo and stood tall.

"Bo Rider is not your leaker. I'll be in my office trying to discover who is."

The Chief stalked from the room, slamming the door behind him. Bo swallowed a blistering retort. Joe Adams mumbled something like he had a report to finish and fled like a deer on opening day. Naomi blinked her enormous eyes, grabbed her purse, and slid out the door.

Shellie beamed an affable smile. "See, it's back to you." She fluttered the papers she'd been showing Hal when Bo first stepped in.

"I wrote down every word your doctor said. Bo Rider, who are you really?"

Mismatched blood types surfacing in a diabolical way. His mom had assured him she had given him birth. Bo's heart surged in his chest. Like the others, he had enough of this grilling session. He refused to be a lamb led to the slaughter.

"Do you know how ridiculous you both sound? I've served our country honorably and I've been cleared for materials you can't get within a hundred yards of."

When Bo rose to leave, Hal jumped up, pressing a hand on Bo's hurt shoulder. Still he refused to cry out.

"Don't touch me, sir." Bo stepped back, ready to take a swing if need be.

"Rider, because of you, the President and the Secretary of State are busting my chops, blaming me for Arab uprisings. I am a man of peace and you have single-handedly ruined my life's work. Sit down." Hal glared, tearing off his tiny glasses.

"Bo, do as he says. Don't make this any worse. You're not going anywhere in the embassy. You've lost your State Department clearance."

Hal, a man of peace? What a perfect cover for the man Bo was beginning to believe could be the infamous mole within the U.S. Government. Bo remained statue-like, glaring at Shellie and then Hal. Kangas had been right all along. He trusted no one. What stung was that Bo had failed to trap the real mole.

"Shellie, take your best shot, only you'd better not miss."

Hal twirled his glasses. "I look no further for the leaker inside this embassy. Bo Rider was born in the Philippines."

"That's in my personnel file. What of it?"

"Rider, enough of your insolence." Hal lunged forward, thumping his hands on the table. "The terrorist group, Abu Sayyaf, was thick as thieves when you were born in the Philippines."

Shellie ducked her head as if in pain. "I'm sorry it's come to this. I run a tight ship and to think you slipped in under my watch."

Shaking her head sadly, she unlocked her briefcase and pulled out a plane ticket. "You leave tonight. It grieves me that you are *persona non grata* in Israel."

"I want you out of here yesterday, Rider." Hal shoved on his glasses.

All Hal needed was a rubber nose to be the star of this circus. Bo pocketed his ticket without looking at it. "A bit drastic, don't you think?"

Hal's neck mottled purple above his silly bowtie. "State doesn't think so."

"Corporal Knight will take you to your apartment for travel clothes. The embassy will ship your personal effects stateside," Shellie explained, her pink lips drooping like a dead flower.

"My things are in my office."

Bo had almost made it out the door when Shellie stopped him with a hand.

"We're performing a security sweep in your office. Allowed items will be shipped with your household goods."

Hal's cell phone rang and he whipped it out of his pocket. "Yes, I'll be right out."

"Clara wants Julia to know she's disappointed in her. I will send in the Marine Guard."

Hal stormed from his office. If his situation wasn't so precarious, Bo would have burst out laughing at these clowns. He could have warned Kangas that his State Department career would burst into flames. But he was surprised how deftly Hal had made Bo the suspect. Clever fellow, but hopefully not for much longer.

"You might as well have a seat until Corporal Knight takes you home en route to the airport." Shellie picked up her cell phone and turned to Bo. "Any questions?"

"I planned on helping Dad with his recovery and flying home."

A slight smile rose at the corners of her painted lips. "Because he's quite a folk hero with the Israeli Navy, they are assisting."

"What's their plan?"

"Marine guards will remain with your folks at the hospital. When Mac is released, the Israeli Navy will spirit him out of the country and back to the U.S."

Bo continued to stand, ignoring the ache in his back. He wouldn't give her the satisfaction of looking weak. She busied herself with papers in her case and Bo clenched his jaw. What a willing sidekick she'd been to Hal's outrageous accusations. Naomi Rabin had acted peculiar, and her shifting eyes brought a memory roaring back.

She'd been talking to Babar at the embassy's holiday party and he was teaching her Arabic. Bo narrowed his eyes, recalling that Babar worked at the Jordanian Embassy. Perhaps Hal had staged this whole sordid affair, using Naomi and Shellie as accomplices.

The mystery of the mole deepening, Bo itched to call Kangas. But Shellie would never permit him one foot inside Com Center. He might be dead in the water here, but Bo refused to accept defeat.

When he finally did return to Langley, he'd redouble his efforts to topple the mole. Hal's crack about Julia convinced Bo the U.S. Ambassador had gone over the top casting aspersions onto Bo. It was true then: Hal Cohen must be the spy behind the leaks.

24

FBI SPECIAL AGENT GRIFF TOPPING rolled up his shirtsleeves, even though the forecast for the late December day was for more snow and lots of it. Elbow deep in paperwork he didn't relish doing, he adjusted the height of his chair, hurrying to finish his monthly car report. He was due to leave in ten minutes when his fingers froze on the keyboard and he stared at the screen.

He'd messed up. His Bureau-issued Chevy was way past due for an oil change. Rather than admit failure in the report, he phoned his buddy at the local garage and got lucky. The mechanic was working until New Year's Eve so Griff could bring in his bucar later that day.

Much relieved, Griff indicated the oil change being completed that day and hit submit, officially filing his report. His boss, Ricardo Diaz, needed to sign off. Griff shut down his computer and swiped his winter coat off a hook. His desk phone rang. Diaz needed him ASAP. Griff paused, coat in hand. Had Diaz found the discrepancy in his report already? He hurried into his supervisor's office.

"Shut the door," Diaz barked.

Why such secrecy for a car report? Griff closed the door and sat down, perplexed.

"Get up, Topping. You won't be here that long."

Griff's eyebrows shot up. "Oh?"

"HQ just phoned. Director Harmon wants you downtown pronto."

Griff had to think. Could he meet the FBI Director and still get his bucar serviced before close of business? If not, he must rescind his car report immediately. But he'd already sent it via the computer to Diaz.

He returned his boss' glare, intrigued why Director Harmon wanted him. He suspected Diaz had no idea so Griff didn't ask. Instead, he waited. Finally, his boss revealed his curiosity.

"Topping, what's the Director telling you that he can't say to me?"

Griff lifted his shoulders in an exaggerated shrug.

"Your 'I don't have a clue' look won't fly. Why are you being summoned?"

"Someone called to send me there," Griff replied. "What did HQ tell you?"

Diaz narrowed his eyes behind gun-metal glasses. "For you to be there by one, in an hour. I'm not in the habit of interrogating the Director's assistant when he calls."

"Perhaps you're due for an award and Director Harmon wants my opinion. Or, he wants an update on the lack of funding for my anti-terrorism task force." Griff couldn't hide his smirk.

"Enough." Diaz raised his hand. "Move your carcass and when you get back, I want to know what mess you've landed in."

Griff backed out of the room, thinking furiously. He had to leave in minutes to reach HQ. That gave him forty-five minutes tops to chat with the Director before scrambling to the garage in Manassas for his oil change at four. He had no leeway for traffic. Worse, snow was falling.

His mind percolating at the speed of light, Griff phoned his car buddy at the garage, disappointed when the answering machine came on.

"Hey, guys. It's Griff. I may not be there until after four, but no matter when, it's imperative you change my oil before you close up!"

He clicked off the phone and hustled down to his car, sweat pooling under his arms in spite of lightly falling snow. Reaching FBI Headquarters in record time, Griff grabbed the first parking spot he saw, cramming change into the meter.

No stranger to the Director's office, Griff knew the drill, the difference being on past occasions he had a fair idea of what he faced. Not this time. He stepped into the penthouse suite atop the Hoover Building on Pennsylvania Avenue at precisely two minutes to one, feeling apprehensive. Not only had he broken speeding laws, he'd parked at a meter expiring in twelve minutes.

Griff greeted the receptionist with a somber jaw, befitting the aura of the Director's office. "Special Agent Griff Topping, northern Virginia office. I am to report here at one."

"Agent Topping," she echoed, staring at her computer monitor. "Be seated. Someone will come for you."

Griff found a stiff-backed chair, passing time observing the Special Agent typing on a computer at a desk outside the Director's office. Another desk sat empty, the agent no doubt off for the holidays, trying to burn up "use or loose." Griff would be losing his unused vacation time in three days, the end of the year.

Last time the Director had summoned Griff, he had ordered him to conduct a highly discreet investigation. Griff had done his duty, delivering his findings and notes to the Director. Griff tented his hands, seconds ticking by and worry building into skyscrapers in his mind. But he hadn't violated any regulations warranting discipline from on high. What was it all about?

He checked his watch, the minute hand reading one o'clock. The gray-suited agent rose from his desk, motioning Griff to follow.

"Director Harmon is ready to see you."

A joke about working over the holidays died on his lips at the grave look in the other agent's eyes. Did he know what ordeal lay in store for Griff beyond the door? He gulped, following the agent's gray back into the inner sanctum.

Director Harmon strode forward receiving him with a warm handshake. "Good afternoon, Griff. I am pleased you could arrive on such short notice."

"Yes, sir."

Things couldn't be so bad if Director Harmon was "pleased." The gray suit left and Griff noticed two other men in suits standing by a cluster of chairs by Harmon's desk. Who were these guys? Harmon made introductions: Wilt Kangas, Director of CIA's National Clandestine Services and his assistant, Frank Deming. The men shook hands.

"I've heard of your previous good work with us," Kangas said, dropping his hand.

Kangas' stoic face and intense stare exuded an aura of power. So this was Bo's boss at Langley. Frank, the quiet type, had trustworthy eyes. What in the world did the CIA want with Griff? Harmon pushed a fourth upholstered chair into a circle and took command.

"You are here because the Agency asked for you. Wilt and I share a good relationship so I have agreed. Wilt, brief Griff on his next assignment."

All eyes turned to Kangas. Adrenaline pumped through Griff's veins. He straightened his back.

"Griff, in one of your past global investigations you learned the identity of our covert operations agent, Bo Rider."

Startled by the mention of Bo's name, Griff simply told Harmon, "You recall Bo and I worked together on the Chinese defection at the United Nations."

"You both handled the matter discreetly and our agencies appreciated the outcome," Harmon admitted.

"A serious allegation has been leveled against Bo," Kangas rumbled. "I believe it is unfounded. Griff, we need you to investigate."

Frank nodded, sharply interjecting, "The Agency doesn't want Bo's colleagues to know he's under the microscope."

"Right!" Kangas bellowed, rounding his fists. "Our agent will approve of your skill looking under rocks and finding the slime who seeks to smear him. Are you up for the task or are you biased either way? Tell me straight."

Griff didn't know what Bo could have done wrong, but if Griff were falsely accused, he'd want an ace investigator covering his backside.

"Sir, I have great respect for Bo, both as a man and as an agent pursuing our nation's best interest. I'll do whatever I can to find the truth."

Kangas slid forward in his seat, slapping his hands on his knees. "Excellent. Let me bring you up to speed."

IN THE NEW YEAR, on the second day of January, Bo gripped handles of a two-line kite, fluttering the fabric jet fighter in gusty winds. His collar bone was feeling well enough that he'd taken his arm from the sling.

"Dad, let me!" Gregg cried, jumping on the sand, his legs flashing in the sun.

"It's tricky flying these kites. You don't want her taking a nose dive."

Bo straightened the plane and using both hands in perfect unison, he buzzed the kite along the beach. Pulling slightly on the right line, he edged the jet higher and higher into the cloudless sky, making it hover like a drone ready to strike. If only he could manage his career so adroitly. Kangas had put him on administrative leave.

So what if the Agency deposited his paycheck? Bo was *persona non grata*, with only Frank still taking his calls. The floating kite made him realize he must stop stewing over his breach with Langley. Hal Cohen had started the ball rolling against him and Shellie had skillfully pushed him into the ditch. How long could he let life tick by until the Agency reinstated him?

The kite soaring above his head, Bo angled down the beach with Gregg dogging close to his heels like a puppy eager for a bone. The kid in Bo urged him to keep his kite, but his brain told him to let his son have a go.

"You ready?" Bo shouted over his shoulder.

Gregg shot up straight as an arrow, excited to show the tricks he could do with the fighter jet flying in the sky. Bo motioned Gregg to stand in front of him facing the kite. He let Gregg hold the handles before Bo relinquished command.

"Feel the strength of the wind in your fingertips? Watch my hands as we pull one line and then dive like a jet toward the water."

Bo tugged the left line and the plane plunged toward the waves. "Now, see how I work the right line? She'll blast upwards in no time."

The kite climbed, stopping still in the air.

"Don't move the lines too fast or she'll drop to the sand."

"Let me, Dad!"

Bo jerked his hands from the lines, giving Gregg total control. His spirits rose watching his son dance the jet high in the sky. But in seconds, the plane crashed to the water's edge.

"Dad, she's going under!"

Bo raced on strong legs to save the kite from being gobbled up by fierce waves in the Gulf of Mexico. He hauled in a soggy mess, the jet's wing broken, smashed just like Bo's career.

Crockett Taylor, Bo's father-in-law sauntered up. "You killed your kite. No big surprise."

"Did you come to throw water on your grandson's parade?"

"I warned you not to fly her in such gusty wind."

"You did, but Gregg and I are having fun anyway, aren't we, partner?"

Gregg's lower lip trembled. "Can we get her up again, Dad?"

"I'll fix her later. Too bad Granddad Crockett didn't get a chance to see you fly her."

"Yeah, she's toast." Gregg kicked at the sand, his head down.

"Bo, you have a phone call from D.C. You run back to the house and save the world while Gregg and I hunt for fiddler crabs."

"Can we, Dad?"

"Sure. I'll even help after I learn what's happening."

Gregg and Crockett hopped down to the foamy water and Bo hiked across the busy highway with a broken kite wondering who was calling. Crockett hadn't said, but then his crusty father-in-law had few words for Bo. He hopped onto the porch, glimpsing the phone receiver on the glass-top table. The place was quiet. Julia had gone shopping with her mom and Glenna.

Unsure how to react, Bo cautiously said, "Hello?"

"It's Frank. Wish I could escape this Virginia snowstorm. Eight inches of snow and they're still shoveling us out. I spent last night at Langley on your old cot, delaying my move."

"I was showing Gregg how to fly an acrobatic kite." Bo breathed easier at the upbeat lilt in Frank's voice. "What's the good news?"

"We've asked an FBI agent to dig into your background to clear the allegations."

"Why can't we resolve this among ourselves?"

"Kangas doesn't want State claiming we whitewashed the outcome."

"Not the Bureau, Frank," Bo complained. "They live to embarrass us."

"You know an FBI agent named Griff Topping."

Standing there on his in-law's porch, Bo swallowed. "He's the one investigating me?"

"Yes, and he's already started."

Bo felt stunned, unable to move. He dropped to a wicker chair, the idea of Griff investigating him slicing through him like a hot knife.

"I feel your angst, but Kangas wanted Griff so you'd know we are fighting for you."

"Thanks," Bo muttered. The kite slipped to the floor.

"You should've seen Kangas turn beet red when he told the FBI Director he wouldn't rest until you are back at Langley. You know how ferocious Kangas can be."

"Tell me about it. He wouldn't even let me step foot in the Agency when I returned from Tel Aviv. His message is loud, but I'm no idiot. He thinks I have leprosy."

"You sound like you're giving up, but don't. The word from Kangas is that you do not, I repeat do *not* contact Agent Topping until it's over."

"Not even 'hi, Griff, it's your buddy Bo, who pulled your fat out of the fire more than once'?"

"Seriously, I'll monitor things from my end. Stay in Florida and have fun for a change."

"I'm trying to, Frank, but it's like I've been frozen out down here in sunny Florida. I'm used to working alone, but this is a terrible kind of loneliness."

"After my wife was kidnapped, I slipped into a world all my own. I heard people talking, but what they said never reached inside. Is it that kind of alone?"

"Yeah, except for my father-in-law's disapproval of my loafing at his house. That reaches me." Bo leaned his elbows on the table, knocking off a basket.

Tiny, pink shells scattered by his feet. He reached to pick some up, hearing Frank's sigh. "Buddy, you're not alone. I'm only a phone call away."

"I appreciate your support, Frank. Don't worry about moving out of our house. We're staying in Florida for another couple of weeks. Julia wants the kids to forget the horrors of bombs going off in Israel."

"How is your dad recovering?"

"Some retired Israeli naval officers are hosting Dad's rehab. They'll be putting him on a plane for Norfolk next week. Julia's praying for him to get safely out of Israel."

Frank hung up and Bo scooped up the shells, jamming them in the basket, a fire welling in his belly. Had his friend Griff become part of the conspiracy branding Bo a traitor?

AFTER GRILLING BURGERS for his family and the frosty in-laws, Bo stuffed his mouth in silence, listening to Crockett boast how he soared off giant sand dunes along northern Lake Michigan in a hang glider.

"I flew over the big lake faster than an eagle."

Gregg bounced on his chair. "Can I try it sometime, Dad?"

"We'll see," Bo said, biting into the last of his juicy burger.

He wiped mayo off his chin and Julia flashed him an adoring smile.

"Glenna and I bought fresh-squeezed orange juice for breakfast," Julia said. "Tell your brother about the orchard we visited near Sarasota."

"You missed out, Gregg. Grandmama helped me pick oranges right off the tree. A conveyer belt separated the fruit and then they made juice."

"Miss Smartypants, Dad and I flew a jet fighter on the beach. I stomped on the sand making fiddler crabs dive in their holes."

His kids vied for the prominent place with Crockett egging them on. Bo wouldn't correct the kids in front of his in-laws. He brought his plate to the kitchen before grabbing a fishing pole and his cut bait, reaching the edge of the dock with the sun falling toward the horizon.

He pierced the meat with a sharp hook, casting his line out into the shimmering Inter-coastal waters, not interested in fish. His bait barely hit the water when a great Blue Heron glided over, its thin legs extending behind. With exaggerated flare, the bird landed behind Bo, tilting its head and with his yellow-ringed eyes watched Bo's line.

"Dinnertime, huh?" He jigged the rod with his one good arm, the events of Israel revving through his brain.

Judah Levitt had drawn Bo to Mossad HQ, insisting a mole had tunneled deep into the U.S. Embassy and telling Bo Mossad would meet only with him. Bo had flown to Langley, met with Kangas, and devised an Ops plan, inserting a series of computer memos with decreasing classifications. Only he'd never rooted out the spy.

The spy, whoever he was, must be burrowed in ocean-deep. Could Mossad's intel be faulty? Nagging questions needed answering. How did Hamas learn that Bo, a CIA agent, had been sent to the embassy before he'd even entered its walls? More troubling, why did bombs show up wherever Bo went in Israel?

The tug on his line burst his thoughts and he swiftly reeled in a six-inch silvery fish. The lanky bird stepped closer, crooking its neck. Bo removed the fish from the hook and on a whim, threw the fish near the heron's feet. With one giant swoop the heron grabbed the flopping fish in its beak, tossing it slightly so as to grab the fish headfirst. The bird began swallowing it.

Convinced he wasn't really fishing, but helping a lazy heron get his dinner, Bo baited his hook and hurled it back into the water. Memories of the two bombings loomed. So did a recent discovery that Dad had foiled a boatload of arms runners to protect the young nation of Israel. While Mac might have forgotten it, apparently Hamas never did.

In talking on the phone yesterday with his dad, Bo didn't feel right asking about the boat incident. He'd simply said he was recovering in Florida, revealing nothing of the Agency putting him on leave. Mac was looking forward to getting home and starting rehab in Hampton.

The sun dipped further west with the heron gobbling three more of Bo's fish, catching the last one in mid-air. His tummy comfortably filled, the bird flew away and Bo reeled in his line, securing the hook in an eyelet of his rod. He leaned over to gather bait remnants when a hand clamped down on his sore shoulder.

"Come up dry as usual?"

Bo looked into Crockett's steely eyes.

"I can take your abuse, Crockett, but leave my kids out of it."

"You don't deserve such a great family." Crockett jerked up his square jaw.

"Because I was overseas when Julia miscarried?"

Crockett pushed his face into Bo's. "You took our baby daughter to Germany. In her time of need, you were off fighting wars."

"You only think of yourself," Bo shot back.

"I could say the same for you, Rider. Always traveling the world trying to better yourself for that company you work for."

Bo had never told his in-laws he worked for the CIA, putting forth instead his cover job as corporate recruiter for United Search Associates. That was the same employer his kids thought he'd worked for until he'd gone to Israel for the State Department.

"Father, stop! You promised to keep your harsh comments to yourself."

Julia was bearing down on Crockett and she wasn't finished.

"I am thankful Bo survived the bombing. He and I are perfectly happy and so are the kids. We appreciate staying here, but if you don't shape up, we're leaving."

Crockett lowered his head and stomped back to the house, saying nothing.

Her pretty lips drawn in a straight line, Julia took the rod and cut bait from Bo.

"Honey," he stammered, "sorry to cause grief with your father. He's been angry with me since we lost the baby."

She adjusted the sling around his neck and under his arm, running her hand along his rough cheek. "I don't blame you. You were fighting for our country and I was content waiting for you. Somehow, God allowed the baby not to be born. But we have been blessed with two beautiful children."

"I need to sit," Bo said gruffly.

He didn't want Julia to see his tears. They walked over to a small bench on the dock where a few minutes before he'd been fishing mired in his dilemma. Julia snuggled against him gently and started singing, her lovely voice comforting his aching heart.

"A love to last, our whole life through, my darling, I love you."

Her lilting song turned to humming and in the waning January twilight, Bo and Julia reclaimed their love for each other.

25

That night with a million stars shining over his head, Bo stood on the dock listening to *woosh, woosh* of water lapping against the shore. Dolphins and manatee swam out in the dark, wild creatures existing without light, living by instinct. Bo felt like he was sinking below tumultuous waters. He pressed his arm in the sling against his chest feeling like a diver with empty air tanks and no clue how far he had to swim before reaching the surface.

"Gregg's gold coin for your thoughts. They're worth more than a penny."

Bo flinched at Julia's soft voice in his ear.

"You nearly scared me off the edge."

"I won't let you fall over. You've been sitting around Florida too long and my father is getting on your nerves."

"Has he said anything to you?"

"Not since you two alpha males snarled at each other."

"Inexcusable," he managed.

Bo faced her, the moon and stars giving enough light to see her worried eyes. He didn't like causing her stress, but what should he do? She slipped a cool hand into his warm one.

"Bo, I've been talking with my mom. She's eager for us to stay, but I think it's time we head home."

She did? Would being so close to Langley rub him raw? Julia must've read his thoughts.

"We've tossed around remodeling the first floor bathroom. Our lounging on the beach won't pluck out the old tile or glue in new vinyl."

Bo kissed the top of her head, inhaling the delicate smell of lavender. His heart stirred at her touch and his mind began forging a path ahead. He had someone to live for, Julia and his kids. No matter what Crockett thought or if the Agency threw him overboard, he'd rise to the top and finish the race, just like he'd always done in his life when facing trouble.

"When should we leave?" she whispered, her voice trailing away in the night air.

"I promised Gregg and Glenna we'd cruise for dolphins and see Disney."

Julia chuckled. "I'm ready to spend a day in Magic Kingdom with my favorite man."

She tugged him toward the house, but Bo stopped after a few feet. "You go on in. I've something to mull over."

"Don't be brooding over my father's caustic ways."

"Julia, I need to think about what you said."

"Like what?" she demanded.

Bo nearly laughed she looked so comical standing there in the moonlight with her hair pulled up and her hands on her hips. A smile erupted on his face.

"If you must know, my mind is buzzing about tile. Can I get a better deal at a big box store or Hank's Hardware?"

She released her hands from her hips. "You love the smell of sawdust and fresh popcorn at Hank's. Besides, he'll coach you. I'll be homeschooling for the rest of this term, so you can bring Gregg with you."

As Julia walked away, words he'd heard in Israel seized his thoughts.

"I hope you know what a wonderful woman you've married," Julia's friend Dr. Van Horn had told him. Bo hadn't appreciated his wife this much since the day they exchanged vows and drove off in his old Mustang. Julia had been absolutely stunning in her white wedding dress.

Bo ran to catch her before she disappeared in the house. "Honey, wait for me."

TIME PASSED IN FLORIDA with Bo's father-in-law refusing to speak with him. Bo and Julia treated the kids to a boat ride looking for dolphins. Glenna dropped her camera over the side and a sudden storm had the boat captain racing for shore.

Heavy rain didn't quit for days. Gregg moped on the lower bunk, playing with his handheld video game waiting for the sun to pop out so he could find beach treasure. Bo sought to interest him in the drawing for the bathroom remodel, promising his son he could help Bo rip out the old tile. Gregg shoved aside his video game.

"Cool, Dad."

Nothing lifted the gloom until Julia turned on a DVD about Jerusalem telling the kids they had to watch it and pen an essay about their time in the ancient city. That got the kids writing and Bo remembering all he knew about Hal Cohen, the "Wolf and Dolphin."

Sunday afternoon the others left in the van for shopping and burgers. Bo had just poured a soda and spread his blueprints on the kitchen table when his mom phoned.

"We're finally home. Your dad's resting."

Bo rolled up his drawings, worry eclipsing his remodeling plans.

"You weren't flying home for a few days yet. Is something wrong?"

"Everything is right for a change. Dad is regaining strength in his good leg. We're conferring with a rehab specialist in Hampton in the morning."

"Super! Julia and I will be heading home to Great Falls soon."

A long pause.

"Mom, did I lose you?"

"Life is topsy-turvy for you, but could you fly to Hampton first? Dad and I miss you and our grandkids."

"Say no more. Let me talk to Julia. They're out for dinner, but we all want to see you. Are you up for company?"

"Your presence, son, is exactly what your father needs."

"Give him my love," Bo said, wiping his eyes.

Seeing Dad and receiving his guidance was what Bo needed too. He'd just clicked off when his cell phone rang. Bo pulled it off his belt and answered. A few minutes later, after he'd hung up with that caller, he made a decision. While he'd tell Julia about Mom's call, he would keep the second one to himself, until after he returned from Tampa.

He'd be leaving at first light, but would the reason for this trip bring him any closer to getting his life back?

AT SEVEN THE NEXT MORNING, Bo downed a bowl of cereal and kissed Julia before the kids were even awake. Thankfully, Crockett let Bo drive his Crown Victoria. Bo viewed his father-in-law's gesture as a peace offering. Everyone else could fit easily into Sheryl's van.

Bo drove over the bridge heading for I-275, which would take him to Tampa's International Airport. Bo had taken his arm out of the sling so he could drive, but his left shoulder rebelled, aching as he gripped the wheel.

He lowered his left arm, driving with his right and wondering what Kangas would do if he discovered Bo's destination, a secret also to Julia. He reached the airport, passing the car rental turnoff. Guess if they weren't leaving for Virginia soon, he should rent a car. Bo didn't want to owe Crockett anything.

He spiraled up the ramp to short-term parking. Based on Griff's orders, he'd be meeting the FBI agent at the burger joint near the arrival flight tram. Bo entered the tiny restaurant, smelling fries cooking. He spotted Griff nursing coffee.

He scooted on the bench. "Am I late? I rose at dawn and drove like a maniac."

"I'm early," Griff said, extending a hand. "Must have had a tail-wind."

"So what's the rush to get together? I understood we weren't to have contact."

Ignoring Bo's question, Griff nodded at the stubble on Bo's face. "That the new you?"

"Yeah, after two bombs exploded in my presence, I'm growing the beard and hair long. I want to stay alive."

"The scruffy you gave me a start, but you may enjoy a moustache like me."

Bo's hand traveled to his chin. "Kangas' warning against talking to you keeps me up at night. What if the Agency doesn't bring me back in?"

"Kangas will approve of this meeting, once he knows the results," Griff said, leaning forward. "I need your DNA."

That rattled Bo. "What for? I thought you wanted to ask me about who might be behind my demise or other things Kangas might have revealed that I was working on."

"Bo, I need your sample."

"Will getting my DNA satisfy those jokers at State?" Bo kicked his legs out in the aisle.

"Forget them. That's not why I'm here."

Bo felt so far out in the cold, he might as well be in Siberia. Griff was nice and all, but FBI agents operated within Bureau hierarchy. What had Kangas told Griff, really?

Bo lowered his voice to a bare whisper. "What did Kangas tell you about the Wolf? His paws are dirty."

"I know enough." Griff removed the lid from his foam cup, taking a swig before snapping the lid shut. "A DNA match will tie this package into a nice tidy conclusion."

"Shellie had to cause a fuss about my dad's blood type. Have you spoken with her?"

"Sure you don't want coffee?" Griff raised an eyebrow at Bo.

"Okay. I ask and you don't answer. What else do you need besides cells from my mouth?"

Griff chuckled. "Stories from your youth that I should know."

"Like did Dad tell me how his boat killed a bunch of Palestinian gun runners?"

"Something like that."

Bo adjusted his back, already aching from the hard bench, and looked out the window at planes landing. What was his first memory? There was Mom, her long hair drifting past her shoulders. Bo had wiggled into an empty box and she pulled him out by the legs.

"No, Dad never told me. He was pure Navy, kept his trap shut. My first recall is Mom unpacking boxes. Wanderlust's in my blood. Dad was at sea, but Hal Cohen is way off base."

"We won't discuss the Ambassador." Griff held up his hand. "I wondered if your folks were married when you were born."

"Sure."

"Then had your mother been divorced when she met your dad?"

"Griff, I have no idea," Bo snapped, his nerves on edge. "I don't think so."

"I realize this is difficult. You said your dad went to sea a lot."

"My parents still seem greatly in love."

"Did you attend any schools where you were forced into ritualistic behavior?"

Bo scratched at his whiskers. "I attended public school in the Philippines until I was eight or so. Memories are hazy, but I never attended a madrasah, if that's your implication."

"Bo, I'm going to expose these accusations for what they are. Pure nonsense. I take pride in solving difficult cases. I'll unravel this one quickly, but correctly."

Bo leaned back, staring at Griff, an agent he'd always respected. Did he trust him to flush out the bad guys? Griff returned Bo's intense look and Bo saw truth. Griff was the man to clear him, if anyone could.

"That's good enough for me."

"Let's swab your cheek. I have a fast turnaround here, so I can jettison back to D.C."

They walked into the terminal where Griff asked Bo how his family was holding up.

"Gregg and Glenna are resilient," Bo said, pocketing his hands. "They're playing checkers and baking cookies with their grandparents. Julia is homeschooling them. It's hard for her because she loved Israel, especially the religious history of Jerusalem, and she's lost that."

By the men's room, Griff raised a hand, stopping Bo at the entry. "Wait here."

Griff went in, hurrying back out. "A man's in there. Once he leaves, we'll get this done."

Within a minute a young fan decked out in a Ray's jacket strolled out.

Griff motioned Bo inside. "Let's go."

Bo followed Griff into a handicapped stall. "I have to swab it myself, for the chain of custody."

"It's weird standing in a stall with you."

"Yeah." Griff laughed. "I didn't want anyone seeing us come in together. That's a good way to get arrested."

Bo saw nothing humorous about the situation. Griff moved fast, pulling a vial from his inside jacket pocket. Bo opened his mouth and Griff swabbed inside his cheeks. Then Griff pulled the swab back into the tube, replacing the cap.

"Presto, we're done."

Bo swung open the stall door and a stooped man with white hair looked at them oddly. Back in the terminal, Griff lightly tapped Bo's good shoulder.

"That was painless enough, wasn't it?"

Bo grimaced. "Are we done?"

"I'll take good care of this." Griff slapped his jacket pocket. "Frank will advise you."

His jaw firmly set, Griff walked away. Bo turned and hopped on the elevator, getting off at his garage level. Griff had asked things about Mom and Dad which Bo knew nothing about. His back and neck ached as he eased into the roomy Crown Vic.

When he reached his folks' house in Hampton, he'd better ask to see his baby book. He'd make copies and fax them to Frank, who could pass the entries along to Griff. That might help solve something. But what mystery of Bo's life did Griff hope to solve?

26

G riff consulted the weather over a solid week, until warmer temps and clear skies arrived. Within the hour, he reached the Manassas airport and was in the thick of his preflight routine, wishing Dawn, his usual co-pilot, had joined him. But this mission was top secret.

Griff radioed the control tower and being cleared to taxi, he stopped at the end of the runway completing his checklist. Finally he adjusted his sunglasses, turned into takeoff position, and accelerated his flying club's Cessna 172 Skyhawk down the runway. Pulling back the yoke, he lifted into the air like a bird.

He liked keeping his private pilot skills current. Nice that Director Harmon had permitted Griff to lease the club plane for this trip. Fortunately the thermals helped him reach the Hampton airport in about an hour. He secured the plane, chocked the wheels, and after grabbing his trusty GPS, he hiked over to the car rental office. All they offered was an orange compact.

With no choice, he squeezed behind the wheel and drove off in his tiny pumpkin, following voice prompts from the British woman who tagged along. He chuckled, thinking how Grandmother Topping, who still lived in Cornwall, would smile over the verbal commands given in such proper English. If in the end the plane and car rental exceeded his government allowance, Griff would pay the difference without complaint. This chance to log in extra flying hours made any cost worth it.

As Griff rounded the corner onto the street where Bo Rider's parents lived, the British lady piped, "You have reached your destination." He turned off the GPS, craning his neck to see the street numbers, finally rolling to a stop in front of a tidy ranch in the Hampton suburbs.

Dread dogged his footsteps to the front door. Bo's dad had sounded perturbed when Griff had called to arrange the interview. Before he pushed the doorbell, a fit looking man of about sixty-five, leaning on crutches, opened the door.

"Agent Topping, I presume?"

"Yes, I'm here for Douglas MacArthur Rider. This proves who I am."

With a flip of his wrist, Griff opened his leather credentials revealing his photo and gold FBI badge, which glistened in the bright sunshine.

"That's me. Vivian brewed fresh coffee and baked homemade rolls." Mr. Rider scooted back with his crutches.

He even managed to pull the door open wider for Griff to enter. Inside the foyer, decorated with family photos lining the wall, Griff detected mouthwatering smells of cinnamon. Maybe the Riders would be cordial after all.

Griff sniffed deeply. "Thanks. The aroma tells me that she made something wonderful."

"Kitchen is this way. We'll load up and talk in my den."

"I hoped to meet Mrs. Rider," Griff replied, looking askance at the empty kitchen.

Mr. Rider poured coffee into two mugs. "Here's cream and sugar if you need them."

"No, sir. I drink mine black same as you."

"Oh? Were you Navy?"

"No, but," Griff said balancing a small plate and roll atop his coffee mug, "an FBI agent on surveillance or catching a cup at fast food joints has no time to doctor it to taste."

Griff picked up Mr. Rider's cup, balancing his plate as well, and followed behind the retired Navy captain who clunked his crutches along the way. He used his crutch to shut the door behind him before pointing to a comfortable chair for Griff. Mr. Rider balanced on one leg before dropping into the seat behind his desk. Griff deposited the coffee, glimpsing photos of a younger uniformed Captain Rider in several poses with ships.

The den, with its nautical theme, felt cozy. Griff began to relax. He hoped Mr. Rider would too in his familiar surroundings.

"Vivian is upset by Bo's troubles and asked to be excused." He sighed. "My wife is downstairs ironing my shirts that don't need pressing."

"Sorry to cause tension, Mr. Rider, but this meeting is crucial to your son's future."

"So you said on the phone. We'll get farther if you call me Mac."

"And I'm Griff. I consider Bo a friend, having worked with him on, well, matters of mutual interest. That's why his agency asked me to conduct this inquiry."

"Bo means the world to us, which is why you're sitting in my favorite chair."

Griff didn't know if Mac was upset or jesting. Rather than take offense, Griff bit into the delicious roll. "This is tasty," he said aloud, wondering if the Riders were hiding something grievous to Bo's career.

Mac sipped his coffee. "Bo claimed the embassy moved him and his family for security reasons. I know about the bombing, but frankly, Griff, I think they yanked him home because of this hogwash about him being adopted."

"Exactly what I aim to find out."

"So you're my son's friend. Did he tell you about the day this occurred?" Mac asked, pointing down at his wounded leg.

"You were skiing near Mount Hermon. Had you noticed anything unusual?"

"Bo and I had gotten back out of his rental to find my sunglasses. We'd made it a few feet when the car exploded, sending shrapnel deep into my leg."

Griff drank coffee before saying the obvious, "You both could've been killed."

He wanted Mac to keep talking to compare his memory of events with Bo's.

"No one seems sure who the terrorist wanted to wipe out," Mac said, adjusting his frame in the chair. "But I figure they were after him. How anyone could think my son is a security risk after all he's endured for our country is beyond me."

Mac forced down his cup, spilling coffee he dashed away. "It really has me steamed."

"Sir, being retired Navy you're familiar with overlapping bureaucracy. The Agency had Bo searching for a leaker at our embassy in Israel without telling State about their suspicions."

"Typical Langley."

"Did you work with them when you were a Navy commander?"

Mac munched his roll, giving Griff time to sip his coffee, rationing the brew to last beyond his final bite of cinnamon roll. Once finished, Griff explained what else he knew.

"The embassy's Security Director Shellie Karnack believes Bo is behind the leaks."

"Excuse my bias," Mac said, lowering his voice. "That woman is plumb over her head. Probably trying to prove she's fit for her job."

Griff shrugged in agreement and Mac leaned on a crutch, shifting his weight beneath him.

"That's why I retired from the Navy. When they began putting women on ships bound for war, I had enough. Women shouldn't be fighting in wars with men and against men."

He stopped long enough to empty his mug. "Sorry for slipping off track, but I understand that Karnack woman was present when the doctor commented on Bo's blood type not matching mine or Vivian's. She leaped to the conclusion Bo is a spy in the embassy. She's nuts!"

Griff seized the opportunity. "What is the explanation? Is Bo adopted?"

"No, he's not adopted! There's a screw-up in the blood typing done at the hospital."

"So it's your position Bo's blood matches yours."

"It has to match one of ours. We were married when Vivian gave birth to him, unless you're suggesting she messed around while I was at sea. Even if that were so, her blood would match Bo's."

Griff fidgeted in his seat. "Sir, I'm uncomfortable asking these questions, but someone has to. I want to clear Bo."

"Our son is lucky you're the guy tagged to end this farce."

"Agent Karnack theorizes that because Bo was born in the Philippines, he's a plant by terrorist groups in the Philippines raised to sabotage the U.S. from within."

"Hogwash!"

Mac tried to stand but collapsed into the chair. He seemed worn out by the ordeal.

"Do you need something, Mac?" Griff asked, halfway out of his chair.

"Justice for my son," Mac snapped. "Karnack's confounded theory confirms mine. She's in way over her head. She actually believes terrorists placed Bo in the family of a U.S. Naval officer to indoctrinate him? What's scarier is that no one at State is examining her crazy mind."

"You were stationed in the Philippines when Bo was born, correct?"

"Yup, I was a young naval officer on a submarine based in Subic Bay. Military families are used to their kids being born outside the U.S."

Griff patted his jacket pocket. "Here's an easy fix. I've brought DNA kits with me. If you and Mrs. Rider will give samples, we can resolve the matter. If you won't, we can't."

Again Mac started to stand without his crutches before again slumping back in his chair.

But his voice was firm. "We'll do it. Vivian is as impatient as me to help our son."

Griff jammed his note pad in his pocket and launched from the chair to help Mac stand.

"Thanks, Griff. My arms need more weightlifting to handle the new me. You bring our cups to the kitchen and I'll call Vivian on my cell. We've worked out a little system."

Griff gathered the cups, walking slowly behind Mac to the kitchen. Amazed by his stoicism after losing his foot, Griff could see where Bo got his courage. Like father, like son.

"Griff, find a seat in the living room and I'll be right back."

The living room, with vases of burgundy silk flowers and strategically placed baskets of pine cones, held no hint of Mac's past Navy life. Griff perched on the edge of a wing-backed chair, eyeing photos taken of Bo with his family at the beach. The neatness of the room, as organized as a magazine layout, brought a strange memory to mind.

A while back, before Bo had left for a foreign assignment, he'd given Griff an envelope to hold for him, which Griff always thought contained Bo's last will and testament or letters to his kids. Bo had retrieved it when he returned. The way his mom kept everything in order seemed just like Bo. Like mother, like son.

Griff consulted his notes, wanting to privately ask Vivian about her months before Bo's conception, but opted for DNA tests to answer any offensive questions. He looked up at sounds of rustling in the kitchen and saw Vivian rinsing out cups in the sink. Moments later, she extended her hand to Griff in a friendly gesture, anxiety showing in her nervous eyes.

"I'm Vivian. I had hoped to leave all this business to you men." She turned to Mac, who stood on crutches right by her side.

Mac gestured for Griff to take a seat. "I told Vivian about your DNA request."

Bo's parents sat on the sofa with Vivian sliding forward, her hands on her knees. She gazed at Griff, her lips twisted and tears pooling in her honey-colored eyes.

"As the mother who endured morning sickness and the pain of giving birth to Bo, I pledge he is not adopted nor was he placed in our home to destroy our government. I cradled him many nights, nursing him through colic and flu. Bo is the same boy we raised. This is absurd. Are we so politically correct that someone can't tell that Ambassador and agent their ideas are beyond the realm of reason?"

Griff removed a handkerchief from his back pocket, handing it to Vivian. "It's clean."

She blotted her eyes, asking, "Does Bo know you want our DNA?"

"I guess he does. I'm sure he'd approve."

"Why would he?" Vivian dropped the hankie, her eyes round.

"Bo and I have worked together on dicey matters, gaining a mutual respect. Not long ago, he brought me an envelope to hold while he was in another country. If anything happened to him, he wanted me to give his family the contents."

Mac and Vivian traded skeptical looks, a cloud passing over Vivian's face. "Do you think it has something to do with this matter?"

Griff hadn't even considered that possibility, but he recovered quickly.

"I think it held his will and letters for family, maybe even for you. Bo could have left the envelope with others, but he trusts me to do the right thing at the right time."

Mac nodded. "Bo's boss picked Griff to conduct this inquiry from the agents in the FBI."

Griff removed the DNA kit from his pocket adding, "I won't let Bo down or you either."

Vivian sagged back onto the cushion. "I want to tell you about Bo's birth."

"Sure." Griff alerted to a possible new clue. "Just understand I'm not insisting."

Vivian looked at Mac, who pursed his lips, but gave her a curt nod to go ahead.

"Mac wasn't there and neither was that embassy agent."

"I sure wish I had been with you for our son's birth," Mac interrupted with a growl.

"Mac, you were deployed," Vivian said. "We lived off base in a small home. I had a difficult pregnancy and received little support halfway round the world from our families."

"I warned Vivian it would be rough, but she insisted on living in the Philippines."

Vivian patted Mac's knee gently. "Let me tell my story."

He grabbed her hand and their tentative glances at Griff made him curious if there was more to Vivian's story. He leaned forward expectantly.

"After dinner one night, I was early into my ninth month, or so I thought. I began having false contractions, but they grew quite severe. Fortunately we had domestic help and she was used to driving our car on errands. I phoned her and she rushed me toward the Navy hospital on base, but my water broke. In all the excitement she took me to the hospital at Olongapo City."

Vivian patted Mac's knee again. "We military wives adjusted to circumstances and it's a good thing we did. Bo was born within thirty minutes. He was a big full-term boy. I'll never forget how the nurses enjoyed fussing over our son. They mostly had Filipino babies born there, unlike the Navy hospital. So my fair-haired little Anglo boy received lots of pampering."

She rose, gripping his handkerchief. "Agent Topping, I gave birth to Bo. He is not adopted. My DNA sample will confirm it."

"Mine too!" Mac said, slapping his good knee.

Griff carefully lifted one of the two vials. "After I swab inside your mouth, I'll be much closer to proving the Ambassador and agent wrong."

Vivian opened her mouth like a patient waiting to say "Ahhhh." Playing the country doctor, Griff inserted the giant swab into her mouth, dabbing the inside of her cheek and gums. He pushed her swab into the vial, replacing the cap and writing Vivian's name on the outside.

Mac scrambled up from the sofa, leaning on his crutches. "My turn," he chimed as if not wanting to be left out from exonerating Bo. He opened his mouth and Griff took his sample, securing the second vial with Mac's name on it.

"I want to fly out before the storm moves in. Thanks to you both. I'll be in touch."

Griff secreted both vials into his inside jacket pocket. Vivian walked him to the front door, folded his hanky, and handed it to him.

"Bo and Julia are bringing our grandchildren in two days. I'm grateful you came today."

"Give him my warm regards and tell him I'll hurry these results."

Griff dashed to his rental car and on the drive to Hampton's airport, his mind pulsed with questions. What *had* Bo put in that envelope? Was it a confession?

27

Julia Rider pulled into the driveway of a modest ranch home in Hampton, Virginia, enjoying her in-law's gracious hospitality. Vivian loved fussing over Bo and the grandkids and even Mac seemed to thrive, proudly showing Bo the new tools he'd purchased for carving wood. The past few weeks had flown by with Bo and his dad each carving and painting wooden birds, their oyster catchers seeming so life-like.

Julia shoved the car in gear, squinting at the dashboard clock. Frank Deming would be arriving in a few minutes. She snatched the keys, grabbed her bag of groceries, and raced inside the front door. Vivian greeted her with a concern.

"What time do I collect Glenna and Gregg from the Living Museum?"

"The program ends at four. That should give me enough time for my meeting."

"Mac and I thought after Agent Topping's visit," Vivian lowered her voice, "that we had answered all his questions. Why is someone else coming?"

"I have no clue. That's why I found the program about Virginia's history. The kids are out of the house and Bo is carving a bird in the basement. None of them will overhear what we say. They've been through enough."

"You all have." Vivian sighed. "Mac's asleep. He didn't eat much lunch."

"No? I was busy getting the kids ready, I'm sorry I failed to notice."

"He's my worry. For your meeting, I set up a tray of hot cocoa in the family room."

Julia kissed her cheek. "You're the best. I bought turkey subs and fruit for supper."

She arranged her purchases in the fridge, leaving out a box of cookies. A loud thump on the front door snagged her attention and Julia scurried to open it before the knocking woke Mac. Frank looked frazzled, holding a bouquet of daisies, which he handed to Vivian.

"Mrs. Rider, these are for you, for storming into your house at the last minute. I-95 was a nightmare of slush covering the highway."

"How nice, young man. I'll find a vase and show them to Mac after his nap."

Julia made introductions, then brought Frank to the den where she was surprised to find Bo standing at the window, hands cupped behind his back.

"I thought you were downstairs with your birds."

"No chance." Bo whirled around. "Frank, mind if I sit in? Somehow I don't like the idea of the Agency sending you to question my wife behind my back."

Frank stuck out his right hand and Bo grabbed it.

"I'd feel the same way," Frank said. "But I'll violate no orders in talking with you."

"Cocoa anyone?" Julia asked, pouring out a cup.

Frank thumped his arms. "Sounds great. I'm chilled."

"Count me in too, hon."

Frank looked around the den while Julia poured cocoa in two more cups. While she appreciated Bo's support, Frank was no stranger. He'd been a regular for Sunday dinners, with Bo grilling burgers and Frank playing board games with the kids. He'd also been staying at their home until he moved into his new place this past weekend. Because Frank's wife had been kidnapped overseas and never found, Julia had a soft spot for him.

She handed out the steaming cocoa before settling in a wing-backed chair. Bo sat opposite her with Frank across on a small sofa, a table with a schooner encased in glass separating them.

"Griff already interviewed my folks last week." Bo paused, sipping cocoa. "Your call wanting to talk with Julia is curious. Has Griff uncovered something new?"

"He's not briefed me yet," Frank replied, turning to Julia. "We believe the Ambassador viewed a website looking at your homes in Israel and Virginia. Do you know why he'd do that?"

"Frank," Bo interrupted. "He shouldn't know where I live. I've long suspected he's—"

Frank shot Bo a silencing look and took out a handheld computer.

"It appears someone concentrated on your homes," Frank insisted, holding his fingers over the small computer, ready to type her answers.

"Oh!" Julia's cheeks flamed. "Clara brought up our homes on a global photo site."

"Where were you when she did that?"

"In her husband's office. Why?"

"Did you suggest viewing your homes or did she?" Frank asked as he typed.

Julia peeked at Bo, wanting to speak with him alone, but that might give Frank the wrong impression. Julia had nothing to hide.

"Clara acted kindly to me and the kids. Are you investigating her?"

Frank typed and then addressed Bo. "A Marine security guard revealed that Clara routinely used her husband's secure computer."

Bo smoothed his moustache. "Did the MSG notify Shellie about that?"

"No. He went behind her back in contacting the Agency. Julia, I need to ask a few more questions to tie things together."

"Clara's my friend. I hope Langley isn't blaming her."

"I'm sure it's routine, honey," Bo said, reaching over and touching her hand. "Frank has no agenda other than the truth."

She rose from the chair, leaving her hot chocolate on the table. Was there a sinister side to Frank's inquisition? Perhaps she shouldn't defend Clara. After all, she hadn't called Julia since she left Tel Aviv, nor had she returned her voice messages.

"What else do you want to know about Clara?"

"Did she log into the Ambassador's computer?"

"Yes." Julia's tried to picture the night of Clara's foundation reception. "She said Hal's computer didn't require certain filters so she could access more websites."

"Didn't that sound like a security threat?" Frank probed.

Julia shrugged. "It never entered my mind."

"Think carefully," Frank said. "Did Clara log off the computer before you left Hal's office?"

His fingers moved quickly as he typed. Julia looked away. Silence became her friend as she tried to recall the simple detail. So much had happened since the night where Julia sought to help Clara's foundation. Bo glared at her, his arms crossed. Surely going on the computer with Clara hadn't caused the bombings, had it? Julia's heart lurched and she dropped to her chair.

"I need to think without you both staring at me!"

She closed her eyes and then she remembered.

"Clara did not log off."

"How do you know for sure?" Frank demanded.

Julia comprehended little of how computers worked. If hers turned on when she pressed the blue button, she happily typed e-mails, leaving technical details to Bo. But this time Julia had the answer. She even beamed a smile.

"Clara showed me an aerial view of their Long Island home. When we left Hal's office, her beautiful house was still on the screen. I thought it made a terrific screen saver."

"How long did you and she spend on Hal's computer?"

"Ten or fifteen minutes at most."

"Did Clara inspect any other sites?"

"She visited her foundation's website to show me the good she's doing for Israeli women fighting breast cancer."

That ought to satisfy Frank, Julia mused. She hoped so because she heard Vivian rattling her keys out in the hall.

"Did you access Hal's computer any other time with her?"

"No."

"Ever log onto his computer yourself when you were in the embassy to see Bo?"

"I rarely went into the embassy to meet him."

Where was Frank going with these pointed questions? Julia peered at Bo. His lips were drawn into a tight grimace and his eyes had grown stormy, as if lightning flashed in them.

"To be clear," Frank intoned as he typed, "you, Julia Rider, never used the Ambassador's computer to open e-mails or stuff like that."

"Frank, are you suggesting that *I* have done something wrong?"

Julia leapt from the chair, her blood reaching a boiling point. "Do you think I caused Bo and his dad to almost be blown to smithereens?" Her voice rose to a fever pitch.

Bo came alongside her, putting an arm tightly around her shoulders. "Dial it down a notch. Frank's doing his job. You can't take it personally."

Tears magnifying with shame and anger, Julia leaned against Bo's strong chest.

"I see how hard it is for you to work for the Agency."

"Julia," Frank said standing, "I didn't plan to come across as a jerk. With all that's happening at the embassy, I can't say more, but the tiniest detail may lead to the truth. You're a key part of my search."

"Are we finished?" she sniffed, wiping her eyes.

"Yes." Frank nodded.

Julia wanted to crash on her bed; she felt enormous relief.

"I'll walk you out," Bo told Frank. "Julia, why not go with Mom to get the kids?"

"That's a good idea. And you should check on your dad while we're gone."

Julia trotted down to the hall bathroom, hearing the front door close. Bo joined her leaning against the bathroom doorjamb; she splashed cold water on her cheeks, dabbing her face with a clean towel.

"Are my eyes red?"

"You look fine, honey."

"Frank thinks I did something wrong."

Fresh tears stung her eyes and Julia pressed her palms against her lids.

"No he doesn't."

Bo reached out for her and she fell into his arms, glad for his strength, but then Bo suddenly pulled away.

"Frank wants to tell me something out in his car. If you see us talking out there when you leave, don't be worried."

"Am I in trouble?" Dread sizzled through her body.

"Not at all. It's about a cat straying into our house and things like that."

He tapped the edge of her nose, leaving Julia alone to wonder why Clara had asked to see their homes. Had it been an innocent search or something more ominous?

BO PUSHED THE HEATER in Frank's car to high, patting his arms while Frank stowed his handheld computer.

"It's freezing out here." Bo wished he'd snagged his coat.

"If you were still in Florida, I could have questioned Julia in the warm sunshine."

Bo faced Frank with a frown. "You did come across pretty strong. Julia's worried, but I promised she's not the target. Am I right?"

"Yes, but we still don't know who kicked you out in the cold. I have a new concern."

"By the serious glint in your eye, I have to ask. Does it help me or hurt?"

Frank drummed his fingers on the steering wheel drawing out the suspense. Bo slugged him on the arm. "Quit kidding around. We're talking about my life here."

"It's Shellie." Frank forced a chuckle. "She's being sent to FLETC as a trainer."

"I never dreamed State would break up the dynamic duo. Shellie was adept at covering for Hal. He must be throwing a fit."

Bo tried to picture Shellie fitting in at the Federal Law Enforcement Training Center and didn't think much of her leadership skills.

"Georgia is a far cry from Tel Aviv," Frank replied, turning the vent toward his face. "Kangas and I think Shellie had lax security, allowing outsiders like Clara to access Hal's computer."

Bo flexed his numb fingers. "I don't think she is qualified to train newbies."

"At least she'll be out of our hair. Langley is sending a team to examine operations. Griff will be overseeing things."

Bo's eyebrows arched. "Kangas has wanted Hal under a microscope, for good reason. But what about Mike Spencer?"

"The Chief is clicking his heels down the halls of Langley until he retires next week."

Bo opened the handle, but Frank stopped him with a hand.

"A stray cat is roaming around. Ten inches of snow fell and I put out tuna fish. When I locked up the last time, the cat was sitting in the driveway. Sorry if I have caused you trouble."

"By the time we get home, the cat will be long gone, taken in by one of my neighbors."

"Say, your neighbor Carver Washington is a nosy sort. He stopped me several times questioning what I was doing in your home."

"I forgot to tell him you'd be staying." Bo sighed.

Just as Frank turned down the heater fan, Bo watched his mom and Julia back out the driveway. He waved, but Julia stared out the window looking hurt. They drove away and Bo turned his mind to what Frank was saying.

"I kept him at arm's length."

"Okay, I'll give Carver a call, which reminds me. Tell Kangas I'm losing ground carving birds. I need to be back at Langley."

With that Bo hopped from the car before Frank could give him any bad news, like it could be years before the Agency reinstated him with honor.

28

Bo walked through the front door and crept down the hall, listening by Dad's bedroom door. *Kaboom.* Bo bounded in, finding Mac standing there looking disgusted, a crutch under his left arm.

"Dad! Are you all right?"

Bo hurried into the room spying the other crutch on the floor next to an empty glass. Liquid was seeping into the carpet.

"It's just water. Guess I'm not used to these fool sticks."

"Your rehab is making you stronger every day. Let me grab a towel."

Bo stepped over to the master bath and pulled a towel from the linen closet. He handed Dad the other crutch before blotting up the water. Mac hobbled out the door and down the hall, with Bo shadowing him until they reached the den.

"I'm gonna read e-mails from my old Navy buddies. Grab us coffee and join me."

Dad settled into his desk chair and Bo filled a mug in the kitchen returning with an extra, each mug supporting a plate with a muffin on top. Mac raised his eyes from his computer.

"I heard loud voices before. Where are Julia and your mother?"

"They're picking up the kids at the museum. An Agency official was here asking Julia about some events at the embassy. Things grew heated."

"Trouble is etched on your face, son," Mac said, narrowing his eyes.

Before he could deflect Dad's concerns, Bo's cell rang. He swiped it off from the table. It was Julia, calling to say she and Vivian were taking the kids to a movie and then for tacos.

"You need to take your mind off things," he told her. "I saw your face when you left."

"Glenna enjoyed watching a film about Mount Vernon and Gregg wants to be president someday."

Bo played along. "Good for them. Tell Mom that I'm sharing coffee with Dad."

"I bought turkey subs. They're in the fridge."

"Honey, try to have fun. Everything will work out, I promise."

Bo hung up. Mac just stared off into space, like his mind was on autopilot.

"What's wrong, Dad?"

Mac turned to Bo with a start. "I was thinking about the toll my Navy years took on you and Vivian. She had more responsibility for raising you. I missed out."

Bo grabbed a photo of Mac standing with his crew on the bridge of his last sub.

"Dad, you probably don't know how greatly you have influenced me. Your naval service is why I went into the Army."

"Really!" A grin erupted on Mac's worn face. "Why Army and not Navy?"

Bo laughed. "Because we had Army ROTC in high school. If we'd had Navy ROTC, I'd be a naval officer like you."

Bo picked up another photo of Mac in uniform, realizing how Dad had instilled in him a sense of honor and duty to country. A mental picture flashed in his mind when he'd been about four years old.

"When I was little, I wore your uniform hat and practiced saluting. It came way down over my ears."

"One Halloween you wore my white gloves and brought 'em back with caramel apple on the fingertips. Your mom cleaned them up good as new."

As Bo brought over the photo, he pointed to a colorful striped ribbon and medal against the background of Mac's white uniform jacket.

"I know the service ribbons, but what's this medal?"

Mac pushed out his bottom lip, gazing off as if lost in a long ago memory.

"They pinned that medal on me as a young lieutenant the year before you were born. Had you already been born, I probably wouldn't have earned that."

"Why not?" Bo slid the photo back on the shelf.

He sat down across from his dad and waited.

"I was new on subs and out in the Pacific on the *USS Dayton* in a typhoon-like squall. We weren't affected much by weather, because we ran submerged. A message alerted us that a B-52 bomber had crashed and the crew bailed out. We were directed to the site, surfaced in heavy seas, and began searching."

Bo hung onto Mac's every word because he rarely, if ever, talked about his service.

"Did you do any good?"

"After searching for hours, we found some of the crew in a life raft, but couldn't get close to them. Forty-foot waves had us bobbing around like a cork. Sometimes our screw even lifted out of the water. We fired several lines that couldn't reach them."

Bo gripped his cup, feeling the tension his dad faced. "What happened?"

"I was a pretty good swimmer, so I grabbed a line, jumped in the water, and swam to their raft. Once I secured the line to their raft, the sub crew pulled us all aboard."

"Wow!" Bo jumped from the sofa. "You saved the entire crew?"

"The guys on the raft were barely alive due to exposure," Mac replied, shaking his head. "A few others we never found. I was awarded the Navy and Marine Corp medal, the one thing I have in common with President Kennedy."

"How so?"

"JFK was awarded the same medal for saving his PT crew when his boat sunk in World War Two. He swam from one abandoned island to another in the Pacific looking for help."

Bo sat down, desperate to keep Dad talking. "Your medal should be called the 'swimmers medal' since that's how you both won it."

His dad was a real hero. Bo wished he could get Dad some kind of medal for losing his foot and bottom half of his leg in that horrendous resort bombing. Mac ate his muffin, washing it down with coffee. Bo did the same, figuring Dad needed a rest from his exciting saga.

In time Mac nodded at the photo. "That's the only medal on my uniform. I received other commendations as I rose to captain, but none of them came with a memento for me to display."

"What kind of commendations?" Bo leaned forward.

"I was in special ops so highly classified they weren't even acknowledged. Oh, some notation was entered in my service file, but nothing to attract attention."

"You mean like the time your sub rammed a fishing boat?"

Mac squared his jaw. "Yes, I was on a special op."

"You mean it wasn't an accident, which is why the Palestinians haven't forgiven you."

"I skippered the USS Dayton. We sat in the Mediterranean off the coast of Israel and got a classified message about a fishing boat steaming for Israel loaded with arms for Palestinian rebels. At first we were told to locate it, which we did. We reported its location asking for further instructions. I was ready to blow that baby out of the water."

"Did you get clearance?" Bo asked, sensing his dad's dilemma.

"Nope, the Administration didn't want us to fire, afraid they'd appear to be taking sides. I proposed a possible accident. After much delay, I received the go-ahead, surfacing in the dark of night with no moon. I claimed we couldn't see the fishing boat until impact. We rescued some militants, transferring them to an Israeli patrol boat sent to the scene."

"Were they carrying weapons?"

An energetic smile lit Mac's face.

"We turned the militants over to Mossad who had given us the original intel. After stiff interrogation, the survivors admitted they carried explosives and shoulder-mounted rockets."

"You worked with Mossad?" Bo watched Mac's eyes but didn't say anything about his own work with Israel's Intelligence Agency. At least Bo had until Hal pushed him out.

"Yup." Mac fingered his mug. "I never knew how my name was so widely circulated, but that's what irritated the PLO at the time. Course, they were terrorists to the core until we made Yasser Arafat a negotiating partner in shrinking Israel to the size of New Jersey. What a tragic mistake."

"And Hamas has replaced the Palestinian Liberation Organization, but still commits terror in the name of peace." Bo took time to drain his cup.

"The PLO correctly assumed we helped Mossad. That wasn't my last time doing so."

Bo's eyes widened. His dad had worked with Mossad all these years?

"What's on your mind, son? Your gears are turning."

"It's astonishing. I mean—"

"How about a refill?" Mac interrupted. "Then I'll tell you things about the CIA."

Filled with wonder, Bo hustled to the kitchen, retrieved the pot, and determined to discover Dad's secrets, he practically ran back to the den where he filled both mugs. Bo set the glass pot on the corner of Mac's desk atop a stack of magazines and got comfortable on the sofa.

"I'm all ears."

Mac's eyes twinkled as he sipped the hot brew. Bo could hardly contain his curiosity and he wanted to rush the tale. Finally, Mac lowered his mug.

"After my sub's 'accident' with the Palestinians, I found the *USS Dayton* being tasked to deploy SEALS for underwater operations. I deposited Army Rangers on foreign beaches. I even thought if I avoided promotions and remained a skipper, one day you might board my sub for delivery somewhere when you became an Army Ranger."

Bo plunked his elbows on his knees. "One time a sub landed us onto a beach in a raft, but that happened after you were supervising operations from behind a desk."

"Those kinds of operations got me kudos I can never brag about."

"What about the Agency?"

Mac leaned on his crutch, adjusting his weight on his chair.

"My foot still aches, only it's gone."

"I'm so sorry, Dad. Do you need me to get anything for you?"

"No, I'm not helpless yet. Let me tell you about the CIA, then I'll take a hot shower."

Bo crossed his arms, feeling stymied. Shouldn't he be doing more to help Dad? But he realized that Mac, once a tough sub commander, still had plenty of guts.

"I was shoving papers at the Pentagon and this guy popped into my office. I'd never met him, but had received two earlier cryptic phone calls from him. Know who visited me?"

Bo shook his head.

"Mr. Wilt Kangas."

Bo's head jerked back. "You're kidding."

"Thought you'd say that. After two of my special ops I told you about, I received a call from Wilt Kangas, operations officer at CIA's Clandestine Operations. Later I learned he was the one who requested my sub when the Agency needed help."

"Dad, that's amazing. He's my boss."

Mac waved a hand in the air. "I'm getting to that. So he'd call me up, real friendly and because we weren't on a secured line, he started talking as if we were school chums, pretending like 'thanks for giving my son a ride on your sub. Johnny enjoyed it and I'm so glad you brought him back safely. Hope someday I can return the favor.'"

"Cool, Dad." Bo's respect for his dad continued growing.

"Hold your horses. A guy shows up in my office just before I retire, says he is Kangas, the guy who tasked my sub to deposit assets for laser targeting. He tells me how SEALs or Rangers would sneak to sites of known terrorists and mark their hideouts with a laser. As a result, our drones put a missile down a chimney."

Bo remembered doing those very tasks but said nothing, wanting Dad to finish his story.

"After Kangas explains he recruits people to work in his CIA unit, he taps a file he's holding, telling me that he used a Ranger group and one of the guys was Bo Rider. In checking your background as a possible CIA agent, he realizes I'm your dad. He says if he offers you a job, I should consider it thanks for my assisting him years earlier."

"Wow! I've briefed Mr. Kangas dozens of times. He never admitted knowing you."

"He impressed me as a serious 'need to know' kind of guy. I figured he was testing my reaction to your working for the Agency, maybe hoping I'd encourage you."

Bo's mind reeled with the nuances of Dad's life. It was incredible how his life continued to intersect with Bo's career. "Why haven't you mentioned Kangas before?"

"I raised you to make sound decisions and knew you would," Mac said, standing with his crutches. "I'm off to the shower. How's the bird carving coming?"

"Slow. I miss the work, Dad."

"To everything there is a season or so I believed in my naval career. Carving wood, using your hands, gives you plenty of time to think about what's important."

He shuffled off to the bathroom and Bo felt a lump in his throat. What did Dad mean by that last quip? Bo opened the fridge to assemble supper. The way he figured it, the rest of the family wouldn't be back for a few hours yet, giving Bo more time to prime Mac's story-telling pump.

29

In the middle of the night after listening to melodic sounds of Julia's deep breathing for too long, Bo decided to read a book. He slid from beneath the coverlet, pulling a robe over his pajamas. He snuck down the hall, longing for a snack, but he didn't want to wake the others.

A lone slice of apple pie Julia had brought home called his name. He grabbed the plate, carrying it to the den where he snapped on the lamp. Bo ate the pie with his fingers, his eyes landing on the photo of Dad in uniform and zeroing in on the medal pinned to his chest.

Where did Dad keep that Navy and Marine Corps medal? Bo would love to see it and even hold it in his hands. His dad sure surprised him, dropping how Kangas had approached him about Bo working for the Agency. Bo searched his mind for past clues, coming up short. Had Kangas directed CIA recruiters to Bo when he'd been with the Army Rangers?

Nothing Kangas had ever said or done revealed his prior knowledge of Bo. Despite Dad's humorous tale about him and Kangas covering each other's backside, the truth stung. Over the past few weeks, Bo had heard nothing from Langley about unmasking the mole and Bo coming back to the fold. He couldn't escape the brutal conclusion, his years of valued service counted for nothing. In short, Bo's career was over, kaput.

Bo turned on his dad's computer, logging into his own e-mail account. Nothing but junk from security firms. However, the last one from Frank caught his attention:

The state-of-the-art conference unveiling the latest technology will be held in Tel Aviv March 15. International security experts will display new drones the size of hummingbirds, backscatter radar, and GPS tracking devices for industrial uses.

Bo reread Frank's e-mail. Was it his way of saying Kangas wanted Bo to attend the Tel Aviv conference? The possibilities were endless and Bo eyed the clock. At two o'clock in the morning, he'd have to wait six hours before calling Frank.

As he typed a reply, a dreadful possibility dawned on him. Maybe Frank was preparing Bo for the inevitable letdown, hinting he should find a corporate recruiter who'd hire him. The sugary apple pie turning to lead in his stomach, Bo erased and typed a new e-mail to Frank:

Are you attending the security conference? Am I going along or should I find myself a job? I feel the irony; a fake corporate recruiter pinning my hopes on some nameless corporate recruiter. I'm in a storm with no life raft. Don't leave me floundering out here. Bo

He shut down the computer, his mind a cauldron of hopes and fears. Would he ever charge back into the game of high-velocity cat and mouse that he thrived on? Bo snatched a book from the table and flipped open to the middle, wanting to blot out his tortured thoughts. He sat with the book on his lap for a while until his mind started going numb.

Suddenly, someone touched his face. He jolted awake, seizing a hand and twisting it.

"Ouch! It's me, Julia."

He dropped her hand and his defenses. The book fell to the floor.

"Sorry, honey. I fell asleep in Dad's chair."

"I woke up and became concerned when you weren't in bed. I love your being next to me at night," Julia said, kneading her wrist.

She sounded okay with his being on the outs with the Agency. If Kangas called him back maybe she'd raise a ruckus. Bo shook his head, unsure what to believe about his future. Julia had always been his biggest champion.

"Are you okay?" he asked, changing mental gears.

"You surprised me more than anything, grabbing me like that. What are you reading?"

Bo had no idea. She bent down, snatching up the book that had fallen to the floor. Her face blossomed into a lovely smile.

"Dr. Van Horn's book about the end times. I gave this to Mac to read. What do you think about Armageddon being fought in the Jezreel Valley?"

He fumbled for a reply. "Ah, I didn't read that far into it."

"I miss Israel in spite of the violence we survived." Julia sat on the couch hugging the book. "My life has come alive just stepping where Jesus walked."

"Honey, I'd give anything to be *anywhere* for the Agency."

"It's freezing in here." Julia tightened her bathrobe around her neck. "What's going to happen to us, Bo?"

"Frank e-mailed me, providing a clue. We'll wait and see."

Bo rose, and pulling her from the sofa, he took the book from her hands. Beneath the shelf holding Dad's photo, he folded Julia into his arms. Here he was warming her from the cold while he was a spy set adrift in the cold, and no one at the Agency besides Frank seemed to care.

GRIFF TOPPING SPENT A FEW MINUTES waiting to be cleared through security at Langley. Though he'd been an FBI agent for years in northern Virginia, this was his first excursion inside the secret agency. He waited another twenty minutes, twiddling his thumbs in a remote and windowless reception area for Frank Deming to escort him inside.

Click, click. Griff snapped to attention as Frank swiped his ID badge at a turnstile. He greeted Griff with a grin.

"Sorry for the delay. I never know what might erupt around here."

Griff extended his hand. "I haven't been peppered with so many questions and requests for documents. Any second I expected a doctor to come at me with a tongue depressor. This is as bad as getting a physical."

"Almost," Frank laughed. "That's why we usually meet folks off site. But you need to comb through Bo's file and our files never leave the premises. Here's your temporary ID."

The two agents turned through the stile, with Frank telling Griff the badges they'd just swiped would record everywhere they went in the building. Soon their elevator delivered them to the suite of offices marked "Director National Clandestine Services."

"Griff, you will work in the Director's small conference room. You may read Bo's entire personnel file, but notes must be brief. I will photocopy every word you write before you leave."

Griff's eyes swept the room, void of any décor except the long table, six chairs, and one safe looking like a file cabinet. He tried to envision Bo as someone other than the man he'd come to respect, refusing to believe he was anyone else. If the CIA's background checks were half as thorough as their office security, it would be difficult for a spy to reach Bo's level in the Agency.

Frank spun a dial on the corner safe, and turning the handle, bolts clattered. A drawer slid open and he selected a file, placing the monster, measuring a good five inches thick, on the table.

"Hope you can plow through this today."

Griff sat at the table, flipping open the cover. "It will be strange reading about Bo, but someone must."

"I'm at my desk if you need anything."

Griff searched recent events on the top keenly aware Bo's life would pass through his fingertips. Thumbing to the bottom, he found papers highlighting Bo's recruitment and background investigation. Griff returned to the top page, interested in a sticky note that looked like it had been hurriedly placed there.

Frank, Hold this award nomination until results of inquiry are known. WK

Griff's eyes consumed the memo beneath the sticky note. Bo had been nominated for the Intelligence Star. Griff let out a sharp whistle—that award was given posthumously to spies who died in service. Only occasionally were recipients still active like Bo. Francis Gary Powers, the CIA pilot of the U-2 spy plane shot down by Russia, had received the Intelligence Star.

Director Kangas had lauded Bo for "voluntary acts of courage under hazardous conditions." Griff absorbed the harrowing details: Bo had infiltrated enemy-controlled areas of Iraq and Iran, received injuries from an exploding IED, and after recovering, rescued captives. Bo neutralized an enemy weapons system more lethal than a nuclear weapon. Those Bo rescued and the specific weapon system had been omitted from the memo for security reasons.

Griff made some notations, but suddenly tossed down his pen. Frank wouldn't let him leave the Agency with these facts. Instead, he skimmed Kangas' memo trying to memorize key phrases. This was the same Bo who ate with Griff and Eva at Rob's Deli, but neither of them had a clue of Bo's heroism, he was so unpretentious.

And because of two hacks at State who had accused him of being a mole, Bo had been basically sacked. Anger boiled within Griff. He snatched up the pen, tapping it against the table. Bo deserved the Intelligence Star. Moreover, Hal and Shellie needed to be taught a lesson. Where should Griff look next?

He realized he'd forgotten something important. Prayer was somewhat new to him, but Dawn had taught him how to reach out to God. He uttered a silent plea for God in Heaven to lead him to the truth for Bo's sake and his family.

Griff then plunged straight to the bottom, digging out Kangas' recommendation that Bo be recruited to the Agency from the Army when he was a Ranger. The file noted he was the son of Douglas MacArthur Rider, commander of the submarine *USS Dayton* and officer in the CIA Special Activities Division.

"Ah, hah," Griff chuckled aloud.

So Mac had been a CIA officer serving the Navy, but he hadn't let it slip in talking with Griff. Seemed he needed to sharpen his interviewing techniques. His eyes flying across the pages, he read how Mac's sub collided with a fishing boat loaded with weapons destined for the PLO in Israel. Griff stopped at Mac's photo standing next to four fishermen on the deck of the *USS Dayton*. After rescuing the militants, Mac had turned them over to the IDF. Griff finally understood why Bo was CIA.

More pages, more standard stuff about Bo's original polygraph. Nothing adverse was noted. Regarding his family, Griff scratched a few notes about Bo's parents, Douglas MacArthur Rider and Vivian Rider, nee Pierce. Bo had been born at Rizal Hospital in Olongapo City just as Vivian told Griff. He scanned the Certificate of Report of Birth form required by the State Department and prepared by the U.S. Consulate, indicating Lieutenant Commander Rider was assigned to the sub base at Subic Bay during Bo's birth.

Battling frustration at finding nothing definitive, Griff saw no evidence the CIA had ever scrutinized Bo's birth in the Philippines. Still, his past seemed straightforward. Griff found nothing supporting Hal's theory that Bo was a covert plant for a Filipino terror group.

"Knock knock." Frank appeared in the doorway. "Ready for java?"

"I drink it black."

Frank disappeared. Griff dug through more reports about Bo's stellar career. Blah, blah. Nothing suspicious. Then a second memo snagged Griff's attention.

Bo received the Distinguished Intelligence Medal for his work leading to the dismantling of a secret Chinese weapons system. Adrenaline pulsed through Griff. He'd helped Bo follow Chinese diplomats in New York City. The conclusion had been spectacular, but Griff never knew Bo had taken such tremendous risks in China.

Frank returned with coffee, offering to take Griff to the cafeteria for lunch when he was ready. Griff stood and stretched his back.

"So Kangas nominated Bo for the Intelligence Star."

Frank shut the door. "I wanted to remove that memo, but Director Kangas told me to leave everything. His agreement with your FBI Director was to let you see it all."

"That's my understanding." Griff sipped the coffee, enjoying the warmth.

"I can't tell you how this pains me. Bo is one of our most talented agents."

Frank sat, twisting his hands as if wanting to divulge something else.

"What's on your mind, Frank?"

"Bo has earned the Intelligence Star, but when he needs encouragement, we can't give it to him, or even let him know he's been nominated. If he ever receives his Star, it'll be done in-house with Agency people present. Not even his family will know about it until he's gone from the Agency or dead."

Griff nodded, holding his cup. "I see he did receive an Intelligence Medal. I worked with him on that New York matter."

"Now you know why Director Kangas wanted you to investigate this ridiculous charge. Bo's been singing your praises around here."

"I respect Bo. He's the reason I'm here."

Griff lifted the pages of the file where he'd inserted the pen. Frank took the hint, leaving the room. Time passed and Griff was ready for lunch when he stumbled upon a Mossad report.

Israel's Intelligence Agency had interrogated the man tackled by Eva and Bo. Turned out that a man by the name of Gath Ramla, a member of Hamas' military wing, had sent the bomber to the bakery. Griff studied Ramla's photo and his mind alerted. Was there something familiar about Ramla? Griff made a note and closed the file.

He stuck his head out the door and Frank gazed up from his computer.

"I'll take you up on lunch if you can get away," Griff said.

Frank rose from his desk. "Yeah, I'll secure Bo's file."

"Wait! I need a magnifying glass."

"There might be one in the supply cabinet. What's up?"

"You'll see.

Frank hurried away returning with a hefty glass. After handing it to Griff, he closed the conference room door. Griff thumbed to the spot at the bottom of the file.

"I'm looking for a photo of Mac and his sub. I thought it was by the report about his career in CIA's Special Activities Division." Griff turned a page. "Here it is."

He stared through the glass at Mac on the *USS Dayton* with the four fishermen.

"Do any of these supposed fishermen look familiar?"

Frank studied the grainy picture with the magnifying glass. "Nope."

Griff flipped to the recent photo of Gath Ramla walking down the street. His pulse skyrocketing, he snatched back the glass.

"Look! He's the same guy! The 'fisherman' standing by Mac is identical to Mossad's photo of Ramla, the terrorist who inspired the bakery bombing."

Frank took the glass, comparing the two pages. "Wow! Griff, you've made a huge breakthrough. Could Ramla be holding a grudge after all this time?"

"Copy my notes and the two photos, which I want Bo to see."

Griff pocketed his pen, astounded by a discovery he'd almost missed. His idea to compare the photos must have flowed from his prayer for God to reveal the truth.

30

After lunch, armed with his notes, Griff raced back to his office where he hurriedly prepared a lead for the FBI Legat at the U.S. Embassy in Manila. He included the file number, certain the special digits would alert the Legat that Director Harmon was monitoring Griff's investigation. He figured that would mean fast action.

He reread his message to the Legat: *Request records check for Ernest King Rider, aka Bo Rider, to establish subject's true identity. Need all files in support of Certificate of Live Birth for Ernest King Rider born July 17, 1977, at Rizal Hospital, Olongapo City, Philippines. Investigate hospital records for infant's birth and for mother, Vivian Rider. Review prenatal medical treatment of Vivian Rider at Subic Bay Naval Hospital and treatment at Subic Bay Naval Hospital for Ernest King Rider, aka Bo, as infant.*

With the push of a button, Griff sent the request electronically. Then he called Eva, grateful she answered.

"I expected your voice mail," he told her.

Eva laughed. "Griff, I must've known you were calling. Budget cuts axed our receptionist so every call goes to voice mail. What's up?"

"I haven't heard from you since the video of you and Bo terrorizing people in Jerusalem with a bomb went viral."

A long pause and then Eva said, "After my photo flashed around the globe, ICE sent me home to work. That's where you reached me. Calls are diverted to my home phone."

"Want to know the latest developments in your bombing?"

"I'm cut off here. Do you know something I don't?"

Griff switched to his sarcastic voice. "Eva, it's me Griff. I always know what's happening and yes, I know things you should."

"My three kids are in school but are due home soon. Scott's at work, so I can't meet you anywhere. Want to stop by on your way home?"

"I can be there in forty minutes."

"Guess I'd better get out of my jammies and robe." Eva sighed.

"I've always suspected when talking with folks in their home virtual offices, they have bed head and are wearing p.j.'s."

"Hey Griff, I rescind my invite," Eva fired back.

"You'll be sorry."

"Bye, Griff."

EVA WAS CURIOUS what Griff had learned of the bakery bombing in Old Jerusalem. She hadn't told Scott much about it, but when her photo popped up all over the World Wide Web, it had been confession time. Scott had hugged her and talked of her changing jobs. As time passed his concern dwindled, mostly because she stayed at home bored out of her mind.

Eva burrowed into her dresser for a warm sweater, realizing how much she missed working cases. She and Griff had busted terrorists, kicked in doors on search warrants, traveled the Middle East posing as scientists, and rappelled from helicopters onto terrorists' ships. They'd risked danger, receiving bumps and bruises together.

She pulled on black slacks and a sweater, tossing her soiled jeans into the laundry. She had more time with family working from home, but Griff's call started her thinking. If ICE didn't reinstate her soon, she'd have to think about plan B, whatever that was. Maybe she'd push Griff to find an opening at the FBI.

Three noisy kids clamoring to pull off their boots brought her running to the mud room.

"How was school?"

"Boring," Andy piped, throwing his jacket on the floor.

Her teenage daughter Kaley smiled, showing her braces. "I earned an A on my essay."

Marty sat on the floor, his face growing red as he yanked on his boots.

"Let Mom help. Andy and Kaley, go finish your homework in your rooms."

"Do we have to?" they whined in unison.

"Yes. I have a meeting."

After helping her youngest son, Eva brought him upstairs to read a book. Pounding on the front door got her scurrying to let Griff in before her kids came back downstairs.

Griff hugged her shoulders. "I just read how close I came to losing you in Jerusalem."

"It's great to see you again," Eva said, thumping his back.

Griff scanned her from top to bottom. "You cleaned up for my visit."

"Yeah, it is a work day."

She led him to the dining room table, grabbing the pot of fresh coffee she'd brewed on the way. "Fill me in before three kiddos invade our privacy. You've ten minutes, tops."

"Have you spoken with Bo since he survived the second bombing?"

Eva nodded. "Briefly after he arrived at his in-laws. He's grateful to be alive and I thank God for answered prayer."

She recalled Bo's desperate tone, but rather than share that tidbit, she'd wait for Griff to reveal his news. She filled a cup as Griff eased into a chair, sadness rippling across his face.

"Not only has the Agency brought Bo and his family to the States, he's banned from the CIA."

Eva's spirits sagged. Bo faced rejection along with the danger he'd been in?

"They think he made himself a target?" she asked incredulously.

Griff gazed intently. "I'm going to tell you something you can never repeat."

"Most of what we work on we cannot repeat."

He leaned in close whispering, "I'm investigating Bo."

"Griff! For what?"

"I'm his only hope. His boss asked me to clear him because of my past work with Bo. The FBI Director agreed."

His shrug revealed he wasn't happy with the assignment and Eva didn't blame him. She poured more hot coffee, thinking she'd have to brew more if Griff didn't divulge what he knew.

"What do they claim Bo did wrong?"

"The international fuss caused by you, my former partner, throwing a bomb in Jerusalem compounded Bo's clandestine search for a mole burrowing into the U.S. Embassy in Tel Aviv."

"For two bombs to go off, he must have been getting close." Eva grimaced.

"Mac Rider lost his leg below the knee. Did Bo tell you of his injuries?"

"Yes. He was mending. I give thanks we weren't injured or killed in the first blast."

Griff nodded, his hands gripping the cup. "The Israeli hospital discovered Bo's blood doesn't match his folks."

"I don't understand."

"Bo has type B blood. Both his parents are type A blood and so it's impossible for them to be his parents. The Ambassador says Bo leaked intel because he's a plant from some terror group."

"That's absurd!" Eva cried, jumping to her feet.

"You and I know it, but it's up to me to prove it."

Eva planted her feet, crossing her arms. "In my book, Bo is a hero. The Agency certainly knows what he's done for his country. I want to help."

"Sit down," Griff scolded. "I'm far from finished. Did you know Bo received the Distinguished Intelligence Medal?"

"No, but I'm impressed. Those are rare." Eva slowly settled back into her chair.

"He received it for our China case involving the U.N."

"Really!"

"He performed heroic work inside China, actions he never admitted to me."

"Me either. Griff, what are you going to do?"

Sweat rimmed her hairline as Eva considered how torn Griff must be and how distressing this investigation must be for Bo. She'd been so busy with life she forgot to be a friend to him.

Griff arched his brows. "DNA tests should clear things up, but I don't have the results."

Stunned at all Bo was dealing with, Eva wanted to unravel the mystery. When she told that to Griff, he opened a thin folder.

"Here's your chance. Look at this photo."

Eva stared at a large man's head, full beard, and dark eyes, feeling shock.

"It's Goliath! He walked in the bakery around the same time as the bomber."

"How do you know his name is Goliath?"

Eva lunged from her chair. "You have to find out his real name. I pointed this huge guy out to Bo, calling him Goliath."

"Tell me everything he said and did in the bakery."

"Bo saw him leave the bakery moments before I chased the terrorist who left the bomb."

Griff pulled out a small pad, scratching a few notes. "Goliath fleeing ahead of the explosion shows his guilty knowledge."

Returning to her seat, Eva snatched up the photo. "Was this taken on surveillance?"

"Score another one for Eva. Mossad sent it to me. The guy you and Bo tackled identified Goliath as his handler after Mossad talked nice to him."

"Sometimes I wish we could use their tactics."

"The photo was taken after the second bombing. Bo reported seeing Goliath outside the ski resort shop before his rental car was obliterated."

Eva heard a thud upstairs. "My kids are getting antsy. If Bo observed Goliath, shouldn't that persuade the Agency Bo is loyal?"

"They believe Mac was targeted by the second blast."

Griff explained how Mac's sub rammed a fishing boat loaded with weapons for Palestinian militants. Then he palmed his moustache. "Eva, I can't believe it, but one of the militants Mac rescued was a much younger Gath Ramla, a militant with Hamas. He is your Goliath."

"There you go." Eva slapped her hand on the table. "Motive and opportunity. Ramla was in the bakery directing the guy we grabbed. Why is he trying to kill Bo?"

"I think he's all about revenge for his dead cohorts on the fishing boat. Bo was a handy substitute for Mac. Goliath probably didn't get the word Mac would be visiting Bo."

Eva raised a finger in the air. "I know. I know. There's a leak in the embassy. They did know Bo's father was coming and Goliath planted the bomb at the ski resort."

"Which brings us full circle." Griff slid the picture back inside his folder. "This photo confirms my belief our embassy leaks like a sieve."

"Are you saying these bombings prevented Bo from tracking down the leaker?"

"That's the size of it. I'm heading to Tel Aviv for a security assessment."

Eva scrunched her hands together. "Your evidence proves Bo is innocent. Goliath wouldn't kill his own source of information within the embassy."

"Wrong," Griff said, looking tense. "Bo could leak to a cohort, who gave info to your Goliath, Gath Ramla. Maybe Ramla doesn't know where his intel comes from. I know this, we have to stop him."

"My mind is turning in a thousand directions." Eva jerked her head at laughter upstairs.

"And I can hear my ten minutes are up," Griff said, rising.

Eva laid a hand on his arm. "I'm straining at the leash, buddy. Slacking off isn't me."

"Your ID of Goliath should push Mossad to act. I'll include in my report how you saw him at the bakery. That should pressure the Agency to send your statement on to Mossad."

Eva walked Griff to the door. "I'm going to call Bo and encourage him to hang in there."

"Pray I'll untangle this mess. It's weighing heavy on Bo. I need the DNA report."

Griff slipped out the door just as Marty trailed down the steps from upstairs, his hands clutching a truck.

"Mom, my wheel fell off. Can you fix it?"

Eva knelt at his side, deciding to call Bo after dinner. She owed him more, but maybe she could help in other ways too.

31

It had been a week since Griff requested records from Manila. He dashed back from an early lunch, opening his e-mail folder. Hey, he finally had a response from the Manila Legat. With great anticipation, he opened the file. His eyes fled down the screen:

Inquiry at U.S. Embassy and Rizal Hospital failed to locate evidence re: Certificate of Live Birth for Ernest King Rider, aka Bo Rider. All hospital records prior to 1980 were destroyed by volcano.

Griff stared in disbelief. He blinked, reading the brief response a second time. He could only close the document, disappointed. What should he do next? Even if he searched the Federal Records Center, he'd unearth some musty form, most likely a copy of what Bo already submitted with his CIA application. Stymied, Griff knew hospital records would have affirmed Vivian's account of her hurried delivery at the off-base hospital.

He typed the bad news into his summary report, defeat building with each keystroke. In five minutes he'd leave to follow a software designer who was meeting a Chinese businessman, so he shut down his computer. Yet claims of espionage against Bo continued to puzzle Griff and he heaved a sigh.

Why didn't he have the DNA results in hand? When he'd last called her the FBI lab tech complained, "I'm up to my eyebrows in pending tests."

Perhaps a friendly call wouldn't hurt. He grabbed the phone, calling Carol Howland. Rats. She'd just left for lunch, or so the secretary said. Forced to leave a message, Griff yanked on his jacket and hurried to his bucar, hoping this other case wouldn't take all afternoon. He was eager to corner Carol before she left for the day.

GRIFF REACHED THE FBI parking lot in Manassas at four forty. He raced to his office, tossed his jacket on the back of his chair, and dialed Carol Howland.

She answered and Griff could hear her typing on her keyboard.

"It's Griff again."

"Agent Topping, you read my mind. I just finished my report and was about to call you. I noticed by the case number that Director Harmon is directly involved."

"What's your conclusion?" His pulse started to rise as he anticipated her reply.

"There is no match."

"No match! What do you mean?"

"The sample you submitted from Ernest King Rider does not match the DNA for Douglas MacArthur Rider or Vivian Rider."

Stunned beyond words, Griff forced his mind into gear. "Can you give me a certainty of percentage, like ninety-nine point nine percent?"

"We're not even calculating a percentage. It's at the opposite end of the scale."

"The opposite end?"

"Listen. Nada, no match, no way. My report will be ready for you tomorrow."

"There's nothing more we can do?"

A long pause. "You don't mean to suggest that I should falsify my report?"

Griff balled his fist. "No! It's just that I felt certain there'd be a match."

"Is this a real case or some quality assurance gimmick testing my lab?"

"Of course it's real," Griff snapped, his patience reaching its limit.

"The names Douglas MacArthur, a famous Army General, and Ernest King, a famous Navy Admiral, make me suspicious."

"Carol, I can safely say these people are strong military supporters and name their children after American heroes."

"You wanted a different result and I hate giving you negative news."

"It is what it is. Send your report. Thanks for your help."

Griff pushed his chair back, his mind whirling. Who was Bo Rider? Hospital records destroyed, by a volcano no less. Carol couldn't have dreamed up a stranger scenario. Eva was a savvy investigator, one of the best, and she believed Bo was for real. Griff considered himself a decent agent and fair judge of character. How could he be so far off the mark?

Bo's CIA file had disclosed he was a hero and no terrorist. Photos pointed to Eva's Goliath, Gath Ramla, as the planner and executioner of the bombings. Griff's own scratchy notes summed it up: *Shellie Karnack, Embassy Security Director, and Hal Cohen, U.S. Ambassador, suspected a leak. Blood type different from parents. Not adopted. Is Bo Rider a mole?*

What did Shellie and Hal see that both Griff and Eva had missed?

Working as special investigator to Director Harmon meant Griff had no partner to rely on and his idea tank hovered on empty. He'd seen with his own eyes the results of Bo's secret work for his country. The public would never know of his accomplishments, maybe not even his wife or kids. Something smelled horribly wrong. He picked up the phone and called Eva.

"It's Griff. Where you at?"

She laughed. "Sitting here at my virtual desk. Why are you calling my cell?"

"I assumed you were out tracking some terrorist. Call my office on a landline."

Seconds later his desk phone rang. "Eva, remember the spook I'm shadowing?"

"How could I remember it? You never told me."

"Yes I did, at your house the other day."

"Griff, think," she said, her voice sparked with sarcasm. "You never told me about any spook."

"You're right, my brain is rattled. This case you know nothing about, well the DNA records came back negative. His DNA doesn't match his parents and he's not adopted."

Total silence.

"Exactly, but DNA doesn't lie." Even saying that hit Griff's stomach like a cement block.

"And there are no birth records?"

"Destroyed by a volcano. His folks filed a form with the embassy claiming Ernest King Rider was born. That's the extent of his past."

"School records?"

"Bo's elementary school closed its doors fifteen years ago. It's like it never existed."

Eva sighed. "Can his mother add anything? Maybe there was a mix-up in the nursery and Mom was given the wrong baby."

"I hoped it would be something simple. Vivian was on her way to the U.S. Naval hospital, but the housekeeper drove her instead to a local hospital. Seems that Bo, I mean our guy, was the only non-Filipino baby in the hospital. Not much room for error there."

"Someone is alleging he's a plant from some Filipino terrorist group, right?"

"Yeah, people in the State Department."

"That's not saying much," Eva sputtered. "If he were adopted in the Philippines at age twelve by Americans, it might be plausible even if he was an Anglo child. But his parents have cared for him since birth. How can State allege something so crazy?"

"You're not helping. I need a logical explanation or you-know-who's career is toast."

"I have an idea. It may turn up nothing."

"Go ahead. I'm desperate."

"Americans must submit a copy of their birth certificate for a passport. You-know-who probably has several, a personal passport, an Official Diplomatic one, and probably another half-dozen in other names."

"What's your point?" Griff wiped sweat from his forehead.

"Ask State to search for every American male born during the same week in the Philippines and the names of those who subsequently applied for a passport."

"What are you saying, that he might have been accidently switched with another baby during a post-natal visit at the U.S. Naval hospital or something?"

"I don't know. I'm grasping at straws."

At least Eva had come up with a viable plan. Griff fired up his computer.

"I owe you, but I have visions of me traveling the world taking DNA samples from twenty men, all the same age."

"If I brainstorm anything else, I'll call. I don't buy the double spook scenario. I have too much respect for our friend."

"Me too."

Griff hung up and in moments he prepared a request for the State Department passport applications just as Eva had suggested. If this didn't jar loose some evidence, Griff was under water and so was Bo.

32

Three weeks flew by with Griff doing surveillance on the Chinese businessman. Bo's dilemma, however, stayed glued to his mind. On Wednesday, he finished a surveillance report, when the office assistant dropped a stack of papers on his desk with a thud.

"You'll be working late. Looks like you ordered a ton of passport applications."

"Is that what you brought me?"

"About a dozen," she shot back and stomped off.

"Thanks," he called. "I've been waiting for these."

Griff quickly plucked off the top application.

Donna Marie Higgins, born July 18, 1977, in Manila looked at him from a black and white photocopy of her passport photo. Donna was female, but at least Griff's request had been understood. She'd been born in the local hospital the day after Bo.

Griff sorted applications in two piles, women in one and males in the other, ending up with seven females and five males. Bo's photo sat on top. Moving aside the ladies, Griff slid Bo's passport application from the pile and everything matched what Griff already knew.

One of the three remaining applications surprised him. Vivian Rider had said Bo was the only non-Filipino baby born at Rizal Hospital on July 17, but here was a photo of an Anglo male born at the same hospital on July 16. Did baby Daniel have a connection to Bo? Griff set Daniel's file aside as a possibility.

He thumbed through the apps. Sure enough, another boy had been born at 2:27 a.m. a mere five hours after Bo. However, since baby Theo's birth occurred after midnight, his birth date was July 18. Griff hurried to locate phone numbers via the computer. It took several calls before his plan coalesced: He'd fly to Tennessee in the morning. As Griff eliminated two remaining males, he felt encouraged. Perhaps he'd stumbled onto an innocent solution to Bo's problem after all.

GRIFF PULLED OFF the busy highway onto a rough country road becoming steeper with each mile he drove. Trees rose up, their branches hanging over the road forming a ghostly tunnel on the March morning. After yesterday's phone call, he'd grabbed another

DNA vial, arranged for a flight and rental car. Adrenaline surged through Griff as he climbed and he shoved the car into first gear. Was he really minutes away from solving the elusive mystery of Bo's birth?

On the mountain road, traffic thinned to a trickle. Griff ascended through curves on the alert for his next turn. All of a sudden he passed a lone driveway marked by a reflector and he braked hard. Griff hit reverse, then cranked a hard right, following the asphalt. Good thing he'd picked a warm day to come. He'd hate to navigate this hill on sheer ice.

Griff arrived at a tall iron gate, which neatly separated two stucco walls bending on each side. Wrought iron letters above the gate announced "Lands Beginning," just as he expected. Griff rolled the car beside a small control box, lowered his window, and pushed a button.

A computer voice greeted him with, "Do not trespass. Survivors will be prosecuted."

Spotting no microphone, he yelled, "It's Griff Topping. I am expected."

Again the computer barked orders like an electronic drill sergeant. "If you are a requested guest, the gate will open. Move forward, but stay put until the gate closes or you will be sorry."

The gates swung inward and Griff drove through, stopping on the yellow line as instructed, curious about the owner. It took about twenty seconds, but then the gates closed. Griff followed the asphalt drive, winding along trees and flower beds, gaining altitude as he went.

Had he traveled a mile since his turnoff? He finally rounded a bend and there in front of him was a long and low ranch house with a connecting four-stall garage. He pulled into the circle drive, parking close to the front door. Griff gathered his leather portfolio and patted his sport coat pocket. Yup, he was ready for the interview.

He hiked up a few cement steps, wind whistling down his shirt collar. After banging a large brass door knocker a few times against the heavy oak door, Griff was greeted by a shorter but fine-looking man with a well-exercised physique.

"If it isn't Griff Topping, FBI super-agent. Come in if you must."

Griff stepped inside, flipping open his leather credential case with the inlaid gold badge.

Unlike most people, Theo took time to read Griff's credentials before handing them back.

"So you've convinced me, you are *the* superman."

"I'm a Special Agent, but many times I wish I was a super-agent. You must be Theo."

"Bingo! Since you're the real thing, I'll even shake your hand."

Griff folded his credential case back into his pocket, hiding a grin over Theo's peculiar funny bone. Being greeted by that idiotic computer voice after the meandering driveway should have been Griff's first clue. He examined the large foyer, his eyes settling on a knight in shining armor glaring from the corner as if it would cut Griff to pieces with its sword at any moment.

"Nice place you have here, but remote," Griff quipped. "Good thing you provided detailed directions or I'd be in some civil war battlefield by now without a gray uniform."

Theo slapped Griff's back. "A sharp one. It might be fun. Come with me and we'll see."

Griff followed his enigmatic host toward a complete wall of large windows. Theo talked over his shoulder, "I promise not to put your interview on air. As I said on the phone, though I own radio and TV stations, technology gives me freedom. Gaze upon my Shangri-La and live."

Griff admired the scene, a vast meadow falling away from the house, bare limbs of bordering trees appearing like starving sentries. He glimpsed beyond brown horses grazing through the trees to the highway, imagining what a plush view Theo would have in summer.

Theo clasped his hands behind his back. "I wouldn't trade my heaven for the clatter and bustle of city. I accomplish all I need to from my office downstairs."

Noting Theo's serious tone, Griff pointed below. "Is that the road I took up here?"

"If you hadn't spotted my reflectors, you'd be on the mountain wandering around."

"Lucky me. I'm a trained investigator." Griff flashed a grin, seeking to move Theo along.

He must have taken the hint because Theo remarked, "Tell me about your investigation into the Philippines."

Griff relaxed on a leather sofa while Theo perched in a chair adjacent to the couch, looking like a bird wanting to fly over his mountain. Griff opened his portfolio, reminding Theo of their phone conversation: that Griff was investigating twelve persons born near Subic Bay, Philippines, around July 17, 1977.

Griff looked up from his notes. "I'm not free to disclose much, but it may involve someone assuming another person's identity."

Theo shifted his position, looking directly at Griff.

"So you found me. I was born in the local hospital a day later. What next?"

"Tell me about your childhood."

Griff wrote nothing for fear Theo would stay guarded. Rather, he lowered his arms and listened to Theo's tale.

"My parents lived in the jungle as missionaries. My older sister, Beatrice, was born as were other missionary babies in the city. Near my delivery time, my parents traveled from the jungle, taking a hotel room in the city until I was ready to pop out."

"You were raised in the Philippines?"

"When I turned seven, my folks grew tired of jungle life."

"Oh?" Griff leaned forward. Perhaps their reason for leaving would shed light on the case.

"No big mystery. I fell off a rope swing and busted my arm. We left for medical help and never went back. Too many mosquitoes," Theo added, swatting the air around him.

It was then Griff noticed Theo's left arm did not extend all the way.

"So I've heard. Are your folks still living?"

Theo raised his jaw, blurting out, "Griff, are you a Christian?"

"I'm a brand new believer. Why?" he asked, hoping to deflect Theo's curiosity.

"Which denomination?"

"I'm not sure."

Theo made an arc with his crooked left arm. "What do I call you, Catholic, Methodist, Baptist, Presbyterian? What kind of church do you attend?"

"A large Bible Church in Virginia, outside Washington. Does it matter?"

Theo's lips turned into a lopsided grin. "You don't seem to recognize my family name, so I'm having fun. My father is well known in Christian circles."

"I'm not familiar with any Van Horns." Griff shrugged. "No disrespect to you."

Theo jumped off the leather couch, striding over to the windows. With his back to Griff, he added, "It's refreshing to meet someone who is not interested in me because of my father, Dr. Hendrik Van Horn. He's the theologian who teaches prophecy on radio and TV."

"I'd say congrats, but then you might be offended," Griff joked.

Theo slowly turned wearing his lopsided grin. "Topping, you're all right. A sense of humor goes a long way in this miserable world. My secret's out so call me Ted."

He leaned over, picked up a book from a corner table, and handed it to Griff.

"Flip over my father's book about Israel and see his photo. Maybe you saw him on TV."

Ted said that so pointedly, Griff sensed a test. He turned over Van Horn's book. A man held out his arms across a body of water.

"He's distinguished with his graying hair. I might have seen him on television."

"Perhaps on one of my stations. Father and I buy and sell many stations, though we are separating them from the rest of the ministry. I am buying him out."

Griff filed away that morsel. "The birth certificate issued by the U.S. Consulate lists you as Theo. You prefer Ted to your given name?"

"I'm going out on a limb here, but is Griff short for Griffin?"

Griff simply smiled.

Ted returned to the sofa. "So you understand why I did not care to go through life being called Theo after Van Gogh's brother. Once I started school in the States, I became Ted and fought off bullies with my good right arm."

He paused, squaring his chin. For a split second, Griff saw a small boy who never fit in.

"All set?" Ted asked. "My interview with the new governor starts in thirty minutes."

"You're on the air like your father?"

"I broadcast freedom and justice issues only, which are my passion."

"You'd enjoy a tour of FBI Headquarters. Give me a call if you're in D.C." Griff handed Ted his card. "You could help me with another item before I leave."

"You want my father's autograph?"

"Yeah, in gold lettering." Griff chuckled. "Seriously, I need your DNA sample. Here's your chance to further the cause of justice."

"How so?" Ted asked, a glimmer in his eye.

"By helping me eliminate and narrow down hundreds of other leads."

Before Ted objected, Griff lifted his hand. "Your sample will be used for that sole purpose and will be destroyed immediately unlike samples from convicted criminals."

Ted lifted his head slightly. "You go around the country demanding people surrender their rights and genetic history?"

"I'm not demanding. Just hoping you'll assist my investigation."

"And I liked you, Topping. I'll pass on your little request to my attorney."

Griff reached inside his coat pocket and thrust a folded piece of paper into Ted's hands.

"In case you didn't cooperate, I brought my big guns."

Ted opened the folded paper. "What is this?"

"A Federal Grand Jury subpoena ordering your appearance in Alexandria, Virginia, next week. Show your attorney. In fact, bring your attorney along, but he or she must wait outside."

"I have to fly from Chattanooga?"

Griff sensed Ted softening, his aversion to traveling to any city apparent in his eyes.

"Yes," Griff replied. "The Grand Jury will request your DNA sample. You'll be free to leave Virginia once you give a swab from your cheek. Refuse and you'll be jailed for contempt."

Ted launched to his feet and began pacing in his own living room. "You are acting tough because I asked to speak with my attorney."

Griff shook his head, knowing he'd leave with Ted's sample.

"Having it your way is no problem. You'll be paid a mileage allowance or airfare as long as the airfare doesn't exceed the mileage allowance."

"Fine for you, Topping. You want to snatch me away from my important work."

Griff rose to his feet. "I came to your mountain top, sparing you inconvenience."

"Okay." Ted stopped pacing. "I'd rather give you the sample right now."

"Without your attorney's advice?"

"Yes, then we can forget about your little subpoena."

"I'm afraid we can't do that." Griff smiled. "I served the subpoena and have no authority to take it back."

Ted slapped his thigh like a petulant child. "Great. What can I do?"

"Here's my suggestion. I take your sample and tell the Grand Jury you furnished DNA in hopes of avoiding the trip. If the Chairperson feels there's no need to question you under oath, they'll send you a letter granting you relief."

"What are the chances your 'suggestion' will fly?"

"With your sample, I'll recommend the relief."

"Time's ticking. I cannot keep the governor waiting."

Griff removed a vial from his inner coat pocket, relieved Ted would comply.

"All I have to do is run this cotton swab around the inside of your cheek."

Ted stepped closer and snapped, "Do it," before opening his mouth. Griff maneuvered the implement between some expensive looking teeth, swabbed Ted's cheek, and retracted the swab back into the vial, replacing the cap.

"We're done."

Griff strode back to the entrance with Ted hot on his heels.

"You will take care of the Grand Jury then?"

"If I need anything more, I'll call you."

Ted opened the door for Griff. "When you first phoned, I suspected you were investigating an adoption agency in the Philippines."

Griff jerked his head around. This could be the answer. "Why did you think that?"

"Through the years my father and I had many disputes. He and I are different and I have accused my mother of adopting me in the Philippines."

Griff shook Ted's hand. "I've heard colleagues say something similar. A curse of youth."

He hurried to the rental car, wondering if Ted's DNA would provide the missing link or if he'd fly to Phoenix to meet Daniel, who was born the day prior to Bo.

Griff waved a thank-you at Ted, but the large wooden door had already closed.

33

The week following Griff's return from Ted Van Horn's mountain ground slowly. He submitted Ted's DNA to the lab, so far hearing nothing. Rather than fly to Phoenix on a potential goose chase, he immersed himself in an old file referred by the Bureau of Indian Affairs. Fat chance of getting money back from the fraudulent claimant after all these years.

He doodled across a clean legal pad when his ringing desk phone saved him from the case he had no heart to pursue.

"Griff here," he barked.

The clatter of suspenseful music blasted his ear. Had he heard something similar on TV?

More slowly he said, "Hello, this is Griff Topping."

"Hey Gibbs, it's Abby. You finally got it right."

Music played and he had no idea who was calling. "Sorry, you have the wrong number."

"Don't hang up, Gibbs. It's Abby. Agent Topping, don't you watch *NCIS*?"

Griff roared in laughter. "So I did recognize the music."

"I downloaded it on my smart phone. This is Carol, your Abby in the DNA lab. That makes you Gibbs and I'm gonna make your day."

"Make it then."

"Remember samples you sent from Douglas MacArthur Rider and his wife Vivian?"

"The ones that didn't match their son, Bo."

"Well, I'd like to give you a happy tap on the back of your head. You've done good."

"Is Ted Van Horn a match for the Riders' son?"

"Ninety-nine point nine, eight percent."

"Oh no!"

"Oh yes! Is that bad, Gibbs?"

"Yeah Abby, I mean Carol, it is. That means a hospital in the Philippines accidently or intentionally switched two newborns. This is going to shock a great many people."

A sigh in Griff's ear and Carol asked, "What will you do?"

"Run DNA on Ted's folks. They could be the parents of Ernest King Rider, aka Bo. If not, there's a third set of parents out there."

"Cool. I'm reuniting families instead of identifying criminals. Keep me in the loop, Gibbs. I love it."

"Thanks for the fast response, Carol. You've thrown the ball back in my court."

He replaced the phone handset, a new quandary boiling in his mind. How to kindly tell Bo that he wasn't the son of Mac and Vivian Rider? And would the test results clear Bo as the embassy leaker? Whose son was he, really?

Griff faced another dilemma. Should he send Director Kangas a memo or simply call Langley? He stared at the wallpaper on his computer screen. No, the risk was too great; whatever Griff wrote would end up in Bo's personnel file. He phoned Frank Deming, Kangas' capable assistant, instead.

Frank seemed eager for results, asking, "Have you good news?"

"Ah, no. Does Director Kangas want a memo on the DNA results or a verbal update?"

"Nothing in writing until this muddle is resolved."

"Should I drive to Langley?" Griff looked at his watch. He could be there in an hour.

"The Director's out of town. Brief me over the phone if you're secure."

"I am, but I take no pleasure telling you that Bo is *not* the son of Mac and Vivian Rider."

"Ugh, I can't believe it! I've known Bo for years. He's a square-shooter."

"My sentiments exactly. I suspect the hospital switched two babies. Maybe it was intentional, I don't know. There are two other sets of possible parents."

"Where do we go from here?" Frank asked.

Griff grunted into the phone. "I am taking the first plane to Tennessee for another round of who-dun-it with Ted Van Horn. I have a hunch."

GRIFF RACED FROM THE NASHVILLE AIRPORT, no stomach for another cryptic meet with Ted. But he couldn't think of an alternate way to resolve Bo's true identity. Griff had urged the Assistant U.S. Attorney to send Ted a letter canceling his Grand Jury appearance. He'd called yesterday to arrange a second interview and Ted had asked, "Something wrong with the cells in my mouth?"

"I'd rather discuss it in person," Griff had replied, "but this is no joking matter."

"It's your dime. I'm not flying to Virginia," Ted had said and hung up.

Today's drive from the airport was easier because Griff knew the drill. Ted swung open the massive wooden door before Griff's fingers could grab the knocker.

"If it isn't my super-agent. Where's your yellow cape?"

"I fly, but in airplanes."

"Come in." Ted stepped back and gesturing to the living room. "I had a strange feeling I hadn't seen the last of you."

The two men paused, looking out the windows at horses romping around a fenced-in meadow. Griff pocketed his hands, dreading the turmoil to come.

"I couldn't bring myself to tell you over the phone."

"We'd better sit. I don't want to become faint and bash my head on the floor."

A replay of his last visit, Griff sunk to the sofa and Ted in his side chair. Griff pulled up on the crease of his slacks, getting more comfortable and looking Ted in the eyes.

"You were right."

"About what?" Ted asked, running a hand through his hair.

"DNA confirms Hendrik Van Horn is *not* your father."

Ted's whole body pitched forward. His eyes bored into Griff's.

"How can that be? Are you sure?"

"There's no room for doubt."

"You've compared my DNA with my parents?" Ted wet his lips, no doubt reality seeping in. "I mean Hendrik and Adriana Van Horn?"

"I need their DNA, but I have samples from a retired Naval officer and his wife. Theirs' is a perfect match with yours."

Ted straightened his back, planting both hands on his knees. He said nothing.

Griff cleared his throat, telling Ted how the officer had been stationed at Subic Bay on July 17, 1978. "His wife delivered a boy in the same hospital five hours before you were born."

"Are you implying the wrong parents took me home?"

"Maybe the hospital staff brought you to the wrong room. I detest bringing you such news. While I know who you really are, I don't know what happened to your parent's son." Griff felt stricken even saying it. "Ah, I mean the baby Mrs. Van Horn had."

"Who are my bio-parents?"

Griff shook his head. "I'm not cleared to tell you yet."

"You're not *cleared*? This is my life. What gives the government the power to decide if I can learn my true identity?"

"It's more complicated than your life. Recall I'm investigating a possible impostor who is using someone else's identity."

Ted's eyes grew wide and Griff palmed his moustache. "Rather than tell the Van Horns about your true identity, I came here first. I'd like your assistance in approaching them."

"You mean with my folks who you say really aren't my folks?"

Ted glared and Griff saw hurt deepening around the edges of his brown eyes.

"I've talked to your bio-parents and they are terrific people who are cooperating fully. I plan to ask the Van Horns for help in identifying their birth child."

"Do my birth parents know about me?"

"Not yet. You're the first to know."

Ted turned to stare out his windows. "I tried convincing myself when you called again that I'd be finished with you. It seems you're the hand to my arm and we need each other."

"Will you call Hendrik and Adriana to introduce me? It might soften the blow."

"Can we wait a few days, while I make sense of it all?"

While Griff understood Ted's shock, he needed him to make that call.

"I refuse to fly over these mountains again and you're not coming to Virginia."

Ted looked at his watch, letting out a tortured sigh. "Let's go to my office and call Father. I mean Hendrik Van Horn, a man I never knew."

His once booming voice trailed away and Ted hurried from the room, leaving Griff to follow, wondering if he'd done right in dumping such astonishing news on Ted without forewarning. Suspicion lodged in Griff's brain. Hendrik Van Horn probably wouldn't take too kindly to Griff and what he needed him to do.

34

G riff strode into Ted's office a floor beneath the living room concerned Dr. Van Horn might not be available. It felt like he'd stepped into a TV set ready for filming. The commercial broadcast camera perched on a tripod dolly and studio lights dangling from the ceiling evoked a synergy in stark contrast to the idyllic meadow beyond sheets of expensive glass.

Interior walls built of cedar wood were crammed with photos of Ted and the Van Horns taken on various sets. Griff noticed a coiffed woman talking into a headset and typing on the other side of built-in glass windows. Ted offered no explanation.

Griff sat in a chair across from a carved desk, waiting for Ted to place the phone on speaker. *Beep beep* of a speed dialer and two rings later, a friendly female answered, "Dr. Van Horn's office."

Ted swiveled his head to speak into the phone. "I dialed Father's direct line."

"He is leaving to meet your mother for lunch. Can he call you back?"

"It's important."

"Hold on."

The line went silent and Ted swiped back his hair nervously. "Griff, my folks live in Colorado Springs. Father's television ministry broadcasts from there."

The desk phone chirped alive. "Ted, your father will phone in a couple hours."

"Sorry, but an FBI agent from Virginia is in my office. I need to speak to him now."

The line went mute again. In seconds, the stern voice of an irritated father barked, "What's this about? I warned you not to sell the Roanoke station to a syndicate. They were far too eager, but you couldn't resist their inflated offer. The Feds are onto something."

"Father, you're on speakerphone."

Hendrik continued his tirade. "The Feds take their D.C. cases to Alexandria, which is why it is called the rocket docket. Their jurists are conservative and always convict. If this FBI agent is from Alexandria, then you've landed us in one whale of a jam."

Ted's face turned crimson, blood vessels protruding in his fore-head. Griff didn't interfere, but discomfort grew as he tried to ignore Van Horn ripping into Ted. Besides, he'd chosen a skimpy chair that didn't fit his six-foot-frame. Ted grabbed the receiver.

"Father, you won't let me wiggle in a word. The agent can tell you."

Ted thrust Griff the phone, heading upstairs. Griff listened. Hendrik had grown quiet.

"This is Special Agent Griff Topping, assigned to the FBI office in Manassas. I have interviewed Ted for a special case. I suggested he explain things to you, but he's deferred to me."

"Agent Topping, we will cooperate fully. I told Ted that I suspected the syndicate buying our Roanoke station, but he rarely listens to his father."

"My meeting with Ted has zero to do with broadcast licensing, which is why I asked him to break the news. My investigation involves the birth of boys born at Rizal Hospital in Olongapo City in nineteen seventy-seven. I must locate the families of those babies."

"Ted was born there."

"Correct, and the FBI has DNA. I hate saying this, but he is not your son."

"That's absurd!" Hendrik groaned and then became deathly silent.

Griff allowed the man a moment to absorb the shocking news.

Finally Hendrik sucked in a loud breath. "Surely, a mistake has been made. Neither my wife nor I submitted DNA samples for comparison."

"The FBI compared Ted's DNA with a former naval officer and his wife. She gave birth in the same hospital as Mrs. Van Horn within five hours of your child. Test results confirm Ted is the biological child of the captain and his wife."

Dr. Van Horn's breathing became labored and Griff felt a twinge of guilt. What a crude way for Hendrik Van Horn to discover his son was not his son.

"Sir, did I lose you?" Griff asked.

"No. I am more stunned than I have ever been in my life."

"Ted is too, sir."

Dr. Van Horn peppered Griff with questions. "How can I break this to my wife? How do we find out what happened? Who is our real son?"

"I had hoped Ted and I could tell you together; however, if you and Mrs. Van Horn will submit DNA, I can compare yours to a sample from a man born within the same twenty-four-hour period. It's possible the babies were switched in error or intentionally."

Taking in short breaths, Dr. Van Horn said, "This shocks me, but explains things I will not trouble you with. Was one other boy born in Rizal Hospital around July seventeenth?"

"I have found three born within twenty-four hours of each other, including Ted."

"And you have DNA from only one of those boys?"

"Two. Ted and another boy born within five hours."

Dr. Van Horn grunted. "I am not telling my wife. She is undergoing chemo for breast cancer. In a month I arrive in D.C. for a Christian broadcasters meeting. I may bring Ted's mom, ah, Adriana. We can discuss things after she's regained her strength."

"I am sorry to hear about your wife."

A tattered memory of Griff's first wife dying of ovarian cancer shot through him like a stray bullet. But he recalled God's tender mercies in bringing a new life and Griff felt composed.

"Our prayers are being answered for God's healing," Dr. Van Horn said quietly.

"Sir, I will add her to my prayers. I have seen power there in my life."

"Thank you. We need prayer to solve this tangle without more hurt. I do not understand how the Lord allowed this, but His ways are mysterious. There is a reason and I mean to find it."

Was it Griff's imagination or had the hard edge disappeared from Dr. Van Horn's voice? Griff thought he heard footsteps so he gave the man his e-mail address.

"What else do you know about this sinister switching of babies?" he asked Griff.

"Before I tell you more, we need to identify your son."

"And how long will that take?"

Griff's hands grew moist holding the phone. "Without your DNA, time marches on."

"This is incredible." Dr. Van Horn cleared his throat. "May I speak with Ted?"

At that moment, Ted entered his office carrying a tray with two cups and pecan rolls, setting these on the desk.

"Ted just arrived. I'll put him on."

"One more question, please."

"Sir?"

"You want to compare our DNA with that of another. Is it from a living donor?"

A slight smile formed on Griff's face. "Yes and here's Ted."

Griff handed Ted the phone. Silently he picked up coffee and Danish before slipping upstairs to give Ted much needed privacy to talk with the man he'd believed was his father for more than thirty years.

Taking a moment in the foyer, Griff drained the coffee and ate his roll, wondering how to tell Bo the Riders were not his bio-parents. A wiser course would be to convey the shocking news eye to eye, man to man. Would Bo's reaction end their friendship?

HENDRIK VAN HORN ATE a lonely dinner, his heart aching. Adriana had gone to sleep early, which was fine because he did not want to even hint to her what Agent Topping had divulged. Hendrik felt crushed and stripped of everything he once held dear. To leave the jungles with a son, only to find out so many years later they had taken the wrong child home was more than he could bear.

He pushed away the half-eaten plate of chicken and vegetables, wandering outside to the wide deck. Here he bowed his head to God under millions of stars on the frosty night, sweat dotting his forehead and his heart pounding wildly.

"Almighty God," he breathed out a whisper. "Help me cope. For thirty-five years I considered Ted my son and tried to train him right. You know my concern over his choices."

Tears flowed from his eyes as the full weight of his failure hit him squarely in the chest. He'd been wrong. Something needed to be said before God would hear his prayer.

"Forgive me, Father, for not honoring the son you brought me. Guide Ted and his wife, Ramona, in their future steps. My time as his father is over."

Hendrik wept openly and as he shed tears long suppressed from years of turmoil with Ted, grief began to lessen. Trust, ever so gradually, filled his heart and mind. God was not through with him yet. Another thirty-five-year-old man lived and breathed in the world, a man Hendrik might one day call "son."

"Almighty Father, thank you for peace I do not deserve. Thank you for your Son, Jesus."

He rubbed his lower back, putting a hand on the door handle ready to step inside when a dreadful thought assailed him. Perhaps the man who would be his son had never heard of Jesus. He should do something about that right away. With a new purpose springing in his steps and bubbling in his heart, Hendrik strolled to his office where he took paper from his desk drawer, making notes of everything the agent had told him.

There was not one moment to lose. He placed a call, leaving a stern voice message: "This is Hendrik. Call me as I need your help on a most urgent matter."

35

Precisely at ten o'clock the next morning, Hendrik brought Adriana a cup of green tea and a light breakfast, as was his custom when not traveling. He found her resting on the sofa, her feet in slippers, gazing out the window at the Rocky Mountains. Snow fell, dusting aspen trees and loading evergreen branches with heavy white ornaments from the heavens.

"Martha baked cranberry scones, but they are hot." He grimaced. "I burned my tongue."

Adriana lifted her arms for the tray, her gray eyes rimmed in red.

"Didn't you sleep well, Rik?" she asked in a hushed voice.

Hendrik smiled. He hadn't heard her use his nickname in years.

"I rose early to arrange a business meeting. Did I disturb you coming to bed so late?"

Adriana lifted a delicate cup to her pale lips, taking a long sip before answering.

"I awoke thinking of the Philippines. Remember the night Ted was born?"

Hendrik's heart quivered. She must have overheard his phone call yesterday with the federal agent. Was this the time to confess the truth?

"We traveled by foot for three hours to get you to the local hospital," he replied.

She looked into his eyes and gently put her cup on the tray.

"We named him Theo after your brother. He was such a beautiful baby with big eyes. I'll never forget how as a toddler he ran through the jungle, pretending he was chasing tigers."

Hendrik moved the tray from her lap to the table, then pulled a chair closer.

"We loved mission work until Ted fell from the swing, breaking his arm. After we left the village, he never seemed the same little boy. Something changed."

Adriana briefly shut her eyes. "Yes, our sweet boy grew into a man who differs with you on most subjects. Even his flying to visit me seems a stretch for him. It's hurt me, Rik. He rarely calls Beatrice, his sister, preferring to hide with Ramona on their mountain."

"Sweetheart, that's his choice and we must let him live the way he sees fit."

Hendrik sought her eyes and she returned his tender look.

"Theo called me this morning, sounding perturbed. Is there something I should know?"

Martha, their housekeeper, walked into the room with hands on her hips. "Your ten thirty appointment is here. He came early but says it is urgent."

"Take him to my office. I will be right along."

Martha spun on her heel. Hendrik placed Adriana's cold hands into his, forcing a smile.

"Theo and I traded harsh words yesterday and I need to ask his forgiveness. Pray for my relationship with him."

Tears pooled in her eyes. "I have long known things were not right between you two."

"We will talk later."

Hendrik lifted the tea things to her lap and hurried from the room. He had business to finish before he disclosed to his wife Ted was not the baby she bore. But how strange she should dream of the night he had been born. Perhaps God was preparing her.

He passed Martha polishing the hall table, saying over his shoulder, "Prepare a special dinner for us, Martha. Your comforting chicken pot pie would go over well I should think."

Martha shoved her cloth in her apron pocket. "I shall start potatoes and simmer the chicken. I had not decided if Adriana would have an appetite."

"She will have."

Hendrik turned the knob to his office, greeting a slender man wearing a brown leather jacket, sunglasses hanging lazily by an arm from the top pocket.

"Dylan, I appreciate you arriving on short notice."

"I beat the snowplows out of my ranch. The roads from Pueblo were tricky but I made it."

Hendrik handed Dylan Burns a folder and blue book.

"That is my son's baby album, where you will learn the name of a missionary woman who bore a baby in Olongapo City when Adriana had our son. Read my notes first."

Dylan opened the file and Hendrik paused by the window watching snow pile on the outside deck. He'd woken up feeling strong, but facing Dylan pained him more than he realized. The former State Trooper joined him by the window.

"Do you buy that garbage Ted isn't your son? Is someone trying to blackmail you?"

"Keep your voice down. I called my D.C. lawyer and after placing calls, he assures me Special Agent Griff Topping can be trusted. You are the best private investigator west of the Mississippi. Will you make this number one priority?"

"To rein in this Griff Topping guy?"

"No! To find Dorothy Ramsey and her son. Adriana wrote in Ted's baby book the other boy's name is Daniel Ramsey, born July seventeenth or sixteenth."

"And when I find Dorothy or the son?"

"We cross that bridge when we have to. Time is of the essence. Get me something."

Dylan took his orders, leaving Hendrik satisfied the PI would find the Ramseys. He hurried back to Adriana where she'd moved to an overstuffed chair, her eyes closed. He waited and in a few minutes she looked at him with open eyes.

"I have been praying, but my burden for Theo is not lifted."

"There's a reason why, Adriana."

"Are you ever going to tell me?" Fresh tears hovered on her lashes.

Hendrik held out his hands, pulling her up and helping her to the sofa where he spread a small quilt over her lap.

"Your dream has convinced me to confide in you," he said, his voice breaking.

It did not become any easier, but he shared everything the agent had told him.

"Can it be true!" she cried, tears streaming down her cheeks. "Where is our baby?"

"I hope to find out with the FBI's help. The agent wants our DNA, but we should wait until you feel stronger. Did I do the right thing?"

Adriana leaned against him trembling. "You want to protect me, but Rik, all I want is to find our child before I die."

With both arms, he held his wife's frail body, silently beseeching God to save her.

"You are going to beat this cancer, my dear. What should I tell the agent?"

"Call him this very moment. See if he will come for our samples."

Hendrik punched in the number, weight shifting from his heart to his shoulders.

"This is Griff."

"Hendrik Van Horn calling. My wife and I want to give specimens. I am sorry to cause delay, but I have been wrong more than once in the last few days."

"Tell Mrs. Van Horn I've been praying as promised. I can arrange for an FBI agent from our Colorado Springs office to take your samples in a day or two and will call back soon."

"Adriana and I need to find the truth," Hendrik said before ending the call.

When he told Adriana the FBI agent was praying for them, her face turned rosy, the gray pallor vanishing. She touched his hand. "Call Ted and ask his forgiveness."

"I have wronged the boy, wanting him to be me. I now see he is the man God made him."

"No parent is perfect; however, we should hold off telling Beatrice."

His head drooped. So many explanations to give family, the board of directors, and staff. What about the media? They could easily make it appear like he and Adriana had done something wrong. Complications mounted as fast as seconds ticking by.

He picked up the portable. "I'll phone Ted from my office."

"Rik, tell him we love him as our son."Adriana's lips parted in a half-smile.

Hendrik stepped from the room, snow swirling outside the window a mirror to the doubts churning in his tortured mind, none of which he shared with Adriana. Maybe he never would. She considered Ted her son, but did Hendrik? Did he ever?

HENDRIK WATCHED ADRIANA gain strength since they had supplied their DNA. The fight within her to locate their son simply amazed him. While he vowed to do everything to help, this news Dylan Burns had just lobbed threw him off his game. He wanted to call foul.

In his den, he gazed out the window not seeing the tree-lined bluff. Rather with fists clenched, his mind burned with a dilemma. Should he dismiss Dylan or keep pressing on? He uncurled his right hand and faced Dylan, who leaned against the stone fireplace; his sunglasses perched crookedly atop his head.

"Dylan, what do you mean Mrs. Ramsey has disappeared?"

A speedy shrug told Hendrik nothing.

"I paid you a hefty five grand and you grin, saying she's gone?"

"Right. There's nothing more to tell you."

"Where is her son, Daniel Ramsey?"

Dylan yanked a cigarette pack from his front jacket pocket. "Don't worry, I gave up smoking. I think better with one between my lips."

"Ridiculous."

Hendrik marched up to his ace investigator, aiming his eyes, nostrils flaring. He had to bury his emotions and not let Dylan see how this family situation had upset his usual steel-like attitude. He refused to give up the search.

"Tell me everything," Hendrik commanded.

"She died in Phoenix. Her son had her cremated. No grave, no marker, no anything."

Hendrik's fight had not fizzled. "I hired you to find our son, no matter the cost."

He detected a twinkle in the ex-state trooper's eyes, but all Dylan did was smack the cigarette pack on his right palm.

"Daniel Ramsey sold his Long Beach home, moving a month ago. Proceeds will be deposited into Ramsey's bank account. The broker has no forwarding address and neither does the post office. Ramsey's phone is disconnected. There's no obituary under Mrs. Ramsey's name and no police record for her or her son in Arizona or California. But I tried one last trick."

A shudder ripped through Hendrik. The answer might seriously disrupt his life's work, but there was no turning back.

"What did you do?"

"The broker gave me the bank account number and I deposited a check for one hundred dollars with a note written in the memo line asking Ramsey to call me."

"And if he fails to see your notation?"

"I wrote it was an installment of a loan his mother had given me. When he finds an unexpected deposit, he'll order the check and call me."

"You've wasted your hundred dollars."

"Not mine. It's on your bill. You said this was important."

Hendrik took a step back. "Forget Daniel Ramsey. I want you to unearth everything about a Navy officer named Douglas MacArthur Rider. He may figure in this matter."

"Why pay me? Your secretary can look him up on the Internet."

"Ted says Rider and his wife bore a son on the same day. I want *you* digging."

"Where does Rider live?"

"Find out! I need to talk with the man ASAP."

Dylan shoved the cigarette pack in his pocket and taking out a tiny notepad, he made notes with a miniscule pencil. He flipped the whole caboodle back into his pocket.

"What if I don't find your Navy man?"

"Adrian and I will wait for the FBI to analyze our DNA," Hendrik moaned, slumping into a chair behind his desk. "I don't like trailing behind, gathering up crumbs."

"I consult for the SecNav. Stand by for my call." Dylan sped away.

Hendrik heard bare tree branches rustling against the window-pane. He stared at the bleak scene, willing Adriana to live and not give up. But at that moment, not locating their son before the federal agent felt like total failure.

36

Bo Rider wheeled his Austin-Healey into the visitor parking lot at CIA Headquarters in Langley, estranged from his career, his life. He drove here because Frank had phoned. Bo shut off the car mentally replaying their earlier conversation.

"It's April Fool's Day. Is this some joke?" Bo had cracked.

"Bo, believe me when I say Kangas needs to see you."

"Like your pretend Tel Aviv conference about hummingbird drones. What was that?"

Frank had simply replied, "Come at ten. I'll meet you out in reception."

Bo's mind veering to the present, he jerked the keys from the ignition. He was back at the Agency, just like he wanted. Yet, he had no clue if he'd leave reinstated or walk out fired, his career over. The end. Kangas could rake him over the coals and send him on his way to oblivion.

Until Frank's call, Bo found the last months mind numbing. The kids seemed lost in their own home until the elusive stray cat had returned. Both Gregg and Glenna fed the ragged cat bits of tuna until they officially adopted the gray and white cat naming him Shadow.

He slammed the car door, letting off pent-up steam. Frank hadn't even admitted things looked good. Bo had walked a couple yards when his conscience assailed him. He should rejoice even to be alive using both legs, unlike Mac. Julia loved him. Glenna and Gregg were happy, enjoying their mom's homeschooling. They'd traveled as a family to Florida, Hampton, and spent time combing the D.C. monuments.

Bo forced himself to face the next turn in his life. Yet no matter how he tried to muster the old swagger, his legs felt like wooden sticks as he entered the main door. There was Frank waiting as promised and he thrust out his hand.

"Great to see you back here."

"Am I back, Frank?"

"I'm betting you are." Frank beamed a rare smile. "Kangas took one look at Griff's report and ordered him to his office. They are both eager to brief you on the outcome."

"What does his report say?" Bo could barely breathe.

"I don't know, but let's find out."

Whatever happened, at least Frank was a true friend. Things took a turn for the worse when the security guy at the entrance acknowledged Bo but refused him entry until Frank presented a pass. The moment they arrived at Frank's desk, Frank pointed at Kangas' door.

"Get in there, buddy. I'm cheering for you. And Bo, you have friends."

Bo nodded, but no words eked out his dry throat. The door swooshed open. Kangas marched around his desk, shaking Bo's hand like he hadn't seen him in years.

"About time you got here, Rider."

Griff pumped Bo's hand asking, "How you holding up?"

Okay, they were glad to see him, but what next? Would Kangas exonerate him or kick him out? Bo couldn't decipher Kangas' guarded look; the old spy master always had been adept at giving away nothing. Kangas nodded to a leather chair on casters and sat in one.

"Bo, you're cleared of any wrongdoing."

At those fantastic words, Bo actually breathed. But what did Kangas mean, really? Would Bo be relegated to a boring job like Frank's?

"We owe Griff thanks for mighty fine work. You're reinstated, but we need to discuss your next assignment."

Bo lobbed his eyes at Griff and then Kangas. "Will I be told what caused my temporary separation?"

"You will," Kangas nodded, his stern look hiding something.

Bo squirmed on the rolling chair. "Why do I sense there's more?"

"Getting back to work at Langley is one thing, but you will have major adjustments in your personal life. Griff discovered you are not adopted. Your blood type differs from your parents because you were raised by folks who are not your bio-parents."

Bo's mouth opened, but he couldn't respond, not one word. His heart pumped mega-blood to his brain, which might erupt at any second.

"It's a shock, I know," Griff said leaning forward. "When you were born in the Philippines, another American boy was delivered at the local hospital the same night. Through some inexplicable error, you were given to the wrong mother. The mistake was never discovered. Instead of being Mac and Vivian Rider's son, you were born to Hendrik and Adrian Van Horn, confirmed by DNA testing."

"All this time I'm someone else?" Bo's throat burned with raw emotion.

He didn't know what to say and searched Kangas' stoic face.

"Wait!" Bo exploded. "Did you say *Hendrik* Van Horn?"

Griff raised his eyebrows. "Right, he's a theologian."

"We met. I didn't even like him." Bo's mind whirled. "Julia aided his Israel tours."

Bo paused, drawing in a deep breath.

"I don't mean I do not like him. It's just that he's not as good as Mac, my dad." Bo stopped, hurt building in his chest.

"Rider, your parentage makes no difference to me, but Mac is tops in my book."

Bo faced Kangas, bursting to speak. "Yeah, Dad told me how you and he go way back."

Kangas merely grinned. Bo rose and began striding behind the chairs.

"I met Van Horn's son. I mean my dad's son. Van Horn introduced me to Ted, who's about my age, but shorter. I found Ted rude to his old man."

"Sounds like Ted, or Theo, which would be your name," Griff remarked. "One of the first things I noticed is Ted's about as tall as Mac and you are Van Horn's height."

Kangas got up and clapped Bo on his shoulder. "Griff will brief you on details. I'm excusing you both to an available office, but then we must revisit your mission in Israel."

"Yes, sir!"

The idea of going back after the mole relieved some of Bo's angst. He needed time alone to comprehend what the peculiar discovery meant for the rest of his life.

Kangas dropped his voice. "Our embassy's computer system was recently compromised. Someone used Hal's password to hack in, the intrusion occurring while our people watched Hal and Clara enjoy a bottle of wine and dinner at a Tel Aviv restaurant."

Bo glanced at Griff, uncomfortable with Kangas speaking of the problem so freely.

"I already briefed him on what you were doing," Kangas said, flicking a hand at Griff. "Director Harmon loaned him to us until we eviscerate this mole. You two put your heads together. We talk in an hour. Our national security is at great peril."

BO'S BRAIN HAD ALREADY SPUN into overdrive, but when Griff finished telling about his search and DNA evidence, Bo sat speechless.

Griff pressed forward. "You and Ted have different parents than the ones who raised you. There is one positive result. Kangas is happy you're back on his team. Ready to find our leaker?"

Bo could hardly process Griff's discoveries and he started talking, words gushing out in a torrent. "It's too bizarre. I worked undercover using pretend names, but Skip Pierce always knew he was Bo Rider. Now who am I? Theo Van Horn? Instead of a military hero, my father turns out to be some religious nut."

"No." Griff raised a hand. "He is an authority on the Bible. I read one of his books."

"I never go to church unless it's for a wedding or funeral. When I met Van Horn in Israel I paid him no attention, though Julia is a big fan."

"When will you tell her?"

Bo thrust a hand through his hair, unsure how to answer, finally managing, "I need to stay sane by focusing on the mission. We have a mole to catch."

"One more thing. Are you ever going to contact Dr. Van Horn?"

Bo scowled. "Maybe someday before my kids graduate from high school."

"Glenna and Gregg are his grandchildren. What about Ted? He's Mac Rider's real son."

Bo shoved both hands over his ears, squeezing the sides of his head.

"Stop it! Stop it! You're killing me."

Griff laid a hand on the table. "Let me tell you something. Though I wasn't religious, I studied the Bible and have accepted God's truths and plans for my life. I hope you'll discover what it means to be on a personal footing with Christ. When Kangas asked me to clear you, I prayed God would bring favorable results. I never imagined the miracles He would perform."

"Enough. I don't share your optimistic outlook." Bo moaned, dropping his hands from his ears.

"Yet, you've found your birth father. I'm thankful God allowed me to be a part of the solution."

Bo blinked rapidly, wanting to move on. "What's next?"

"Tell Julia. Then I'll arrange for Ted to meet Mac." Griff thought for a moment. "You should probably contact the Van Horns and I can help make that happen."

"What's your plan, some cruise for the happy family in the Caribbean?"

Griff shook his head. "I'll be advising the Van Horns of the DNA results. Hendrik is coming to D.C. for a conference. You could meet with him then."

"I met him, remember?" Bo shrugged, not anxious to repeat the event any time soon.

"The longer I put off the inevitable, it becomes a raging giant."

Griff took out his cell, but Bo shook his head.

"Cells won't work in here. We have ways to render it useless."

Griff slid a desk phone over and eyeing Bo said, "Use the secure phone."

"Hate to have you on the other side of an interrogation."

"You might want to record his number."

Griff opened his address book. Bo rolled his eyes but wrote down Van Horn's number, then dialed. Griff leaned in toward the phone. A pleasant-sounding lady answered.

"Mr. Van Horn's office. May I help you?"

"FBI Special Agent Griff Topping calling from Virginia."

"Mr. Topping, let me see if he can be interrupted."

Griff smiled as the line went mute. "He'll have time."

"Agent Topping, do you have news for us?"

"I do, but I hope you are sitting down," Griff said gazing at Bo.

"Yes, I am. I mean *we* are. Adriana is beside me. You are on speakerphone."

"Remember I told you Ted's DNA matched a naval officer who was in the Philippines?"

"Have you located the Navy commander? I couldn't."

Bo wondered what Van Horn meant, but Griff let it pass.

"Sir, DNA reveals your son was erroneously given to Navy Commander Douglas MacArthur Rider and his wife Vivian. Their son was placed with you. Your son was raised by the Riders who named him Ernest King, but they call him Bo."

An audible gasp and faint sounds of weeping gushed from the phone. Van Horn's comforting voice spoke low in the background, "Now we know for sure, my dear."

Quiet absorbed the Langley office and Bo felt compassion. They didn't deserve to learn over the phone Bo was their son. He wanted to sock Griff in the arm.

Van Horn said abruptly, "The name Rider is familiar perhaps because I met a Bo Rider in Israel. Does he work for the State Department?"

"He does, sir." Griff pointed at the phone, prodding Bo to say something.

"And does he have a beautiful wife Julia and two precocious children?"

"Correct."

Van Horn's voice faded away, but Bo heard a few words: "Adriana, you will never believe." A pause and, "Our son and his family are wonderful. Must be a Divine appointment."

Then Van Horn spoke into the phone. "We tried preparing ourselves, but it is hard to explain the sorrow, the joy we feel. God makes no mistakes so we pray He will reveal His plan."

"Are you attending the D.C. conference on Thursday?" Griff asked.

"Why yes. I would like to thank you in person."

"You might like to see someone else in person. Bo is here and I have you on speaker."

Adriana's soft voice echoed over the long distance, "Bo, will you meet me in D.C.?"

"Did you hear that?" Van Horn asked. "My wife is not well, but she wants to travel."

Griff raised his eyebrows, flashing Bo a questioning look. Bo could only swallow.

"I'm excusing myself so the three of you can talk. It's a pleasure helping you find each other. I have been truly blessed." With that Griff left the room.

Bo opened his mouth but had no words for his other father and mother.

"Are you there, Bo?" Van Horn asked.

He must say something. He cleared his throat. "Do you remember me and my family?"

"Certainly, your lovely wife introduced us by the tour bus in Tel Aviv. Our son, I mean, Ted surprised me at that time with a visit. How is Julia?"

"Missing Israel and your tours. So are Glenna and Gregg."

"Thank you for sharing that. She is a special woman."

Bo relaxed just a bit. "Julia knows nothing of this discovery. I need time to absorb the reality of being someone other than who I thought I was for the past thirty-some years."

"Fair enough. We still have not come to terms with our son being taken away from us."

"I'll call you at this number tomorrow," Bo said before giving Van Horn his cell number.

"We could share a meal together; however, we shall levy no demands on you."

"That's fine. Take care."

Before Bo hung up, he heard soft crying. Repercussions hit him like a tidal wave. Mom and Dad would be crushed. He swung open the door, facing Griff who was talking with Frank.

"Griff, I have to be the one to tell Mom and Dad. Just what do they know?"

37

Bo's morning began like the others since he'd returned home from Hampton with sun peeking through the blinds and his feet hitting the floor. But after today, his life would be flipped upside down forever. Julia was already up, no doubt also feeling pressured to make everything perfect for Hendrik and Adriana's first visit.

Down in the kitchen Bo found coffee Julia had brewed. He drank the dark roast in a few gulps setting his mind to mow the lawn. Sweat trickling into his beard and streaming from his armpits, hot liquid probably wasn't such a good idea on the warm April morning.

He stared out the window at fresh brown spots in the grass. New mole hills? Bo plunked down his coffee, mulling over how to stop the beasts from ruining his yard. He swung open the cupboard barely missing Julia's head as she jetted into the kitchen, carrying a laundry basket.

"Whew, that was close. I'd like to keep my head, but my mind has blown a circuit. I've made so many lists you'd think I'd have it all together."

Bo took her laundry basket, setting it on the ground.

"You're folding towels for me?" she asked.

Her eyes sparkled with such good humor that Bo's heart leapt. He put his arms around her and kissed the top of her head.

"I know you're elated to have Van Horn as a father-in-law…" His voice ebbed away.

Bo didn't want to say aloud what he was thinking.

Julia rubbed his back. "You will be too. Dr. Van Horn was great with the kids in Israel."

"So I'm supposed to go through life calling him Dr. Van Horn. Please."

Bo closed his eyes, trying to recall meeting him in Tel Aviv, but the only vivid memory was his car exploding at the ski resort, taking off his dad's foot. Only Mac wasn't his dad.

"Yes, Mac is my dad!" Bo hissed, curling his fists.

"Bo, what's wrong?"

He started. Julia looked at him with surprised eyes.

"I don't care how wonderful Van Horn is, Mac will *always* be Dad to me."

When Julia grabbed his hand, seeking to comfort him, emotions Bo had locked away threatened to overwhelm him. He turned away.

"Bo," Julia whispered his name. "I don't understand how you feel, but I know Mac and Vivian are your parents and grandparents to our children. We love them. That will never stop."

Bo leaned against the counter. "You're right," was all he said, blinking his eyes. He needed to bottle up his runaway ache before Gregg and Glenna came downstairs.

"I need breakfast," he added, rummaging for a box of bran flakes and a bowl.

"Bo, wait. There's something else I want to say."

He stopped pouring out cereal.

"This afternoon, we open our home and hearts to Hendrik and Adriana. Imagine how they, your mother and father, feel taking their son home to a village, feeding him, raising him, and all the time you have been lost to them. I know the real you, Bo Rider, and I know what they've missed all these years. Think of that when you unlock the door."

Bo stood at the window, his mind a complete blank, like a giant eraser had blotted out his thoughts. His eyes caught green grass with its tangled weeds waiting for him to cut it. He heard Julia's words, yet nothing sank in.

A jolt of caffeine made his heart start racing and he poured out cereal, barely aware Julia left the room and was stuffing clothes in the washing machine. Eating his bowl of breakfast, a memory wafted through Bo's brain. Intervening years dropped like falling acorns.

He was graduating from Army Ranger training, wearing his dress uniform. Mac gripped his hand, delight brimming from his eyes. "Son," Dad had said with a smile, wide as the Potomac. "You make your mother and I proud, signing up to serve your country. Never forget our freedoms rest upon your shoulders."

Even back in his Virginia kitchen he could envision his mother Vivian's beaming face. A day to remember, Bo rinsed his bowl in the sink, grinding remnants in the disposal. If he'd been raised by the Van Horns, he'd be stuck behind a TV camera making videos of tourist sites in Israel. Because Mac and Vivian raised him to love his country, Bo served with honor.

He straightened his back, shoving his feet into his grass-cutting shoes, black socks and all and snapped open the door. In the garage, he pressed the button to the overhead door and fired up his lawnmower, not caring how famous or great Hendrik Van Horn was. He couldn't take away from Bo the man he was or the fine upbringing his parents had given him.

Two hours later, his lawn mowed, weeds whacked, and mole peanuts crammed into the ground, Bo trudged into the kitchen. Julia had fixed a light lunch of salad and cheese sandwiches on pita bread. He wasn't hungry so he stalked upstairs without stopping, catching a handful of cashews off a side table on the way.

Julia found him in the master bath in front of the mirror, holding up a book with Van Horn's photo.

"Do I look like him?"

She peered at Bo and then the photo. "Your chins are similar. And he has thick hair. So do you, only yours is wavier."

Bo lowered the book. "You read his stuff, then started going to church with the kids. The Agency sent us to Israel and you were excited because of Van Horn's teaching about the Jewish people. You joined his tours. Can you believe he's my father?"

"It is like a dream come true," she laughed.

Bo whirled around.

"Stop it! Not to me, it isn't. I feel like a traitor to Dad and Mom. Even having the Van Horns over here feels wrong."

"We've been through worse. Remember the two bombings you survived?"

Bo swallowed. "Yeah."

"You lived for a reason. Let Gregg and Glenna enjoy their new set of grandparents."

"I suppose so. We'll get through it somehow."

Julia scratched his back through his damp t-shirt asking, "What about lunch? Should I save your plate in the fridge?"

"Tell you what. I'd like to rewind the clock to when Kangas ordered me to Israel. I wish I'd said no and put in my walking papers. I wish I'd never met Van Horn or even heard of him."

SPRING WAS IN FULL BLOOM throughout D.C., but Griff Topping paid no heed to the explosion of cherry blossoms lining the streets. He parked the bucar behind the Marriott, trying to decide how much to share privately with Hendrik and Adriana Van Horn before they visited Bo and his family.

As agreed, he knocked on the hotel room at two o'clock, greeted by the man Griff had seen on a book Ted had showed him. Griff flipped open his credentials and Hendrik Van Horn showed him to a smallish room with an extra chair. A delicate-looking lady, wrapped in a beige shawl matching her light brown eyes, sat on a love seat.

"Adriana, this is Agent Topping."

Griff gently took her thin hand. "I know Bo very well."

"Thank you for finding our son," Adriana said, a shy smile gracing her luminous face.

Griff pulled up a chair, sitting across from them and beginning his speech.

"Bo might want to tell you certain things but won't in front of his kids."

Hendrik moved slightly forward in his seat. "Oh? Is there a problem?"

"When you met him in Israel, did Julia tell you that he works for the State Department?"

"Yes."

Griff smoothed his moustache. "Bo is really employed by a secret agency. His embassy assignment was part of his cover, in a long career of covert operations. I say this because parents are usually told at some point, but never learn much more."

A somber glint shone in Adriana's eyes. "His children don't know of his dangerous job?"

"Correct. While Julia knows who he works for, she rarely knows much else. I was tasked to find his bio-family after he was injured in a terrorist bombing. Doctors discovered his blood type didn't match either parent."

Adriana jolted in the chair. "Bo was in a bombing. Was he hurt?"

"Yes, but he is recovered. Bo is highly decorated for clandestine work he's performed in enemy countries." Griff held out his hands, palm up. "However, his awards remain secret."

"Are you sure he is all right?" Adriana asked, twisting a hankie in her feeble hands.

"Bo is back to work."

Hendrik looked at his watch. "We should leave soon. We are due at their house by three."

"Need directions?" Griff asked.

"I made sure the rental car came equipped with a GPS. Agent Topping, we appreciate you telling us this much. We will take our cues from Bo."

Griff stood to leave. "Please don't repeat any of what I just told you."

"Of course not," Hendrik said, but by the door, he posed a quiet question.

"What may we tell Ted about Bo?"

Griff stopped in his tracks. "Bo has talked with the Riders about the tragic mix-up. They will be meeting Ted. Mac Rider was a submarine commander and a national hero in his own right. Leave it to him to correctly describe Bo's career to Ted."

"May God bless you, Agent Topping."

"He already has. Bo is fortunate to have you for parents. Enjoy your time today."

38

Bo paced up and down his drive, doubts bombarding his mind like artillery fire. He didn't feel comfortable calling them Mom and Dad, but what should he use? He couldn't very well keep calling him Dr. Van Horn. Maybe he should use their first names and not worry about it.

He stooped to investigate upturned earth and sure enough another mole had tunneled along the drive's edge. Bo stomped his feet pushing down the dirt, rehearsing what to do when they arrived. Shake her hand or peck her cheek? After all, Adriana had carried him for nine months. What about Hendrik; would he criticize Gregg for hiding that old Israeli arrowhead?

Bo's foot smoothed the earth, his mind focused on Gregg's question over last night's dinner. Julia had passed Glenna the breadsticks, saying "Remember Dr. Van Horn, the man who led our tours in Israel? He is really your grandfather."

Gregg had dropped his pizza on his plate, staring at Julia and Bo with sparkling eyes.

"Are you guys really my mom and dad?"

"Yes, buddy," Julia had replied. "You look just like Dad and Glenna's blue eyes are just like mine."

Bo had ruffled Gregg's wavy hair. "Finish your pizza and we'll work on your car."

And he'd stayed with his son in the garage painting Gregg's soapbox derby racer, the subject of Gregg's birth never coming up again. The Van Horns were late.

He kicked a pebble, launching the tiny rock down the cement drive, shaking loose a memory of the time Ted had appeared in Tel Aviv, catching Hendrik off guard. The resulting conversation had crackled with tension. A horn blaring made Bo jump in his driveway.

He watched a dog dart in front of a blue sedan as it careened around the curve. The hound ran off and Bo steeled himself for the next chapter of his wild ride. Though the Van Horns had sounded friendly on the phone, he should've gone to their hotel instead.

The sedan jerked to a stop in front of the house, but Bo waved them into the driveway. He found himself swinging open the right door for an elegant-looking woman with light brown hair. Before he knew what was happening, she enfolded him in her thin arms. He gently hugged her, afraid to hurt her. She smelled fresh, like summer flowers and he heard her say, "My son."

When Bo pulled back, tears glistened in her eyes that were so like Gregg's and his own gray eyes that he blinked, the word "Mother" sticking in his throat like sawdust.

"Thanks for coming," he blurted, swallowing raw emotion.

Good thing Julia had kept the kids inside. Were they peeking out the window? Before he knew it, a hand grabbed Bo's with force.

"Great to see you again, Bo. We last saw each other in Tel Aviv."

Whew, no mention of being Hendrik's son. He didn't want to break down in the yard.

"Yes, sir. You remember Julia and our kids, but … ah … Adriana hasn't met them. You must be tired after the long flight and everything."

Hendrik seized Bo's forearm. "I'm fine, but you are right. She is exhausted."

Bo didn't need to hear more. Quickly, he caught her hand in his, cradling her frail, cold fingers, aware that this woman was his mother.

"Let's get you inside, Nina. Wind is picking up. My family is anxious to meet you both."

"You lead the way, Bo," Hendrik said, a smile broadcasting approval for Bo's care of Adriana.

Not such a bad beginning Bo thought as he led Nina up the walk. Inside the front hallway, Gregg and Glenna raced over, wearing their best clothes and happy faces.

"Meet Nina," Bo said. "That's what I called my grandma when I was younger than you."

Glenna handed her a picture, which Nina grasped with both hands. "How beautiful! Did you paint this?"

Glenna nodded, her cheeks shining pink. "It's our view from the Tel Aviv apartment. The blue water is the Mediterranean Sea."

"And you gave me this," Gregg chimed, digging a gold coin from his pocket.

"That's my grandson." Hendrik laughed heartily. "He nearly caused a riot protecting his arrowhead."

Julia corralled the kids to the couch and they got comfortable with the Van Horns in the middle. Bo chose a far chair while Julia pulled a chair near Adriana, saying, "I'm delighted to meet you. Dr. Van Horn taught me so much about the land of the Bible. He's changed my life."

"My dear, please call me Adriana. Rik told me how helpful you were to him."

Hendrik nodded and said in a friendly tone, "Rik is a name Adriana first called me when we met. We are informal folks and I would like it if you all used that name for me."

Bo watched the scene unfold like some heartwarming movie he was directing. What should he do next, hold up an "applause" sign? Julia supplied the answer.

"Gregg and Glenna have homework upstairs."

"Do we have to, Mom?" Gregg asked. "Rik and Nina just got here."

"It will take you ten minutes to write about your favorite living hero. Come down when you're done. Scoot."

Glenna curtsied before skipping upstairs. Gregg placed the gold coin on the center table where Rik could see it, thumping his feet all the way upstairs. Bo felt a strange urge to follow his son and avoid the inevitable time alone with Rik and Adriana.

"What sweet and smart children," Adriana said, her face glowing like sunshine.

"Thank you," Julia replied. "I hope you enjoy Dutch pea soup."

Rik clapped his hands together. "You remembered. It's my favorite."

Bo saw Rik's jaw dip, tension easing from his face. No problem there. It had all transferred to Bo.

Julia brought Glenna's painting over to Adriana. "I also sliced several types of Dutch cheese. Glenna helped me bake fresh raisin bread and create a special dessert."

"The kids are excited by your being here," Bo safely added. "Glenna's painting shows how much they liked Israel."

"Will you return there again?" Rik wondered aloud.

Bo swiped his hair. "It's complicated."

"Why not show Rik the porch you built last year. Adriana and I want to become better acquainted." Julia faced Bo, shooting a sort of message with her spirited blue eyes.

"Okay." Bo glared back. "This way, Rik."

The last thing he wanted was to be cornered by the man. Too late now. Bo prepared himself for an awkward ten minutes before Julia called them to dinner.

BO PUSHED OPEN the glass French doors leading to the four season's room.

"Let me show you what Julia calls a porch and I consider an addition."

"Your whole family is wonderful," Rik pronounced, walking in first.

Bo didn't feel like talking to Rik about his life, not yet. He'd show him the room, hoping to stall the inevitable for as long as possible.

"A contractor from Julia's church roughed it in. I finished the interior. If I'd done all the work, it would never have been completed."

Rik ran a hand along the built-in shelves, which made a nice perch for family photos. He perused collages of Gregg and Glenna's first steps, riding their bikes, and dressed up as tin soldiers for a school play.

He sat on a love seat, and crossing his long legs, said with a grand smile, "Bo, you look just like your mother."

"When did you meet Mom?"

Bo's heart pounded, realizing Rik wasn't talking about Vivian Rider but Adriana Van Horn. He picked up a marble clock Frank gave him last Christmas. The second hand sweeping across the gold face made him think about what a weird time he was living in. When he'd finished this room last fall, he didn't know he'd be sitting here chatting with Rik, his father.

"I'd barely brushed on the last coat of paint before we were sent to Israel," Bo said, putting the clock back on the antique table.

"Your work is top-notch and looks like a contractor built the whole thing."

Bo shrugged off the compliment. "We're back in Virginia sooner than we expected. It's good we had not rented out the house."

Rik came over, sitting in the chair a breath away from Bo, and lightly touched his knee. Did Bo see concern in his eyes?

"Can we talk without the kids hearing?" Rik asked.

"Yeah," Bo mumbled, not wanting to go wherever Rik was headed.

Rik lowered his voice anyway. "Adriana and I do not want to say anything to put you or your family at risk. Agent Topping told us about your secret work and why you left Israel."

"He shouldn't have done that."

Bo leapt up, stalking over to the slider doors. Griff had no business butting into his life. A voice echoed in his head, *Yeah? Griff is why you're in the clear at the Agency. Stop being a jerk.*

Pushing out a sigh, Bo faced Rik. "Listen, even my kids don't know what I do. Julia knows precious little of my true work and I intend to keep it that way. The danger is real enough without her worrying about me every minute of the day."

"Adriana and I are grateful for you and the risks you take. Allow me to say how much we thank God for keeping you safe."

Bo refused to discuss his Agency work any further. He straightened his back. "Please. I want you and your friends to know I work for the State Department."

"We will protect you with our lives. Are you willing to hear something?"

At the anxious sound of Rik's plea, Bo scooted to a chair. "I'll listen."

Rik crossed his legs again as if winding up for a long tale. Bo tamped down an urge to fling open the slider and run outside. He had few friends and besides his family, he didn't seek close relationships. Rik was talking and Bo tuned his ears to hear.

"I have studied the Jewish people and Moses, who was taken from his Hebrew home. You're familiar with the man who led the Israelites from Egypt thousands of years ago?"

"From what I could tell, Charlton Heston played a great Moses in the movie."

Rik smiled. "So he did. Thousands of years before, when Pharaoh ordered all Jewish baby boys killed, Moses' mother hid him in a basket along the Nile River where he was found by Pharaoh's daughter. She took him as her son. Imagine the government's top official raised Moses, which prepared him to ultimately save the nation of Israel from the Egyptians."

"I am overwhelmed." Rik briefly stopped talking to gape at Bo. "You, my son, were taken from our home and raised by an official of our government. I can only wonder if God will use you in a strange and mighty way to save His people in modern-day Israel."

Bo's face flushed, warming his ears. This line of Rik's made him squirm.

"I hope you don't have the impression that I'm more important than I am."

Rik waved his hand dismissively. "You met Ted briefly. He was raised in the home where you should have been and he is not serving his country. So you see, I believe what happened is part of God's providence."

Bo seized upon the mention of Ted to escape his growing unease. "How is Ted handling the discovery he has different birth parents?"

"With him, I never know," Rik said, his substantial shoulders drooping. "He will meet with the Riders, or so he told Adriana. Even though we raised Ted there are times when it is like we have nothing in common."

"This quagmire isn't easy for any of us except for Gregg and Glenna. They think you are great. So does Julia."

"And I see you don't. Bo, time will reveal God's plan. Adriana and I care for Ted and we always will. But God has given us a greater capacity to love. Will you allow us to shower you and your family with our love too?"

Bo blinked away Rik's intense look. What could he say? No, leave us alone. Nothing was the same. Even returning to the Agency had seemed awkward. Yet, neither Rik nor Adriana was to blame.

In that moment, compassion welled in Bo's chest and he felt moved to do something, but what? Then he recalled the Van Horns had no grandchildren. He had an idea, but with Adriana recovering from breast cancer, would she be up to it?

He had one way to find out. "How about spending time with Gregg and Glenna while you're here?"

"You propose the very thing to speed my wife's recovery. God bless you, Bo."

Rik offered a hand, which Bo clasped, an odd sensation overwhelming him. Respect for a man he'd recently shunned grew in his heart.

"I have another question for you."

Bo dropped his hand. What shoe would fall next? Since he had no idea what motivated Rik, Bo was prepared to answer, "No!"

Rik smiled. "Adriana and I want to take you and your family with us to Israel, at our expense. She hasn't traveled much with me the last few years. With God calling His people to Israel, we believe prophecy is being fulfilled. The time is right."

"What are your thoughts on the Middle East peace process?" Bo asked.

"God will protect His people despite enemies piling weapons on all sides. I'd like to tell you a bit more about Bible prophecy for the end days, which began with Moses helping the Jews escape from Pharaoh. Joshua led them to victory into the Promised Land."

Bo's mind tumbled. When he'd met with Judah Levitt at Mossad HQ, Judah told him about the warrior Joshua and two spies hidden by a woman, but Bo couldn't recall her name.

"Joshua is a hero to the Jews. I know that much," he replied.

Rik arched his heavy brows. "God infused Joshua with strength and courage to defeat opposing armies despite every power against them."

"My Israeli friends seem enamored by the ancient commander."

"Picture this, Joshua, a commander like your father, Mac, having to cross the Jordan River with thousands of people and animals. But it was spring, so it would have been swollen from Mt. Hermon snow melt, the very place you and Mac were skiing. Then a miracle happened. God rolled back the rushing water, roughly a mile wide and brimming over the banks."

Bo had no idea of any of it. Still he asked, "Is that legend or did it really happen?"

"I believe the Bible is true, inspired by God." Rik leaned forward, his eyes bright. "Perhaps you have not heard about God's promise to Joshua."

Bo lifted his good shoulder in mock surrender. "Nope."

"Wherever the Israelites set their feet, God promised to give them that land. Some of your CIA people are familiar with His sacred promise."

Bo searched his mental files for something he'd missed about Joshua, coming up empty. Ever since his concussion, his memory had unfortunately become more fallible.

"Rik, I won't talk about what goes on there."

"I will talk and you listen. A year ago, I met with one of the Agency's leading analysts on the Middle East. He invited me to a luncheon at the Willard Hotel in D.C."

"Does your expert have a name?" Bo asked, crossing his arms. He had a sneaking suspicion Rik sought Bo's respect and he wasn't buying the ploy.

"Retired General Jake Hobbs."

One of Bo's eyebrows rose, but he kept mum about having met with Hobbs before he flew to Israel. He'd found Hobbs a treasure trove of helpful intel about Mossad's efforts to infiltrate Hamas. Bo dropped his arms, his curiosity about Rik intensifying. Just who was he, really?

"I imagine the CIA is a pretty big place. Maybe you've not met him. Anyway, Hobbs picked my brain about something he called 'The Joshua Covenant.'"

Bo stared at Rik, unwilling to be drawn into a discussion about a possible clandestine Op.

"Pretend you don't know what I'm talking about. Fine; however, he did seek my opinion on the IDF's plan to retrieve land promised to Joshua."

"Sir, I mean no disrespect, but—"

"Why did Hobbs meet with someone like me?" Rik interrupted. "Adriana and I lived in Jerusalem with Ted and his sister in the eighties. Even though we eventually moved to Colorado, I've traveled to Israel more than fifty times, meeting with various Prime Ministers. Perhaps the key reason is because I have spent my adult life studying the books of Revelation, Joshua, Ezekiel, and prophetic books of the Bible."

"Sounds impressive," was Bo's guarded reply.

"Hobbs remained coy, but I sensed the Agency had locked onto scuttlebutt about Israel's war plans. The General was trying to discern what the Joshua Covenant might be."

"And you enlightened him?" Bo shot back, marveling at Hobbs seeking advice from Dr. Hendrik Van Horn.

An intense fire burned in Rik's blue eyes. "First I told him what I tell my tour groups. U.S. policy should support Israel. Throughout biblical history, God dealt seriously with Israelites who disobeyed His commandments, but He has handled Israel's enemies more severely."

"What is the Joshua Covenant?" Bo glanced over his shoulder from habit.

"A recent discovery in Israel has received no publicity. An archeologist found a codex, a ringed book of metal pages, made thousands of years ago. It substantiates the account in the book of Joshua and those things I told Hobbs."

"Where is the codex?"

"That I do not know." Rik held up a finger, telling Bo in a harsh whisper, "God piled up the Jordan River in a heap so Israelites could cross into the Promised Land."

"Something like that happened in the Moses movie," Bo said.

"Actually, that was Moses leading his people out of slavery across the Red Sea. This was another miracle years later. The river stopped flowing and the nation crossed on dry ground, priests carrying the Ark of the Covenant, leading the way. So the Jews would always remember His protection, God instructed Joshua to take twelve stones from the middle of the dry riverbed for each of Israel's twelve tribes and pile them up across the River Jordan."

"So the covenant is about twelve old stones being piled up?"

None of this made sense to Bo. He folded his arms, waiting for Julia to announce dinner.

"Stay with me," Rik pleaded. "Joshua assigned each tribe an area to live and prosper. He fought and defeated thirty-one kings. If modern Israel possessed *all* the land God promised to Abraham in Genesis and then to Joshua, Israel would control Lebanon and the West Bank of Jordan, with her boundaries extending into Syria, Iraq, and even Saudi Arabia."

Bo wrapped his mind around a larger Israel, imagining the uproar.

Rik continued. "God gave the Israelites land known as the West Bank and Gaza. It took them many years to gain the land, but they eventually lost it as the Jews were scattered by their enemies. God withdrew His protection for a time, but now He is bringing the Jews home."

Though he had read about Assyrians and Babylonians fighting in the area and the Jewish people being dispersed, how those events related to modern-day Israel Bo didn't comprehend.

"Okay, you've convinced me. I'll read one of your books. But tell me, what is the Joshua Covenant? It might help my future work."

Rik swiped at his eyes and swallowed. "One day Israel will occupy the whole Promised Land. My Israeli sources say their government is using the codex as proof God made the promise thousands of years ago. They believe when Arab nations or other enemies attack, God will help Israel regain possession of all the lands fulfilling the Joshua Covenant."

Bo's heart rate quickened. Did anyone at the embassy know of the Joshua Covenant? Could the mole access intelligence about the codex?

"And you told Hobbs all this?"

"Yes. And I encouraged him to fix a U.S. response."

Hobbs had mentioned none of this to Bo. Before he questioned Rik, Julia bounced onto the porch.

"Everything all right in here? Supper is ready."

"Rik was asking if we'd like to visit Israel with them. Interested?"

"Wonderful!" Julia's magnetic smile disappeared. "Bo, is it safe?"

"I'll talk to Frank. For now, Rik and Adriana want to spend time with the kids by themselves. Have any ideas what they'd like to do?"

Julia took Rik's arm, sharing how Glenna wanted to photograph the baby panda at the National Zoo and Gregg longed to see the *Enola Gay* at the Air and Space Museum in Chantilly.

"They also want to visit Williamsburg. We're studying John and Abigail Adams."

Julia's voice faded away and Bo stood alone, his mind spinning. Was it possible Rik was correct about God intervening in Bo's life? Why else would he be hearing about the Joshua Covenant when no one at the Agency, not Hobbs, Frank, or even Kangas had ever told him? Maybe they all knew but he had no need to know until now.

A sudden idea gripped him. He'd sneak back to Israel and finish the job with Judah and Griff's help. Yet, he needed to learn from Judah Levitt if Mossad linked Goliath to the ski resort bombing. Bo walked to dinner, wondering if he'd seen the giant man. Or had he been a phantom before Bo's world had gone black? There must be a way to know for sure and he intended to do everything to discover the truth.

39

The next morning, Griff Topping hurried to reserve the small FBI conference room. Good, no one was inside. He placed a sign indicating the room was in use, which it would be when Bo Rider arrived in a couple minutes. Griff filled an insulated urn with hot black coffee, empathy flooding his heart for Bo, whose real identity was Theo Van Horn. But during Bo's entire life no one knew him as that man.

Griff paused. Had he correctly explained the names in his report? He dashed up a floor to his office, booting up his computer and navigating to the page. Okay, he'd connected the right dots: Bo was known by the name Mac and Vivian Rider had chosen for their son, who was the real Bo, using the name Theo as chosen by Hendrik and Adriana Van Horn.

He exited the computer, puffing out a sigh. If he was confused, how must Bo feel?

The intercom buzzed on his desk interrupting his mental journey and the receptionist announced, "Theo Van Horn is here. Says you're expecting him."

He wasn't expecting Theo. What could he… Wait. Griff would find out.

"Show him into the conference room. I'll be right down."

After gathering notes he'd taken of Bo's personnel file, Griff walked down the stairs and into the conference room. A tall man stood cradling a cup, perusing the Wall of Honor, a photomontage of FBI agents killed in the line of duty.

"Hey, Bo, I'm still getting used to your close-cropped beard."

Griff didn't say that with his hair waving over his ears, Bo looked like Hendrik Van Horn. Instead he asked if meeting the Van Horns helped cushion the blow, adding, "They seem terrific and proud to have you for their son."

"You've lost far too many." Bo gestured at the photomontage.

"How was your conversation with Mac and Vivian?"

Bo faced Griff, dark hollows under his eyes. "They're my parents and always will be. Why do I feel like I'm ditching the folks who loved me when I stayed out too late and wrecked Dad's car? They saw me through basic training, Dad toasted me at my wedding, and

Mom scurried between my bedside and Dad's after the bomb blew off his leg."

Bo choked back a sob and Griff placed a hand on his shoulder.

"Eva and I are praying for you, if that's of help."

Griff dropped his arm and took a seat at the conference table, hoping Bo would join him. Instead, Bo remained by the Wall of Honor, sipping coffee.

"Julia is asking God to help me. Something's holding me up, yet I'm stuck in mud. Do I change my name? Because I'm never going to be known as Theo Van Horn."

"Then why give that name to the receptionist?"

"Testing it out, I guess. I don't like it," Bo said with a definite shrug.

"My advice, be yourself. You haven't changed from the man you are just because your blood type is different from Mac and Vivian's. Who cares?"

Bo stared at Griff as if those words were sinking in. Was it Griff's imagination or did a dark cloud lift from Bo's eyes?

"What you say makes sense," Bo said, pulling up a chair. "But finding out I was switched at birth has been worse in some ways than the firefight I survived in Iraq last year."

Griff poured coffee from the urn. "Will you see each other in the future?"

"I have no clue. Anyway, I'm back at the Agency thanks to you."

"We need to figure why Shellie Karnack stoked the flames. She didn't have our country's interest at heart, I think."

"What's her motive?" Bo set down his cup with a *thwack*. "Professional jealously because I am CIA and she never will be? Or a power struggle to stay on Hal's good side?"

"It's a kettle of stinking fish and I intend to help you snare the bottom feeder. Did you know Hudson Engle, the MSG commander, went behind Shellie's back to tell the Agency Clara Cohen used Hal's computer?"

Bo rubbed his beard, nodding. "Frank interviewed Julia about Clara's sneaky online habits. She even cajoled Julia into divulging our addresses in Virginia and in Tel Aviv."

"She's suspect number one." Griff held up a finger.

"What?" Bo jumped up, fuming. "You're after Julia! That's why you called me here?"

"Settle down. Being away for months has fried your brain. Clara is suspect number one."

"Number one means you have a number two." Bo sank back into his chair.

Griff lifted a second finger.

"Her husband, Ambassador Cohen. And number three is someone you know pretty well."

"Not Frank? He would never betray his country for love or money."

Griff shook his head. "Of course not, although he was in the loop for your contacts with Mossad. No, Shellie Karnack is a prime candidate for betrayal."

"Our Station Chief approved of her and she acted like my only friend over there." Bo shook his head. "But she has a beef with the Agency not hiring her."

"Okay, you mentioned that twice, something I didn't know about." Griff wrote on a legal pad. "The embassy trio, Clara, Hal, and Shellie, might be colluding together and your blood mismatch provided a ruse to get rid of you."

Bo scratched his beard as if deep in thought. "Or Hal and Clara used Shellie to cover their tracks. Kangas suspects Hal. And Clara befriends my wife to access our addresses. Their Hamas contact follows Dad and me to the safe house, eyes my rental car, and then follows us to Mount Hermon, planting the bomb while we're on the slopes."

"Did Julia ever tell Clara about Federal Agent Eva Montanna coming to visit?"

"I need to think." Bo's lack of total recall jarred him. "We saw Eva and her grandfather after the bakery bomb. It seems I told someone beforehand that I'd take Eva there. Who was it?"

Bo's mind clunked along, but Griff interrupted his train of thought.

"No matter. It's clear to me that you were followed."

"Perhaps Julia told Clara who told Hal who told Goliath about Esther's Bakery. I need to check with my Mossad contact to see if Goliath was at the resort, prior to the blast. "

Griff nodded his agreement. "Eva compared photos and indentified the man on your dad's sub as your Goliath from the bakery. His name is Gath Ramla."

"Then he has vengeance in his heart," Bo bellowed, whirling around. "When he missed me the first time, he must have thought he hit the jackpot with father and son skiing together."

"What lengths will he go to with you and Mac still alive?" Griff's heart shuddered even asking the question. He and Bo needed to take every precaution.

Bo strode over to the honor wall. "I'll update my security system at the house and install more cameras."

"Good idea. I also am pleased Shellie has been separated from Hal. The FBI is keeping an eye on her at FLETC in Georgia. She'll be there a few weeks yet."

"And the Agency has assets in place monitoring Hal and Clara."

Griff joined Bo by the wall, placing a hand on his shoulder. "I've been working on a plan and should be in Israel within the week."

This was it, the moment Bo had hoped for. "Count me in. I'll do whatever it takes to stop Goliath and his minions."

"You read my mind." Griff chuckled. "You'll be traveling to Israel as Skip Pierce, but you won't be seen at the embassy. Mossad is supplying us an off-sight place where we can work."

"Great!" Bo chimed and sparks seemed to fly from his eyes. "Before we head out I have a story to tell you. Ever hear of a guy from Bible times named Joshua?"

"Sure. He's the commander who brought the Jews to the Promised Land."

"Ever read the book in the Bible with that name?"

Griff pursed his lips. "I'm spending more time reading John, learning about Christ's life. Have you started reading the Bible?"

"Sit down, Griff, and I'll explain."

The two agents sipped their hot brew around the table, with Bo consulting notes from his front shirt pocket. "According to Rik and his sources in Israel, scholars have unearthed a secret text of the exact locations of the Promised Land."

Bo quickly explained Rik's startling disclosure of the Joshua Covenant.

"The codex is a new one to me," Griff remarked, feeling stumped. "But Israel hasn't been my field of expertise until now. Who are Rik's sources in Israel?"

"I should have asked him, but I didn't want to ring alarms. He's entrenched over there. Even the Agency asks his opinion on Middle East prophecy, which I haven't begun to unravel."

Griff twirled his pen. "Does Rik work for Langley and you don't know it?"

"All I know is he dumped this mystery on me last night right before dinner. After we ate, Adriana was tired and they left. Maybe we should confer with him while he's still in D.C."

"Call him." Griff walked over to the phone, bringing it to Bo.

"Okay, then I'm running my notes through your shredder."

Bo rang the hotel, putting the phone on speaker so Griff could hear. Catching Rik as he and Adrianna were leaving their room, Bo said, "We had a great time with you both yesterday."

"Adriana and I enjoyed being in your home. We stayed up late talking so we're just going down to breakfast."

"I won't keep you, but are you free to meet with me and Agent Topping later?"

A pause and Rik said, "When Adriana rests this afternoon, I will skip a meeting."

"We'll pick you up at your hotel at two. Griff drives a blue Chevy."

"Is this about the Roanoke stations Ted sold?" Rik asked, sounding anxious.

"Rik, it's not about Ted. Give Adriana my best."

After ending the call, Bo leaned against the table's edge. "If the ancient Joshua leads me to a modern Goliath I may yet see the terrorist who bombed me and Dad in handcuffs."

"I'm praying it will. And Bo, forget Rik's remark about his stations. They're not on the FBI's radar. I need to make travel arrangements and you should tell Julia you're leaving town."

Bo started punching in numbers on the secure phone.

"I didn't mean you should call her this second."

"No, I'm phoning Frank. He needs to tell me everything about Dr. Hendrik Van Horn's connections in the Middle East."

40

Bo peered out the blinds of the safe house window, scrutinizing pedestrians walking below along the Tel Aviv street. Who was that large man ducking into an alley? Could it be Goliath?

All extremely tall men were suspect.

"Hey, Skip Pierce, think it's wise showing your undercover face at the window?"

Bo snatched his finger out of the slat. He'd traveled to Israel sporting a beard, moustache, and hair curling toward his ears, yet he didn't exactly feel invisible. Returning to the scene of his near death, he was wearing fake windowpane glasses. Whatever confused his enemies, so much the better, despite Julia rolling her eyes at his scholarly disguise.

He dropped to a chair across the table from Griff. "I think I saw Goliath down below."

"Gath Ramla lives in Gaza," Griff replied over the top of the newspaper.

"Could be my nerves. I see him everywhere."

"After what you have been through, suspicion keeps you alive."

Bo drummed his fingers on the table. "Julia sent me off with tears in her eyes. She's praying for me every day."

"Dawn prays for me too and I do the same for her."

"Tell me about your meeting with Hudson Engle. Anything new about Shellie's return?"

Griff lowered the newspaper. "The sergeant is reluctant to work for her again at the embassy. He's adamant he tried to stop her from letting Clara and others use Hal's computer and reported her to the CIA Station Chief, Mike Spencer. Shellie pulled rank on the Marine."

"What about the FBI agents watching her at FLTEC?" Bo asked. "Anything suspicious?"

"I assigned an FBI agent to Shellie's pod, so she's observing her closely. In fact, my colleague runs with Shellie every morning before class. Seems normal so far."

Bo rubbed his beard. "Ever grow one of these? It itches. Julia hates it as much as I do."

"Plenty of times I grew one undercover, but after the first week my beard didn't bother me. Once we capture the elusive mole, you can celebrate by shaving it off."

Griff raised his eyes and Bo detected a solemn look.

"What else has happened around here?" Bo asked. "I wanted to be in Tel Aviv before now, but Kangas insisted you needed to secure the safe house, meet with your Legat, blah, blah."

"My time's been well spent. Late one night, with Engle's help, I had an FBI computer whiz examine the embassy's systems. He found a flash drive in a USB port on Hal's computer. The drive was empty but shouldn't have been there in the first place."

"Not surprising. Traffic through Hal's office has been as busy as O'Hare airport."

A noise outside the door startled both agents. Bo hustled over to the security monitor, seeing nothing. Griff strode to the window, peering out.

"A storm is brewing."

"Yeah, they move in fast off the Mediterranean. Probably thunder we heard."

Griff smoothed his moustache with his hand. "The flash drive is being analyzed and processed for prints. Our people think it might have been left from the original installation."

"Or someone with sinister intentions was frightened before they downloaded anything." Bo turned from the security monitor screen. "Check the flash drive for Clara's prints."

"Not only hers, but also Hal's and Shellie's."

"How long before you have results?" Bo pushed up his phony glasses.

"Analysts are working round-the-clock."

"Good," Bo said, bolting back to the table. "Remember what Rik told us about his source in Mossad? Yesterday after I landed, I left Judah an urgent message to call me."

Griff rose from the table, pouring coffee from an electric pot. "I've been thinking about Shellie. Did she suspect you were with the Agency?"

"She knew," Bo shot back. "Told me that first thing and I didn't appreciate it."

"Was she informed you were there to track down the mole?"

"I never told her of my mission," Bo said, thinking of his earlier conversations with Shellie. "You know what?" Bo sprang from the chair. "I saw her several times with a man."

"News flash, a woman being seen with a man is not unusual."

Bo was on to something and he didn't want to lose the thread.

"I just remembered seeing her in deep conversation with a man in the lot outside the embassy gate. At the time, I wondered why she didn't meet him inside the embassy."

Griff set down his cup and picked up his pen. "Describe him."

"All I can see is a fuzzy guy."

"Is he tall or short, skinny or round?"

"Let me think."

Bo shut his eyes, mentally leafing through the past months as if turning pages of a photo album. Then he reached the day when Shellie had hassled Bo about Saul Goldberg's call.

"Shellie confronted me after a Mossad agent called, blaming her questions on the receptionist."

"Noted. Was her fuzzy guy wearing a suit or motorcycle jacket?"

"Ever try to see your face in the mirror after a steamy shower? He's engulfed in fog."

Griff lifted his jaw. "Don't try so hard. Let your recall happen naturally."

"Coffee might help."

Bo poured a cup, his mind straying into neutral while Griff read their sketchy notes of Operation Mole Be Gone. Hot brew refreshed him and Bo recalled Shellie cornering him sipping coffee on the embassy's patio. Things had skidded downhill from there, with Bo's efforts to catch the mole foiled at every turn.

A spy in America's Tel Aviv embassy was dangerous—so many players used violence to achieve their aims. While diplomats lobbied for peace, Hamas and Hezbollah made no secret of their goal to wipe Israel off the map, hatred running deep.

Who lurked behind the embassy walls, using stealth to betray America? If only Bo could remember the man's face. Yet, was Shellie's friend or whoever even important?

Bo sauntered to the window, angling the blinds and watching Israelis whiz past below, some carrying briefcases and others juggling shopping bags. In this thriving metropolis, safety of the Jewish people was razor thin. A man and a woman walked by, the man's hand on her hip.

Bingo! The fog burst. Bo conjured up a snapshot of Shellie's man. In a flash, he saw her at the British Embassy's Christmas party, looking wired as usual, wearing a brown pantsuit. She mingled with four people, sipping tea in a cup. A man came up to her and as he spoke in her ear, he rested his hand on her hip.

"He's tall, about my height. Thinning hair the color of dirty sand. Hands are large with no wedding ring. I looked. His eyes. I can't see his eyes."

"You will."

Bo guzzled coffee, staring out the blinds. Griff stayed quiet, but his pen scratching against paper sounded like screeching chalk against a blackboard.

"I'll be back."

"Not going outside, are you?" Griff stood.

"Not with Goliath on the loose."

Bo stepped into the lavatory where he splashed water on his face, drying his eyes on a clean towel. In the mirror, his tired eyes saw a combo of Mac and Rik Van Horn. He tossed down the towel, refusing to become mired in his own twisted past and vowing to bust Shellie's link with a devious traitor. He stormed from the tiny bathroom.

"Black. The guy has eyes the color of coal, which do not match his light hair."

"He dyes it blond?"

"Possibly. At the British Embassy Christmas gathering, Shellie allowed him to rest his hand on her hip. I thought the gesture more than casual."

"A friend is MI5." Griff shoved aside his notes. "Maybe he can round up a guest list."

Bo thumbed through his wallet. "Last fall, I met Brewster Miles at the British Embassy. He's also with MI5. Here's his card."

Griff took the card, his eyes never leaving Bo's. "You met him before you went home?"

"Yeah." Bo nodded. "Why?"

"Brewster is the friend I mentioned. He may still be in Tel Aviv. Let's give him a ring."

GRIFF FOLDED PAPER into an envelope, having just typed and printed a message for Brewster who unfortunately had returned to London.

"Shane Rollins, the FBI Legat, will send my message to Brewster via diplomatic pouch."

"You have more faith in Rollins than I do," Bo called from the dining room. "He flaps his gums about things he shouldn't."

"Rollins knows better than to read my note. He'd be fired in a heartbeat."

Bo went back scanning the *Jerusalem Times* and other Israeli papers for the latest news.

"Griff, you need to hear this," Bo said, his voice strained. "Iranian-backed Palestinian assailants crossed into Egypt from Gaza's recently-opened border crossing. They sneaked through Egypt's Sinai desert back into Israel near Eilat, launching a three-pronged attack. Using automatic weapons they shot up a bus, killing eight Israelis and wounding twenty-four."

Griff set down the phone, putting his call aside for a moment. "Did Israel strike back?"

"Did they ever. An IDF air strike into Gaza killed a militant leader and three others."

"And the Palestinian response?" Griff asked, knowing there would be one.

"Hamas fired a rocket from Gaza, hitting a school bus, injuring a teen. IDF soldiers helping those victims sustained serious injuries." Bo sighed, pulling off his glasses.

"The circle of violence is endless. I'm calling Sergeant Engle."

"Wait, there's something more. Egypt has withdrawn their ambassador to Israel. "

Griff's hand froze. "I wonder if Israel's enemies have already discovered the codex."

The two agents traded looks, with Bo saying, "And our mole might be right in the middle of the chaos, slipping intelligence to the other side, betraying America."

"Pressure mounts." Griff yanked up the phone. "Sergeant, can you meet at Ben's in thirty minutes?"

"Anything particular I should bring?"

"Your memory of what we spoke of yesterday."

"Yes, sir."

Griff hung up before the call could be traced. He felt safe enough at Ben Ami's, a gem of a restaurant nestled near the U.S. Embassy and a common hangout for FBI agents posted in Israel. He'd remain alert though for anyone unusual. He grabbed his gear, cell phone, and jacket.

Bo put down his newspaper. "Our Secretary of State is in Cairo meeting the newly installed regime. Why am I finding that out in the paper?"

"My bad vibes from State haven't changed, despite you pretending to work for them. I'm meeting Engle at Ben Ami's. Need anything?"

"The juiciest burger money can buy, with loads of fries."

"I'm not much of a cook, but if we had a grill, I could rustle up tasty steaks."

"Your coffee is drinkable, I give you that. Why are you meeting with Engle?"

"He's reviewing his notes about Shellie after my interview with him yesterday. It's a long shot, but he may know her mystery man with the dyed hair."

"If you see suspicious characters riding by on motorcycles, call me."

Griff eyed Bo to see if he was serious. The hard glint in his eyes told Griff that he was.

"You've got my local cell number. I won't be long."

"Don't forget my food."

"You got it, Skip."

Griff hustled to his rental car, which he changed every other day, Kangas having urged him to spare no expenses. In minutes, he parked, eager to get inside Ben Ami's ahead of Engle. He grabbed a seat at a back table, near a side door, appraising the one couple in a corner booth. The twenty-something woman with long black hair stared at her male pal as if he was about to propose marriage. A waiter approached and Griff ordered a fresh juice while eyeing the couple.

A man clad in civvies marched in, his closed cropped hair giving away his U.S. Marine status. Engle carried a leather pad under his arm and sat huffing.

"I was detained by Ambassador Cohen."

"You're still on duty?"

"I have to drive right back. The Secretary of State is flying here from Cairo."

"Yes, I heard. Go ahead and order anything on me."

"No thanks. Mrs. Cohen catered in a swell lunch for the security detachment in honor of the Ambassador's birthday. Hot chicken wings, salad, and fresh fruit. She is a first-class lady."

A different take on Clara from what Bo had said. When the waiter stopped by Griff asked for two burgers to go with plenty of fries. He'd eat with Bo back at the safe house.

"Okay, what did you bring me?" he asked Engle.

"Nothing. I didn't find what I was looking for."

Griff leveled a gaze at Engle, who didn't flinch.

"That is a shame," Griff said in a low voice. "Remember anything else then?"

"I thought hard and long before notifying the Agency about Ms. Karnack allowing unauthorized access to the Ambassador's office."

"What tipped the scales?" Griff leaned back. Was Engle legit?

"One night I stood night watch for a Marine on his birthday and observing surveillance monitors, I saw Ms. Karnack enter with a man. During my rounds, the Ambassador's office was closed, but I heard her inside talking to someone."

"Had she entered with Ambassador Cohen?"

Engle shook his head. "The Ambassador was out of town. The man was about her age and kinda tall. I completed my rounds and she sat at her desk, but the Ambassador's door was still closed."

"Did you see her guest leave the building?"

"Nah. I opened the door and he was typing at the Ambassador's computer. Since my boss permitted him to be there, I didn't challenge him."

"Did you notice his hair color or how long he remained at the embassy?"

Engle paused. "I observed them leave later by the rear door. His hair was blond."

"Have you seen him again?"

"Not since Ms. Karnack left for training in Georgia."

Griff finished his juice. "Do the embassy's security cameras record onto a memory?"

"That's why I have nothing for you," Engle complained. "I searched my records for the date I stood watch for the Marine. I retrieved the correct memory, but it's been deleted!"

Griff's antennae flared. "Deleted? One day was deleted?"

"Correct, sir." Engle's eyes roamed the room before he whispered, "Others were too."

"Do you have the dates?"

Engle gave him a paper. "Memory was erased on those dates in the past six months."

"You do good work. I need a duplicate of the memory, to preserve it. Can you help me?"

"Sir, yes sir."

Griff rose, signaling a close to their meeting. "Call my local number when your mission is complete. Meanwhile," he added, raising a finger to his lips, "everything stays mum."

Engle stood tall, ready for duty, and left the restaurant. Griff settled the tab, grabbing the sack of burgers. He had plenty to tell Bo about Shellie and her mystery man who'd made the embassy his personal Internet café.

Griff hopped into his car. Maybe Shellie had impressed her boyfriend by letting him peruse e-mails on Hal's computer as Clara had done. He drove a circuitous route to the safe house, his FBI instincts telling him there was something more sinister to the charade. Would Griff find the truth before the mole did more damage to Israel and America's security?

41

In the safe house Bo huddled with Griff around the dining room table, feeling on edge. Judah Levitt would arrive any second and Bo worried how the Mossad agent would receive him. Since the ski resort bombing Judah hadn't surfaced until Bo called him upon returning to Israel. He poured out orange juice for a change, enjoying the fresh taste.

Meanwhile, Griff cleaned up, stacking papers on a cabinet. "After Engle described Shellie's companion, I'm ramping up her surveillance."

"Fine for FBI agents in Georgia, but what about Hal? He's within miles of here. Let me snoop around. I'm worthless sitting in a safe house, being 'safe.'"

"You can't leave, remember?"

Bo plunged a hand in his long hair. "We don't want Goliath trying to take me out again."

"Here's an idea, Skip. Plug any holes in your Op."

"Right."

Bo finished his juice and grabbed a pen, focusing his mind on what they needed to accomplish: Find the leaker with enough evidence to prosecute. Secure America's embassy and restore relations with Mossad.

He chewed on the pen, unsure why no one ever accessed his decoy computer data. A knock at the door and he shuffled the papers under a file. Griff rushed over to the security monitor. "Looks like your secret agent is here."

Bo came over. "Yup, it's our friend," he replied, ushering in the Mossad agent, making introductions.

"I took evasive measures." Judah nodded at the closed door. "I was not followed."

Bo gripped Judah's hand. "I didn't think I'd see you again. Thanks for meeting here. We're avoiding the U.S. Embassy like the plague."

"Skip Pierce, you bear no resemblance to my friend Bo Rider," Judah said narrowing his eyes to slits. "You have done a splendid job changing your appearance since we last met."

"I'm like a refurbished computer. This is my new look."

"Join us over here and help yourself to juice or coffee." Griff led Judah to their makeshift office in the dining room. "Bo returned to the U.S. after the ski resort bombing. You may not know the blast resulted in him learning his blood type differed from his parents."

Judah lifted his eyebrows at Bo, who bounded from his chair, waving the glasses around.

"That led Hal and Shellie to concoct a harebrained idea I was a terrorist with Abu Sayeff because I was born in the Philippines. My dad was stationed there." Bo spat these words like so much gravel.

He took up his spot by the window, lifting the blinds. Though he saw no one watching, he remained at the window letting Griff explain how the CIA had assigned the FBI to investigate.

"Bo was accidentally sent home with and raised by the wrong parents. That was the problem short and sweet, and he is here helping me and you sniff out the real rat," Griff said.

"A terrible shock for you, but I have one of my own." Judah's voice had assumed an unfriendly tone and he tossed a manila envelope onto the table.

Bo hurried over, snatching up the envelope. "What's in this?"

Judah's eyes darted at Bo and then at Griff. "No offense upon meeting you for the first time, Griff, but your country speaks out of two different sides of its mouth."

"You opening this or shall I?" Bo asked, tapping the envelope.

Judah grabbed and ripped open the packet, throwing a photo on the table. "Remember our agents saw Ambassador Cohen meeting with a Turkish arms dealer? There he is assisting undercover Mossad agents to load American stinger missiles onto a boat in Cyprus. The dealer believes these weapons will be smuggled into Gaza and that our agents are really Hamas soldiers."

Bo snatched the photo and studied it. "You think the U.S. is assisting the arms dealer?"

"What else are we to assume after your Ambassador's meetings with him? Can you say with certainty your government knows nothing about this?"

"I understand your concern after the rocket attacks yesterday," Bo replied evenly.

Griff leaned in. "A U.S. ambassador allied with an arms dealer is troubling. It hurts our relationships with Mossad."

"I'll call the Agency and ask my boss about the arms deal." Bo gave Judah the photo.

The Mossad agent stroked his beard before saying, "It appears while I work with you for the CIA, some in the Administration are aiding our enemies."

"Such a policy could not be officially sanctioned without it being leaked to the Agency."

"I thought so too, Skip Pierce," Judah said, his voice edged with concern.

Bo laid a hand on Judah's shoulder. "I am sorry for militants killing your people. My dad nearly lost his life, as you know. This kind of violence doesn't sit easy with me."

"I had to bring your ambassador's, how do you say, shenanigans, to your attention."

As Judah slid the photo back into the envelope, Bo told him how Griff had learned other shocking news.

"My birth father is Dr. Hendrik Van Horn, a Christian theologian and foremost authority in the U.S. on biblical history."

"I know of his interest in my country," Judah replied, pulling on his beard tip.

Bo leaned nonchalantly against the wall, testing Judah's reaction. "He explained how Joshua commissioned his men to make a map of the land God gave them."

"You and I once discussed Rahab helping Joshua's spies."

"Yes, the scarlet cord, but I am not talking about thousands of years ago." Bo hopped in a seat, facing Judah. "Ever hear of the codex and the Joshua Covenant?"

"I am surprised you have," was all Judah admitted.

Griff entered the mix. "Rik believes Israel's enemies are after the codex, to embarrass your nation."

"I see you are well informed as it should be among friends."

"You should have told me about Joshua and the secret codex." Bo crossed his arms. "I might have better understood the real threat at our embassy. It's like fighting an armed man with my hands tied behind my back."

Judah lifted up his hands. "When I come for help, you squeeze me, but I will share this. The article you speak of is preserved in a vault beneath Mossad HQ. The last time Bo visited, you were a few steps away from this treasure."

"You mentioned nothing of a secret vault."

"Need to know, my friend."

"Now is the time for us to know," Bo said, holding steady eye contact with Griff.

Judah's lips formed a thin line. "Many seek to destroy evidence of God's favor to us Jews. My Prime Minister has briefed your government at the highest level about Israel's vow to one day occupy the original borders Joshua mapped out."

"All issues are on the table." Griff opened a file. "Bo and I have discovered someone searched the embassy computer system using the search word 'codex.' We'll keep looking to learn who was interested."

Judah poured coffee from the carafe, taking a long swig.

"This tastes good," Judah said, lowering his cup. "Mossad would like to coordinate a matter with you."

Bo's mind traveled at the speed of sound. "What matter?"

"Gath Ramla to be precise."

Bo's eyes darted to Griff's. "We've been briefed on the intelligence memos you forwarded to the Agency on Ramla. Our code name for him is Goliath."

"An apt name for your nemesis," Judah spat. "The Palestinian seeks revenge for acts of courage by Commander Mac Rider, Bo's father. Excuse me. I mean the man who raised Bo."

"To me, he is my dad. Call him Mac."

"He is a hero to us all," Judah replied. "The terrorist Bo and the female agent tackled following the bakery bombing confessed that Goliath, who ordered the bombing, is a highly placed officer in Hamas, adept at sneaking into Israel from Gaza. When he rigged a bomb at the ski resort, he came close to achieving revenge on Mac."

Memories of the blast on that snowy afternoon flooded Bo's mind. Anger spiked in his chest and he dug at his beard, wanting to tear it off along with Goliath's head.

"I will never forget the evil giant," Bo said, his voice a bare whisper. "Each time I gaze from a window, my eyes see him."

"Very likely. Our people observe him occasionally in Tel Aviv."

"Then arrest him!" Bo's rising voice revealed his growing agitation.

Judah lifted his chin. "This is where we need to coordinate with you. Remember Sadie Lamb, the American teaching school in Gaza, now being held by Hamas?" Judah fixed a penetrating gaze upon Bo. "She was captured after meeting with your station chief in Tel Aviv."

"Don't assume she is with the Agency simply because she talked to Mike Spencer."

Judah laughed, slapping the table. "We assume nothing; however,

Hamas thinks she is your spy. Goliath ordered her seizure and supervises her captors."

"I want to secure her release. But are you suggesting if we ignore the spy in our embassy," Bo snorted, "Goliath lets her go free?"

"Goliath will never allow Sadie to be freed," Judah said softly.

Griff shattered the momentary silence with a question of his own. "Judah, are you concerned her meeting with Mike Spencer leaked from the embassy?"

"Of course. And if we do not first plug the leak from your embassy, Goliath will kidnap other Sadie Lambs, or kill them as he tried with you, Skip Pierce."

Bo put on his glasses. "I'm listening."

"The day after Sadie's kidnapping, Hamas seized our IDF soldier, Herzl Abraham, as he dispersed rioters near Gaza. Hamas illegally detains him. Through recent surveillance on Goliath, Mossad has located where Herzl and Sadie are being held."

"Let's get them out!" Bo said, ripping off his fake glasses. His anger began fueling a possible strategy to free the captives.

Judah's intense eyes never left Bo's. "We should agree on our strategy. Stop the leak, then launch the rescue."

"To be clear," Griff said with narrowed eyes, "you're not afraid an arrest of the spy will get Herzl killed?"

"I want Herzl back yesterday." Judah paused, his voice thick with emotion. "Our plan is to draw Goliath from Gaza, capturing him the moment our rangers raid his Gaza hideout."

Bo drummed his fingers on the table. "Do you believe Goliath is the spy? If so, how's he gaining access?"

"Someone is working with him," was all Judah said.

"Okay. So we find his 'someone' and then lure Goliath from Gaza. How do you propose doing that?" Bo asked, tapping his glasses against his thumb.

"Griff sends a communiqué to your embassy saying Bo Rider returns to Tel Aviv. Include your hotel arrangements and everything. Goliath steps right into our trap."

Bo lunged at Judah across the table. "You'd use me like a piece of cheese?"

"Wait!" Griff held up a hand. "Judah's on to something here. We set up the traitor who is disclosing our movements and rescue our teacher and Israel's soldier."

"I want justice for what happened to my dad, but you're not the cheese. I am!"

Judah spun out of his chair and walked over to Bo. "Goliath is a rat, but you are no mere decoy. What you and I performed in the dark of night in Iran was more dangerous."

"I agree there, but he's tried twice and failed."

Bo had to think, but adrenaline pumping through him made it difficult to concentrate.

Judah grasped his shoulder. "Mossad will call upon an entire team to free Herzl and Sadie. We will keep Goliath from knowing you are in Israel until the precise moment we launch the raid."

"No!" Bo shook off Judah's hand. "He's found me and each time a bomb went off. You can't control what he knows."

Griff held up both hands. "Will you agree we can at least solidify a plan?"

"I'm trying not to picture my wife, kids, and parents without me."

"With God leading, our mission will succeed," Griff said matter-of-factly.

The powerful look in Griff's eyes revealed the federal agent meant he was trusting in God to bring a positive result. A mental image tore through Bo's mind. Before he'd left for Israel, he'd walked into the master bedroom for his jacket and found Julia on her knees beside the bed. She hadn't risen right away, but when she did, her face had radiated peace. Unlike the past when she'd tried to hide her tears, she had smiled and her words from that morning echoed in his mind.

"I asked God to protect you with ten thousand angels," Julia had said. "That's in the Bible. I have to believe you will make it back to us."

Bringing his mind to the present, Bo moistened his lips, unwilling to tell the other agents of Julia's prediction. Did he believe it himself? As he considered the strength of his wife's faith, the wall he'd built against Judah's proposal began to crumble.

"No one in my family is safe with Goliath walking a free man. I'll do it."

42

Bo awoke the next morning, surprisingly refreshed despite the looming mission. He showered beneath a skimpy spray and dressed in jeans and a khaki shirt, the truth hitting him with the force of a Mack truck. Why had he agreed to be the decoy luring Goliath into the trap?

"Julia better be right that I'm coming home," he muttered, sliding on his glasses.

He wasn't superstitious, but three strikes meant you were out. Shellie once said that; had she been making a threat? Bo decided to forget trimming his beard. He wouldn't cut his hair either. Grabbing a toothbrush, he stared in the mirror trying to decide if he should dye them both when a rap on the bathroom door startled him. He pulled it open, facing Griff.

"I smell coffee," Bo said. "I slept in later than I wanted. Have you eaten?"

"Bagels are toasting. Brewster arrives in thirty minutes bringing what we asked."

"That gives us time for breakfast. I'm starving."

Bo tossed down his toothbrush, following Griff to the kitchen. Griff poured orange juice and Bo spread cream cheese on cooling bagels, curious about Brewster Miles, the MI5 agent Bo had conferred with. Only he'd told Bo he was on loan to MI6, Britain's CIA.

"You're pretty confident about this Miles?" Bo asked, his knife poised in the air.

Griff placed the juice on the table and sat beside Bo. "Do I trust him?"

Bo placed a bagel in front of Griff before biting into his own. "Uh huh."

"Remember El Samoud, the terrorist who headed up the Armed Revolutionary Cause?"

"Yeah," Bo mumbled as he swallowed, "the terrorist spin-off group from Al Qaeda."

"I was on Eva's Terrorism Task Force and crossed paths with Brewster. The three of us posed as scientists going to an island where ARC had their headquarters. I snuck aboard their mobile command ship and installed a device. I was scared to death, but Brewster and Eva covered my back. I'm here to talk about it."

"I guess you have reason to trust him." Bo still wasn't sure about bringing in a Brit.

Griff sipped his juice. "Like I learned to trust you after our New York City job."

A knock at the door. Griff scurried over to the security monitor, admitting their guest.

"Brewster, it's great to see you again. I understand you and Bo have met."

"Pleasure is mine, mate. Bo, do I recall you are with the State Department?"

Bo laughed. "I never set foot at Foggy Bottom. Langley is where I hang out."

After shaking hands all around, the three agents convened their meeting at the dining room table with Griff taking the lead.

"We have a chance to work together; however, Bo complains we're using him as bait."

"Unfortunately, it seems the only way to stop a terrorist before he kills someone I love," Bo replied, taking off his pretend glasses and twirling them. "Did you locate any video from your embassy's Christmas party?"

Brewster set his carrying case on the table, then opened it, plugging in an electric cord. "I have the memory card from that night and a digital display. I hope you spot the fellow with your Security Director on this small screen. The entry camera should show every guest arriving."

Images started, with Griff asking the Brit to speed the film. "At least until Bo sees someone familiar."

Brewster adjusted the speed, with Bo watching guests climb the embassy steps. Several men in suits and one woman in a long dress left the party. Then no one came or went for some seconds.

"I entered your embassy using my real identity and it felt strange," Bo said as the film flickered past.

Griff said to Brewster, "You should know Bo is now in Israel using his undercover identity, Skip Pierce."

Just then Bo spotted Shellie. "Back up! Stop on the woman in the brown pantsuit."

Brewster played back the video, with Bo pointing, "There she is."

"Shellie was in charge of security at our embassy," Griff jumped in.

"She has been shipped to the States to train new security officers at the Federal Law Enforcement Training Center. We're trying to prove she allowed unauthorized people to access embassy computers."

Brewster's finger hovered over the machine. "Should I switch to another camera angle?"

"No. Stop when you see me arrive at the party."

Time passed in silence. Bo stared at grainy images of men and women ascending the steps. He saw himself enter the building, then Griff snapped, "Back up. Skip's new disguise is brilliant, but I just glimpsed a clean-cut version of Bo Rider enter the building."

Brewster rewound. "My word, lad, you look like a true diplomat without your beard and longer hair. I was watching for you and failed to recognize you."

"I don't look much like a piece of cheese now. A private joke, but the fact you didn't spot me on the video is reassuring." Bo adjusted his glasses. "Play a bit more. I haven't seen the suspicious man I recall from the reception."

A steady flow of guests coming and leaving continued, but their faces became harder to identify as darkness descended. Bo saw himself hurrying down the steps.

"You better stop the video." He sighed. "The suspect I saw talked with Shellie at the reception. With me leaving, this camera angle missed him."

Brewster switched to a video with a different camera angle. "Watch the main corridor and embassy employees getting on and off the elevators near the reception hall. But I hope this is not bad news for my government."

Griff folded his arms, looking askance. "What do you mean?"

"Your target may have never arrived," Brewster replied, clearing his throat. "Perhaps he was already in the British Embassy because he works there."

Bo secretly hoped that to be the case, otherwise this effort would lead nowhere. He flashed a thumbs-up and Brewster increased the speed. Many of the same people Bo had seen entering the embassy mixed in the corridor before exiting off-screen. Then he saw him.

"Wait! Run it back."

Brewster did and Bo glimpsed a tall man with blond hair walking from the elevator.

"It's him!" Bo cried, pointing. "He's the guy I saw talking with Shellie."

The video played and Bo watched the man standing in the corridor for some seconds before walking out of sight.

"The lavatory is further down the hall. He might have gone there," Brewster offered.

Soon the man reappeared and waited in the hall, his hands clutched behind his back. Suddenly Shellie stalked into the corridor, facing him. They possibly spoke, but then she turned. After the briefest moment, the unidentified man followed her into the reception room.

Bo leaned back, relieved. "Our search has ended."

"Are you sure he is the one you saw with Shellie?" Griff demanded.

"Oh yes. The fuzzy guy is burned in my memory. How he approached her from behind, placed a hand on her hip, and spoke in her ear."

Griff tapped his temple. "And how did she react to his touching her that way?"

"She didn't, which made me uncomfortable for her. I don't think a woman would accept a stranger doing that."

Brewster turned up the speed. "I want to see if they come out together. The man looks familiar. If I am correct, we have reason for concern."

Bo watched his own image enter in fast-motion and proceed to the party. Much later the unidentified man came out again, lurking in the corridor speaking to no one.

"That's him," Bo hissed.

Griff squinted at the screen. "I can't tell. The film is quite grainy."

"With his height and blond hair, it's him."

"To be on the safe side," Brewster intoned, "I'll slow it down. See what he does."

Brewster returned to real speed and then it happened. Shellie Karnack hurried from the reception hall, sweeping by the man. Their mouths didn't appear to move, but they walked to the elevator, entering it together.

"Uh-oh! Did you see that?" Brewster asked, sounding unusually ruffled.

Griff was first to respond. "They know each other but are careful not to appear familiar."

"This is terrible, chaps," Brewster lamented, stopping the video. "I do not recall his name, but I have encountered him. He works in our Foreign Service."

"What does he do for your country?" Bo pressed.

"I am not sure he does anything for *my* country, but he should not be assigned here. Last I heard he had a do-nothing job at Whitehall in information technology, what we call IT."

"A do-nothing job? Really, Brewster?" Bo jabbed his index finger at the MI5 agent, then curled his finger. "Keep it coming. I smell another rat here."

Brewster twisted his lips. "Before meeting you last November, I had been in London where I watched a military attaché from Russia's embassy day and night. Twice your man on the video was observed drinking at a pub with the Russian. His hair seemed darker then."

"If our guy is a Russian agent, what is he doing at the British Embassy in Israel? He should be behind bars," Bo growled.

"I was on surveillance, so I do not know his name. MI5 questioned and polygraphed him, but nothing was proven. They relegated him to the basement with access to nothing."

Bo was stunned by the admission. "Your snake has wriggled out of the basement."

"We have to find out what's going on here." Brewster ran back the video. "I will pause when I have a clearer view of his face."

"Stop right there," Griff said, pulling out his cell phone. "I'll snap his picture at the point he sees Shellie and another when they appear together on screen."

As Griff took the photos, Brewster turned to Bo setting his jaw.

"I will contact Whitehall for this chap's name."

"A meager start, Brewster. Griff can show his mug to our Marine sergeant who observed Shellie bringing your IT guy into our embassy and using the Ambassador's computer."

Brewster's face turned to stone. "MI6 should know why he is assigned to our embassy. Be assured I mean to run it to ground."

"This explains why no one in the U.S. Embassy fell for the decoy memos I'd placed in our system." Bo rose, darting to the window. "*Someone* had already told this guy that CIA agent Bo Rider was coming to Israel. And that someone is most likely our mole."

"Let's get to work," Griff ordered.

Adrenaline pulsed through Bo. He whirled around, hoping this was no red herring.

"I agree. This is our best lead yet."

BO'S AGITATION GREW with each passing day. Would their Ops plan, the one where Bo would be dangled like bait, ever come to fruition?

At four in the afternoon the following Sunday, he opened the door to the safe house. Brewster Miles breezed in carrying his leather case, a box, and a sack. He walked straight to the dining room table, where he dumped the box and sack.

"I bought some fabulous Israeli cake for your midday coffee. There's also pretzels coated with sesame seeds."

"How did you know I'm ravenous?"

"I've been holed up in safe houses in Paris, Vienna, and even in Moscow."

That was one positive result from the time spent in the safe house; Bo was beginning to appreciate Brewster's fine qualities.

"Help yourself to coffee," Bo told him. "I'll cut the cake."

Brewster poured steaming brew into a tall mug. "Where is your sidekick?"

"At the embassy for show-and-tell. I expected Griff before now. He knows you're coming."

Bo sliced off two chunks of cake, wrapping the rest for Griff. He and Brewster ate their snack in silence, Bo wiping his mouth on his sleeve. Without warning, he heard someone press the door code outside. He jumped up. Through the peephole saw a scowling Griff. Bo stepped aside and Griff stormed in, tossing his jacket on the chair. Bo shut the door.

"Someone followed me from the embassy. I drove clear to Jaffa before I lost him. Then I switched rental cars. They made me take the tiniest green car on the planet. My knees were bumping the wheel."

"Who tailed you?" Brewster called from the kitchen.

"A Land Rover, dark blue. Male driver wore shades. I couldn't get a license number."

"Sit down and cool off over some cake compliments of Brewster." Bo handed him a plate and Brewster brought him a steaming cup.

Griff dug into the cake, and Brewster took a file from his leather case.

"A courier sent this from Whitehall. Drum roll please. Hosni Malik is the tall, blond man playing friendly with your Security Director."

"Is he the same guy who met with the Russian attaché in London?" Griff asked between bites of cake.

Brewster frowned. "He most certainly is. I find Hosni Malik a curious figure."

"May I?" Bo held out his hand. "I'd like to read the file myself."

Brewster handed the file to Bo and his eyes tore through a few typed pages.

"He's Egyptian, immigrating to Britain at sixteen with his father, over twenty years ago. His mother died when he was two weeks old. Educated at Cambridge."

"Not much to go on." Griff plunked down his fork.

Bo slapped the file on the table. "Brewster, tell us what's not written here."

The Brit didn't answer. He rose, and taking Bo's usual spot by the window, he peered out. "I do not like Griff being followed."

"Hey, I didn't like the Rover on my tail either. Things are escalating and we'd better decide our next move if we're going to snag this spy and neutralize him."

"With Shellie Karnack in the States, Ambassador Cohen has new freedom to operate. So does his wife," Brewster observed.

Bo wanted to bring Brewster back around to Malik. "Could Shellie be contacting either Hal or Malik from Georgia?"

"Our Washington Field office is quietly pulling her phone records," Griff said, making notes. "We should avoid putting her on alert until we've exhausted all other possibilities."

"The chocolate cake stoked my appetite." Bo reached across the table, tearing open the bag of pretzels. "Griff, did Sergeant Engle recognize anyone in your digital photos?"

"Yes. He identified Malik without hesitation. The tech who found the flash drive on Hal's computer is still here from Washington. I talked to him and he's afraid someone used Hal's computer to download classified files onto a similar flash drive."

Brewster helped himself to a pretzel. "What was on the original flash drive, the one he found? That might point to our next move."

"Nothing." Griff swiped at his moustache. "The FBI tech believes one drive could have already been filled and the clean one inserted in Hal's USB port. Something or someone scared away the mole before he or she could download anything onto the clean drive."

Bo leapt up. "Who is behind this? Engle said he hadn't seen Malik at the embassy since Shellie went to the U.S., but Hal still works in his office. Can't State recall the Ambassador for bogus training in D.C.?"

"That's a brilliant idea," Griff lowered his voice to a bare whisper. "Our tech suspects the mole installed a Trojan Horse or keystroke program capable of launching on command at some future date. If

Hal isn't here to log onto his computer, the spy is frozen out and learns nothing."

Bo shook his head furiously. "Clara uses Hal's computer. She also has to be sent back."

"Griff, are you saying the spy set up a site in his or her own lair and has a window into everything typed on Hal's computer?" Brewster's eyes blazed.

"Yes and even worse, it's possible the mole can garner ever-changing passwords for Hal's computer, giving the spy free access to roam the network and open entrée to our embassy."

Bo sat at the table, tapping Brewster's file. "Even from the basement of Whitehall, he could know our every move."

"If a Trojan Horse or keystroke software has launched and we were to query the system, it might alert the spy we're on to him. Your colleague is a menace." Griff rose to stand by Brewster.

Brewster looked crushed. "A Brit spying on America is *not* working for Whitehall."

"Take no offense, but I'm afraid that remains to be seen," Griff said, nodding at Bo. "There's only one thing to do."

"You want me to leave." Brewster took his file and snapped shut his case.

"Stop!" Griff barked. "You're under no suspicion. We must be more diligent in keeping our own counsel. Agreed, Bo?"

"Yes, but don't either of you forget I am the decoy."

Bo narrowed his eyes, feeling troubled. Though Brewster seemed a great guy and all, some of the world's most treacherous spies had spawned from Britain. One of their Cambridge scientists had handed the Soviets U.S. secret plans for the nuclear bomb at the end of WWII.

Griff motioned them back to the table. "It's time to let Judah know we are launching Operation Cheese Caper. Bo, have the Agency send a message to the embassy of your imminent return to Tel Aviv. We'll be all over the response to that."

"Before I go public and risk another bomb attack," Bo said, "we should pressure State to recall the Cohens. We need to discover what else Malik knows."

"We'll put round-the-clock surveillance on him."

Brewster straightened his tie. "I shall not let you down. Whitehall is stalling me on why Malik was freed from its bowels and how he ended up in Tel Aviv. Once I learn those facts, Operation Cheese Caper can proceed full throttle. Give me a day or two."

"Any chance you can get me his fingerprints? I want our lab to process them." At Brewster's nod, Griff added, "I used the embassy's secure phone to run down print analysis on the flash drive from Hal's computer."

"Whose prints are on it?" Bo's voice sounded strained to his ears.

"A smeared print with unidentifiable chemical residue."

"No usable print. No way to trace the chemical. Chaps, we are dealing with a pro and not an innocent intruder," was Brewster's take.

No kidding. Bo stomped to the window, angling the blinds with a clatter.

"Thinking about Clara drawing Julia into her intrigues makes me crazy," he whispered, not sure if either Griff or Brewster heard.

It didn't matter. The mole was out there, breathing down their necks and Bo was doing nothing but talking in constant meetings. Their team moving forward an inch at a time was pure torture. Drip, drip, drip with no end in sight.

43

For Griff Topping, the most dangerous aspect of Operation Cheese Caper was just around the corner, literally. He slouched in the rear seat of an unmarked car in the dead of night. Only Tel Aviv pulsated with bright lights and young people roaming the streets, laughing and skipping into nightclubs dotting the avenues. He hoped the partiers were oblivious to their mission—foreign intelligence operators creeping into the home of their Egyptian-born target for evidence.

Brewster turned the rental car down a narrow street leading to a quieter neighborhood, shooting a glance at Griff over his shoulder.

"Malik boarded the flight to New York taking him to Jacksonville, Florida, right?"

"Yes," Griff replied, his knees bent. "I suspect he'll rent a car and visit Shellie in Glynco, Georgia."

It was his own fault his knees ached; he'd chosen to ride in the back behind Oliver Sterling, the bow-tie-wearing computer techie MI5 had sent from London.

"Oliver, once Griff gains entry into Malik's residence," Brewster said, slowing the car, "you have twenty minutes to find all unauthorized equipment or data."

"Will one of you agents be with me the whole time?"

"Griff will instruct you every step of the way," Brewster reassured his fellow Brit.

Hopefully not holding his hand. Griff muffled a sigh. Oliver had never participated in an officially-condoned burglary, which gave Griff pause. So did the motorcycle buzzing behind the rental car. He leaned forward so Brewster could hear.

"Did you find out why your foreign service sent Malik to Israel after he had met with a Russian military attaché?"

"I was given two possible answers."

"Typical spy mumbo-jumbo. Someone messed up," Griff grunted.

"You're spot on. Or, the Foreign Office wrongfully surmised he was not a suspect."

Oliver twisted in the front seat, craning his head sideways. "Hosni Malik is a genius. He is a danger to any intelligence service computers."

"Brewster, this is beyond belief. My British grandfather would turn over in his grave. Didn't you guys learn anything after Kim Philby defected to Russia?"

"Admiral Topping is one of England's most distinguished heroes. There are still a few committed ones left. Do not lose hope in me."

"Brewster, I pulled you in because you wear a white hat."

Brewster jammed on the brakes. "I do not care for that motor bike. He stays behind me."

"Can't you lose him?"

"We're almost to Malik's."

Silence enveloped the slow-moving car until the motorcycle finally roared on by.

Brewster grunted as if relieved. "I insisted MI5 send Oliver because he trained Malik and he knows what Malik should rightly have in his possession."

"Your compliment rings hollow, old chap. It is too risky sneaking into someone's home." Oliver turned to stare out the window.

"Keep your hair on. What you and Griff are about to do is vital to our security."

Brewster wheeled the car around the corner with uncharacteristic speed. Griff sensed he was growing touchy over Oliver's fears, which erased the last shred of Griff's confidence in a positive outcome. Suddenly he recognized the neighborhood from yesterday's reconnaissance. Griff pulled on latex gloves, gathered up his tool kit, and tapped Brewster on the shoulder.

"Drop me at the corner. Once inside I'll call on the radio and Oliver can join me."

"I will watch your backside from the car," Brewster promised, pulling to the curb.

Griff opened the passenger door, nudging it closed to make no noise, and strolled back down the street, slipping between two multi-story apartment buildings. It was so quiet in the confining space—he heard no one talking or even dogs barking—that it unnerved him. Griff breathed deeply to calm his claustrophobia, then stopped near an alley, carefully peering around the corner of a high fence.

Whoa! Seventy feet away a man hurried straight for him. With no time to retreat, Griff flattened against the fence standing motionless. He didn't even breathe. The man hurried past without looking toward him.

Griff clutched his tool kit, crossing the alley to the side of another apartment building, where he easily found the ground level entrance to Malik's apartment. Holding a pen light between his teeth, Griff inserted a tension bar and a pick into the lock, gently massaging the tumblers. It refused to budge. Sweat broke out on his forehead. With a sleeve he wiped his eyes.

He eased the tension on the bar and repeated his moves, his brain warning him to beat it before a nosy neighbor phoned the local police. Griff said a silent prayer and steadied his hand, tapping the pins some more.

To his amazement the bar slid easily. He pushed open the door, listening for alarms to sound. None did and he saw no alarm panel. In total darkness, his senses on high alert, Griff flashed his pen light around the small foyer before keying the mic on the portable radio.

"All is well. Send my assistant."

Two clicks of the squelch. Okay, Brewster responded without speaking. Griff walked lightly down the hall to a small bedroom and with the aid of his tiny light, he spotted a laptop on a desk near some books. He'd just opened the center drawer on the desk when the earpiece from his radio crackled.

"Take good care of him. He is scared."

Griff clicked his microphone twice letting Brewster know he copied. Did the MI5 agent think Griff wasn't scared? He'd have to be crazy not to be nervous committing a burglary. Still, the Op must be worse for Oliver, the techie being neither trained nor paid for covert action.

After checking the rest of the small apartment and finding zero of interest in the bathroom or kitchen, he returned to wait by the front door. In seconds, a breathless Oliver arrived carrying a backpack.

"Agent Topping, just show me the computers."

"There's one in the bedroom."

Oliver began unzipping his backpack as he followed Griff down the carpeted hallway to the bedroom where he handed Oliver a pen light.

"Computer's on the desk. Gadgets are in the drawer. I'll do a more thorough sweep and keep an eye on the front door."

"Um … might someone find us here? I thought the owner was out of town."

"He is," Griff snarled. "Be quick about your business. Did you put on your gloves?"

"Yes." Oliver clicked on a tiny flashlight and lifted a laptop from his backpack.

Griff left Oliver alone to probe the secrets of the computer world. He hurried to look in the shower and bathroom cabinet, ignoring musty smells of used towels. Finding a hair, he slid the potential evidence into a glassine envelope. In the kitchen, he pulled open cupboard doors, doing a double take with what he saw in the freezer.

Did those foil-wrapped packages contain drugs? Griff unwrapped a bundle, surprised it contained currency. He opened the rest, finding close to thirty thousand Euros. A rapid-fire decision made, he snapped photos with his cell phone camera and rewrapped the bundles. He eyed the sparse living room. A sofa, but no books or magazines. Griff figured Malik must spend all his spare time on the computer doing who knew what.

Beneath the sofa cushions, his fingers rattled something like paper. He yanked out a torn photograph of two people. He didn't want to turn on the light and so instead, he memorized where he'd taken the photo from. Opening the door to the fridge for light, he snapped photos with his cell.

"Police car!" Brewster hissed in Griff's ear. "He is slowing down to eyeball my car, so I am moving down the street. Stay alert. He drove toward the alley behind Malik's."

Griff double-clicked his mic before heading to the bedroom where he laid a hand on Oliver's shoulder. "Quiet. A police car is driving by."

Through a crack in the curtain, Griff saw headlights fill the alley. He ran to the front door, locked it, and returned to the bedroom. Though it was dark, he saw the police car stop behind Malik's house. Griff held his breath and Oliver seemed frozen like a statue.

Suddenly a spotlight swept the other side of the alley, then across the bedroom window. Griff ducked involuntarily. Had he triggered a burglar alarm? At the sound of a two-way radio, he heard a muffled voice. His mind calculated at the speed of sound. One thing was in his favor.

Mossad would vouch for him if Griff's actions were in Israel's national interest. Good thing Mossad had sanctioned this insertion into Malik's home. Yet, Griff didn't want the embarrassment of being caught by local police. He listened to Oliver's harsh breathing as if any second he'd have a heart attack. The tech was a liability, a loose cannon who would blab his head off to get out of a jam.

Finally the lights passed down the alley and Griff saw the beautiful red glow of taillights. Soon the alley grew dark and Brewster announced, "All clear."

To his credit and in spite of the scare, Oliver got busy downloading data to his computer from Malik's laptop.

"I say," Oliver grunted as he finished sucking what he could from Malik's computer. "I found dozens of cords, but no hard drives or thumb drives. Where is your spy's hidden cache?"

"What's a thumb drive?" Griff asked, shining his tiny flashlight along the floor.

"Small metal things you insert into the USB port. About the size of a gum packet."

"Oh, you mean a flash drive."

His heart rate returning to normal, Griff went to work finding something they could use against Malik. He slid open the bedroom closet, tapping each shoe hoping something would fall out. The shelves held folded sweaters, but nothing hidden between the folds. He patted each pair of hanging trousers, suddenly declaring, "Something feels like gum."

Oliver hurried over, thrusting his hand into the pocket.

"By George, you've found them."

He snatched out two flash drives and rushed to his computer saying, "Remember which pocket these came from. You can have them back in a jiffy."

Groaning, Oliver started downloading and Griff returned the torn photo beneath the sofa cushion, wanting to finish their search before the police car returned. In each drawer he opened in the living room, he anticipated some big find, but he found nothing incriminating.

Griff stepped in the bedroom in time to hear Oliver say, "Bob's your uncle!"

"Who? I have no uncle named Bob."

"That may be, but I found enough to believe Malik is our man."

"What did you find?"

Oliver handed Griff the two flash drives. "I will tell you when we reach the car. I do not like it in here."

"Fair enough. How much longer do you need?"

"I am done." Oliver zipped his backpack.

Griff called Brewster for a pick-up in three minutes. Then he turned to Oliver, ordering him to leave nothing behind. Oliver clutched his backpack like a life preserver. Griff returned the drives to the trouser pocket, then led the way silently out of the apartment and into the alley. The duo hopped into Brewster's car.

Rather than trade high-fives—the MI5 agent had already started driving off—Griff leaned forward, slugging Oliver's shoulder.

"You're in the big league. How does it feel protecting your country?"

"Brilliant! I found volumes of evidence. He erased files most innocent people do not bother to erase. I will know more when I evaluate his content."

Griff tapped his shoulder. "Oliver, did you lose it in there? You said Bob was my uncle."

Brewster chuckled. "Griff, being part British you should know 'Bob's your uncle,' is saying 'Bingo!' in the States."

Griff scrunched his knees, finding Oliver's oddities far from funny. He was antsy to brief Brewster and Bo about the frozen cash and the torn photo. First, Brewster had to drop Oliver at the airport so the tech could perform his analysis in the safety of Whitehall. Would that or the money bring them any closer to catching the mole?

44

When Griff and Brewster returned from the clandestine search of Malik's apartment, Bo sensed escape from the monotonous safe house was at hand. He gave back Griff's cell after studying the photo.

"What is your opinion?" Brewster asked from across the table.

Bo flexed his fingers, sensing they were close to liftoff. He steeled himself for action.

"It's one-half of her face, but that's Shellie sitting with Malik in a restaurant. If we could identify the place, we might locate witnesses to their close relationship."

"Malik has returned from the States." Griff put his cell phone in the holder with a snap.

Then with a nod, he asked Brewster to share the latest on Malik.

A rustling sound at the door brought Bo leaping to his feet and pushing an eye against the peephole.

"Judah Levitt is here," Bo said turning. He watched Brewster's lips curl. Did the Brit have some beef with Mossad?

"Too many people coming and going from here," Brewster said, his brow creased.

Bo went over and laid a hand on his arm. "I felt that way about you jumping in the fray, but Griff vouched for you. Judah and I worked a dangerous Op in Iran. He's seriously scary, but oh so good. See for yourself, Brewster."

He opened the door and greeted Judah who stopped abruptly when he saw Brewster.

Griff introduced the MI5 agent, chuckling. "Our discoveries have turned us into a mini-UN."

"Let us hope we succeed in stopping Goliath," Brewster said in all seriousness.

Judah nodded, pulling on his beard.

"It's time to act in our mutual interests." Bo forged the way to the dining room. He was so ready to get his Op moving.

Four agents from three different countries nabbed seats around the table, with Griff consulting his notes and telling Judah how he and Brewster searched Malik's apartment.

"Evidence found by the FBI computer tech proves he tampered with computers at the U.S. and British embassies."

"I have information to share about Malik," Brewster added.

Bo held up a hand. "First let Griff bring us up to speed on Malik's activities in Georgia."

"He spent an entire day with Shellie Karnack. We don't know if his time with her in Georgia was strictly social and if she's naïve—"

"Or something more sinister," Bo interrupted.

"We have had a tail on Malik since his return from the U.S. Did he meet with anyone else while there?" Judah wanted to know.

"Not on the ground, but get this. Our FBI agent saw him trade valises with a Russian KGB agent on his flight from La Guardia to Jacksonville." Griff looked down at his notes. "The Russian agent opened the overhead, removing Malik's valise. In turn, Malik left the plane with a similar-looking case from above the Russian's seat. They did not speak."

Judah rose, pouring himself hot coffee in the kitchen. When he returned to the table, his dark eyes were edged with concern. "Malik is in collusion with Russia. The plot thickens."

Griff flipped a page on his pad. "The Russian stayed in Jackson-ville for two days, returning to LaGuardia on the same flight as Malik. Guess what?"

"They switched bags a second time," Bo answered.

When Griff said, "Yes," Judah banged down his cup.

"Malik must have a Russian handler in the region. Hamas receives time sensitive intelligence from your embassy on a regular basis. I suspect the valises held cash or even computer software. The Russians are adept at playing both sides in the Middle East. They send intelligence to Hamas using their contacts in Egypt."

"Open these," Brewster said, passing three packets around the table. "Malik was born in Egypt and his extended family lives in Cairo. Whitehall analyzed his three flash drives. The first one had a keystroke program and, gentlemen, it is serious. Malik had continual access to British and American computers."

Bo's heart pumped furiously, his eyes tearing through the rest of Brewster's material. "It says here that his second flash drive held copies of embassy messages, including U.S. directives and Israeli policy for Hal's upcoming summit with the Palestinians."

His eyes landed on a crucial sentence. "Wow! Malik hacked into orders for my coming to Israel. He even knew my arrival date."

"Exactly." Brewster tapped a file. "His final drive contained something strange. Photos of ancient Hebrew carvings our archivist thinks are copies of an ancient book found in Israel."

"He couldn't find ancient Hebrew documents in our embassy," Bo said.

"Nor in ours," Brewster added with a grimace.

Bo and Brewster turned to Judah who took his time scanning the file. Griff looked on, palming his moustache expectantly.

"Malik should not have these." Judah squared his jaw, fire dancing in his eyes. "These are closely guarded by our government. I fear your spy has hacked into our sensitive war plans and has copies of our ancient texts."

"Did Malik steal what I think he has?" Bo raised his eyebrows.

"Hakarat ha'emet," was all Judah said.

"My Hebrew is rusty." Bo removed his glasses. "Care to decipher?"

Judah pointed at a photo of the ancient Hebrew text. "I said, 'we must be strong and brave.' Malik has obtained an exact copy of the ancient survey written by Jewish tribes for Commander Joshua."

"The codex," Bo whispered.

Griff shifted on his chair. "What's the fuss? Anyone can open the Bible and read how God promised land to the Israelites."

"My friend, these surveys are secret and have never been released to the world. They justify our future plans to regain every inch of land once lived in by Jewish tribes. It is our Promised Land from the Mediterranean to the Euphrates River, all given to us by God. His land covenant encompasses parts of Egypt, Syria, and Jordan. Can you imagine the outcry if this becomes known?"

As Bo smoothed his beard, he felt compelled to add, "Malik's clandestine photos prove one thing, Griff. That Dr. Van Horn is right about the Joshua Covenant."

"The entire Arab world will erupt in flames if even a portion of the codex is released," Judah said. "But no matter what arrows they fire at us, someday Israel will be as large as God intended her to be."

Brewster's face had turned gray. "Chaps, listen. MI5 downloaded the flash drive, but we do not know what Malik will do or has done with the original. Did he give a copy to the Russian agent?"

"Perhaps he is holding the codex photos for a larger future payment," Bo offered.

Judah's eyes glittered in the bright light. "Though our enemies deny part of their land was originally Jewish territory, Israel will fight to the death to remain alive. When attacked we will recapture our land."

Bo rose from the table, finding his perch at the window. Glenna and Gregg had walked the streets where Jesus did, almost losing their father to a hate-filled maniac. Uncertain of Malik's true intentions, Bo had to act.

He clenched his fists, facing the others. "Malik is in league with Russian foreign agents and most likely Goliath, the Palestinian who won't stop trying to kill me and my dad. He is an enemy to each of us and must be stopped!"

"Let it be so," Judah agreed, his quiet voice holding force of his convictions.

"MI5 stuck Malik in a do-nothing job *after* discovering he met with Russians two years ago," Griff interjected. "He ends up in Tel Aviv, with Shellie inviting him into our embassy. Something smells."

"Brewster, how do you propose uncovering his friends in your government?" Bo wondered how many superiors Brewster would have to challenge before learning the truth.

The British agent drew out his pipe, whacking the empty bowl against his palm. "My wife convinced me to quit smoking, but this old friend serves a purpose. I have scattered red meat at Whitehall. We shall see which wolf gobbles it up."

"We all agree Malik and Goliath must be caught." Judah looked directly at Bo, as if cuing him to respond.

Bo returned to his seat, knowing the risks involved with Operation Cheese Caper were off the charts. Was he ready?

"Suddenly I feel like a piece of cheese about to catch the giant rat Goliath."

"You and I signed up for danger, my friend."

Bo pushed hair behind his ears. "But I never expected to amble down the street wearing a sign saying, 'Here I am, come kill me.'"

Griff sought Bo's gaze. "Look around you. With our expertise, we can do this."

Unwilling his friend should discover how much he wanted to settle the score, Bo dropped his eyes, determined to avenge the damage and pain Goliath had caused Mac, his dad.

"Okay, I'll have Kangas alert the State Department. Bo Rider returns to Israel for IDF training in the Negev Desert."

"When Goliath races to find you, we free the hostages from the hideout in Gaza." Judah flashed a rare smile at Bo. "Do you want to help Israeli commandos free your American teacher?"

Bo straightened his back, pondering his dilemma: Free Sadie Lamb or face Goliath and give him the justice he deserved.

"You'll make the right choice," Griff said. "Meanwhile Brewster and I will tighten the noose on Malik and Shellie."

Judah pushed himself up from the table. "You have been in the safe house too long."

"If you mean I'm going nuts from isolation, I agree." Bo shoved on his glasses to make his point.

"No, no. You could be discovered here."

Bo's heart thudded. "Are you saying we're already compromised?"

"Mossad cannot guarantee you are safe. We move you in the morning."

Bo had another idea, but would Judah agree?

"Dr. Van Horn speaks in three days at a Bible conference in Nazareth. I could spend time with him while Griff and Brewster are relocated."

"No." Judah raised his thick eyebrows. "I am uncomfortable with you appearing in Nazareth, an Arab town, until we neutralize Goliath."

"Try this. For the next two days, Van Horn is in Tiberias. I can rent a car."

"Only if Mossad drives you there and brings you to the new safe house."

Bo stared into Judah's eyes, his grave stare speaking volumes.

"Agreed, my friend," Bo replied.

But was spending time with Van Horn in the Galilee a wise decision?

45

Water rippled silver beneath scorching sun as Bo looked out from the hotel's open patio. At least he'd found shade while Rik Van Horn finished his phone call inside. Bo toyed with his fork, pushing around an unappetizing pile of lentil salad and wondering what was so important Bo couldn't hear it.

Well, he didn't begrudge Rik keeping secrets, having his own that he'd never share in a million years. Like his soon-to-be role as cheese in a trap for Goliath bent on destruction. A vision of the evil green witch stirring her cauldron flashed through his mind. As a boy, the flying monkeys in *The Wizard of Oz* movie had intrigued him, but he'd been aghast by Dorothy's stunning discovery in Oz. The wizard, an old man working buttons behind a curtain, had no power to grant her wishes.

Bo forced his eyes to the shimmering Sea of Galilee. Would Rik and Julia's belief in God come crashing down in similar fashion? He had to admit there was something real about Julia's faith. She'd become stronger and happier since she began reading her Bible and going to church. Bo pulled out his cell, then his fingers froze. Kangas had forbidden him to call home.

Instead, he mulled over the Op, the truth embedded into his mind. Stopping Goliath wouldn't be as easy as tossing a bucket of water on him, making him melt. Bo's desire for vengeance stirred. He thrust down his fork. It had been a mistake to come see Rik.

"Sorry to be gone so long," Rik remarked behind him.

Bo craned his head, watching Rik take his seat only to stare at Bo's half-eaten plate.

"You don't enjoy the lamb kebob?"

"It's fine. I should clean my plate like Mom taught me, because other children had none."

"Vivian Rider is a wise woman. I look forward to spending time with her."

"She and Dad raised me with good values, but we never ate lamb." Bo forced a grin. "The longer I stay in Israel, I'm getting used to the strong taste."

"I'll settle the bill."

Bo dug into his wallet. "Not for mine."

"It would please me to treat you on occasion."

"Maybe this once." Bo sighed, shoving his wallet in his back pocket.

"I would like to show you a special place. Do you have time?"

Bo didn't know what to say. He'd already decided to leave and meet Judah a day early. Brewster and Griff should be settled in the new safe house and the Mossad agent reading the paper at the far table would drive Bo there. Without warning, a pang of guilt shot through him.

Would he always feel remorse over his tense relationship with the man who fathered him? He watched Rik toss shekels on the table, all the while his eyes seeking Bo's. Something about his beseeching look made Bo relent.

"The hot springs are known for therapeutic properties," he said.

Rik placed a hand on Bo's arm. "We'll drive farther south, if you care to go with me."

Bo imagined Julia's hurt look if he reneged on his duty to Rik. She sure had taken a shine to Rik and Adriana, almost as if she were their own daughter. Out of respect for his wife, Bo said, "For you, Rik, I have all day."

The man's face brightened like a thousand suns. Bo exchanged his glasses for sunglasses, wondering what he might learn about Rik before the day's end. What more might he learn about himself?

B O RODE ALONG the seven or so miles down the highway, listening as Rik shared how he'd seen God fulfill several prophecies in his lifetime. "When the State of Israel was created in 1948, I was a toddler, but my father lauded the news with great enthusiasm."

Bo turned to Rik surprised. He'd never once thought of Rik as a child, never even asking where he grew up. Before he could fire off a question, Rik continued talking about his love for Israel.

"Secondly, tribes from Ethiopia, Russia, and Europe began gathering in the land God provided for them. The Jewish people regaining control of Jerusalem after the Six Day War is equally important."

"If what you call 'prophecy' is done, why keep coming to Israel? What are you looking for?"

"I am thrilled to meet Jews that are flocking to Israel from all over the world after being dispersed for thousands of years. These happenings are written in God's Word as needing to be fulfilled before the end times. That is why I believe the rapture is near."

Bo looked in his side-view mirror. "I saw a bumper sticker once that said, 'The driver will be missing in case of the rapture.' I thought it meant rupture."

Rik laughed. "Do you want to know what it really means?"

"Sure." Bo shrugged.

"The Bible tells us that when we least expect it, Jesus Christ will descend over earth with a shout and the trumpet of God. All those who have accepted God's gift of forgiveness, both living and dead, will rise to meet Him and go to heaven," Rik said, his voice ringing.

Bo just stared at Rik. It all sounded so strange, like some space movie.

Rik's hands gripped the wheel tightly. "Those who are not taken will be surprised by what happens after Jesus claims His own. Seven years of intense fighting and death will follow."

"Julia told me some of your teaching."

"Bo, I tell it straight from the Bible. After seven years of tribulation, God's forces will fight evil in what is called Armageddon. After that Satan will be bound for a thousand years and Jesus will reign in Jerusalem from a new Temple."

Too much for Bo, he blocked out the rest, his eyes focusing on the black Mercedes squeezing in between their bumper and a vegetable truck. No big deal. It was the Mossad agent trying to keep up with Rik's fast driving. Just then Rik wheeled around a bend and Bo caught his breath at the sight of sparkling water and a halo of mountains.

"Adriana completed her chemo," Rik announced, casting a sideways glance at Bo.

"Is she feeling better?"

"Yes, but not well enough to accompany me on this trip. Perhaps next time."

"Julia will want to know about Adriana's health."

Bo's cell phone rang and he pulled it out telling Rik, "It's probably my team."

"Are we on?" he barked into the phone.

"Bo! It's me, Julia."

"Honey! How great to hear your voice." Bo's lips formed into a wide smile.

"For me too," she giggled. "Frank Deming called to see how we're doing and I asked if I could call you. He gave me the number. I so wanted to talk with you."

"I owe Frank for that. Rik and I just mentioned your name."

"When he phoned last week, he said he'd be going to Israel. I hoped the two of you would get together."

So Rik kept in touch with Julia, but he hadn't mentioned that to Bo. And this time Bo had told his wife where he was going without even thinking. In the future, he'd be more careful.

"How are Gregg and Glenna doing with their studies?"

"I'm busy grading tests, but we drove down to see Dad and Mom."

"You drove all the way to Florida to see your folks?"

"Not quite. We're in Hampton, with yours."

Bo cast a sideways look at Rik but asked Julia, "Is Dad all right?"

"He spends so much time in rehab, Mom sounded lonely when she called. I thought we should come down. I'm helping her redecorate their bedroom."

"Tell them I'll call when I can."

"We miss you, Bo."

He peered at his watch, worried about talking on the phone too long.

"Would you like to speak with Rik?"

"Just give him our love."

"Will do. He said Adriana has finished her chemo."

"Isn't that great? She called to tell me."

"You talked with her?"

"Yesterday. She had another reason for calling. She wants us all—"

Static crackled in Bo's ear. "Julia? Can you hear me?"

More noise. Their connection had been lost.

"Julia and the kids send their love," he said, clipping his phone back in the holder.

"I happily receive such a gift. You have a delightful family. Adriana and I had fun visiting the zoo with Glenna and Gregg." Rik turned into a parking lot filled with cars. "You'll see where the Jordan River and the Sea of Galilee merge. This site was closed after the Six Day War, but recently reopened."

"Does this place have military significance?" Bo kicked his legs out of the car, stepping into the blazing sun. Perhaps he and Rik had something in common after all.

"To me it is a key site of the Christian faith."

"Oh."

Bo walked beside Rik along the stones, shade from palm trees cooling his head. He insisted on paying the fare to go in and Rik brought him to a newly constructed overlook.

"Tradition says Jesus was baptized by John the Baptist in these waters. Do you know that part of history?"

"Can't say I do," was Bo's quick retort.

"You would find John, the cousin of Jesus, an interesting fellow. He ate wild honey and lived in the desert. You could probably relate to his lifestyle."

"I've lived like a vagabond for my country." Bo laughed lightly, tugging his beard. "Did this John have a beard?"

"No doubt; however, he felt inadequate to tie Jesus' sandals let alone to baptize Him."

"But weren't they cousins?"

Bo turned around, seeing twenty or so people in white robes standing behind them. Had he been tricked into attending some church service?

"Jesus encouraged John that by baptizing Him, John would fulfill God's plan so he consented. Just like you are an instrument used by the State Department," Rik winked at Bo, "John accomplished God's purpose. I'm trying to do all I can on earth to do the same."

"What does it mean to be baptized, Rik? I understand none of this." Bo felt his hand creeping to his cell phone, hoping Griff would call about the Op.

Rik jerked his head over his shoulder. "See those folks in the white robes behind us?"

"Yeah," Bo replied tersely.

"They are like the Israelites that Moses led across the Red Sea out of slavery and Joshua took across the Jordan River into the Promised Land. These people are Christians, forgiven by Christ. Their wanting to be baptized is symbolic—being dunked under the water is like Israelites being enslaved to the Egyptians and our bondage to sin. Coming out of the water symbolizes what Christ did in forgiving our sins and publically testifies we are ready for a new relationship with God."

"Hmm."

Rik turned to Bo. "Did you know the name Jesus means Joshua in Hebrew?"

"No, I should brush up on my Hebrew. Julia wants to be baptized, but why? She's a wonderful woman."

"Jesus went under the water too," Rik said, touching Bo's arm. "The moment He came out, heaven opened and God's Spirit lighted on Him, a voice from heaven saying, 'This is my Son, whom I love; with Him I am well pleased.'"

"You think that was God talking about Jesus?"

"I believe it happened just as the Bible says it did."

Bo blinked, feeling out of his depth. He saw a man with a crown of gray hair and a white robe walk into the water.

"I think about what Julia has," Bo said. "I'm not completely without spiritual interest."

"Glad to hear it. We are created with a desire for God. We find Him when we open our hearts and minds to Him."

Bo gazed into the bluish water, amazed by the man being dunked. He came out wet but smiling like he'd just won a million bucks in the lottery.

"Julia gave me a Bible and your book about Jesus being a Jewish carpenter. When I came to Israel last fall, I had no time to read."

"You're interested in woodworking. Jesus studied under His father, becoming a carpenter to provide for His mother. He started His public ministry at the age of thirty."

"Creating shelves for Julia kept me busy while I was off work. During that time I made another decision."

"About your next project?" Rik asked, sounding interested.

"When I finish this job I'll study up on how to be a Christian."

Rik smiled. "Becoming a Christian is an act of intellect and faith, but Bo, you sound as if you have already decided."

He did? Bo searched his mind. "I guess I have."

Rik took a small Bible from his pocket and flipped through some pages. "You and Mac were both military. Let me tell you about a soldier and what he thought of Jesus."

Bo spotted Judah's Mossad colleague leaning on the railing. Bo doubted the agent would ever be baptized here.

"Okay, Rik. What do you want me to know?"

"Jesus was walking to Capernaum on the northern shore of Galilee, about twenty miles from here, when a centurion came asking for help."

He looked up at Bo. "We're talking about a Roman soldier whose servant was at home paralyzed and in terrible suffering. Jesus said He would go and heal Him, but the soldier said he did not deserve to have Jesus come under his roof."

"What happened?" Bo found himself curious about the Roman soldier.

"The centurion said if Jesus would say the word his servant would be healed, just like he was a commander used to having authority with soldiers under him. He said, 'I tell this one 'Go,' and he goes;

and that one, 'Come,' and he comes. I say to my servant, 'Do this and he does it.'"

"He was used to giving orders. I can relate."

"The soldier's faith in Jesus as the Son of God was so great he knew Christ could utter a command and the servant would be healed."

Bo looked over Rik's shoulder at the Bible page. "And was his servant healed?"

"Jesus said to the centurion, 'Go! It will be done just as you believed it would.' And you know what, Bo? The servant was healed that very hour."

"Hmm," Bo grunted.

Rik closed the Bible, replacing it in his pocket. "Jesus didn't tell the soldier to go and study a course. The soldier believed in Christ's power to save and heal. Christ honored his faith right there on the spot. You've told me of your desire, now tell Jesus."

"I have no idea how to do that. Jesus no longer lives on earth."

"You do that by praying to Him. Julia has."

"How do you know she did?"

"She told me. Then she began learning how Christ wants her as His follower to live."

Bo's mind was spinning out of control.

Julia had been easily convinced to come to Israel because she'd read Van Horn's books. She couldn't wait to see the land where Jesus lived. Then she and the kids toured Israel with Van Horn while Bo settled into the embassy. It didn't take long for Mossad to tell Bo about the mole in the embassy and for Goliath to surface trying to bomb the living daylights out of Bo and Eva and then Mac, who Bo had always believed was his father. Now he stood here where Jesus dipped below the water talking about Jesus with his biological father.

Rik startled Bo out of his mental turmoil.

"I do not care if you ever look upon *me* as your father. But I pray you will know how much your Heavenly Father loves you. He sent Jesus to die for you."

Bo gripped the cell phone attached to his side. "You're saying because I've decided to become a Christian, I already am."

"Accepting Jesus is a gift. We pray to God admitting we need God's forgiveness and asking Him to come into our lives. He forgives us through the blood Jesus shed. We are no longer strangers, but are His sons and daughters. We are made whole and will have life for all eternity. That's the essence of a Christian."

From the corner of his eye, Bo saw the Mossad agent talking into his cell phone. He raised a hand at Bo and started walking to his car.

"Rik, I appreciate this time together. I really do, but I'm being summoned."

Bo shook his father's hand and Rik grabbed hold, directing his gaze into Bo's eyes.

"Thanks for spending a few days with me. I will not forget it."

"Me too. And I will see you later," Bo said, wondering if he ever would.

46

Back from his unexpected time with Rik along the Galilee, Bo strode into a drafty warehouse on the outskirts of Ashkelon a few miles from the Gaza border, a question hounding his steps. Would State's phony message to the U.S. Embassy about Bo's return secure Goliath's capture?

He'd seen the missive to Hal, pinpointing Bo's meeting with IDF intelligence officers at their training center in the Negev at Israel's southernmost tip. The electronic message also contained false information that Bo would arrive in Eliat tomorrow before heading to the training.

Bo dropped to a chair, scratching his beard and desperate for Judah's prediction to come true: that Gath Ramla, aka Goliath, would learn of Bo's visit through Malik and be seized at Eliat by armed commandos.

He surveyed the gathering spot for another dangerous mission: Operation Cheese Caper. Pungent smells of paint and varnish assailed his nose and he stifled a sneeze. Two vans from a Palestinian painting company stood ready, their doors open. In seconds, Israeli commandos would board, their faces darkened and military gear hanging from every possible spot on their bodies.

"I hope these guys are as prepared as they look." Bo felt seriously on edge.

"They are, my friend. We wait an hour and leave in complete darkness."

Bo whipped his head around, facing Judah who had also rubbed dark grease on the exposed skin around his beard.

"I promise you, Judah, if we rescue Sadie Lamb, I'm shaving off my beard first thing."

Judah pulled a long knife from ankle holster, overhead lights glinting off the sharp blade.

"This is yours to use *when* we retrieve her and Hertzl."

"No thanks." Bo waved him off. "I'll wait for my electric shaver back home."

"Your choice, but I want you armed. My spare knife and holster are stowed in the van."

Judah handed Bo the knife, then removed his ankle holster. Bo attached the blade beneath his pant leg, straightening his back.

"Do your people know where Goliath is?"

"They are following him in Gaza." Judah leaned closer. "At last report he headed for the border crossing, on his way south."

Bo sneezed, wiping his nose with a hankie. "How can you stand the stink, Judah?"

A gleam in his eyes, Judah asked a trio of commandos, "Who smells anything?"

The three commandos shook their heads in unison, prompting Bo to grin. "I see. I'm the pampered American and the odd man out."

"This place smells better than some holes I have crouched in around the world. Mossad has a saying, 'All circumstances bring opportunities for victory.' Tonight we will be victorious."

"How long have your operatives been running this painting company?" Bo pocketed his hankie.

"Two years in Gaza. Recently they moved to a smaller warehouse near the refugee camp in Jabalia. That is when we discovered where Sadie and Hertzl are being held. The Palestinian painters for our company enter Israel each day and return every night to Gaza. They are on friendly terms with the Palestinian and Israeli border guards."

Bo pointed to the commandos nearby. "I hope their eyesight is more acute than their sense of smell. Do all twenty go with us?"

"Yes. They have been practicing for months to achieve this rescue. You and I are in the first van with nine commandos. The rest go in the remaining van. A third commando team is sweeping into Eliat to capture Goliath who should be there looking for you."

Bo stepped back, assessing the room. A basketball-sized toy with rubber treads maneuvered toward Bo and Judah, operated by a commando using a handheld device equipped with a stubby antenna. The mechanized toy stopped by Bo, tipping back on its haunches like a pet animal, the antenna protruding from its back. It aimed a gun barrel right at Bo.

"Meet Scorpion," Judah said.

Bo leaned forward to examine the gun. "What's it capable of?"

"Watch out!"

Bo flinched and Judah jumped back with a booming laugh.

"Scorpion has just sent your photo to the operator. If the operator doesn't like you, he pushes a button and Scorpion's built-in Uzi automatic will pump you full of 9 millimeter slugs."

"I needed Scorpion at the bakery bombing. Eva and I could have taken out Goliath and saved a lot of grief."

Judah nodded solemnly. "With terrorists plotting and hiding throughout Israel, Scorpion is extremely quiet, but lethal. It saves lives. Tonight it goes ahead of the commandos ensuring the coast is clear."

Bo was impressed. He saw another weapon in the hands of a burly commando.

"What is he carrying?"

"The Uzi's ninety-degree stock peers around any corner ahead of the commando, who remains protected by the wall. I will show you the genius of our latest weapon."

Judah asked the commando to demonstrate and then told Bo, "Pretend you are on this soldier's team."

Intrigued, Bo followed the commando along the outer wall of a room built inside the warehouse. When the commando reached the corner, he raised the weapon, which aimed its barrel around the corner. The commando huddled against the wall, but Bo saw a small screen on his back flash a picture of paint cans around the corner out of sight. If the cans had been a living enemy, the commando could fire without exposing himself or Bo.

Bo hustled back to Judah, excitement for the Op building in his belly. Mossad's brilliant tactical teams, better trained than Bo had been with the Army Rangers, reassured him. With the sophisticated weaponry, they had every chance of accomplishing the impossible.

"As we say in the States, that's awesome."

"I call it the smart gun. Scorpion had made nighttime visits, leaving the Gaza painting warehouse and sneaking down to where the hostages were being held."

"Did your Uzi-carrying weapon actually see Sadie and Hertzl?"

"Yes. We now know they are shackled and guarded by two militants. These terrorists are Islamic Jihad, affiliated with Hamas. They fire rockets from Jabalia into nearby Israeli towns."

Judah handed Bo an Uzi. He gripped the powerful weapon. "Who am I shooting with this mighty gun?"

"You remain in the van during the raid. We will bring Sadie out and you guard her until we secure Hertzl."

Bo studied the weapon, noticing a silencer. "What am I authorized to do?"

"I know your work. Do what you have to do."

The team leader walked into the middle of the room, and instructing the commandos in Hebrew, all eyes were fixed upon him. Occasionally a commando raised a hand in response to the leader's question.

Judah whispered in Bo's ear, "When the painting vans return to Gaza, the Palestinian border guards will search each van."

"And if an American is found going in?" Bo had to admit it was possible; he could be captured by Hamas and held for ransom. Or worse, killed.

"You seem like one of us, Skip, with your full beard. Say nothing and you will not give away your accent. Also, we have another secret weapon."

"I'm all ears, Judah." Bo's heart pulsed in anticipation. These Israelis were full of surprises with their arsenal of bendable Uzis and stinging Scorpions.

"Chocolate."

"The bars explode when the guards open the package?"

"Hardly," Judah laughed.

And then he explained. "This past week, the drivers told the guards they are painting a Jerusalem candy store and have treated them to all kinds of chocolate. Thus, they have not been searched. I pray to Jehovah our ploy works again tonight."

Bo wasn't used to putting his safety in the hands of others. His nose began to tickle and he blew out another sneeze. He had to trust that with Griff and Julia praying this Op would succeed.

DARKNESS OF NIGHT GAVE THEM ample cover and two painting vans rolled toward the Gaza checkpoint. In the first van, Bo caught his breath, not wanting to make a sound. He covered his nose and mouth in case he sneezed. He and Judah crouched on the floor leaning against the sides, along with nine camouflaged commandos. One pointed his silenced Uzi at the rear doors.

Judah put a finger to his lips, nodding up front. Arabic chatter made blood surge at Bo's temples. He fixed his eyes on the rear doors, coiling his legs beneath him. Suddenly laughter broke all tension and the van drove through the checkpoint. Bo breathed.

Two commandos high-fived each other. Judah leaned over to Bo, speaking softly, "Now the second van must get through."

Bo flashed Judah a thumbs-up thinking, *God, you know me and what you want me to do.*

"I have news in my earpiece," Judah hissed. "Our Eliat team says Goliath is not there."

"You're just finding out?" Bo asked, his heart pounding.

"They were tailing him in Gaza, but Goliath has disappeared."

"The man is worse than a snake sliding into its hole. I only hope Malik hasn't discovered Griff had visited his apartment. He might slip away from Griff and Brewster's surveillance."

Judah tapped his earpiece. "Second van is through. We arrive in fifteen minutes."

Bo rode in silence, wondering about the Israeli commandos. Were they married with kids? What were they thinking about while he was thinking about them? These tough dedicated guys reminded him of his Army Ranger buddies with whom he'd bonded during times of war. He knew little of Judah's personal life, only that his wife and child had been killed years ago.

Goliath's face towered in Bo's mind, taunting him. Bo blinked, shutting out the vision of his wicked foe and gathering strength from Julia's prayers for him.

A few turns later and the van stopped. A commando cracked the rear door ajar, setting Scorpion on the ground before closing the door quietly. Judah manipulated toggles and images flickered on a small screen covered by a red filament. Bo crouched on his knees.

Judah tugged on his sleeve. "Scorpion must travel half a block. Be patient."

In Hebrew, Judah called out progress in a hushed voice, leaving Bo to study faces. Most team members were stoic, giving Bo no clues. Suddenly every commando raised his weapon.

Judah whispered, "Scorpion has arrived where the hostages are held. A guard just walked out, smoking a cigarette. Scorpion is staying still and watching."

He barely quit talking when his screen flickered. Judah began pressing buttons and barking orders. The rear doors flew open and Mossad's highly-trained commandos burst out.

Judah remained calm, briefing Bo. "The guard spotted Scorpion and went to investigate. Scorpion killed him, so the team is making their entry. I am going in. You remain here."

Before he rushed out, Judah jammed a finger at Bo's Uzi. "Shoot only if necessary."

Bo hadn't heard gunfire from Scorpion and hoped he wouldn't hear any. He crept to the rear windows, covered with a porous painter's graphic, every one of his senses on high alert. He watched for the slightest movement.

Someone rushed the van. Bo raised his Uzi, prepared to shoot. At this time of night was it friend or foe? Judah hurried up, carrying a body over his shoulder. Oh, no. Maybe they'd be taking a dead soldier back to Israel.

Bo pushed open the door. Judah was winded as he dropped the body down gently.

"Sadie is alive," he huffed before scurrying off.

Sadie began whimpering. Bo slid her along the bottom of the van and closed the door. He watched out the rear, trying to comfort her at the same time.

"Sshh. You are safe."

He peeled duct tape from her mouth. "I am an American. You've just been rescued by Israeli commandoes."

Using the knife Judah had given him, Bo cut plastic ties holding Sadie's feet and hands.

"Can you move to the front of the van? The team should return soon."

Sadie wiped her face sobbing, "I'm free. I'm free."

"Sshh. Please remain quiet."

A sob seemed to catch in her throat. "There's an Israeli soldier in that building too."

"Yes. He's our next mission."

She dropped her face into her hands, crying softly.

"Sadie, are you all right? Can't you move?"

"I was shackled for so long." She stretched her legs, rubbing them and then on all fours Sadie crawled to the front.

Out the windshield, Bo spied a car racing around the corner and dimming its lights. He tensed, listening to every sound. Tires crunched. The car stopped right in front of the van. Bo slid his finger to the Uzi's trigger.

A large man bolted from the car carrying an AK-47. He ran to the van, flashing a light in through the driver's door, but the partition with the small window behind the driver's seat prevented any light from reaching the rear of the van.

Who was he? Bo couldn't see the man's face. He hoped commandos would spot the interloper and disarm him before it was too late. With no radio to alert the team, Bo drew shallow breaths, his entire body sizzling with energy.

Heavy steps outside. The man shone his light through the window graphic on the rear doors. Bo held his breath and the worst thing happened. The rear door flew open. Light blinded Bo for a split second. Sadie gasped. Bo ducked his head. The man reached in. At that moment, Bo glimpsed no face paint. This man was no Israeli commando.

On enemy soil, Bo's finger itched on the trigger. The intruder raised his gun. Before he or Sadie could be shot, Bo squeezed, letting off a blast of muffled flashes. The man fell backwards, dropping his gun and flashlight.

Sadie screamed. Bo jumped out the rear barking at her, "Be quiet or you'll get us killed."

He picked up the flashlight, aiming the light on the intruder. He rolled the man onto his back. There was a pattern of bloody wounds from the man's belly to his throat. The light reached the man's face. It was Goliath!

Bo checked for a pulse and finding none, he strained all his muscles dragging and heaving the giant man into the rear of the van. Sadie shrank into the front panel, weeping. Bo retrieved his gun from the ground and had nearly closed the door behind him when a commando raced full tilt to the van, carrying another body.

Behind him, Judah sped toward the van. Bo used his boot to open the door, revealing Goliath's body. Judah and the commando halted, but Bo waved them in, keeping Goliath's identity a secret for now.

"This interloper opened the back door, ready to kill us with an AK-47. I had to fire."

"Hertzl is safe." Judah climbed in. Reaching for the IDF soldier, he loosened plastic ties and tape on his mouth.

Herzl let out a moan, slumping over. Judah spoke to him in Hebrew while the commando sprinted off.

Judah straightened, telling Bo, "They are wrapping up. No casualties for the good guys."

"Bravo." Bo steadied his arms, hardly believing Goliath had tried to kill him.

"What is with the man?" Judah nodded toward Goliath's body.

Bo breathed a tormented sigh. "He drove up, lights off, and swung open the rear door. He raised his weapon. Before he shot me and Sadie, I took him out in self-defense. I had no option."

"I wonder if he knew we were coming," Judah asked softly, rolling up the tape.

Bo held up Goliath's AK-47. "He carried this. I don't think Gath Ramla will be arriving at Mossad's trap in Eliat."

A strange mix of exhaustion and relief filled Bo. He shined the light on Goliath's face.

"Meet my nemesis. I do not cheer his end, but he will no longer pursue my family."

Judah laid a hand on Bo's back. "Your prayers have been answered."

The commando team piled in, each showing surprise at the unexpected body. The last team member crawled in cradling Scorpion in his arms like a puppy.

Bo leaned back, guilt seizing him, burning his eyes. In the short battle pitting Bo against Goliath, Bo remained alive. Yet, he was no ruthless killer. He could never tell Julia or the kids, but he had a feeling Mac would be grateful Goliath no longer posed a threat.

He secured the Uzi, reflecting on the near tragic turn of events. Had God's hand protected him once again or was it mere coincidence? He longed to ask Rik what he thought, but knew he'd never be able to tell him how he'd shot Goliath.

Yet, Goliath had been his enemy who wanted nothing more than to wipe out Mac, Bo, and anyone else close to him, even his children. Bo was grateful to be alive, but he couldn't help wondering if God approved. This was justice, but revenge had begun seeping into his heart.

A few days ago, Rik had urged Bo to seek God's forgiveness. Maybe this was the right time to do so. They still had to pass through the checkpoint at Gaza. Would someone else in Goliath's network be waiting to spring a trap on Bo?

47

The next morning snapped open for Bo like a broken window shade, his feet landing to the floor with a thud, his ears turning to a loud humming noise above his head. He ran to the window and looking out saw nothing unexpected. Bo hustled to the kitchen of yet another safe house where he brewed coffee. His stomach awash in acid, he needed food. He yanked open the small fridge, pulling out a carton of dried fruit, and sliced off a hunk of bread.

Setting his meager breakfast on a plate, he knew two unresolved questions needed answering. Was Goliath on his way to the hostages when he stumbled on the van? Or did he have advance warning Bo would be in Gaza?

Bo sat at the table, frustrated the bait hadn't worked. The embassy message to entice Goliath to find Bo in Eliat had failed big-time. Yet somehow he'd survived with Goliath meeting his eternal judgment.

He'd just torn off a piece of bread when a deep voice from behind his back startled him.

"Goliath is dead. How come you haven't shaved off your beard?"

Bo whirled so quickly to face Griff that he nearly toppled from the chair. "I'm not celebrating until I have answers."

"We wrapped up things neat and tidy by my book." Griff reached for a mug. "Sadie Lamb will arrive soon at Landstuhl where she'll receive medical treatment after her captivity. I guess she has an inflamed tooth that needs extracting."

Bo chewed his bread before responding. "She was in a lot of pain."

"Goliath's death means you and your family are safe. And Mossad—"

"I know," Bo shot back, "they recovered Hertzl, their IDF soldier. But here's what I need to know. Why was Goliath in the wrong place?"

Griff sat across from Bo, helping himself to coffee. "You shot him before he killed you. Sounds like God answered my prayer for your protection."

"You don't understand. The leak didn't work."

Both men were startled by the front door lock turning. Bo jumped up, grabbing a knife from the kitchen drawer, wishing he still had the Uzi. Griff swiped an empty soda bottle off the counter, both agents preparing to defend themselves.

A surprised Judah walked in carrying a newspaper. "I did not want to wake you by knocking, but I see you are already hard at it."

"You should be more careful next time," Bo said, dropping the knife with a clatter.

Griff set down the bottle, plunking back into his chair with a sigh. "We're in a quandary."

"Care to enlighten me?"

"How did Goliath manage to sneak up on me in the van with Mossad hot on his trail?"

"You may want to read this," Judah said, bringing over an English version of the newspaper.

Bo seized the paper and read aloud, skipping unimportant details. "Soldier freed. Sadie Lamb is finally released."

Judah snatched back the paper. "No, this small article beneath the fold."

Bo followed Judah's finger, again reading aloud, "IDF forces near Ashkelon stopped a vehicle. Inside were found Gath Ramla and two other Palestinians. A shoot-out ensued with Ramla and his militant friends being killed before a highly explosive vest detonated. Ramla was a highly-placed terrorist in Hamas."

Griff shook his head. "But Bo killed Goliath."

"Not by Mossad's telling. Only our team will ever know. We don't want Goliath's son coming after you."

Bo crumpled the paper in his hand with a sinking feeling. "Goliath has a son?"

"Do not worry, my friend. He is twenty years old and believes his dad was killed by our commandos. We have plenty of enemies. One more cannot hurt Israel."

"Okay for you to shrug it off, but I want his name and everything else on Goliath's son."

"Consider it done. We have, as you say, other fish to fry. Shellie Karnack lands at Ben Gurion International airport in two hours."

Griff guzzled the java, wiping his moustache. "I'm hitting the shower and can be ready in ten minutes."

"Brewster will be calling to advise of us Malik's whereabouts," Bo reminded. But his mind was revolving around Goliath's son.

Judah poured coffee, sitting across from Bo. "After investigating what happened with our Negev team, we think Goliath gave them the slip so he could stay in Gaza to receive a delivery of arms from our Turkish friend. He is the one photographed with Ambassador Cohen."

"How deep does this go, Judah?"

"An octopus has eight tentacles. We have severed one and have many more to lop off."

Hadn't Bo heard an octopus could re-grow a severed tentacle? With a shudder, he reread the article about Goliath's death, vowing to ensure the terrorist's son never learned of Bo or Mac Rider.

AT A TRAFFIC LIGHT in Tel Aviv, Griff Topping snatched a hurried look over his shoulder. His passenger in the backseat silently gazed out the window, drumming her fingers on her knee. Griff had placed Shellie Karnack behind him to keep her off guard. He'd also engaged the safety locks to prevent her from jumping out. Her flight from the U.S. had arrived twenty minutes late, which meant Brewster and Bo were already waiting at the embassy.

Traffic began moving again. Griff sped forward thinking how Shellie had snorted when Griff showed his credentials, identifying himself as FBI. So far, she'd said nothing on the ride.

Griff spoke over his shoulder. "Shellie, you haven't asked why I met you, so I'll tell you what you may have guessed. I was sent to the embassy in your absence to assess security."

"I see," was her reply.

Griff turned the corner. As they neared the embassy, Shellie found her tongue.

"Security audits are conducted by teams from State Security. Why is the FBI involved?"

"More than embassy security is at stake. You've been relieved of duty."

"What? I work for Ambassador Cohen. I demand to see him at once."

Griff saw in the rearview mirror her cheeks were blazing red. He would let her stew in her own anger before revealing all. He eased to the security gate, waiting in line. In minutes the Marine security guard cleared him for entry. Griff parked behind the embassy where he pulled the trunk release and removed Shellie's bags.

She hurried around to the back. "Put my bags back in there."

"I won't be giving you a ride home. Someone else will."

"Oh."

She snatched the handle of her large suitcase, wheeling it off in a snit. Griff closed the trunk and rolled her carry-on, managing to hold the door open for her. On the elevator, she stabbed him with her eyes and Griff stifled a laugh. Special Agent Shellie Karnack had no idea of the trouble she faced. They placed her bags in the security office.

"I want to collect my things if I no longer work here," she sniffed, heading for her desk.

"Stop," Griff ordered. "We're meeting in the conference room and you're invited."

"What do you mean by 'we'?"

"Come along and find out."

Griff escorted Shellie from the security office and they rode the elevator in total silence, though he could almost hear her mental gears grinding. In the conference room, Griff didn't wait for her to get comfortable. He sat across from her, leaning forward.

"I am in Tel Aviv because you alleged Bo Rider leaked intelligence from the embassy. My investigation exonerates him completely."

Shellie clunked her purse on the table. "You're here to harass me for suspecting Rider wasn't who he claimed to be?"

"It's not my job to harass you, but to find out if you did your job. Guess what I found?"

Shellie returned Griff's stare with deadpan eyes. "Astonish me."

"You allowed a grave lapse in security. On several occasions, data has been deleted from the embassy's security cameras."

Shellie pulled out a silver tube, flipping it open. In the tiny attached mirror, she applied pink lipstick, which Griff saw matched her nail polish. He ignored her primping and slapped a portfolio on the table.

"You were seen entering the embassy after business hours with Hosni Malik."

She pressed her lips together, closing her lipstick tube. "There's nothing illegal about my bringing a guest into the embassy. I've also visited him at the British Embassy."

"Have you seen him lately?"

"How could I see Hosni? I've been in the States for weeks and you picked me up at the airport." The hard tone of her sneer matched her icy glare.

"True enough, but when were you last with Hosni Malik?"

"Several weeks before I left Tel Aviv."

"So you haven't been in his company since leaving Israel for Georgia?"

Shellie nodded, the glint in her eye daring him to contradict her. In reply, he opened the portfolio and removed some photos.

"Quit playing games."

"What game are you playing, Special Agent Topping?" she asked, her upper lip curling.

Her act was pure bluff and Griff intended to crack her. He laid out several photos.

"These pictures were taken of Malik getting into a car with you when you met his flight at Jacksonville. That was two weeks ago, Special Agent Karnack."

"Okay, so we're involved." Shellie slid her chair out from the table. "We felt we should keep our relationship on the QT."

Suddenly, Griff snatched the buzzing phone in his pocket. He answered and listened.

"Bring it in here," he finally replied.

He ended the call, his eyes locking onto Shellie's. "Your little charade is over."

The door opened. In sauntered Bo wearing latex gloves and pulling Shellie's large bag behind him. He was followed by Brewster Miles.

"Shellie, meet part of my team. You remember Bo. The other gentleman is Brewster Miles from British MI5."

Her left eyebrow lifted a fraction. Bo hefted her suitcase onto the table and began unzipping it. Shellie jumped to her feet, a loud protest exuding from her pinched lips.

"You've no right to tamper with my bag."

Griff pointed to her chair. "Au contraire, Ms. Karnack. As Security Director, you placed signs in prominent places warning anyone entering the embassy that they and their personal effects are subject to search."

Shellie dropped to her seat, her painted lips drooping. Bo whistled sharply and removed from her bag a stack of currency. Placing it on the table, he thumbed through the bundles of cash.

"You secreted thirty-seven thousand dollars, all in new, crisp one hundred dollar bills."

"There's no law against keeping my savings in cash."

Griff tapped surveillance photos of her and Malik. "There is if you have just been seen meeting with the agent of a foreign government, a meeting you have denied."

As though to embarrass Shellie more, Bo delicately lifted skimpy underwear and laid her garments on the table. Then he removed from beneath the fabric of her suitcase a manila envelope, which he opened, carefully sliding out a document between his gloved fingers.

"Your hidden envelope contains a top secret Memorandum of Understanding between the U.S. and Israel. It outlines secret defense strategies the Israeli Prime Minister has shared with the Secretary of State. *Someone* downloaded this classified document off an embassy computer."

Shellie's body stiffened. "I have never seen that envelope or document in my life. Obviously, Bo Rider planted it in my suitcase, seeking to frame me for his misdeeds."

Griff glared and he wasn't the only one who trained eyes on her. Bo and Brewster also seemed to observe every twitch of her facial muscles. Shellie rummaged in her purse and Griff leaned in even closer.

"A jury will decide how defense secrets came to be in your possession. You can cooperate, if you choose. Either way you will be charged with violating the Espionage Act."

"That will never stick," Shellie said, lifting her chin. "You have no proof against me."

Griff didn't miss a beat. "You will be detained in the embassy until you are flown to D.C. I remind you of your rights against self-incrimination, which you know verbatim. Remain silent, but if you help us determine the damage, I'll make sure the federal prosecutor is aware of your cooperation. Do you understand?"

Shellie hung her head, giant tears rolling down her cheeks. Griff retrieved a box of tissues and handed them to her.

"It all started innocently!" she cried. "Hosni flattered me. Our relationship evolved into a huge mistake, but the envelope and documents aren't mine. I just picked another loser."

"So Hosni is the culprit, putting secret documents and money in your suitcase without your knowledge?" Griff demanded.

"Check for fingerprints!" Shellie snarled. "You won't find mine anywhere!"

Griff pulled out a form, sliding the sheet across the table. "Read and then sign I advised you of your rights. Meanwhile, we will analyze the envelope and contents for prints. We'll also see what your good pal Hosni has to say about his efforts to draw you in."

"What will you do with him?"

Griff lifted his chin, smiling. "I should think the rest of my team is picking him up at his apartment as we speak."

"Who else is on your team?" Shellie asked, gripping a pen.

"You will have to wait and see."

Griff traded looks with Bo and Brewster, their cue to leave the room with the evidence. After they left, Griff told Shellie, "Commander Engle is guarding the door. You will not be allowed to leave the room until your escort takes you to detention."

"I insist on speaking to Ambassador Cohen."

"He is out of the country, back in D.C. It's unlikely he will return anytime soon."

"I don't believe you."

"Your choice," Griff said, rising.

She dried her eyes with a tissue. "I'm not signing your silly form, either. I'm innocent. Let me at least say good-bye to Zaveda."

"I think not. And I'm seizing your purse and cell phone."

Griff watched Shellie refresh her makeup. He took her lipstick, tossing the tube into her purse. Shellie sat staring at the rights form as Griff left the office. He nodded to Commander Engle, who'd been briefed on Shellie's fall from grace.

Down in the SCIF, Griff found Bo and Brewster talking on a secured phone, with Bo saying into the speaker, "Griff is here. Judah, bring us up-to-date."

"Mossad grabbed Hosni Malik, snapping cuffs on him five minutes ago. He has asked to be taken to the British Embassy. Brewster, will you be leading his questioning?"

Brewster lifted his wristwatch. "Notify your agents I will be at my embassy within ten minutes. I will meet them at security and handle Malik from there."

Griff hustled to the phone. "Bo briefed you on Shellie's response to our questions?"

"Yes," Judah replied. "She sounds tough, admitting only to being duped by Malik."

"I'll send the documents for fingerprint analysis to the FBI lab via airmail."

"Judah, you need to see the memo Shellie hid in her suitcase," Bo said, arranging to meet Judah at Mossad Headquarters in thirty minutes.

Griff remarked hurriedly, "I'll remain here and see if Shellie changes her mind once she ponders the hornet's nest she is in."

48

Bo wove through heavy traffic determined to reach Mossad HQ within thirty minutes as he'd told Judah. But an unruly protest made him navigate unfamiliar side roads. At a stoplight, he switched to the left turn lane, glimpsing the driver off to his right. Bo's heart nearly stopped.

The man behind the wheel of the gunmetal gray Mercedes looked so much like Goliath, with a huge head and bushy beard. The light turned and the Mercedes sped off, with Bo memorizing the license number. Could the driver be Goliath's son?

Bo rushed to the Institute, his heart hammering in his chest. Judah had yet to give Bo the details of Goliath's twenty-year-old son. Entry into Mossad was thorough as usual. Saul Goldberg met Bo with a worried frown.

"You bring news for us?"

Bo tapped the leather folder under his arm. "I can't say it's good. Take me to your leader, as Judah and I must talk in private."

Saul led Bo along the labyrinth to the secure room underground, shutting the door behind him, leaving him alone with Judah, who flashed a rare grin.

"We at the Institute are pleased with your help. Shooting Goliath, you have lived up to your legend. We may call upon you again."

Bo felt his ears warm. He did what he did so Bo and his family could live. But what about Goliath's son—would he be an even sharper thorn in Bo's side?

"I think I just saw Goliath's son."

Judah's eyes flashed. "Near Mossad?"

"On the drive here. And seeing that Goliath look-alike nearly gave me a heart attack. I memorized his license number."

Judah snatched up the phone, calling someone at his HQ to run the plate. When he hung up, Bo tapped the folder he carried.

"I found out why Goliath failed to take the bait."

"Tell me. Our Eliat commando leader is embarrassed."

Bo took off his glasses. "Given Shellie's relationship to Hosni Malik, we assumed he'd downloaded software giving him access to the embassy's computer systems."

"Yes, yes." Judah pressed his elbows forward.

"Though Malik had keystroke software and a Trojan Horse program, his information came directly from Shellie who downloaded what he needed onto flash drives."

"So your former Security Director acted only with Malik and not Hal Cohen?"

Bo nodded. "Although Hal and Clara were recalled to D.C. on a pretext, I've since learned Hal met with the arms dealer at the insistence of the State Department to placate the Turkish government. Hal leaked nothing, but he won't be returning to Israel."

"Good to know." Judah fingered the scar in his eyebrow. "Has Brewster's questioning of Malik revealed his motives or who he is working for?"

"The interrogation continues." Bo handed Judah a four-page document. "Read this and tell me the impact of its being leaked. I made a copy of the document we found hidden in Shellie's luggage. We are processing the original for her fingerprints."

Judah's eyes traveled across the pages and Bo sat in silence dreading his reaction. Page after page, Judah read on until flipping to the bottom of the last page, when a dark shadow passed across his face.

"We know Malik is part of the Brotherhood in Egypt and in league with Hamas. It now appears Goliath and Malik worked like brothers, with Malik feeding intelligence to Goliath who destroyed their enemies."

"And if Malik is released from custody, he can just as easily use Goliath's son to perpetuate their ring of hate." Bo felt trapped in an evil vortex.

Judah's nostrils flared. "If Malik passed this top secret document to a Russian agent when they exchanged valises, it could provoke war. I must notify my superiors at once."

"I was afraid you'd say that, which is why I brought you this memo ASAP."

"Remember God's promise to Joshua?" Judah asked, spreading out the four pages.

"That He would give the Israelites land wherever they placed their feet?"

"Yes. After Joshua fought to claim the land, my ancestors lived in places now belonging to Jordan, Syria, and Egypt. The moment Israel became a nation we were attacked and defended our land. Your government was an ally to Israel, supporting us in the world theatre."

Bo sensed where his comments were going. "We remain your greatest friend."

"I wish it was so, but your government has acted more sympathetic to our neighbors who seek to annihilate us, requesting we justify why we should not return to our sixty-seven borders. We gained these lands in self-defense."

Because Bo had taken out Goliath in self-defense, he too might face more violence. He touched the pages. "Perhaps the State Department is encouraging Israel to reach a negotiated peace with your neighbors."

Judah reared back his head. "You are not so naïve."

"No matter my government's policies, I remain your friend."

"A given." But then Judah seized the papers and shook them, growling, "Our Prime Minister gave this secret memo to your Secretary of State putting you on notice that when attacked, we intend to occupy every pebble and every rock of the land God gave our forefathers."

Bo leveled a gaze at Judah. "You plan to retake these lands only if provoked?"

"So the memo says." Judah raised a fist. "But I do not reveal the triggering event. It is too highly classified. It is enough to know the Syrians harass us day and night over the Golan Heights, sending in phony settlers. Hamas does the same in Gaza. And the Brotherhood rises to power in Egypt and Libya. We will not remain docile forever, even if your government removes all support."

"I understand your dilemma." Bo sensed Judah's anguish. "War could break out over the leaking of this memo. By now, Malik's Russian handler is showing it to the Russian president. Soon all our mutual enemies will know Israel's secret."

"Minutes before your arrival, I received an alarming phone call." Judah lowered his voice in the clandestine room. "Mossad intercepted a coded message Moscow sent to a Russian agent in Turkey, offering to sell missiles to Egypt. The Kremlin must already have Shellie's memo."

"I feel like I failed you and your country. Trapping the mole came too late."

"Far from it, my friend. You and your father, Mac, risked your lives for us."

"With Goliath's son on the loose, I'm not shaving this off," Bo said, tugging his beard.

"Let me show you something." Judah pointed at the bottom of the last page. "Key paragraphs are missing. They detail the triggering actions that will cause Israel to launch an attack. Fortunately these were excluded or Shellie would have leaked the truth to our enemies."

"A stroke of genius!" Bo cried.

"Jehovah must have given us the idea. Know this. When one of the events is triggered, we will strike with supernatural force God has always given us. We will reclaim every square inch of land God promised to Joshua."

Bo could have been listening to his newly-found father, Rik's account so closely matched what Judah was saying. Dread for Judah's future filled Bo.

"We should have stopped Shellie before she released this memo. Without proof she was the mole, we sent her to the States. FBI agents her watched closely, but it wasn't enough to prevent her from committing treason."

"Mossad has a saying, 'There is wisdom with many advisers.'" Judah flicked his hand. "Even so, Jehovah remains our greatest ally."

"Does your Knesset share your trust in God's divine promises?"

Judah's face fell. "Many do not, which is a tragedy. However, the Joshua Covenant cannot be shaken by the skeptics among us." Silence engulfed the room. Judah gathered the papers before slapping a fist into his open palm. "I have no fear. Jehovah will *never* let us down."

Bo held out his hand. "And true friendship is not erased by the wrongdoing of others. Count on me to rush to your aid, no matter where I am in the world."

"You will leave Israel soon?"

Bo furrowed his eyebrows. "With Gath Ramla's son on the prowl, I'm not hanging around, waiting for a little Goliath to hunt me down."

"Here is his son's name, address, and phone number. I will get you a recent photo."

Bo memorized the data Judah handed him when the phone rang. Judah hurried to grab it. After pausing he said, "Thank you for checking so promptly."

"Was the Mercedes driven by Goliath's son?" Bo held his breath.

"The auto belongs to a Jewish man by the name of Seymour Livkin. One of our agents will visit him this afternoon. Let us hope he is a different fellow."

Bo breathed, running a hand through his hair. "I have a dilemma and need advice from someone wise enough to omit those final paragraphs from the secret memo."

"At your service, my friend." Judah's black eyes grew darker.

"Julia showed our home addresses to Clara on Hal's embassy computer."

"Hmm," Judah said stroking his beard. "Goliath located you first at the bakery and then the ski resort after following you and your father from the safe house. He knew where you lived in Tel Aviv. Most likely Malik has your home address in Virginia."

"I'm glad my family is not at home. They are going to need security round-the-clock. Talking it through with you helps me realize we should move—and pronto. May I use your secure phone to call my wife?"

"Certainly."

Bo reached Julia's voice mail. "Honey, it's me. You need to visit your folks. I'll call back, but if you don't hear from me in an hour, call Frank to make arrangements."

Worry for Julia and the kids pulsing through his veins, Bo immediately phoned his folks in Hampton, but the answering machine clicked on.

"Mom, Dad, I need to talk with you and Julia. Call my cell right away."

Then Bo punched in Frank's numbers, crushed at leaving a message for him also.

"Frank, it's urgent the Agency's security get with Julia and Mac. Call me ASAP!" Bo shouted into the phone before slamming down the receiver.

Judah nodded sadly. "Another time I will tell you about my family being killed by rocket fire into Israel. Saving precious lives is my goal each morning I awake."

Bo shot out of his chair. "You and I share a common mission, Judah. I'm half out of my mind not being able to reach Julia on the phone. Maybe I should get my kids their own cell phones for emergency."

"Whatever it takes, my friend." Judah angled the memo into a secrecy sleeve. "This goes to the Prime Minister today. Keep me advised on what Brewster learns from Malik. Would you like to see the codex before you leave Israel?"

Bo blinked. "Now?"

Judah nodded, his eyes flashing. "The codex may determine our future steps. As I say, war could be at hand."

Bo instantly recalled what Rik had said about a final battle being waged in the Jezreel Valley. But wasn't that going to happen after believers went to be with God? Bo had to figure all that out, some other time.

"Judah, let me see your ancient document. I am in need of your Joshua's divine powers. It may not be long before you and I are fighting side by side in the days to come."

The two agents walked from the secured room. While Bo was eager to view the codex, his mind was glued to talking with Julia and finding out if they were all right. Would they ever find peace in this life?

49

Anxious to leave Israel, Griff Topping still had an important job to finish. He grabbed every file from the safe in Shellie's old office, which he'd been using since her incarceration back in Alexandria, Virginia. These he stored in his valise along with his ticket for his flight to Dulles.

He snapped shut his valise, ready to leave for dinner with Brewster Miles, when a mail clerk brought a package, return address: FBI Laboratory.

Griff tore it open, scanned the contents, but when he reached the end, he refused to believe the results. He heart pumped mega amounts of blood to his brain, which pounded against his temples. This had to be a terrible mistake.

Cramming the report in his valise, he stormed to the Com Center. Outraged, he called the FBI lab back in Virginia.

"I'm calling for Abby… Carol Howland." Griff snatched out the report. "Yes, I'll wait."

"Hey, Gibbs. I'm not surprised to hear from you."

"I'm on a secured line in our Tel Aviv embassy."

"You're calling because the only prints on the memo are from CIA agent Bo Rider."

"Exactly!" Griff cried, fury building in his chest. "That's impossible. I saw Agent Rider discover the document and he wore latex gloves. Are you sure there are no other prints?"

"It was inordinately clean. No smudges from the heel of anyone's hand, just a set of four fingers, which match Rider's prints he provided with his CIA application."

Griff must be missing something. His eyes flew to the last sentence in Carol's report. Then he pulled out an earlier report, comparing the two.

"Carol, you found a chemical on the photocopied memo. You also wrote in an earlier report how you detected a chemical on a flash drive from the Ambassador's computer."

"Thanks for pointing that out, Gibbs. I'll pull my report and see if they are the same."

Griff did a slow burn for what seemed an eternity until Carol finally chirped, "Okay, I'm looking at the smeared print from the flash drive.

There are two points of identification, but they are consistent with the right index finger of suspect Rider."

"Suspect Rider!" Griff objected.

"Yes, Gibbs. It seems Agent Rider is the only person handling both these exhibits."

"Quit calling me Gibbs!" Griff roared. "This is real life and not some TV show we've landed in."

At Carol's trembling sigh, Griff focused on the chemical's name. "Sorry, Carol. I'm at my wit's end. Your reports conclude the paper and flash drive had traces of the same chemical Chlorhexidine Gluconate. What is that?"

"It's an anti-bacterial product we use to wash our hands after handling contaminated submissions."

"There's your answer. These two exhibits were contaminated in your FBI lab."

"Oh no! The exhibits were analyzed over a two-week period. Rather, your suspect compulsively disinfects his hands."

Griff's mind whirled. "What if Rider was in a hospital?"

"That's possible. Hospitals use Chlorhexidine Gluconate to disinfect patients," Carol replied. "But the flash drive was found in an embassy computer."

"That's it! Rider stayed in an Israeli hospital before the exhibits were sent to you."

"Good. That confirms he's your suspect, Gibbs."

Griff's heart sank. "Carol, consider a small tap to the back of your head my thanks."

He hung up, his mind a blank about what to do. On a whim, he called Eva, desperate for another take on his dilemma. After all, she had suggested Griff order passport applications, which had cleared Bo, only now it looked like Bo had landed back in hot soup.

She answered her phone, saying, "I don't have the results. Give me an hour."

"Eva, it's Griff. I have a problem."

He quickly briefed her on the shocking news.

"Griff, someone is setting up Bo as the fall guy. Who has the most to gain?"

"Shellie's in a Virginia jail cell. Her cohort, Hosni Malik, is holed up at the British Embassy in Tel Aviv, refusing to talk. Cohen and his wife have been sent back to D.C."

"Where are you?"

"In Israel for another twelve hours."

"What can I do from here?" she asked quietly.

"My mind is mush. The FBI tech insists Bo is the suspect. Help me, partner."

"Tell me this. Who could have lifted Bo's fingerprints?"

Griff toyed with his moustache, trying to lay blame. "Eva, any of the above except Malik. I don't think Bo ever met him."

"This may sound odd, but humor me. Did Shellie or Hal visit Bo in the hospital?"

Griff paused to think and in seconds remembered something important.

"Yes! Shellie was in the room when the doctor asked about Bo's blood type."

"Have you examined hospital videos?"

"I should. Bo was unconscious for a brief time at the hospital."

"Run the videos and see if Shellie doesn't show up doing something outrageous. There is no way Bo has committed treason against our country!" she cried, her voice intense.

"I couldn't agree more. Thanks for oiling my mental gears. All is well with you?"

"Ring me up for lunch after you get home. I've an exciting case and must run."

Griff got busy tracking down hospital videos, infused with new energy. Then he decided he should watch embassy videos on the day Bo and Mac went skiing, hoping it hadn't been erased. Something better turn up to clear Bo once and for all. Griff had no heart to tell Bo about the fingerprint results.

Not yet anyway. Instead, he phoned Brewster Miles at the British Embassy.

"It's Griff. We're having a get-together at our embassy at noon. Can you make it?"

"Um, do I need to make a reservation?" was Brewster's guarded reply.

"Just yes or no, if you can be here at that time."

A pause and then, "Count on me."

"Bring nothing and tell no one," Griff added, then hung up.

INSTEAD OF ENJOYING LUNCH at a fine restaurant, Griff and Brewster Miles sat cloistered in the office of Marine Security Sergeant Hudson Engle, reviewing embassy videos. Griff was grateful they had not been erased.

"Focus on the beginning of Bo's hospitalization when he was unconscious."

Shadowy images flickered across the monitor until Griff ordered, "Stop! Back up. There's Shellie."

Engle hit reverse, but Brewster waved a hand. "She is simply going into the lift."

Other embassy staffers zoomed across the screen. Griff tapped a pen on his pad, agitated.

"Any time," he grumbled.

"Wow!" Brewster shouted. "Back up!"

Engle ran it backwards, started the video again until Griff pointed. "There's Shellie leaving the elevator, heading for the rear exit of our embassy. Play it again, Sam."

"That's from the movie *Casablanca*." Engle grinned. "We showed that film last week."

"Yup, a real spy thriller." Griff's eyes never left the small monitor.

The trio watched again as Shellie stepped from the elevator, racing to a door.

Griff turned to Brewster. "See anything surprising?"

"Play it again, Sam," Brewster chuckled.

For a third time Engle replayed that section of the video and Brewster erupted, "I say, old chap, look! She's wearing dress gloves."

"And carrying a manila envelope," Griff said, feeling enormous relief.

Engle stopped the video, zooming onto the envelope. "Why are gloves so crucial?"

To Griff, things were crystal clear.

"Suppose Shellie took sheets of blank paper and a flash drive to the hospital while Bo was unconscious. Wearing gloves, she placed Bo's fingers on the paper and the flash drive."

"That might explain the chemical residue," Brewster gulped, staring at the screen.

"Hold on," Griff urged. "She later slid the blank sheets with Bo's fingerprints into her embassy printer. She then printed out the classified Memo of Understanding, which she had already downloaded."

Brewster bobbed his head, getting into the spirit of solving the case. "Righto, Griff. She also left the flash drive in a USB port with his prints on it. A diabolical woman."

"Shellie insisted we look for prints knowing she wore gloves and we wouldn't find hers. Except she never figured anti-bacterial chemical would cling to the paper and flash drive."

Griff pushed himself back from the table. "This is really scary. What if we had discovered Bo's fingerprints on the flash drive weeks ago? We would have been convinced that Bo was a spy, for sure."

Brewster grabbed his cell phone off his waistband. "My embassy is calling."

"Miles here," he answered. "What do you have for me?"

Brewster shot out of his chair. "I am on my way."

He whirled toward Griff. "Malik is being flown to London. I must see him before he leaves Israel. You and I will stay in touch."

With that Brewster sprinted from the room.

"Engle, make copies of the digital memory and I need it by the end of the day. Have the hospital videos arrived yet?" Griff asked.

"No, sir. Delivery comes again at four."

"Good work, Sergeant. How about lunch? I'm buying."

Griff locked the office and the two men went to find a restaurant. For his part, Griff's stomach gnawed and he could eat a horse.

THREE DAYS AFTER HE RETURNED to Virginia, Griff hurried into his office resolving to wrap up his embassy reports before meeting Director Harmon at two. He passed the receptionist with a wave, but she fluttered a note.

"Some Aussie just phoned. Said you should call back on a secure phone."

Griff read the message. "Are you sure he didn't have a British accent?"

"Could be," she said blushing. "They all sound alike to me."

"Thanks." Griff headed straight for the office SCIF, ringing up Brewster.

"It's Griff and I'm secure."

"Let me go to our SCIF and call you back. Give me two minutes."

Griff gave Brewster the number and hung up. He sped to the coffee station, where he poured a cup, threw a quarter in the honor can, before dashing back to the SCIF.

When the phone rang, Griff answered out of breath. "Brewster?"

"Can you hear me, Griff?"

"What's so important I need to be in the SCIF?"

"Malik was sent to London in shackles with an escort. We didn't permit him to enter his apartment."

"Is he talking?" Griff shot back.

"Hold on, chap. Professional movers packed up his personal effects yesterday. I assisted and had a look-see."

Griff grabbed a sheet of blank paper from the copy machine and readied his pen. "What did you find of interest to me?"

"I am the bearer of good and bad news. Which would you like first?"

"I save the best for last, ask Dawn. She finally figured out why I eat my peas first."

"Tell Bo Rider not to return home to Virginia for the safety of him and his family."

Griff lurched, dropping his pen. "Oh no! Who is after him?"

"In Malik's wastebasket, I found a crumpled piece of paper written in a woman's hand with two addresses. One is the apartment where Bo stayed with his family in Tel Aviv. The second is in Great Falls, Virginia, where I assume Bo lives in the States."

"Correct," Griff said into the phone. "But he sent his family to his in-law's in Florida while he flies home. I'll notify him immediately. I hate to ask your good news."

Brewster cleared his throat. "A second note appears to be in Malik's handwriting with a different Tel Aviv address and a number for a cell phone purchased here in Tel Aviv."

"Could be the decoy info Bo inserted into State's computer system."

"These paper scraps prove Malik and Shellie retrieved secrets from the embassy system. I suspect Malik passed Bo's addresses to his Russian handler who gave them to the Egyptians. By now Goliath's son knows Bo's home address."

"Which means Bo can never return home."

"I think not. Also, I did some digging with Mossad. Shellie's grandfather served in the precursor to Mossad, the Hagana, posing as a wealthy landowner. He was taken captive in Damascus and died there. Mossad believes Shellie gave Malik the flash drive with Israel's ancient codex."

Griff considered the ramifications before saying to Brewster, "So she blames Israel, because the Hagana did not prevent her grandfather's death?"

"When you question her in the future, use this information. It might jar her confession."

"Your diligence never ceases to amaze me, Brewster. Send the evidence via diplomatic pouch. I'll compare the handwriting to Shellie's and process the notes for her prints."

"I will arrange the transfer. My flight leaves soon for London so I had better hurry. Another case solved, working with you and Bo."

"Watch your back. Malik's Russian comrades may be coming to help him escape."

"And yours, good friend. Stop and see me in London."

Griff ended the call, wiping sweat from the back of his neck. Seconds later, he placed a call, anxious to warn Bo.

50

After being dropped by Sergeant Engle at Tel Aviv's airport, Bo just passed through security when his cell phone rang.

"This is Skip," he said, keeping his voice low.

"I hoped to catch you," Griff replied.

"My flight's about to board."

"Listen, don't go home and don't say over the cell phone where you're flying."

Adrenaline shot through Bo like electricity. He pressed the phone against his ear.

"I am listening."

"The Dolphin furnished your address to her friend in handcuffs. If your family is staying where I think they are, I can call, warning them not to travel home."

"Griff, are you sure of this intel?" Bo gazed down the departure terminal. Would he even make it out of Israel alive?

"It's straight from MI5. Change your flight. I will pick you up if need be. Send a text with place and time."

"Ten-four. My family is where you think they are."

Bo hung up, but before he could call Julia, his cell rang again.

"Griff, I haven't rebooked my flight yet."

"Hey, it's Frank. You're at the airport, right?"

"Are you monitoring my movements?"

"A lucky guess. Why are you changing your flight?"

Bo edged out of the main aisle away from bustling travelers toward a side window.

"Dolphin broadcast my home address in the U.S. Can you coordinate with Griff and transfer my family somewhere safe?"

"Yes. I'll have a real estate agent put your house up for sale on the QT. The Director has something for you that can't wait."

Bo forced a sigh. "I need a week to settle the family and find a place to live."

"Oh, you'll have your week, but when you land come straight to the office."

"And if I say no?" Bo pressed the cell close to his ear, curious how Frank would respond.

"You won't when you hear what we have in mind. Unable to say more over the cell."

Bo knew Frank well enough to know he'd never coax him to reveal what was brewing at the Agency. Fine with Bo. He and Frank were both Company Men, through and through.

"Okay, Frank. Do me a favor?"

"I'm already caring for your cat. Anything else, you know that."

"Give me a few minutes to call Julia. Then I want you to tell her about Kangas needing me. You owe me that much."

"And plenty more; however, I already spoke to her," Frank replied.

So Frank had already figured Bo would fly to Langley instead of meeting Julia and the kids in Florida. Where would the Agency take them?

"What did she say?"

"Asked me to say she and the kids are fine. Please call her ASAP."

"I hope everything is okay."

"Sounded that way to me. A car will be waiting for you at Dulles."

"Frank, how long will I be gone this time?"

A quiet pause and then Frank said, "I have no idea, but your bags are already packed."

Frustrated by the Agency jerking him around, Bo pushed the red button on his phone. Let Frank think they were cut off. He punched in Julia's cell number. She answered on the first ring as if waiting for his call.

"Bo! I'm so glad it's you, but then Frank said to expect your call."

"Honey, are you all okay?"

"We are, but I miss you terribly. Frank told me about some security crisis needing your immediate attention."

Bo scratched at his beard and adjusted his bogus glasses.

"I can't say more on the cell. Honey, I could pack it in. Then I could fly right to you."

"Don't do that! Too bad the surprise dinner we planned for your homecoming is off, but we all know your job demands you," she whispered in his ear.

"Except for your dad." Bo could only imagine what negative thoughts Crockett was cramming into Julia's head.

"He doesn't have to know," she replied.

"But you're canceling the party. He'll find out and think I'm ditching you again."

"Bo," she whispered, "we are not in Florida, we are—"

"Not over the cell phone," he hissed. "Frank will contact you via secure phone. Get the kids ready and pack your bags, Julia. Frank will notify me of your new location."

"Bo, wait. I have something to tell you."

"Are you all right?"

"Yes, the security team is like my shadow, but I appreciate their dedication. It's your mother I worry about," came her soft reply.

"Something happened to Mac and Vivian?"

"I mean Adriana. She is having radiation and is so weak."

Bo shook his head. He did not need another complication.

Julia sighed in his ear. "Rik called asking me to bring the kids to see her."

A crush of passengers surged past him in the hallway, reminding Bo to change his flight.

"Honey, I need to make arrangements here."

"My cell is beeping in my ear. I think it's Frank."

"Know how much I love you. Hug the kids."

"Bo, I love you!"

She was gone. Bo hurried to the counter. Standing in line, he flipped open his passport, knowing this was his last flight using his undercover name. With no clue what Kangas had in store for him, Bo wondered who he'd be after Skip Pierce.

Pulled in separate directions, he felt stymied. At least he'd gotten to hear Julia's voice. She and the kids were okay. A daunting question loomed. Should he tell Kangas his career as a CIA agent was over, that he needed to put the security of his family first? Bo shoved his cell in his pocket, firm answers to his future as elusive as his identity.

But then he'd have the entire flight home to decide what to tell Kangas and what path to take, whatever his real name might be.

51

Bo Rider gazed off the expansive deck, life's twists and turns astounding him. Since leaving Tel Aviv, he'd hidden out on a tropical island before flying to Colorado Springs a week ago. He shielded his eyes from the sun, mulling over all the mysterious happenings.

A Palestinian driven by revenge had targeted Mac the Navy hero, putting Bo in the crosshairs. Inspired by Mac to protect and serve his country, Bo had stopped Goliath before the terrorist could shoot Bo and Sadie Lamb.

With Rik being an expert about God's plan for Israel, he'd given Bo intel about Israeli plans to regain their Promised Land. When Shellie tried to frame Bo as the spy, the Israeli war memo about the Joshua territories tripped her up.

"We had a whale of a time at Pike's Peak yesterday. Glad you asked me along."

Bo spun around, facing Rik who held out a blue ball cap, emblazoned with orange lettering, *Broncos*. Bo flipped it on his head, instantly blocking the sun's glare.

"Thanks, Rik."

Bo lifted his eyes to the snowcapped peak, enjoying the incredible view from Rik's unassuming hilltop home. Sounds of uneven footsteps made Bo turn. Mac joined them on the deck, and he leaned against the railing, chewing on a toothpick.

"Whew, you should've warned me, Rik. Fifty-mile-an-hour winds atop that peak. For an old sub commander like me, I'd never been so high off the ground."

Bo lowered his visor. "I'll buy Gregg a new cap. The wind tore his off up there."

"I laughed so hard my stomach hurt," Mac said grinning, "my grandson chasing his cap, always a foot ahead of him."

"His pluck comes from you, Dad." Bo put a hand on Mac's shoulder.

"Speaking of guts, Bo," Rik adjusted his *Broncos* cap. "You put my Barracuda through a few risky turns on the way down."

Bo smiled. What had made their outing special was sharing the day with Gregg, Rik, and Mac. Bo had fun laughing and carrying on with his son, especially since Julia and the kids had been spirited to a safe house near Annapolis after Goliath's death. They were all thinking of changing their names.

Bo focused on the spot Rik pointed to in the distance.

"See those two red rocks. Do they look like camels kissing?"

"Amazing, but they do." Bo chuckled. "I'll have to show Julia."

"Dad!" Gregg yelled. "We're ready to leave. Mom wonders if you're going."

"In a minute," he called over his shoulder.

"I guess we should head out." Rik cleared his throat. "Mac, I want to thank you for arranging our tour. Though Adriana and I have lived in Colorado Springs for years, we are excited to finally visit the Air Force Academy."

"Think nothing of it. The commander and I served together in the Pentagon. I'm looking forward to seeing him again."

Bo had a hard time believing he was standing here with both his fathers, but he no longer felt as tense. He'd been visiting here for a week along with Mac and Vivian, the father and mother who would always be his folks. Rik and Adriana had arranged the family outing hoping they'd all forge closer bonds. Everyone had come except Theo Van Horn, who Julia kept calling Bo's brother, only he wasn't.

Rik tipped his cap to Mac. "I want to thank you for something else."

"What, for riding in the front seat of your Barracuda with Bo?"

"I enjoyed whooping it up in back with Gregg," Rik answered, a lilt in his voice. "On a serious note, I wish I hadn't put my ministry ahead of my fatherly duties. Despite my mistakes, Ted has excellent business acumen and is doing well with the stations he bought from me. He's assured me that I'm forgiven, for which I am thankful. I want to thank you and Vivian for the fine job you did in raising Bo."

"Oh boy, you wouldn't say that if you'd been there the night Bo wrecked my Chevy Impala. Needed a remodel; new fender, hood, and grill."

Bo reared back laughing. "Okay, you guys. It's not like I'm not here."

With that, Rik extended a hand, which Mac eagerly grabbed. Their eyes locked and after dropping their hands, Mac fired off a salute to Rik. Bo swallowed a lump in his throat, dashing tears from his eyes. How could he go wrong with two such stellar men in his corner?

Rik clapped a hand on Bo's shoulder and then left him with Mac to finish their chat.

"That was first class, Dad. I'm grateful you and Mom flew out here. With everything we've been through, spending time together eases the angst."

"It's been rough, but I'm stronger with my new leg. So you destroyed the destroyer."

Bo shifted his eyes across the colorful rocks. "True, Goliath is dead. But you and I must be vigilant. Will the terrorist's son become a hater of us too?"

"Let's not worry about tomorrow. Enjoy today."

"Yeah, we should, Dad."

Bo gripped the railing, thinking how he'd explain his recent spiritual decision to Mom and Dad. There was a different matter he wanted to talk over with Mac.

"I've been blown using my undercover name Skip Pierce. I need a new one."

Mac raised an eyebrow. "How about Ernest King Van Horn?"

"Nah, that's not me," Bo replied, shaking his head.

"I am glad to hear you say that."

Bo shrugged. "Who am I, Dad?"

"Son, be you. It's unlike you to stay marooned in foxholes. Come out and fight."

"That's just it. I'm fighting myself. The Agency wants me to run a program at Harvey Point, North Carolina."

"I know where it is. This is me, your dad you're talking to, and not some rookie in short pants."

"You'll always be my dad."

"I know that too," Mac shot back, his eyebrows flaring on his forehead. "Are you gonna like having your backside in a chair all day long?"

"It's either that or be at Kangas' whims. Is that fair to Julia and the kids?"

Mac propped his back against a tree the deck had been built around. "I never asked you or your mother if or where I should go. I saw my duty and did it. Look how well you turned out."

Bo gripped his dad's shoulder. "Thanks for believing in me."

"Loving your job is a gift, a true gift most men won't receive. Don't blow it. My executive officer, Hunter Stilling, passed up two promotions to commander because he refused to deal with the politics. Died a year after he retired, but he did things his way."

"You think I should stay working clandestine ops?"

"I think what you think, son," Mac replied, a twinkle lighting his eye.

"Or I travel in and out of countries like Pakistan as a sales rep for a technology firm."

Mac's eyes sparkled again. "Pakistan sounds mighty interesting."

Bo turned toward the house, Mac forging the way, leaning on his cane. Before they reached the steps, Bo asked, "How does Hunter Stilling sound?"

A hand from behind grabbed his arm. "I need a few minutes alone with you, Hunter."

Julia's beautiful eyes drew him in completely.

"Dad, mind if I skip your tour?"

"I approve of your decision to stay with your wife and whatever else you decide," Mac replied before limping away.

"He is a terrific father, just like you are to Gregg and Glenna. Is Hunter Stilling your new undercover name?"

"It seems to fit, don't you think?"

With a smile, Julia looked him up and down. "I definitely like your clean-shaven chin and moustache. Why not try something like Ian Fleming?"

"Too obvious." Bo tossed his head. "What about Foster Stearns?"

"Oh, did he also write spy novels?"

"Undercover, get it, under the covers, as in a mattress brand."

Julia slipped her hand into his, leaning her head against his shoulder.

"You mentioned about going to Pakistan. Is that for real?"

"I haven't decided, honey."

"The four of us will do all right without you. For short periods, mind you."

"You mean the three of you, right?" Bo wondered aloud.

Julia beamed a smile. "I am pregnant, Hunter, Skip, Bo, or whoever you are."

She circled her arms around his neck. Bo returned her embrace, their kiss lasting well beyond the van starting up and sliding down the drive. Finally he pulled away.

"Honey, when—"

Julia pressed a finger gently on his lips. "You'll keep our secret, right?"

His cell phone whirred in his pocket, bursting their special moment. Bo yanked it out of his pocket. When he saw it was from Frank, he didn't take the call.

"After what you just told me, I don't care what Kangas wants," Bo growled. "He can wait to hear back from Hunter Stilling."

Julia's hand in his, the unfolding drama of Pakistan seemed light years away. They walked hand in hand to the far edge of the deck where they joked and laughed until the sun slipped below the hill, the master painter spinning their world purple and gold.

"I have my own little secret," he whispered in her ear.

"You're selling the Austin-Healey and buying us a new SUV?"

"Nice try, but no. Something more intriguing than automobiles."

"That's not the Bo Rider I know."

"Forget cars. I'm serious."

"I see by your set jaw you mean business. Should I be afraid?"

"Joyful is what I had in mind," Bo replied, squeezing her hand. She giggled.

"We have a chance to move to North Carolina. They want me at Harvey Point."

"Bo, are you sure? You don't want to try your hand at whatever the Director has for you in Pak—I mean overseas?"

"I'm more of a family man now than a Company Man."

Julia lifted her pretty chin, her blue eyes burning with a fire that could only come from her pregnancy. Bo swallowed, her splendor taking his breath away. He'd made the right decision, he was sure. But she shook her head.

"Follow your heart, Bo. We'll be fine, all four of us. God promised me so."

"You heard His voice talking to you? Is that like some craving for ice cream?"

"Not His voice out loud. This morning I read my Bible here on the deck, listening to birds singing. Peace flowed over me like the warm waterfall we once swam in."

"Hawaii," Bo chuckled. "You said you were expecting Glenna, just before I shipped out."

"Exactly. And all these years later our family is still growing."

"Rik said something to me in Israel like God is using me to protect His people. Do you believe that's possible?"

"With God nothing is impossible," Julia said softly. "I wish you believed that too."

Bo wrapped her in his arms. "Surprise, surprise, but I do."

"Really?"

"I may not ever be as schooled as Rik in the Bible, but he helped me see God accepts me as I am with my warts and my past. I've given my life over to Him so if you have peace about Pakistan, that's what I want to do, Julia."

"You don't want to live in North Carolina?" she asked frowning.

Was she pretending to be upset?

"Well, if you do, then—"

"Stop it, Bo. I thought of naming our son Hunter, but we'll decide on a new name."

Was she teasing?

"Okay, I have one. Jethro Gibbs after our favorite TV character."

"Think again." Julia slugged his stomach playfully and he crumbled in mock pain.

Straightening, he touched her cheek.

"What's your idea?"

"Douglas Hendrick Rider after both your fathers."

He rubbed her hands in his. "I approve, but we should go in. The air is turning cool. And if our baby is a girl?"

"Vivian Adriana Rider."

"I like it, but," Bo pocketed his hands, "are we safe keeping the last name of Rider?"

Julia nodded, her face shining. "So you approve of both names?"

In answer he drew her to him, savoring the heady aroma of her hair.

"You smell like you just stepped off the beach."

"It's a new coconut shampoo. Glenna bought it for our trip."

"That's our daughter, always doing something special for someone. She's like you. And Gregg is poised for adventure, like me. Who's the baby going to take after do you think?"

"Maybe both of us."

"That might be true, but I'd want our son to be courageous and not wimpy."

"You're calling me a wimp?" She tugged on the ends of his moustache.

"You're perfect."

"Glad you think so, but I lied to you back there by those trees."

Bo's heart took a dive.

"So you really want to live in North Carolina?"

Julia shook her head. "I said the four of us would be okay if you went to Pakistan."

"But you really don't want me going there?"

Her eyes widened. "Oh yes, but it will be the five of us."

"Five? Who's coming to live with us? Your mom without your dad?"

"Bo, I'm carrying twins."

His body twitched and his tongue faltered. He could only stare in her vibrant eyes.

"I had an ultrasound the day before you flew in. I wish you could have been there to see their sweet little shapes."

Her lips trembled, but Bo burst out laughing. He threw his ball cap in the air shouting, "Hoorah!"

Taking her in his arms, he danced Julia around the deck, his heart overflowing with love for his family. He could never have predicted when Kangas sent him to Israel how rich life would become. Still, what dangers lurked around the corner if he took up the post to Pakistan?

Only God in heaven really knew. But Bo was forging a new life plan and was more ready for the future than he'd ever been.

Julia turned toward the slider door. "I'm going in to put on my sweater."

Bo returned to the railing, watching shadows obscure the kissing camels.

"Bo, come in here! See what's on TV." Julia's voice sounded uptight.

He opened the slider, glimpsing imagery of soldiers and artillery on the flat-screen TV.

"Our Israeli friends may need your help," Julia whirled, facing him. "Eli Rosenbaum and his family are in danger."

Concern flooded Bo's mind. "Has it begun then, war over the Joshua Covenant?"

Julia turned up the volume, the reporter booming, "The Brotherhood in both Egypt and Libya is aiming Russian missiles at Israel. They are demanding Israel return to the sixty-seven borders or they will launch, blowing them off the map."

"Julia, I don't know what I can do from here. I can't just call our friends on any phone."

She reached for his hand. "I'm thinking if you're ready, we should pray for the peace of Jerusalem."

"You mean pray out loud, here in the living room?"

"Yes, the two of us, asking God to protect His people and to show us what to do."

This was a huge stretch for Bo, but as he held Julia's hand, he knew one thing. No matter what happened he could rely on the God of Israel, the God who always kept His promises.

The Munsons' Thrillers May Be Read In Any Order.

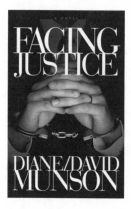

ISBN-13: 978-0982535509
352 pages, trade paper
Fiction / Mystery and Suspense
14.99

Facing Justice

First in the Justice series, Diane and David Munson draw on their true-life experiences in this suspense novel about Special Agent Eva Montanna, whose twin sister died at the Pentagon on 9/11. Eva dedicates her career to avenge her death while investigating Emile Jubayl, a member of Eva's church and CEO of Helpers International, who is accused of using his aid organization to funnel money to El Samoud, head of the Armed Revolutionary Cause, and successor to Al Qaeda. Family relationships are tested in this fast-paced, true-to-life legal thriller about the men and women who are racing to defuse the ticking time bomb of international terrorism.

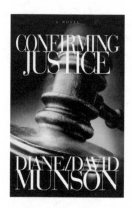

ISBN-13: 978-0982535516
352 pages, trade paper
Fiction / Mystery and Suspense
14.99

Confirming Justice

In *Confirming Justice*, all eyes are on Federal Judge Dwight Pendergast, secretly in line for nomination to the Supreme Court, who is presiding over a bribery case involving a cabinet secretary's son. When the key prosecution witness disappears, FBI agent Griff Topping risks everything to save the case while Pendergast's enemies seek to embroil the judge in a web of corruption and deceit. The whole world watches as events threaten the powerful position and those who covet it. Diane and David Munson masterfully create plot twists, legal intrigue and fast-paced suspense, in their realistic portrayal of what transpires behind the scenes at the center of power.

The Camelot Conspiracy

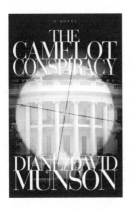

ISBN-13: 978-0982535523
352 pages, trade paper
Fiction / Mystery and Suspense
14.99

The Camelot Conspiracy rocks with a sinister plot even more menacing than the headlines. Former D.C. insiders Diane and David Munson feature a brash TV reporter, Kat Kowicki, who receives an ominous email that throws her into the high stakes conspiracy of John F. Kennedy's assassination. When Kat uncovers evidence Lee Harvey Oswald did not act alone, she turns for help to Federal Special Agents Eva Montanna and Griff Topping who uncover the chilling truth: A shadow government threatens to tear down the very foundations of the American justice system.

Hero's Ransom

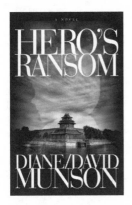

ISBN-13: 978-0982535530
320 pages, trade paper
Fiction / Mystery and Suspense
14.99

CIA Agent Bo Rider (*The Camelot Conspiracy*) and Federal Agents Eva Montanna and Griff Topping (*Facing Justice, Confirming Justice, The Camelot Conspiracy*) return in *Hero's Ransom*, the Munsons' fourth family-friendly adventure. When archeologist Amber Worthing uncovers a two-thousand-year-old mummy and witnesses a secret rocket launch at a Chinese missile base, she is arrested for espionage. Her imprisonment sparks a custody battle between grandparents over her young son, Lucas. Caught between sinister world powers, Amber's faith is tested in ways she never dreamed possible. Danger escalates as Bo races to stop China's killer satellite from destroying America and, with Eva and Griff's help, to rescue Amber using an unexpected ransom.

ISBN-13:978-0982535547
320 Pages, trade paper
Fiction/Mystery and Suspense
14.99

Redeeming Liberty

In this timely thriller by ExFeds Diane and David Munson (former Federal Prosecutor and Federal Agent), parole officer Dawn Ahern is shocked to witness her friend Liberty, the chosen bride of Wally (former "lost boy" from Sudan) being kidnapped by modern-day African slave traders. Dawn tackles overwhelming danger head-on in her quest to redeem Liberty. When she reaches out to FBI agent Griff Topping and CIA agent Bo Rider, her life is changed forever. Suspense soars as Bo launches a clandestine rescue effort for Liberty only to discover a deadly Iranian secret threatening the lives of millions of Americans and Israelis. Glimpse tomorrow's startling headlines in this captivating story of faith and freedom under fire.

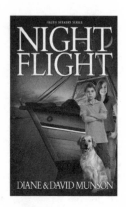

Fall/2012
Night Flight
ISBN-13: 978-0983559023

Night Flight

When Glenna and Gregg Rider's parent adopt a mature Golden Retriever, the children don't know that Blaze is a search dog retired from the Department of Homeland Security. When the young teens discover the dog's skills, they put him to work, without their parent's knowledge, and the family's lives become filled with excitement and intrigue. This heartwarming story is the first young adult thriller by ExFeds, Diane and David Munson.

NIGHT FLIGHT
COMING IN FALL OF 2012